The Lady from
St Petersburg

CHAPTER ONE

The Convent of the Blessed Sacrament, Spain, 1812

The young French lieutenant, flushed and breathless, rushed to the colonel's room and snapped a salute. 'Sir! British artillery has crossed the border.' He swallowed hard. 'And, sir, the lady from St Petersburg is missing.'

Colonel Leblanc, still in his dressing robe, kept his bloodshot eyes on the plate of breakfast before him and acknowledged the first item with a grunt. It was the second that made him look up in alarm.

'In the name of God, what do you mean she is *missing*?' A dozen devils were pounding hammers inside his head this morning.

'The lady is not in her room, sir,' the young man said and cleared his throat, 'and cannot be found in any part of the convent where it is permitted for us to, er, search, sir.' He avoided the expression in the colonel's eyes by fixing his own gaze on the far wall where the regimental guidon stood propped against a large wooden cross, almost obscuring it with red silk richly embroidered with battle honours still resplendent, despite the staining and fading.

The lieutenant had already noted the empty wine bottles and two glasses lying on the floor beside the colonel's campaign bed positioned near the fireplace.

'Madame is not in her room, Colonel, but the sentry in the hall swears he has not seen her leave.'

The new code book! Colonel Leblanc snatched the dispatch pouch which had been delivered to him yesterday and cold fingers of panic ran down his spine as he rifled through the contents. 'Search again for Madame Warshensky-Rostro . . . er, the Russian woman – though I'll swear she's no more Russian than I am! And this time search every room in the convent, d'you understand!' he shouted. 'And I want to see the sentry immediately!'

The bewildered sentry delivered his report to the colonel in staccato style:

the lady from St Petersburg had retired to her room at three this morning; she had wished him goodnight as she passed. At six o'clock four sisters of the convent had joined her in the room for prayers; he had heard them praying; they had left fifteen minutes later.

'And only four nuns walked from the room? You are certain?' Suspicion slid like a snake through the colonel's gut.

'Four sisters, yes, sir! And at seven o'clock two sisters entered the room with a wash basin. And a little later two more came with madame's breakfast tray. Then others carried it away.'

'You fool!' the colonel roared. 'You've been duped by the oldest sleight of hand in creation: they've slipped her out, right under your nose! I'll have you shot for this!'

The colonel realized that the sentry was not the only one to have been duped. 'Bring the Mother Superior to see me immediately,' he bellowed to the young lieutenant, and the sound of a window shutter which had rattled softly all through the windy night now pounded like cannon shots inside his skull.

Two weeks previously, when Colonel Leblanc and his battle-weary regiment had taken the little Spanish town of Tejada, the Convent of the Blessed Sacrament had been requisitioned as a billet for the officers. The Mother Superior had abandoned her own austere accommodation to the colonel, while she and the displaced sisters retreated to the chapel and a few rooms near it with doors that locked.

Now, while the first fingers of sunlight streaked through the window grilles to touch the whitewashed walls, the colonel's heart raced and he again rifled through the papers that had come yesterday with a red seal bearing the insignia of a bee – the emperor's personal seal. The new code book had been in there last night; he could remember that much about what had occurred in the hours before he'd held the lady from St Petersburg in his arms. The flowing red wine and the lady's warm kisses may have rendered him a little boastful but surely to God he had not been sufficiently imprudent to reveal that he had received a copy of Napoleon's new, unbreakable *grand chiffre*?

He groaned. The colonel had not yet reached the age of forty, but this morning he felt two decades older. It was difficult to remember just how much he'd told the woman last night when she'd expressed such tender concern for his personal safety – for the safety of his whole depleted, weary regiment. There had even been a tear in her marvellously blue eyes when he'd let it slip that Marshal Soult was refusing to bring his army from the south to reinforce Marshal Marmont's force when they faced the British soon at Salamanca.

'What agony it must cause the poor, dear emperor to have his marshals squabbling like disobedient children!' the lady from St Petersburg had breathed into his ear.

Dear God! How could he have been such a fool! The colonel rested his head in his hands and swore.

It had long been apparent that Wellington's intelligence officers had broken the standard French code and that the British were reading all captured dispatches. And these days very few French couriers slipped past the murdering bands of Spanish partisans who roamed the country. The British paid the peasants well for information on French military movements.

And now the lady from St Petersburg had disappeared, along with the key to the new code that Napoleon claimed would be unbreakable! The colonel fought a rising nausea as he thought of the court martial facing him when this blunder became known.

The voices of the nuns singing morning angelus in the chapel rose above the clatter of hooves in the courtyard, the jingling harness and the rattle of accoutrements as horses were saddled, sabres sharpened, wagons loaded, and the regiment prepared to march out.

The colonel slammed his palm into the wall and spat an oath. The arrival a week ago of a mud-splattered travelling coach carrying an unescorted Russian lady – a creature of beauty and refinement, golden-haired and in great distress – had caused a welcome surge of excitement amongst the officers in the convent building. Madame Antonia Warshensky-Rostroprovich had begged for the colonel's protection, describing how she had been visiting friends in Spain when the British advance had forced her to flee. She was desperate now to return to her home in St Petersburg.

'I have had a most frightful journey to reach here, Colonel,' she'd told him with touching anguish. 'When I hired this coach, the driver assured me he knew a safe route to the French border, but the wretched man has lost his way a dozen times already, and this morning we were stopped by a band of guerillas who have stolen everything of value I was carrying.' At this point she'd touched a lace handkerchief to the corner of her eye. 'I must now throw myself on the charity of the good sisters of this convent until the roads are safe for a lady to travel again.'

The colonel and his officers had rushed to offer what hospitality they could to the delightful woman with the troublesome surname, and it had been gratifying to see how quickly her composure was restored as they vied for her attention. She laughed at their anecdotes, applauded their songs, drank their wine and seduced their colonel.

Leblanc walked to the window and rested his throbbing head against the cold iron of the grille as he looked down on the branches of the almond trees swaying in the walled garden. The lady from St Petersburg, he suspected, might be past the age of forty but she was still one of the most glorious women he'd ever met. And clever.

Down in the village, the clock in the church tower that had been chipped and scarred by cannon balls, whirred as it geared to strike the hour. Wrapped in his own bitter humiliation, Leblanc failed to notice that, oddly, the weathervane on the roof of the church was not moving with the blustery wind.

He shaved, and was dressed by the time Mother Superior arrived at his door. 'What have you done with the Russian lady who sought sanctuary?' His tone was threatening. 'I demand you bring her to me immediately.'

'I can be of no help, Colonel.' The woman's pale, lined face under the white wimple was composed as she answered. 'I have not seen the *señora* since she prayed with us in the chapel last evening.'

He scoffed. 'Well, I'm told a number of your nuns have spoken with her this morning.'

'I think that is unlikely, Colonel. We are a silent order and the sisters speak only in prayer to our Christ.' The woman stood with her hands clasped against her brown habit 'If you care to look, sir, you will see the lady's coach still stands in the courtyard and the convent's little farm cart remains beside the barn. Do you imagine the *señora* is wandering unescorted through this bandit-infested country?' Her shrewd, dark eyes saw the colonel's confusion. 'I am unable to tell you of her whereabouts, and now I beg you will excuse me while I join the sisters in the chapel.'

She left the room with splendid dignity, and her lips gave no hint of a smile.

Antonia Warshensky-Rostroprovich sat under a little stone bridge two miles from the convent, removed the white wimple, pulled off the thick brown stockings and splashed her feet in the river while she ate the last of the bread and cheese provided by the nuns. The gentle brides of Christ, bound as they were to love their enemies – even the French invaders who for the last four years had left a trail of destruction, rape and pillage throughout Spain – were nonethless eager to help Antonia with her plan to deliver Napoleon's code book into British hands.

Their vow of silence had not been broken; they'd simply listened as she'd explained her strategy. Well before daybreak, a message had been sent to the village priest to stop the weathervane from swinging in the wind – the signal arranged with the partisans to tell them that her mission had been successful – and the nuns who came to pray with her had smuggled a brown habit and wimple into her room.

Each sister had taken away a piece of Antonia's own clothing and she, dressed in the spare habit, had walked from the room with the first group. With her head bowed over the rosary in her hands, she had joined the twenty-seven nuns praying as they walked in contemplation around the cloisters. And later, while the French soldiers ran through every part of the convent searching for her, she worked alongside the sisters who were digging in the vegetable garden.

Her own clothes had been bundled into her cloak and hidden in the wood pile; when the opportunity came, she retrieved them and followed an elderly nun who unlocked a small door in the wall.

'Bless you,' the woman mouthed and made a sign of the cross as Antonia slipped through the portal to the outside world.

'And bless you all, a thousand times over,' she answered fervently. British silver would be delivered to the convent for the aid they had given; Lord Wellington was most particular about such payments.

When the door closed behind Antonia, she raced through a grove of olive trees and down a rocky hillside to an insignificant river where several small, war-ravaged and now-deserted farms stood on the far bank. She had just begun to hurry towards her rendezvous at the bridge when for one moment, from amongst the trees on a far ridge, she caught the flash of sunlight reflecting on glass. Someone up there was watching her through a telescope.

Her heart pounded and, lifting the hem of the brown habit, she ran along the bank. The French had a particularly unpleasant method of dealing with captured spies and, with Marshal Marmont's army probably less than a day's march away, she prayed that the local guerilla leader, Don Julian Sanchez, had received the message from the rigid weathervane on the church and would waste no time in meeting her at the bridge.

Under its arches she dressed quickly into her own clothes and hid the brown habit. She listened, but the only sounds were of water running over the river stones and the wind rustling the leaves of the cork trees. At any moment she expected to hear the clatter of hooves on the bridge above and prayed it would be Sanchez and his men who arrived before any French troops discovered her.

She spread her cloak and sat leafing through the code book, intrigued by the pages of columns listing more than a thousand numbers that held the key to the new cipher. Antonia yawned. She'd had little sleep in the last twenty-four hours, but she knew Colonel Andre Leblanc would be suffering far more when he woke this morning. She felt almost sorry for the lonely, boastful, drunken fool who had made her mission so simple last night.

She took the combs from her hair and tried, with little success, to tidy the strands. If Don Julian Sanchez had any understanding of a woman's need for her toilette set, she prayed he would make haste in returning it, along with all the other personal items his band had stolen from the coach when they'd met her on the road.

Without warning, horsemen burst from the trees covering the slope running down to the opposite bank, and Don Julian's band rode to the water's edge, pulling up with a flurry of clinking snaffles and flying turf. Riding beside the guerilla leader was a British officer in a red jacket, and while the others watered their horses, this man and Sanchez, leading a spare mount, splashed through the shallows and came to a halt beside her.

'Congratulations, Doña Antonia,' Don Julian called with a flamboyant charm as he dismounted. He wore a razor-thin moustache that curled up into sharp waxed tips, and today he was dressed in an expensive, eye-catching blue uniform of his own design. Don Julian could afford to live well and buy the best with the gold the British paid for his attacks on French couriers who crossed his territory.

He took Antonia's hand and pressed it to his lips. 'Doña Antonia, allow me to present Lieutenant-Colonel Lord Matthew Halifax, one of the British army's brave exploring officers.' He bowed theatrically to the tall man who had dismounted and was now registering his irritation at the Spaniard's flowery performance. 'The British Intelligence Service depends on such gallant officers to ride their fast horses far behind enemy lines, gathering information on French armies, French code books, and weathervanes that refuse to move in the wind.' Sanchez laughed at the Englishman's stiff, unamused expression. 'The French shoot at him and chase after him, but his magnificent mount outpaces them all.'

'Señora,' the man interrupted, bowing to Antonia. There was a lean hardness in his form. 'I believe you have something for me to deliver to the general?'

'My mission was successful, Colonel,' she said, continuing to hold the slim book against her breast. 'Am I to assume that it was you I noticed observing me through your telescope this morning?' He had a tanned, angular face with the hint of a cleft in his chin, and Antonia liked what she saw in the hazel eyes that held hers.

'It's my duty to observe everything that happens in this country, señora,' he said in flawless Spanish, 'even nuns who take solitary walks in the morning.' Suddenly he smiled and his face softened.

She passed the little book to him. He slipped it into one pocket, then pulled a purse and a sealed letter from another. 'Lord Wellington is most grateful for your efforts on England's behalf.'

She gave a rich laugh and shook her head. 'Let us simply say that I have wagered heavily on a British victory in this war, and I do this work to ensure I collect as quickly as possible.'

'In that case, señora,' he said, handing her the letter, 'will you accept another request from headquarters?'

She broke the seal, read the message. 'Information from King Joseph's court in Madrid? Assess the strength of Marshal Jourdan's opposition to Joseph's military plans?' She tore the page and scattered the tiny pieces into the running water. 'Ah, yes, poor Joseph Bonaparte! I was a guest of his wife several years ago at their delightful Mortefontaine estate.' She sighed. 'Joseph is a charming man, but he's no warrior. I'm afraid Napoleon expects far too much from his brother.'

'Thank you,' the colonel said, preparing to remount. 'Make contact with our agent in Madrid and he'll forward your reports to headquarters.' He firmed his lips, but the corners of his eyes creased. 'His name is Father Juan, and you'll find him in the *Catedral de San Isidro* when you go there to make your confession.'

Her eyes widened and her brows arched in pretend shock at the prospect of entering a confessional, and the officer's stern expression softened. His face was rather too rugged to make him a truly handsome young man, Antonia decided, and his nose appeared to have been broken at some stage. But she liked the character she saw in him. He looked as if he would be as comfortable in a prize fight as in a drawing room, and when he swung into his saddle she felt a twinge of regret that they were to part so soon.

'Sanchez,' he called, 'you will see to it that the señora reaches Madrid safely?'

'It will be my honour,' the guerilla leader said with a bow. 'Doña Antonia's property, so inconveniently stolen by the *peasants*, will arrive at my camp by nightfall.' He threw back his head and laughed.

'Goodbye, Colonel,' Antonia said. 'Perhaps our paths will cross again one day.'

Matthew Halifax saluted and put his heels to the flanks of his tall grey horse. He rode back over the river and travelled for several miles along the crest of the hills, scanning the landscape with his powerful telescope until he saw a smear of dust in the sky. It rose higher as the morning moved towards midday's heat, and he rode closer until he was able to identify the blue uniforms of Marshal Marmont's column marching north. He assessed the numbers of infantry, cavalry, artillery, ammunition wagons, ambulance wagons, as well as the long baggage train trundling behind in the dust.

Picquets ranging out from the main force eventually observed him on the skyline and made a futile charge. Their musket shots fell far short, and before they were within range, he collapsed his telescope and swung the big, corn-fed Irish hunter that had cost him 500 guineas, and easily outpaced the army mounts pursuing him.

He gave the horse its head and galloped back to headquarters, still thinking of the extraordinarily beautiful woman who was now on her way to Madrid with the partisan band. What drove such a lady into this dangerous network of information collectors? Surely it was not merely for the gold he had just paid her.

If he or any other exploring officer was captured in his British uniform he would be taken as a prisoner of war – a miserable fate, but not necessarily a fatal one. On the other hand, should the French capture the lady from St Petersburg, it would be a different story.

As the weeks passed, Matthew heard that Wellington was receiving messages from Madrid, and all confirmed conflict at court and the ineptitude of the military command in the capital. King Joseph Bonaparte made no secret of the fact that he wanted nothing more than to abdicate and bolt back to a quiet life with his wife in France; Queen Julie was still unwilling to join him in Madrid. When he'd begged his brother to relieve him of his military responsibilities, the Emperor Napoleon – now storming into Russia at the head of his Grande Armée – had sent the King of Spain a scathing reprimand and repeated his orders to engage Wellington's army and drive the British out of the country.

'Gentlemen, we have good news today from Madrid,' Lord Wellington announced to his officers as they gathered in his tent to dine. 'It seems we are likely to meet with only Marmont's force at Salamanca. Marshal Soult is still refusing to bring his army up from Cadiz, King Joseph is in ever deeper conflict with Marshal Jourdan in Madrid and they're ignoring the emperor's orders to advance. In fact, our informant has witnessed King Joseph and the marshal at *virtual swordpoint*!'

Glasses were raised around the dinner table to the lady from St Petersburg and her reports.

'I say, Halifax,' someone called from the far end, 'you're the only one who's actually ever met her, so – come on – tell us what she's like.'

Matthew Halifax shook his head slowly. 'Hard to remember,' he lied. 'We met for only a moment.' When the others scoffed, he shrugged. 'Why should

I remember that particular lady when I have a lovely young fiancée waiting for me in England?'

Actually, Matthew Halifax thought frequently about the lady's extraordinary beauty, and the fire of purpose in her eyes. In moments of self-indulgence he allowed himself to imagine sharing his life with such a woman, and sighed.

Occasionally he thought of his fiancée, Miss Evangeline Fenton, whose letters contained little but descriptions of the balls she'd attended, the latest plays in London and gossip from various house parties.

Several times Lord Matthew had tried – and failed – to compose a letter to her describing the changes that four years of war had brought to him. He was no longer the twenty-two-year-old who had declared his love on the eve of his departure for Spain. His body showed remarkably few reminders of the battles he'd fought in those bloody, filthy years, but words became elusive when he attempted to describe the battering his spirit had endured during the carnage and the grief he had lived through.

His greatest hope was that pretty little Miss Fenton would soon become tired of waiting and write to break off their hasty engagement.

CHAPTER TWO

London

A pair of handsome greys stood in the traces of the barouche hired for the day by Sir Christopher Templeton, and it waited for him now at the door of Mrs Pickett's quiet lodging house just off The Strand. He had arranged a number of significant calls in London before evening and, though none was far from the next, he needed to ensure he did not arrive breathless at any of these doors.

Besides, very few people knew he had arrived back from Malta, and he wanted to avoid any chance meetings until he had completed the crucial business in hand.

Alfred Atkins, who had been the baronet's manservant for the last ten years, was clearly miffed that he'd been given no hint of his master's destination today. ' 'Ave a pleasant day, sir,' he said dourly as he escorted him to the steps of the carriage, and was rewarded by one of Sir Christopher's singularly amiable smiles.

'Thank you, Alfred,' he said, and not by the flicker of an eyelid did he reveal that he was about to face one of the most difficult days of his life – precipitated by the three very angry letters which lay in the pocket of his grey superfine coat.

He gave the driver the address of his first appointment, settled himself into the barouche as it pulled out, and gazed with unseeing eyes at the bustle of the city beyond the window. With his head resting against the back of the seat, he tried to ignore the twinge of pain in his chest as he pondered the future.

At forty-five, Sir Christopher was tall and slim, a widower for fifteen years, a man of impeccable taste, always popular with hostesses at balls and country house parties where he charmed ladies young and old, and carefully left no broken hearts. His features were regarded as pleasant, rather than wildly handsome, but he had kind eyes and a quick smile, and moved through the world with a confident, easy charm.

In the last ten years, those attributes, coupled with a quick brain, had found him frequently sitting with British diplomats at negotiating tables in the United States and throughout the Mediterranean.

Now, as the hired carriage pulled up outside a house in Oxford Street, Sir Christopher knew it was going to take all his finely honed diplomatic skills today to resolve the dilemma raised in the letters which had brought him rushing back to London.

He left the vehicle and walked slowly up the steps towards the door bearing a brightly polished brass plate which announced the premises of William Percival, Physician. Even so, his heart had kicked into an irregular beat by the time his knock was answered.

'Well, sir,' the eminent doctor said with his customary bluntness at the conclusion of the examination. 'What do you expect to hear from me today? Something that changes the prognosis I gave you ten years ago?' His grey eyebrows snapped together. 'I told you on the first day you came to see me that no heart damaged by a childhood bout of rheumatic fever can be *healed* – it must be cared for – but, like so many young men who hear unpleasant news regarding their health, you've refused to accept the fact. It's quite clear you have taken scant notice of my advice, so—'

Christopher Templeton felt like a schoolboy called before the headmaster. 'On the contrary, Doctor, I resigned from the army on your recommendation, and' – he struggled to find some other evidence of compliance – 'and I still take the tablet you prescribed. Perhaps now something stronger is warranted? Something that would steady my heartbeat? Prevent the spells of dizziness?'

The doctor pursed his lips and sat back in his chair to study the elegant man sitting across the desk from him. Then he shook his head and his expression softened. 'No, sir, I can do no more. Your life is in your own hands – er, and God's, of course.'

'How long do I have?'

'Perhaps two months, if you continue to dash about at your present pace. Perhaps a year, if you retire to the country immediately.'

Sir Christopher was no fool, and the doctor's warning came as no shock. More than anything it was a confirmation that he desperately needed to conclude the items of business on today's agenda. And when that was done he'd know how to respond to the three angry letters.

The next call was on his man of business in Fleet Street. Unfortunately, the genial *old* Mr Oswald Grovelly, who'd died the previous year, had left Sir Christopher's affairs in the hands of his son, and an appointment with the tight-lipped, long-nosed *young* Mr Oswald Grovelly proved to be a chilling experience.

'You wish to withdraw *all* your funds, Sir Christopher?' he said with a barely contained sneer as he looked up from the columns in his ledger. He clicked his tongue. 'How disappointing that the large investment you made all those years ago has yielded not one penny. Your assets are now – well, shall we say – extremely light.'

Sir Christopher maintained a practised expression of bored indifference, and silently damned the ferret-faced young man's impertinence. That *investment*, made during the time he was in St Petersburg, had delivered dividends far beyond price, he recalled warmly. 'If you would kindly make haste, Mr Grovelly,' he said with the superior lift of a brow, 'I'm somewhat pressed for time this morning.'

'This will take no time at all, sir,' the man said, dipping his pen into the inkwell and scratching figures onto the page. 'There! Five hundred and seventy-two pounds, nine shillings and four pence.'

The amount was even less than Christopher Templeton had imagined 'Much obliged, Mr Grovelly. I'll take it with me now, and good day to you, sir.' This was a further confirmation that he had no choice but to carry on with his plan.

With the money in his pocket, he set off in the carriage to settle his debts with the tailor, bootmaker and hatter, and several merchants who had served him well.

'Drive twice around the park,' he called to the coachman when he'd attended to these matters, which had left him now with just over £200 in his pocket. Today's business must succeed! He took several steadying breaths, pulled out his gold half-hunter and looked at the time. In ten minutes he was expected in Curzon Street, and at this meeting all his finely tuned tact and diplomatic charm would be called into play. More than his own future depended on it.

'I was surprised to receive your note this morning, Sir Christopher,' said Lord Ramsden, rising from the chair in his splendid library when his visitor was announced. 'I'd no idea you were back in London.' He strode across the marquetry floor with his hand outstretched, and a rare smile on his lips. His lordship's age was little over fifty, but he appeared older, and his bent shoulders hinted that he carried a never-ending burden through life.

'I'm delighted to receive you, of course, sir, delighted,' his lordship said, indicating a chair, 'but unfortunately I am expected in the House within the hour – more problems with the Princess of Wales, y'know, and yesterday's news from the Peninsula has the Whigs baying at our heels.'

'I apologize for this intrusion, m'lord, but I need only a moment of your time,' Sir Christopher said quickly. To delay this interview would complicate his plans. 'I've come to ask just one question.' He cleared his throat. 'Would you have any objection if I was to offer my hand in marriage to your sister?'

He held his breath. Without Lord Ramsden's endorsement this project would fall apart.

For a moment his lordship stared at him, slack jawed. 'Viola?' he gasped and dropped into the nearest chair. 'You want to marry Viola?'

'My Lord,' Sir Christopher said, 'as important affairs at Westminster are awaiting you, please allow me to be brief and completely frank.' Though his breath was becoming short, he spoke with persuasive charm. 'Your sister and I have been acquainted – slightly – for many years, and I've always felt a deep regard for the dignity she displayed in the face of her late husband's ungentlemanly behaviour. I flatter myself to think she has formed a favourable opinion of me also, and that if I offered her my hand, *and* the name of Templeton, she would not be reluctant to leave behind the memory of Mr Otway and his, er, activities.'

'Viola? *You* want to marry Viola? Well, upon my word!' His lordship's shoulders seemed to sag further under the shock 'Why Viola?'

'I must confide my circumstances clearly, m'lord.' Sir Christopher chose his words with the utmost care, for he would never stoop to speak an outright lie. 'I will, of course, inform your sister that as I am not in robust health I plan a quiet life, perhaps in the country.' He leaned closer to his host and lowered his voice. 'Your sister has a kind heart and a tender nature, but between gentlemen, m'lord, permit me to whisper that a younger wife would not suit me at all.'

'Ah!' His lordship took a moment to comprehend the oblique message. 'I see.' Separate bedrooms.

'Of course, it's well known that I am not a wealthy man' – that was an understatement – 'but I assure you I have no debts.' Sir Christopher spoke the truth matter-of-factly, and to his relief, the matter of his finances brooked no further interest.

'Well, upon my word!' said his lordship once more. 'You actually want to marry Viola.'

Sir Christopher took a deep breath before he placed his last card on the table. 'It is not for myself alone that I'm seeking Lady Viola's hand, m'lord.' Again there was an uncomfortable tightness across his chest. 'I have a daughter, Ellen, who is now sixteen. She has been raised very quietly in

Norfolk by cousins of my late wife, and it is high time she was introduced into society. It is my sincere hope that, as your sister has no children of her own, she might graciously consent to my daughter becoming her ward.'

'Well, upon my word!'

'You have no objection to my proposal?'

'My dear fellow, of course not! I hold you in the highest regard. You must speak to Viola straight away.' He smiled again and rang for a servant to bring his sister. 'She quickly regretted running off as a girl with that scoundrel Otway, y'know. Pity she had to wait thirty years for him to break his neck, but at least the creature left her a decent fortune.'

Within seconds, Lady Viola Otway, a plump lady of forty-nine who favoured heavily frilled dresses, rushed into the library, flushed and trembling with enthusiasm. She was fully aware of the reason she had been summoned because she'd had her ear against the library door and had nearly fainted with excitement as she listened to the men's conversation. It was twenty-five years since she'd left Mr Otway and put herself under her brother's protection, and now Sir Christopher Templeton was about to ask for her hand! What a stir this would create in society.

'Oh, Sir Christopher, indeed I accept with pleasure,' she said when he proposed immediately, in front of her brother. 'And becoming mother to your dear little girl will be a joy.' Her soft brown eyes became misty with happiness.

The urgent government business in Westminster was delayed while Lord Ramsden discussed matrimonial, legal, financial and domestic arrangements with his euphoric sister and Sir Christopher. The arrangements were not merely discussed: in typical Ramsden style, they were recorded, signed and witnessed.

Two hours later Sir Christopher rallied his ebbing strength and climbed back into his carriage. Dear God, he'd pulled it off! Ellen's future was now assured, and doors into the greatest houses in England would be opened to her. And it had also been agreed that when she reached the age of twenty-one, she was to receive a bequest of £10,000 from Lady Viola's estate.

When Sir Christopher left the overjoyed Lady Viola in Curzon Street and climbed back into the carriage, the tightness in his chest made it difficult for him to breathe. 'Piccadilly, m'good fellow,' he murmured to the driver, and alighted unsteadily at the premises of his favourite jeweller to buy a gold wedding band.

Now he had only one more visit to make, and they set out for Chelsea.

'Pour me a brandy quickly, Charles,' he said with a sigh when his old friend greeted him at the door. 'Have Cynthia and the children gone for the afternoon?'

Charles Phillips laughed. 'Why the mystery, Christopher? Yes, we're alone. When your note said it was essential for us not to be disturbed, I sent them all off to Hampstead to visit my mother.'

As soon as they walked into the study, Christopher Templeton stretched himself on a chaise while Charles unstoppered the decanter and poured 'I say, old chap, you look rather washed out,' he said, passing the glass. 'A bad trip back from Malta?'

Sir Christopher took two sips of his brandy, then held the glass and stared into the golden liquid for several moments. 'Charles,' he said solemnly, 'as my oldest friend I want you to understand certain facts. I'm not here to seek your advice or comments – I simply want you to hear this from my own lips, because I have no intention of ever mentioning the matter to another living soul.'

He sipped from the glass again, frowning as he marshalled his thoughts. 'Charles, I'd be a fool to commit any of this information to paper, but if some day an explanation for my actions becomes necessary, I want you to be able to set the record straight'

Charles's fine, open face showed his astonishment, but before he could speak, Christopher held up a hand to halt him.

'You're aware that I left the regiment ten years ago because of my weak heart. Well, Doctor Percival confirmed this morning that my days are numbered and—'

'Oh, no, no, Christopher, I'm sure you'll—'

'Charles! No comments, please. Just listen to what I'm saying.' He reached into his pocket and withdrew the remainder of his money. 'I'm going to die – perhaps next month, perhaps next year – and this is the sum total of my worldly wealth, apart from a diamond tie pin, a good watch and this gold-topped cane.' He gave a small, wry smile. 'And, of course, I've made sure the name of Templeton still commands a high price.'

Charles looked at him in puzzled disbelief. 'I know your father had to sell the estate when he lost heavily on his last maritime venture, but he left you a tidy enough little legacy. Ten, twelve thousand pounds? You've never been a gambler, so what the devil happened to it?'

Christopher nodded. 'It all went years ago and I have no regrets, Charles. Remember that year I spent in St Petersburg? There was a lady there – a lady like no other – but where the money went is of no consequence.' He pushed himself up into a sitting position. 'Now, before this news reaches the rest of

London tomorrow, I want you to know that I've arranged to marry Viola Otway next week.'

Charles threw back his head, let out a roar of laughter and slapped his thigh 'Well, Chris—' he began, but one glance at his friend's face told him it was no joke, 'Oh, come, m'dear fellow, surely not – Viola Otway? Good God, she's fifty if she's a day and I'll swear there's nothing but feathers between her ears. She was a pretty little thing once, but you can't be serious!'

Christopher nodded 'Agreed, she is a few years older than I am, but Lady Viola has a sweet nature, no real vices – and two outstanding virtues. In the first place, she's Lord Ramsden's sister and therefore connected to some of the oldest families in the land; and secondly, the late, unlamented Mr Reginald Otway left her with a very great fortune.'

'Her fortune? Is that what's behind this marriage madness? Good Lord, old chap, don't do it! I'll gladly cover whatever you need.' He sprang to his feet and opened the satinwood desk. 'Come now, don't shake your head at me.'

Sir Christopher reached into his pocket and pulled out the three letters that had reached him in Malta. He waved them at Charles and indicated for him to resume his seat. 'These all concern Ellen.'

'Ah, dear little Ellen. She must be, what, twelve now?'

'Ellen has turned sixteen – and I'm ashamed to say it must be at least five years since I last went to Norfolk.'

Charles gave a tut-tut and shook his head. 'You have many praiseworthy points, Christopher, but being a fond father certainly has never been one of them.'

'No, I admit I've never been close to Ellen.' He swung his feet onto the floor and sat for a moment with his elbows on his knees, looking directly into Charles's eyes. 'As this is the day for revelations, my friend,' he said slowly, and with emphasis, 'let me tell you now that I am *not* Ellen's father – though not another soul is ever to know that.'

Charles's jaw dropped. 'You mean Margaret. . . ?'

Christopher nodded and the corners of his mouth turned down. 'I've always felt responsible for what happened to her.'

'I can't believe it! Good Lord, Christopher, she looked on you and me as her big brothers when we were growing up but—' He shook his head in bewilderment.

Christopher shrugged. 'She was eighteen when I took her to a ball at Wychwood Hall and introduced her to – well, no names, just say he was a fellow officer. If a French sabre hadn't finished him off in '95 I'd have killed him myself when I heard he'd seduced her and she was carrying a child. What could I do then but marry her myself?'

'Oh, God! Of course you did the right thing, old fellow, and I know you'd have been a good husband had Margaret lived.' The men sat quietly while somewhere in the house a clock whirred, then struck two. 'Poor little Margaret – she would have wanted her child to be raised by her own cousins,' Charles finished lamely.

'The fact is, Charles, I chose to make Margaret my responsibility sixteen years ago, and that makes her child my responsibility, too. But so far I've failed miserably to play any part in Ellen's life apart from sending Mr Oliver Sharpe £50 each year for her keep.' Sir Christopher blew a long sigh, picked up the thickest letter of the three, then put it down again. 'As you have daughters, Charles, tell me, is it really important for a young lady of sixteen to wear her hair *up*?'

'Eh?' Charles blinked. 'I'm told it's an indication to the world at large that the young lady is leaving childhood behind. Why do you ask?'

'The subject of Ellen's hair is causing concern in Norfolk, according to each of these letters. Mr and Mrs Sharpe, the cousins who have raised Ellen, tell me they have two daughters who wear their hair *up* and who are now both engaged to marry suitable young gentlemen.' He ruffled through the six pages of the letter and shook his head wearily. 'The Sharpes are eager to get Ellen off their hands, too, and it seems she's caught the eye of a new vicar who is coming to the village, but as well as being most uncivil to the fellow, she refuses to do anything about her hair.' He gave a heavy sigh and took another sip of the brandy before he continued.

'The cousins have produced a litany of complaints about the time my cold and ungrateful daughter spends at the vicarage with the elderly Reverend Mr Halliday and his books, and say that if they are to make any sort of a match for her, I must send the money to buy new dresses, and order her to start putting her hair *up*.'

'Ah!' Charles said, trying not to smile. 'A difficult situation.'

'This next letter is from the Reverend Mr Halliday himself, and he chastises me for leaving my delightful daughter's upbringing in the hands of Mr and Mrs Sharpe – "genteel blockheads" he calls them. He goes on to say that I must under no circumstances give my consent to any engagement between Ellen and the dreary young vicar who is coming to take over the parish when Mr Halliday retires next month.'

Sir Christopher unfolded the pages. 'Listen to what the reverend gentleman says about Ellen: "Your daughter, sir, is a remarkable young woman with an intellect that has been my delight to foster over the last ten years. She shows a prodigious understanding of mathematics, astronomy, philosophy, Latin – and her Greek is coming along well. Indeed, had she been born a boy, I would now be hammering at the doors of Oxford to gain a place there for such a scholar!" '

'Good heavens!' said Charles. 'A scholar? That's a worry.'

'The letter ends with a little postscript from Mr Halliday's good wife who declares that Ellen's hair looks perfectly sweet as it is and she sees no need yet for it to be put *up*.'

'The matter appears to be creating something of a stir in the village.' Charles couldn't stifle his laugh.

'But it's this letter from Ellen herself that has spurred me into action. Don't worry, it's brief: 'To Sir Christopher Templeton: (I address you thus as I do not know you sufficiently well to call you Papa!) Sir, I write to warn that if you give your consent to the *appalling* suggestion that I should become engaged to the most *obnoxious* man whom Mr and Mrs Sharpe plan to impose on me, I shall run away *immediately* to London and become an actress. I have the coach fare ready in my pocket And I *absolutely refuse* to put my hair *up*. Yours etc., Ellen Margaret Templeton." '

Charles began to laugh, low, and then unable to contain his mirth, fuller and rounder still. 'And this is the daughter you're planning to introduce into Viola Otway's noble family?'

Sir Christopher finished his brandy and held out the glass for another. 'As you can see, something has to be done promptly about the matter, and tomorrow I intend to be on the early-morning coach to Norfolk.'

CHAPTER THREE

It was late in the day and Sir Christopher was exhausted by the time he was welcomed by the landlord and shown to the best room in the White Swan Inn at Littlewood.

Before he retired for the night, he wrote to Mr and Mrs Sharpe informing them of his arrival in Norfolk and inviting them to lunch with him tomorrow at the inn. Experience had taught him that it was an advantage to discuss sensitive matters on neutral territory, and he asked the porter to have his message delivered to their house, which was situated a little distance from the village.

Despite his fatigue, he slept badly and woke at sunrise, frustrated by his own gloomy restlessness. By the time his breakfast was brought to the room, he had already shaved and dressed, and sat eating at a little table by the window overlooking the gentle village scene below. Shop doors were opening and the townsfolk were going about their business; a hay cart lumbered into sight, and the blacksmith who was lighting his forge looked up and called a greeting to a farmer riding past. He was followed by a shepherd herding his small flock towards the market, and a spotted dog, which was sitting in the middle of the road to scratch himself, jumped up with his tail wagging and chased after a boy who came from the baker.

A great loneliness enveloped Sir Christopher Templeton as he watched the people below moving about with a quiet purpose. What was the sum total of his own purpose in life? Very little indeed! He'd been born and he was going to die. What was there to show for the forty-five years between? A few now-forgotten battles won or lost, a few signatures on treaties that had often been broken by one side or the other. And one glorious, hopeless love.

He had a sense of having passed through life like a gentle breeze over a field of grain – a breeze that waved the golden stalks for an hour, providing no benefit, causing no harm, leaving no trace.

Damn it! He didn't want to marry Viola Otway, he didn't want to saddle himself with the responsibility of providing a future for a daughter who wasn't his. But now there was no going back, so he sighed and picked up his hat and stick, and left the inn to stroll towards the church with its square, grey tower standing beyond a grove of beech trees at the edge of the village. He knew it was too early in the morning to call on the Reverend Mr Halliday.

Nevertheless, he continued to amble in that direction until he came to the gate opening into the churchyard. He wandered through the lines of tilting, lichen-covered headstones, past the ancient church, to the vicarage standing in a wild garden on the far side. He climbed a stile over the wall and followed a gravel path to the front door of the mellow, red-brick house.

Before he could knock, it was flung open and a portly, grey-haired man looked at him in happy astonishment. 'Well, upon my word, I do believe it's Sir Christopher! What a pleasure it is to welcome you. Come in, come in. Martha, m'love, Sir Christopher himself has called!'

'Forgive me for arriving unannounced at this early hour, Mr Halliday,' he said, as the vicar shook his hand vigorously.

A smiling, bird-like woman with white hair appeared in the hall, wiping her hands on an apron, while she bobbed at their visitor. 'I'm afraid the house is all topsy-turvey, sir. We're in the midst of packing, y'see, because the vicar and I are off to Lincolnshire next week to live with our son and his family.'

'Have you spoken yet with Ellen, sir?' Mr Halliday asked as he opened the door into his cluttered study. Sir Christopher shook his head and the vicar's wife bustled ahead to remove books and papers from a big, shabby armchair.

'My husband and I do apologize for writing to you about Ellen's troubles,' she said, inviting him to sit, 'but we are both extraordinarily fond of your daughter, and that affection is behind our concern. Ellen has a sharp brain and – at times – a very sharp tongue.' Mrs Halliday clapped her hands to her cheeks. 'Oh, but never here with us, I assure you! The vicar and I have always found her company delightful and her manners charming.'

Worry creased Mr Halliday's ruddy face. 'What's to become of your daughter, Sir Christopher? What's to become of a young lady who finds joy in the language of mathematics? In the questions raised by astronomy? In the study of natural science?'

Christopher Templeton had no simple answer prepared and, while he struggled to find one, his attention was caught by the sight of a girl and a large, brown-haired dog bounding through the churchyard.

'Ah! Here comes Ellen now,' Mr Halliday said, looking pleased 'She's very early today.'

Sir Christopher held his breath as he watched the tall, lithe girl who bore his name zigzagging her way through the lines of headstones. Her body moved with the lightness and grace of youth; she carried a book in one hand and her bonnet in the other, so that her dark curls flew around her shoulders as she ran.

She and the dog jumped from the top of the stile then, rather than taking the path to the front door, they ran across the grass, leapt over a flower-bed and came straight to the French doors leading in to the study.

'Sit, Hannibal,' he heard her say to the hound at her heels and it obeyed, gazing up at her with tongue-lolling adoration. The vicar opened the door with a greeting and, as she stepped over the threshold, her expression was alive with excitement. She thrust her notebook into his hand. 'I did it! The calculus! See, I've used the second equation and found the answer!'

The vicar showed his delight. 'Splendid, m'dear, splendid,' he said. 'Now, Ellen, look who has come to visit us.'

Only then did the girl notice Sir Christopher on the other side of the room. She drew in a sharp breath and frowned in astonishment; the colour drained from her cheeks. She made a quick curtsy and, as she hesitantly crossed the floor, her extraordinary beauty hit him like a physical force. He could detect little of her mother's likeness in her features and certainly none of her father's. She kept her chin high and her eyes of glittering sapphire blueness regarded him with suspicion.

'My apologies for this unannounced arrival in Littlewood,' he said to her as he would have addressed an adult, 'but your letter led me to believe there was some urgency to discuss certain matters with you.' Here, with consummate diplomacy, he turned to include the vicar and Mrs Halliday. 'And what a happy coincidence for us all to meet here this morning. I'm sure, Ellen, you and I will both appreciate the wise counsel of the vicar and Mrs Halliday on the suggestion I'm about to present regarding your future.'

He noticed how the girl held on to her stiff self-composure while she continued to regard him warily and moved to a chair beside the vicar's wife. Christopher Templeton himself was feeling far from calm.

'At last my years of travel have come to an end,' he said in a deliberately light tone, 'and my greatest desire now is to lead a quiet life – in the company of my daughter, who quite rightly scolds me for having been a shamefully neglectful father.' He had no intention of mentioning the fragile state of his health.

The vicar and his wife smiled at him encouragingly, but Ellen's expression became even more glacial.

'My dear,' he said carefully, 'I have come to tell you that I am shortly to marry a lady of about my own age, and we would be delighted to have you come and live with us.' The girl remained tight-lipped and her eyes narrowed. 'Lady Viola is in a position to introduce you into the wider world – when you decide the time is right, of course. Initially we plan to live on a little estate in Dorset which is owned by her family. A pretty place, I'm told.'

At this, there was a tremor in Ellen's bottom lip and she darted a pleading look towards the vicar.

He rubbed his palms together. 'The wider world! Ah, my dear Ellen, what wonders lie out there waiting to be discovered in the wider world,' he said philosophically. 'Opportunities, lass, opportunities to be grasped!'

The girl drew in a deep breath and when she locked her gaze with Sir Christopher's, he recognized how frightened she was. 'You are inviting me to live with you and your wife permanently?' She made it sound like a challenge.

'Yes,' he said gently.

Her chin lifted further and the awkward silence that followed was broken only by the ticking of the tall clock in the corner. At last she drew in a deep breath to speak. 'I shall refuse to call your wife *mama*!'

'Quite rightly, m'dear. Lady Viola would never expect it,' he said with a sudden rush of relief to hear her oblique acceptance of his proposal. 'Our sincerest wish is to make your life with us a happy one.'

She frowned at his patronizing tone. 'I'd have a very happy life here, sir, if it wasn't for the rush to make me the wife of some appalling man.' She blinked hard and denied any tear a chance to appear, yet when Mr Halliday held out his arms, she ran to him and buried her face in his chest.

'There, there, dear girl, we won't have to stop our work' He patted her shoulders. 'We will correspond – letters to and fro. I trust we have your approval, Sir Christopher, to continue Ellen's study into the work of Isaac Newton?'

'Of course,' he said, and was bemused by the enthusiasm that the vicar and the girl then both directed towards the tome bearing the title *Principia Mathematica* which was lying on the desk.

'I always intended this to be yours, Ellen.' Mr Halliday lifted the volume and presented it to her. 'Keep working on the calculus, and every month you must send me your results.'

Ellen gasped her thanks as she held the heavy book against her small breasts and gave the elderly man a heartbreakingly beautiful smile. 'Oh, Vicar, I promise to treasure this, and I'll keep working through it, you'll see!'

Sir Christopher had witnessed women presented with diamonds who'd shown less excitement than this, and the shadow of that delighted smile was still on her lips when she faced him again.

'Yes, very well, sir, I'll accept your offer, but Hannibal must come, too.' She indicated the shaggy brown beast slobbering on the glass of the French door.

Sir Christopher's heart sank 'Of course, Hannibal is most welcome to join us,' he answered smoothly. Lady Viola's lap dogs were likely to die of fright when they saw the creature, but that was a problem he'd deal with later. 'Now, let us discuss our plans for departure,' he said. 'Would Thursday – the day after tomorrow – give you sufficient time to prepare?'

So it was that when Mr and Mrs Oliver Sharpe alighted from their carriage at the White Swan on the stroke of twelve to dine with Sir Christopher Templeton and to confront him with their litany of complaints regarding Ellen, they were astonished to find the girl already sitting there, pale-faced, in the parlour.

'Indeed, a happy coincidence that my daughter and I should meet so unexpectedly this morning,' he said, producing a display of his well-honed charm as he greeted the forbidding couple. 'I am greatly indebted to you for writing to me in Malta. Now, please, do come and join me at the table while you hear my proposal regarding Ellen's future.'

He called for the landlord to serve the meal – he had ordered the fine roast beef for which the inn was renowned – and while it was carved and the plates were passed, Sir Christopher thanked Mr and Mrs Sharpe for the years of tender care shown to his daughter.

Ellen kept her eyes lowered, and the Sharpes' surprise rendered them temporarily speechless. Sir Christopher used the silence to praise the couple for having raised a young lady with such pleasing manners and air of refinement, and he congratulated them effusively for encouraging her splendid posture, her mellow tone of voice, her modest demeanour . . .

Mr Sharpe puffed out his chest a little, but his wife – a lady with dark, severe hair, a receding chin and an expression of terrifying disapproval – would not so easily be diverted. 'I'm delighted to hear you are pleased with our efforts, Sir Christopher,' she said, 'but I'll have you know it has been a thankless task and has imposed a great inconvenience on our own two daughters.' Her tirade on Ellen's faults began with selfishness, included appalling obstinacy, and ended by warning that the girl was about to send herself blind by reading in her room till all hours of the night. 'The number of candles she wastes is sending us to the poorhouse! Now, if she—'

'I am most grateful for that information, Mrs Sharpe, and I'll ensure our house is well stocked with candles.' The strain of the morning was rapidly sapping his strength and he subtly brought the meeting to a conclusion. After that, as he escorted them all to the door of their carriage, he discreetly handed Mr Sharpe an envelope containing a formal note of thanks for their care of Ellen, as well as his last £100.

It was done! Slowly, Sir Christopher climbed the stairs to his bedroom, swallowed a pill and, before lying down, wrote two messages to be delivered by express: the first was to Lady Viola, telling her the date of his return with Ellen, and the other was to his manservant, instructing him to meet their coach on its arrival in London. That evening he informed the landlord that he had caught a chill and intended to spend the next day in bed.

Despite the pain in his chest, he slept intermittently through the day, swallowed his pills, ate the barley broth brought to his room, and tried not to dwell on the mountain of new responsibility ahead.

It was far more pleasant to let his mind drift to things past, to remember people and places and times when his body was strong and his horizons seemed to have no limit. To remember Paris, Vienna, Naples. To remember the time he had spent with Antonia in St Petersburg. If there was one gem from the past he treasured above all else, it was that year when she'd been the centre of his world.

He'd heard nothing of Antonia since he left St Petersburg, but when he closed his eyes he could still see her, dressed in a low-cut gown of shimmering silver, designed to caress every line of her body as she moved, every glorious curve and swell of it. She was a woman who had been born beautiful, and every artifice that money could buy was enhancing that beauty when he'd first glimpsed her, drifting towards him up the great sweep of the marble staircase in the Winter Palace. Here in the midst of this palace of priceless objects, she was the most perfect of them all.

She'd looked up, their eyes had met and their glances held as she slowly climbed step by step until she reached out a gloved hand to him waiting at the top of the staircase.

In that moment they fell in love, and the brilliance of the great diamond necklace at her throat had been quite eclipsed by Antonia's own radiance. He'd swept her into the ballroom, into his arms, into his life. And she'd loved him in return. Oh, yes, how she had loved him!

It was the damned necklace that later caused the trouble.

Sir Christopher's only regret about the whole affair was that he hadn't killed her husband when he'd had the opportunity.

CHAPTER FOUR

Early on Thursday morning, after a heated altercation amongst the three girls in the Sharpe household concerning the ownership of a length of yellow ribbon – which resulted in much running from room to room and slamming of doors – Ellen set off with Mr Sharpe in his gig. The ribbon was in her hair and Hannibal ran behind the wheels of the vehicle. She waved to neighbours they passed on the way to the village and ignored Mr Sharpe's censorious monologue.

'Behave in London society as you did in my house this morning, young lady, and no respectable family will be willing to accept your acquaintance!'

Ellen's head was turned away and she said nothing. When she was very young she'd learned to imagine herself as a hedgehog with quills that raised defensively at times like this. It was a tactic that was still working well this morning, and she allowed nothing said by Mr Sharpe to touch her. His angry voice ceased only when they pulled up outside the White Swan where a big group of villagers, including the vicar and Mrs Halliday, had gathered to bid farewell to her.

The spotted town dog forgot his fleas when Hannibal charged forward to attack him in their ritual tail-wagging, ferocious play-fight on the green. When Ellen put her fingers to her mouth and blew a whistle, the now well-muddied Hannibal bounded back to her side.

Mr Sharpe rolled his eyes and shot her a look of exasperation, but Sir Christopher smiled a greeting and stepped forward to help her from the gig. The others pressed around her with fond wishes and there were a number of tears when the coach pulled up outside the White Swan with a clatter of trace chains and squealing brake blocks. The coachman, anxious to be on his way without delay, ordered the luggage aboard, took the fares, and opened the door for the gentleman and his daughter.

Two passengers were already in the coach, and two young men in army uniform sat on top. 'Sorry, miss, I can't allow the dog inside,' the driver snapped as soon as he saw Hannibal. 'There's no place under the seats for an animal that size.'

'Very well, I'll sit on top with him,' Ellen said quickly, and the hound, sensing excitement in the air, began to leap about. The two young soldiers looked down with enthusiastic smiles and moved to show how much of the seat remained between them for the young lady.

'Out of the question for you to sit outside, m'dear,' Sir Christopher said quickly. 'Perhaps the dog can sit up there on his own?'

'All seats is for payin' passengers only, sir,' the coachman said adamantly, and before Sir Christopher could speak, Ellen opened her reticule.

'I'll pay Hannibal's fare to London,' she said, and counted out her shillings into the man's hand. She looked surprised at her father's questioning frown. 'It's all right, sir, it's the money I saved to run away and become an actress.'

The two young soldiers reached down eagerly, and with the blacksmith's assistance at ground level, they heaved and hauled the shaggy animal onto the seat between them, where he expressed his delight by wiping his tongue across their faces.

The long journey to London took a further toll on Sir Christopher's health. While Ellen sat reading or wrestling with mathematical exercises in her notebook during the hours of daylight, he pleaded a migraine to avoid conversation with their travelling companions. He swallowed his pills frequently and at each stop to change horses, he used his cane to stretch cramped muscles and walk a little with Ellen and the dog. He felt increasingly weak and at times he was swept by a fear that he might not live long enough to reach the altar and complete his part of the contract with Lady Viola.

'My man, Alfred, will meet the coach when we arrive,' he explained to Ellen when they made their last stop before London, 'and I expect we'll spend a week or so quietly at Mrs Pickett's lodging house before the wedding.' How his body pleaded for rest! 'Lady Viola is arranging a simple, private ceremony, and directly after that we're to leave for the country.'

Because of other passengers aboard the coach, he'd had no opportunity to speak with Ellen privately, and the girl remained an enigma. However, Sir Christopher couldn't fail to notice how male heads snapped in her direction when they stepped from the vehicle at each inn, though she appeared quite oblivious of the attention she was attracting.

Dear God, he thought, no time must be lost in finding some sensible female in Viola's family who could prepare Ellen – delicately – to face the inevitable male attention lying ahead of her on the social battlefield. That was another matter to add to his list of concerns.

And there were more, he found to his dismay, when their coach at last reached London. He could read trouble written on Alfred Atkins' long face the moment the fellow bustled towards them.

'I'm sorry, Sir Christopher, but Lady Viola insisted, *insisted*, I was to pack up everything at Mrs Pickett's and bring it all to rooms prepared for you and Miss Templeton in Lord Ramsden's house in Curzon Street.'

Sir Christopher swallowed another tablet as liveried footmen escorted them to a waiting barouche bearing the Ramsden crest. His lordship's coachman raised the whip to his hat in salute and stoically made no comment about the dusty hound who leapt into the splendid carriage behind the young lady.

'Oh, my dear Sir Christopher!' Lady Viola cried, running from the drawing room as soon as they entered the house. Her soft brown eyes widened. 'And this must be dear Ellen! Oh, I had no idea you were so grown up! And how pretty, too!' She fluttered, pink with excitement, then gave a shriek when Hannibal skidded towards her across the marble hall. A courageous footman stepped forward to restrain him while her two fluffy white lap dogs fled in terror.

'Perhaps he should be taken below stairs and fed?' Sir Christopher suggested breathlessly, and Hannibal was led away.

'And now,' Viola continued with a desperate eagerness to please, 'let me explain that, as the wedding is all arranged for midday tomorrow in St Margaret's, Ramsden felt it would be more convenient for you both to spend the night under this roof. He has arranged a special licence and my dear cousins have been excessively helpful with all the preparations for the service, and some members of the family are coming to dine here with us this evening. As we're to leave for Dorset immediately after the ceremony tomorrow, I thought we should have a little celebration here tonight, because there'll be no opportunity for our friends and family to drink our health when we step from the church, although I am sure we will not lack visitors as soon as we are settled into Fernhill Manor. Such a pretty little estate. Ramsden has made arrangements with his steward down there to have the house made ready for our arrival and some of our servants have gone on ahead.'

She paused at that point only because she had run out of breath and, with her hands clasped against her ample breast, stood glowing with happiness.

Sir Christopher felt his head spin. He struggled for breath. He needed rest. He needed quiet 'Splendid,' he said and grasped the edge of an ebony table to steady himself 'I am astonished that so much has been accomplished in so little time.'

'I am so pleased you approve,' Lady Viola said in a soft, kittenish voice. 'I thought – I thought—'

'No, my dear Viola, your arrangements are excellent. But now, if you will kindly excuse me – a slight chill, you understand.' He tapped his chest. 'I'd like to be shown to my room to rest before dinner.'

'Of course,' she said and signalled to the head footman. 'Ramsden is not yet home from the House, and I think he's bringing one or two colleagues from Westminster to dine with us. Fortunately our Halifax cousins are in town this week, along with the Perrimans and several others, so it will be a merry party tonight, I'm sure.' She smiled encouragingly at Ellen's grave expression. 'I fear the evening will be lacking in young company, my dear, but the family is most eager to make your acquaintance.'

Determined to hide his weakness, Sir Christopher took Alfred's arm and they followed the head footman slowly up the stairs while Viola excitedly led Ellen towards the drawing room.

'Do let us become better acquainted, my dear girl,' he heard her saying 'I am quite beside myself with delight when I think of all the happy times you and I will share.'

Ellen threw a glance over her shoulder at Sir Christopher, and he saw the naked, unguarded dread in her eyes. He sent her an apologetic smile. Poor child: it had never been his intention to throw her straight into the whirlpool like this.

In the drawing room, Lady Viola beckoned Ellen to sit beside her on a chaise. 'Now, my dear, do tell me all about yourself,' she said girlishly. 'What are your interests? Do you play and sing? No? Perhaps you ride? No? The theatre? Balls and parties? No? Oh, but of course, I suppose you are not yet *out*? Well, that is something we will attend to next season. Oh, yes, how wonderful, we'll have a splendid coming-out ball for you.' She seemed unfazed by Ellen's stony lack of response, and her smile didn't slip. 'So, my dear, how did you amuse yourself in Norfolk?'

'I enjoy reading, ma'am, and walking, and I take pleasure in studying mathematics and natural science.'

'You do? How – how interesting,' said Lady Viola, looking worried. Then she took Ellen's fingers and squeezed them. 'I do want you to be happy in this family, so you must ask me for anything you need. New dresses? I have a very clever modiste who will make them for you. What colours do you favour? Dominique will advise the best for your complexion. And I've heard that a new style of bonnet with a pleated crown is becoming very fashionable. I'm sure it would suit you charmingly.'

To Ellen's relief, Lady Viola was interrupted by a footman who came with a message: 'Miss Templeton's bath is prepared, m'lady.'

'Yes, yes, of course,' she said and drew Ellen to her feet. 'Our dear Dominique thinks of everything. How silly of me to keep you chatting here when you must be longing to bathe and rest after your long journey. Come, Dominique will help you decide what to wear this evening.'

Dominique Duprés, who had been Lady Viola's personal maid for the last ten years, had already unpacked the young Miss Templeton's small trunk, and was waiting when her mistress, puffing from the effort of climbing the stairs, bustled into the bedroom with the girl.

'Now, Ellen, my dear, this is Dominique, and she will look after you, too.'

Dominique, a thin, middle-aged Frenchwoman with an interesting, intelligent face, dropped a curtsy. 'It will be a pleasure, mademoiselle,' she said in a softly accented voice, and smiled at the young, dark-haired beauty who was trying hard to smother her discomfort.

'My lady, perhaps you should rest now?' the maid said to Lady Viola with an amiable familiarity. 'I have had Polly take a tea-tray to your room, and she will attend you there until I come to help you dress for dinner.'

'Of course, thank you, Dominique,' she said. 'Yes, do help Miss Templeton now, and if there is anything you need – a shawl, a necklace. . .?'

'I'll see to it, m'lady,' the maid said and gave Ellen a warm smile as her mistress fluttered from the room. A steaming bath stood invitingly before the fire. 'Perhaps you would like your hair to be washed also, mademoiselle? I can brush it dry before dinner,' she said softly and the girl nodded.

Dominique had a deep understanding of human nature and she had grown fond of Lady Viola in the ten years she'd been in her employ. Her ladyship could never be called astute or discriminating, but she was invariably kind-hearted and generous to the world at large. Like everyone else, Dominique had been astonished to hear of Sir Christopher Templeton's sudden offer of marriage, and now her heart went out to the bewildered girl shyly washing herself in the tub.

Was Sir Christopher's daughter aware that at dinner this evening she was to be inspected by thirty-five of Viola's wealthy, elegant male and female relatives and close friends? As Dominique poured warm lavender water to rinse the soap from the girl's thick curls, she worried about the four plain, well-worn dresses now hanging limply in the armoire.

'Mademoiselle,' she said diplomatically, 'as you have brought no dinner gowns, may I offer a suggestion? If I was to stitch a flounce of Flemish lace to the neckline of your white taffeta dress – and perhaps add some touches of red and gold velvet ribbon – the effect this evening would be most elegant.'

'Oh?'

Miss Templeton displayed no enthusiasm, but Dominique was not discouraged. 'And Lady Viola has a little gold locket on a pearl chain that would sit charmingly at your throat,' she added.

Dominique's remarkable sense of style had been cultivated in Paris by her beloved mistress, Countess Louise de Chambord, before the Terror had struck and swept the entire aristocratic de Chambord family to the guillotine. Right up until the end, Dominique had tried to help the countess escape the blade and when her attempts were reported to the Committee of Public Safety, an order had gone out for her own arrest. Penniless, she'd been forced to flee from France and felt herself fortunate to have eventually found a position across the Channel with Lady Viola Otway.

Dominique had soon grown fond of Lady Viola and, with exquisite tact, she'd spent the last ten years steering her new mistress past some of the more unfortunate choices in fashion, which the lady had always been too eager to make. Nobody tittered at Lady Viola's style once Dominique Duprés came into her life.

After a few hours' rest and an iron-clad determination to play the role of attentive husband-to-be in front of Viola's relatives, Sir Christopher stood at her side in the drawing room and charmed the cousins, uncles, sisters-in-law and family friends as they were presented. He gave every indication of delight to be marrying Viola, and the lady's gratitude was touching. He smiled at her happiness, and promised himself never to give Viola cause to regret their marriage, however brief it might be.

At Dominique's suggestion, Lady Viola had agreed that Mademoiselle Ellen should not join the company this evening until just fifteen minutes before dinner was announced. That time, Dominique judged, was more than enough for the unsophisticated girl to be scrutinized by a whole room full of Ramsden relatives.

Ellen smiled for the first time when she was told of the arrangement. 'Oh, thank you, Dominique, I'm so glad about that,' she said, looking at the woman's reflection in the dressing-table mirror as she stood behind her with a hairbrush. 'I've never been in a house as grand as this. I won't know what to say to anyone.'

Dominique's brush strokes slowed when she caught Ellen's glance in the glass, and saw the deep blue eyes fringed with dark lashes peering anxiously at her from an oval face which glowed with health and youth and vitality. God had indeed been generous the day he'd created this young woman, she thought. 'Mademoiselle, simply give them your smile this evening, and I assure you the guests will require no conversation.'

'If you say so.' Miss Templeton gave a shrug and looked doubtful, then as the brush swept the hair away from her face, she frowned. 'Oh, please don't put my hair *up*, Dominique!'

'*Non! Non!*' Dominique sounded shocked by the suggestion. 'However, if I bring it softly back from your forehead? – *voila!* – and from your temples? – *voila!* – and now the strands can be pinned behind your head with this pretty silver clip which Lady Viola has sent.'

Ellen Templeton sighed and eyed the image in the mirror critically. 'Nothing in my life will ever be the same again.' As she voiced the thought aloud, her chin trembled, and she looked quickly at Dominique. 'My dog! Please, Dominique, I must see Hannibal and tell him not to fret for me. Do you know where they have taken him?'

'No, but come with me, mademoiselle, and we'll find him somewhere below stairs.' Ignoring the inquisitive stares of busy servants, Dominique hurried Ellen down a back staircase and along corridors. In the kitchens the cook directed a scullery maid to take them to the stables; and there Hannibal lay curled up, with his belly full, snoring at the feet of a sleepy stableboy.

The lad sprang from his chair and the dog, instantly awake, yelped his delight at the sight of his mistress. 'Stay, Hannibal!' she said, and the leap he was about to make was instantly stalled. 'Sit!'

He obeyed and looked up at her with his tail wildly pounding the floor, accompanied by whines and whimpers of canine joy. She crouched beside him, stroking his coat and whispering into his ear.

'It's all right, Hannibal,' she said at last, then stood and turned to the stableboy, who was gazing at her with wide-eyed admiration. 'Thank you for looking after him. You see, we've never been apart before.'

She stroked the brown head again – as if she was touching a talisman – and Dominique gave an understanding smile. The dog was the girl's last link with everything that had been safe and familiar in her old life. Everything that was now far behind her.

In the drawing room, Sir Christopher was engaged in conversation with one of the Ramsden aunts, when the doors were opened by a footman and Ellen stood framed in the doorway. All heads turned to stare at the flush-cheeked, prettily gowned beauty, and Lady Viola immediately held out her plump arms and swept across the drawing room. 'Allow me to present Miss Ellen Templeton,' she announced eagerly, beaming as she drew her into the room. 'Dear Ellen is to become my ward.'

Lord Ramsden himself hastened to greet her and a soft murmur of approval rippled around the assembled guests. Sir Christopher sighed with relief as he watched the girl being carried slowly around the room on a tide of introductions, eddying from one quizzical group to another. And he also noted her surprising poise as she acknowledged each person with a curtsy and a smile.

It was Ellen's turn to sigh with relief when dinner was announced; in Norfolk they would have dined hours before this, and her stomach ached with hunger. She was seated at the table between two middle-aged uncles and listened with every appearance of grave attention as they explained the network of relationships linking various guests sitting at the table tonight with other families around the country.

She hid her confusion, smiled at them in turn, nodded, and occasionally murmured '*Oh, I see*' or '*How interesting*'. They pressed her for nothing further and eventually turned their discussion to Wellington's victory at Salamanca and Bonaparte's march into Russia.

Ellen ate well, while all around her the sounds of clinking crystal and adult chatter filled the dining room. She saw her father watching her closely from the far end of the table and noted how his tired, grey face seemed to have taken on even deeper creases this evening. He smiled at her and gave a soft nod of approval.

At the end of the meal, while the men stayed at the table with their port, she withdrew to the drawing room with the aunts and cousins, who settled themselves into little groups. Their chatter drifted about, pleasant and aimless, and one exceedingly handsome, golden-haired cousin whom they addressed as Grace, went to the piano and began to play.

Ellen – trying to smother her yawns – sat quietly beside Lady Viola, listening to the ladies' gossip about somebody's recent elopement, and the case against a Devonshire gentleman who was being sued for breach of promise.

'Did you see her at the theatre on Tuesday with Roger Pilkington? That yellow dress was dampened, and quite indecently revealing!'

'Who, dear?' an aunt asked.

'Why, Evangeline Fenton, of course!'

'Oh, Miss Fenton!' Eyebrows were raised. 'I heard reports of her behaviour during the masquerade at Vauxhall last week that would make her dear mother weep.'

'That silly girl is on the way to losing her reputation completely if she continues to ride about town with Major Williams in his phaeton!'

'Poor Matthew,' a grey-haired woman said to the lady named Grace at the piano. 'Is he aware of his fiancée's behaviour? Surely Sebastian has dropped a hint to him?'

Grace stopped playing and shook her head. 'My husband feels his brother has more urgent matters in Spain to concern him at present.' Her smile faded. 'Besides, I've always thought that Matthew made a dreadful mistake rushing into an engagement with Evangeline on the eve of his departure. They barely knew each other, so I could see the whole thing was doomed from the start' She sighed and played several soft chords. 'Matthew tells us very little about the war, but he did say that the lovely big grey horse Sebastian bought for him last year had been killed by a French shell. Matthew wrote that his own injury was slight'

'Is this campaign in the Peninsula never to end?' said a stout woman wearing heavy pearls. 'Why can't we leave the Spaniards to fight their own war?'

Less than a mile away, a footman ran from the home of Sir Thomas Fenton to summon the doctor, while Lady Fenton and Evangeline's two younger sisters hovered by her bed, sponging the sweat from her body and listening to her incoherent ramblings as she tossed on the pillow.

'Can you hear me, my love?' her mother wept 'You must hold on, you must! Lord Matthew will soon come home, and Papa will give you a splendid wedding. You will be the envy of every young lady in London that day and – oh, my dearest girl, open your eyes, open your eyes and look at me!'

The sisters exchanged fearful glances.

'I warned her, I *warned* her she'd catch a chill – but would she listen? No! She insisted on going about with her dresses dampened – and just look what has happened!' Lady Fenton sobbed as another spasm of coughing wracked her lovely daughter. 'Stupid, stupid girl! She might have been a marchioness one day.'

Poor Evangeline gasped, and fought for a breath.

It was her last.

CHAPTER FIVE

London society filled St Margaret's to see Lady Viola change her name from Otway to Templeton. When Sir Christopher entered with his friend Charles Phillips, he tried to ignore the pain in his chest, acknowledged acquaintances briefly and took his seat on the front pew to await the arrival of his bride.

Charles, sitting anxiously beside him, turned frequently to look behind at the people filling the pews. 'Seems as though half of London is here this morning,' he muttered, then made a little sound of surprise. 'Now, who's that delicious creature just arriving?'

Sir Christopher looked around and for the moment forgot his uneven heart-beat. Ellen, with her spotted muslin dress and straw bonnet prettily trimmed with wide cornflower-blue satin ribbon, was creating a wave of interest amongst the wedding guests as she walked down the aisle with the Marquess and Marchioness of Eversleigh.

'That young beauty, my friend, is the sole reason for this whole charade.' Sir Christopher smiled with satisfaction, just as the organ sounded the first chords of the Wedding March and – only five minutes late – Lady Viola entered the church on the arm of her brother. With Charles's steadying hand discreetly under his elbow, Sir Christopher stood and faced his bride coming towards him in an elegant dress of cream and pink silk, and a matching turban with only three osprey feathers. Dominique had ensured that her mistress looked her very best on this day, and Lady Viola's face beamed with happiness as she acknowledged friends and family members in the pews as she passed.

The ceremony was a long, taxing one, interspersed with a selection of choral items chosen by the Ramsden cousins. Sir Christopher felt his last reserves of strength fast disappearing and he was breathless later outside the church when the couple was faced with a flurry of well-wishers. How he dreaded the long trip to Dorset! But he kept his smile in place until they climbed aboard the waiting coach, where Ellen was already seated in a corner with her back to the horses.

'Goodbye, Lady *Templeton*,' voices called, and Viola, delighted with her new title, fluttered her handkerchief from the window as they set off. She was far too elated to notice that her bridegroom's lips had a bluish tinge as he fumbled for the small bottle of pills he always carried in his waistcoat pocket.

'Oh, Sir Christopher, have you ever known such a beautiful service?' she said as she settled into her seat. 'Those dear little choirboys sang like angels; and weren't the flowers magnificent? Aunt Adelaide had them sent up from her gardens in Suffolk – did you see the length of the stems on those white lilies? And, my dear Ellen, you look as pretty as a picture. Everyone said so.' She gave a happy sigh and reached behind the cushion for a box of confectionery supplied by Gunter's. One was always placed there for Lady Viola when she travelled.

She opened the lid and held out the box to her new husband, but he declined and she leaned forward, thrusting it towards Ellen. 'You must try one, my dear. Here, take one of the marzipans. No, not that one, you'll enjoy the pink one much more. Take two.'

Ellen had lifted her hand, but suddenly she dropped it back into her lap. 'No, thank you, I don't want one.' From the corner of her eye she saw her father stiffen at her abrupt tone, and she avoided his expression by turning her head to gaze out the window.

Oh dear, she thought, how quickly those porcupine quills had sprung up to keep Lady Viola at a distance. She knew her father's new wife was simply being kind, but her insistence on Ellen taking the pink confection had suddenly seemed a forewarning that the lady had expectations of controlling every aspect of her new stepdaughter's life. And that would be even worse than enduring the intrusions of Mr and Mrs Sharpe, for at least in their house she could vent her anger. Lady Viola was far too sweet a person to receive the sharp edge of Ellen Templeton's tongue.

As the miles disappeared beneath the carriage wheels, guilt niggled at her and she slanted a glance across at her father. His head was resting on the back of the seat and his eyes were closed; his lips were slightly parted, his breathing fast and shallow.

Lady Viola seemed quite unaware that Ellen had spoken abruptly to her, or that her new husband was clearly unwell. Her chatter flowed on randomly as she took another bonbon from the box and bit into it.

'Yes, Grace and Sebastian are having a folly built beside the lake at Eversleigh Hall. Such a lovely estate,' she said, addressing Ellen. 'I was so pleased to see them at the church this morning. After all, it's not as though

Miss Evangeline Fenton and Matthew were married, so I'm sure it was not necessary for them to go into mourning.' She opened her reticule, found a handkerchief, and dabbed the corners of her mouth before she continued.

'You see, Ellen, dear, the Marquess of Eversleigh's younger brother, Lord Matthew Halifax, is fighting with Wellington in Spain, and this morning news came that his fiancée, Miss Fenton, passed away last night.' She clicked her tongue and rolled her eyes heavenwards. 'Pneumonia! Poor Sebastian must now write to his brother and break the dreadful news.'

When Lady Viola next paused for breath, Ellen spoke softly. 'Ma'am,' she said in an attempt to make amends for her earlier curt tone, 'may I please have one of your sugared almonds? I'm very fond of almonds.' Her father's eyes opened. Did he recognize her small attempt at bridge-building?

Viola cheerfully thrust the box forward. 'Almonds? Oh yes, of course! And see, there are some lovely big walnuts here, too, so take—'

'No, thank you, ma'am, this is the one I would like. Just this one,' Ellen said firmly, then took a small almond from the corner and popped it into her mouth. When she glanced across at her father his eyes were closed again, but she thought she saw a faint smile on his grey face.

Exhaustion at last caught up with Lady Viola and she dozed frequently while Ellen took out her notebook and wrestled with a fresh mathematical puzzle. Dominique and Alfred, travelling ahead, were waiting at each inn when the Ramsden carriage arrived, and Ellen noticed the maid's deepening frown as she watched Sir Christopher alight.

'Fortunately we have not far to drive now,' Lady Viola announced as they sat down to refreshments at their last halt. She gave her new husband a reassuring smile, then signalled a servant to carve her a second slice of ham. 'I'm sure, Sir Christopher, you will find our visit to Fernhill most refreshing, and I know you, Ellen, dear, will enjoy it tremendously because we are acquainted with a number of very charming young ladies and gentlemen nearby who are sure to fill your days and evenings with entertainments.' She glanced across the table, and pointed to a veal pie. 'Yes, I'll have some now, thank you. Where was I? Oh, yes, did I tell you that our Rigby cousins are coming to stay with us for a week or two? And the Symes-Andersons will be calling in on their way to Devon.'

Sir Christopher, ashen-faced, made no comment, but when it was time for them to reboard the carriage, Dominique drew Lady Viola aside. 'M'lady,' the Frenchwoman said with the sweet firmness in her tone that always persuaded her mistress to listen, 'we must consider some way to help Sir Christopher overcome the *chill* that is clearly making him unwell.'

'Oh! You think the change of air will not be sufficient?' Lady Viola blinked and showed concern.

'M'lady, may I suggest that Sir Christopher's health would benefit greatly from a period of complete rest and quiet, away from the – the delightful activities you are planning for the guests.'

'Oh, yes, thank you, Dominique, I should have considered that. How selfish my own happiness has made me. Yes, Sir Christopher will need a quiet room where he will not be disturbed by young people in the house.' Lady Viola sighed.

'Perhaps, m'lady, a convenient bedroom for him could be made up in the parlour at the end of the south wing? That part of the house is little used and there are no stairs to climb. Should I send someone ahead to ask the housekeeper to prepare it?'

'Oh, yes, a splendid idea, my dear Dominique. What would I do without you?'

Set in a deeply wooded park, Fernhill Manor sprawled on a rise that gave distant views to the sea. The red-brick house itself was an ancient, unpretentious pile to which various wings had been added over the generations, and seen from a distance, the skyline looked a jumble of high-pitched eaves and twisted brick chimneys.

When the carriage at last pulled up at the big oak door, the steward, the housekeeper and a line of servants waited to welcome Sir Christopher and Lady Viola Templeton, and Miss Templeton. Sir Christopher needed the assistance of Alfred Atkins as well as a footman to enter the house, and he was taken immediately to the isolated room that had been prepared for him in the south wing.

There was a general flurry of activity in the rest of the house as boxes were unloaded and carried upstairs to be unpacked. A maid escorted Ellen to her room, along corridors that were full of twists and turns, up steps and down steps, past big rooms and small rooms that seemed to follow no particular plan. The curtains at all the big mullioned windows were faded softly, and throughout the house the floorboards creaked, the woodwork shone and everywhere smelt of beeswax and lavender.

Ellen fell in love with Fernhill Manor. It was a friendly, rambling old house that didn't intimidate her the way Lord Ramsden's great London mansion had done. When she was shown into her own big, sunny bedroom she flung the windows wide open and looked out onto terraced gardens and woods that dropped into a shallow valley leading down to the sea, a mile away. She hoped their stay in Dorset would last for ever.

Hannibal had arrived earlier with the luggage and as soon as the maid had helped her to wash and change her clothes, Ellen went looking for him in the stables.

He barked when he recognized her footsteps approaching and danced about her legs as they ran from the stableyard, across the terraced gardens, and down a winding path that led through the woods to the valley floor.

The blue sea in the distance beckoned, and she was gasping for breath by the time they reached the cliffs. The wind carried the tang of salt and seaweed; it ballooned her skirts and tousled her hair, while overhead the seabirds cried as they wheeled and swooped along the chalky cliffs. The white-crested water below lapped the long, empty beach and Hannibal bounded along the clifftop in a frenzy of canine excitement.

It was he who discovered the steep, narrow path leading down to the beach and she followed him, slipping and sliding on the loose surface until they were both running across the shingles to the water's edge. The dog plunged straight in and, within moments, Ellen had discarded her shoes and stockings and, with her skirt hitched up to her knees, she splashed through the shallows with him.

With her head thrown back, she spread her arms and turned full circles. They were here alone – utterly, blissfully alone with only the birds and the sea and the cliffs to watch them. 'Oh, Hannibal, if only life could stay this way,' she said aloud, but the wind snatched her words and lost them. Nothing remained for ever.

It was dusk before Ellen took the weary Hannibal back to the stables where the head groom cautioned that Lady Viola had sent servants to search for her. 'Her ladyship had fears you were lost, miss,' he said with a twitch in his eye, which might have been a tiny wink. 'Now, if you please, miss, I'll escort you to the house meself, just to assure Lady Viola you've come to no 'arm.'

As soon as Ellen stepped into the hall, Lady Viola rushed to embrace her. 'Oh, my dear, I was so worried that something dreadful must have happened! I thought you might have fallen off the cliff or be wandering, lost, in the woods and slipped in to the river. Oh, I am so happy to see you have not drowned!'

'I'm sorry to have caused you to worry, ma'am,' Ellen said. 'Hannibal and I spent a very pleasant afternoon, though I'm afraid we walked further than I had planned.'

To Ellen's embarrassment, her stepmother's eyes filled. 'I'm so sorry, my dear, it's entirely my fault that you were left without company. I've neglected you dreadfully. I should have arranged for a companion to come and sit with you, but matters will take a turn for the better tomorrow, you'll see.'

Lady Viola's good spirits quickly returned, but Ellen's heart sank when she learned that while she was out, several of the neighbours had made calls at Fernhill and a busy social schedule had already been arranged.

'Squire Hawkswill has invited us to a picnic on his estate tomorrow,' Lady Viola chattered on, 'and everybody will be there for you to meet but, of course, I had to tell the squire that Sir Christopher will be unable to accompany us because Doctor Parker insisted he must remain in bed and receive no visitors for at least two weeks.'

A jolt of alarm shot through Ellen. 'My father called for a doctor?' she asked.

'Actually, I think it was Dominique who suggested it,' Lady Viola said, blinking. 'Your father was not well pleased, I gather, and refused to allow Doctor Parker to bleed him, but I'm sure Sir Christopher will soon be up and about again if he follows the doctor's instructions.'

Later that evening, after Lady Viola and Ellen had dined, Dominique sat with them in the drawing room while they discussed fashions illustrated in the latest edition of the *Ladies Magazine* and decided what dresses should be added immediately to Mademoiselle Ellen's wardrobe. Lady Viola agreed enthusiastically with Dominique's four initial suggestions, and Ellen could hardly believe her ears. Four new dresses! And no arguments?

Lady Viola cheerfully brushed aside Ellen's thanks as they later said goodnight, but instead of going straight upstairs to her bedroom, Ellen asked a servant to show her to her father's room in the south wing.

Her light tap was answered by Alfred, who opened the door a few inches to peer out, shook his head and put a finger warningly to his lips.

'May I come in to say goodnight to my father?' she whispered shyly and he looked shocked by the suggestion.

'Sir Christopher is asleep, miss. Mustn't be disturbed,' he whispered back. 'How is he?'

'Bad chill. Needs his rest.'

'I see,' she said and felt her bottom lip quiver. 'In that case, when he wakes, please tell him I was enquiring.'

She felt heavy-hearted and close to tears as she went up to her bedroom. Why did everyone insist that her father had a chill when he was clearly ill with something more serious? The knot of anxiety in her stomach tightened. She needed Hannibal's company, but he was far away in the stables. A great, smothering loneliness enveloped her, and once she was in her nightgown, she lit another candle on the writing table, opened the *Principia Mathematica* and set out a mathematical problem that took her until the early hours of the morning to complete.

The days at Fernhill Manor ran into weeks, and Sir Christopher kept to his bedroom or sat reading in the walled garden on sunny days. Ellen went each evening to enquire politely after his health, and every evening he politely assured her from his pillows that it was improving. Then he'd enquire about her day, and she'd tell him politely that it had been very pleasant, though it wasn't strictly the truth.

Actually, she felt as if she was living in a beehive, with Viola's friends and relatives, male and female, young and old, happily swarming in and out daily. They carried Ellen off with them to parties at neighbouring houses where she would listen to their music, learn dance steps and card games, and hear the latest gossip about people she didn't know.

When at Fernhill, the days buzzed with activities indoors and out, and the young ladies discussed fashion or filled their sketchbooks with pretty scenes, and worked on their embroidery. And flirted with the young gentlemen.

The older ladies spent much of their time matchmaking.

Ellen still felt uncomfortably tongue-tied with strangers, even the ones who were clearly trying to be sociable. It was the men – young men mainly, but not exclusively – who were the ones most eager to be in her company, and they found every opportunity to be alone with her, often so close that she could feel warm breath on her cheek or the brush of their fingers on her arm.

One brash young man, one of the Rigby cousins named Tobias, whose father had just bought him a commission in the army, was someone she regarded warily after he slid his hand under her hair on two occasions and tried to stroke the nape of her neck.

Tobias was a pale, sharp-featured young man, with a thin-lipped face beneath carefully waved blond hair, and when she'd scolded him sharply for touching her, he'd laughed, put an arm around her waist, pulled her against him and planted his mouth on hers.

That was when she brought her knee up so skilfully between Lieutenant Rigby's legs that he instantly sank to the ground with a howl. The daughter of the blacksmith in Littlewood had once told her all about that very effective strategy. But rather than deter any further contact, it seemed to add fuel to the detestable young man's determination to kiss her again.

Tobias Rigby became her annoying shadow, which the older ladies thought most amusing. 'Ah, yes,' said his mother on a quiver of laughter when they saw him standing behind a shrub in the garden to surprise Ellen as she passed,

'Toby will always fall in love with the prettiest girl at any party.'

Ellen's escape from Lieutenant Rigby's attentions was to take Hannibal for long walks along the beach. If she was approached, one soft word of command to the dog produced a display of wolfish ferocity that quickly deflated any man's hope of sharing Miss Templeton's company.

On days when the weather kept everyone indoors, Ellen slipped away to a secluded little room she'd located in the south wing where she could lock the door, quietly get on with her studies, and write to Mr Halliday with news of her progress.

After a period of complete rest, Sir Christopher's strength improved sufficiently for him to leave his bed for longer periods and walk about a little. Doctor Parker was a fussy little bald-headed man who irritated him greatly, but he had been persuaded to continue the myth of the *chill* when speaking with Lady Viola about her husband's health.

'Say nothing about the condition of my heart, Doctor,' Sir Christopher had insisted 'I must tell her myself, when the time is right.' And that time was growing closer, he had to admit. But not yet. He wasn't ready yet.

From his big south-facing window he was able to watch Ellen and the other young people when they were in the garden. She usually came to his room in the afternoon, but she was still as aloof with him as she was with the party of young people he could now see cheerfully setting up a game of bowls on the lawn.

A tall, handsome youth, the heir to the neighbouring estate, was speaking earnestly to her while she held herself stiffly, unsmiling. What the devil was wrong with the girl? Sir Christopher asked himself. She was lively enough each time he'd watched her bounding through the garden with that damned hound.

Something must be done quickly to improve her apathetic attitude towards human company, he decided at last, and struggled to rally his failing strength. To Lady Viola's delight, he announced that he would join the party for dinner that evening. It was not something he anticipated with joy, but the need to prompt his daughter into a semblance of sociability was becoming urgent.

He asked for Ellen to be seated next to him at the dinner table and attempted to include her in the banal conversation he was having with Tobias Rigby's mother who was sitting opposite them and holding forth tonight on the benefits said to be gained from regular sea-bathing.

'I have taken a house at Brighton for a few weeks – Tobias does so enjoy bathing – and I believe this time the girls and I will be brave enough to try it, too!'

Sir Christopher murmured his congratulations, but Ellen kept her eyes on her plate and made no attempt at the art of conversation. He turned to her and asked if she would like to attempt sea-bathing one day, and she smiled politely, murmuring that she was sure it would be pleasant, then returned her attention to the plate. Sir Christopher felt his patience with her growing very thin when every other attempt to engage her in conversation failed as well.

It wasn't until after dinner, when the gentlemen had joined the ladies in the drawing room, that he caught a surprising flicker of enthusiasm in Ellen's eyes. While Lady Rigby's daughters sang a duet at the piano, Ellen unhesitatingly accepted an invitation to join two middle-aged cousins at a card table that had been set up at the far end of the room. The gentlemen were known to be keen gamblers, and one called to Lieutenant Rigby to be the fourth player.

'What game this evening, Miss Templeton?' one cousin asked as he shuffled the cards.

'*Commerce?*' she answered quickly, and as the game progressed, Sir Christopher saw that Tobias Rigby's concentration was clearly on Ellen, not on the cards dealt to him. And she was steadily lightening his purse.

As he continued to watch Ellen closely, a knot of worry tightened inside him when he recognized how skilfully she played the cards in her hand. And how much she enjoyed the game. The rules of *commerce* were simple – a matter of picking up and discarding cards until a three-card flush was collected. Ellen played fast, but never recklessly. Luck had its part in the game, of course, but he could see her unwavering concentration as she watched the table, obviously remembering what cards the others had already discarded, and winning more hands than she lost.

He stood behind her, observing how she coolly trounced the gentlemen, and it suddenly reminded him of the way Antonia had played at the gaming tables in St Petersburg. He gripped the back of Ellen's chair to steady himself. How ridiculous it was to compare the gloriously golden Antonia Warshensky-Rostroprovich with this stubbornly unforthcoming dark-haired child who was, after all, playing for no more than a few pennies at the table this evening.

It wasn't as though she was risking a great diamond necklace that had once belonged to the Empress Elizabeth. Antonia! Sir Christopher's pulse quickened as he recalled her expression the night she lost that damned necklace at the gaming table, and he'd later told her of his arrangement to buy it back before her husband discovered it missing. That episode had cost him almost every penny he'd inherited, but he had no regrets.

At the end of their game, Ellen stood up from the table, swept her winnings into her reticule, thanked the gentlemen, and rejoined the ladies near the piano.

Tobias Rigby trailed behind her.

What strange, ironic twists fate took, Sir Christopher thought as he later made his way back to his bedroom. If Antonia had not gambled away her diamonds that night in St Petersburg, his own inheritance would probably have remained intact, and there would have been no necessity for him to marry Lady Viola to rescue Ellen from a life of poverty.

Of course, Antonia had vowed that she would find some way to repay him, and he knew she'd truly meant it. Just as he knew it would be impossible for her to do so. He sighed. Antonia owed him nothing.

But now he must find some way to curb Ellen's enthusiasm for gambling or she'd be at risk of some day losing everything he'd just worked so assiduously to arrange for her future. He sank into reflection: Antonia and Ellen. They both occupied his thoughts as he lay in bed and waited for his pills to do their work.

Antonia! What joy they had found together.

Ellen? It was difficult to find a warm place in his heart for Ellen when she seemed determined to keep herself at a distance. He didn't know her at all.

CHAPTER SIX

When the household woke the following morning, the view beyond the windows revealed a sky covered by grey, wind-driven clouds that seemed to be sinking with the weight of water in them. Lady Viola's plans for a picnic party on the top of Hackthorne Hill had to be abandoned when the rain began.

'Do let's play hunt the thimble,' called one of the female cousins after breakfast, and the young people romped through the house while the fire was lit in the drawing room and the adults gathered in there to read, play chess, or doze the morning away.

Lady Viola smiled at all the youthful exuberance. 'Enjoy yourselves, my dears,' she called, 'but remember Sir Christopher is sleeping, so please avoid running through the south wing.'

Ellen tolerated the games and the increasingly obnoxious attentions of Tobias Rigby until an opportunity came for her to slip away while he was being blindfolded for blind man's buff. She snatched the *Principia Mathematica* from her bedroom and ran with it down a back staircase, into the south wing, and locked herself in the chilly little room that had become her sanctuary.

She sat at the table and blew a sigh of relief that the entire Rigby family was leaving for Brighton tomorrow. Another day spent fending off Tobias's groping fingers might persuade her to let Hannibal's teeth do their worst, preferably on some place that would cause the arrogant young lout great discomfort when he sat in his saddle. With that gleeful thought, she opened the book and picked up her pen.

When the time came for lunch, it was not simply hunger that drove her to rejoin the party. Lady Viola worried if she thought Ellen was alone – and therefore must be lonely – and couldn't be persuaded that this was never the case. But Ellen didn't want her stepmother to be worried; she was growing fond of her.

'Oh, yes, I enjoyed the morning very much indeed,' she said when Viola asked, 'and I suppose there'll be more games this afternoon.' She didn't add that she planned to avoid taking part in these ones also.

Lady Viola made a habit of retiring to her room after lunch, and when Uncle Albert asked Ellen to join him for a game of draughts in front of the fire, she accepted. In the drawing room, several aunts worked on their embroidery, a trio of younger cousins sitting in a corner giggled over somebody else's sketchbook, and Tobias Rigby was nowhere to be seen.

Ellen and Uncle Albert played two ponderous games before he nodded off to sleep in the middle of the third. She quietly put away the pieces, left him snoring softly in his chair and hurried back to Isaac Newton, waiting for her in the bare little room in the south wing.

When she swung open the door, she froze with horror. Tobias Rigby was sitting at the table; he looked up and gave her a sly, wet-lipped smile. 'Ah, at last she appears! The Marchioness of Mathematics, the Countess of Calculus, the Princess of Parallelograms!'

Her precious book was open. He had a pen in his hand and she saw that he had 'decorated' the frontispiece with a collection of big, lopsided hearts and his initials intertwined with hers. 'See, you'll never forget me now!' He snorted when he laughed.

Her jaw dropped and an incandescent rage consumed her power of speech; she threw him a look of pure hatred and reached for the nearest weapon. It was a poker standing beside the cold hearth and she advanced towards him with it in her hand and a look of murder in her eyes.

He tittered and sprang up from the chair as she swung the weapon. He pulled away and it merely clipped his shoulder, but he gave a yelp of pain, then backed towards the door, laughing. She raised her arm again and he sniggered at her fury while he edged out of the room and into the corridor. And still she came towards him brandishing the poker.

But rather than cool his ardour, her attack had seemed to inflame it, and when he spread his arms to block her exit from the south wing, the lustful gleam in his eyes struck a chord of alarm deep inside her.

She dropped the poker, snatched her book from the table and, clutching it tightly against her, bolted down the twisting corridor towards her father's room at the far end. His door was ajar and when she ran in without knocking, she saw him standing by the window in his velvet dressing robe, looking out at the rain.

He turned to her in surprise, then smiled. 'Oh, splendid, Ellen, I was just about to send for you to hear the good news: you and Lady Viola will be able to try a little sea-bathing after all because Lady Rigby has kindly invited you both to stay with them at Brighton for a week or two.'

Ellen's face paled. 'A week or two in that company? God spare me! I'd prefer to spend a week or two down a coal mine!'

She heard a gasp from behind and spun around. To her mortification she saw Lady Viola and Dominique standing on either side of the bed, where they'd been adjusting Sir Christopher's pillows. Her stepmother's face crumpled as she burst into tears, and with her hands to her mouth, Lady Viola ran from the room; Dominique followed her to the door, then paused.

There was a long moment of stricken silence as Sir Christopher stared at Ellen in disbelief 'How dare you! How dare you insult Lady Viola and her family!' he said at last. Sir Christopher never raised his voice, but its tone was chilling. 'You are an arrogant, ungrateful young woman, flaunting your superior airs. Nature has blessed you with advantages in body and mind' – it was rare for him to stumble over his words, and it was a measure of his anger that he was doing so now – 'advantages of birth, for which you can take absolutely no personal credit. And yet you display no humility and dare to insult the generosity that is offered.'

Ellen flinched, but didn't look away. Her face was devoid of colour, her lips trembled, and the works of Isaac Newton slipped from her fingers to hit the floor with a thud.

'I don't know – I don't know what to do!' she cried. 'Oh, why did you bring me here?' The angry bitterness in her words shocked him. She turned and ran from the room, brushing past Dominique, who was hovering in the doorway with an expression of dismay.

Sir Christopher drew in a sharp breath as pain shot through his chest and he took an unsteady step towards his armchair. Dominique closed the door and rushed to help him. A few minutes later they saw Ellen and Hannibal running past the window, through the misty rain, across the garden and down into the gloom of the woods.

Sir Christopher groaned. 'In the name of God, what more does she want?' he said in a voice tight with frustration. 'I thought the Ramsden connections would provide the advantages that I could never give her, but it seems I was quite mistaken.'

'No, no, monsieur,' Dominique said, crouching beside his chair, 'forgive me for speaking boldly, but surely you misjudge Mademoiselle Ellen. She is a child and sees nothing but uncertainty around her, and that uncertainty makes her afraid.' He was about to object, but Dominique continued nervously. 'Monsieur, do you not understand that mademoiselle has just two things in her life of which she can be absolutely certain: she can trust the loyalty of her dog, and she can trust the numbers she uses in her mathematical calculations. These don't lie to her.'

Sir Christopher looked away and rubbed a hand across his lips as he gazed through the window at the gathering dusk. The maid stood slowly and took a step back, looking down at him.

'Forgive me, monsieur, but your daughter's greatest need is to be able to trust you, too, and that she is unable to do. She understands you just as little as you understand *her.*' He swung around with a frown of angry surprise, but Dominique would not be silenced. 'Oh, how often I see her concerned glances when you pretend to others that your health is improving. She fears for her father who will not permit her to hear the truth, yet—'

She stopped abruptly and dropped her gaze, aware that she was grossly overstepping her position. At her feet, Ellen's heavy book lay open where it had fallen, and as Dominique picked it up she saw the love-sick nonsense that had been scrawled on the frontispiece. 'She clings to childhood, monsieur, because she fears the unknown world beyond it.'

Without speaking, she passed the book to him, and he studied the desecration. 'You're a wise woman, Dominique,' he said, frowning, 'and perhaps your assessment is correct' The trace of a smile flickered in the corners of his mouth. 'Sadly, my daughter is facing womanhood with a coward for a father.'

Night was falling by the time Ellen entered the manor by a side door and learned from a servant that Lady Viola was upstairs in her room. She trudged up the back staircase feeling cold, damp and miserably ashamed of her outburst.

Dominique had been hovering in the corridor and hurried to meet her when she reached the head of the stairs. 'Oh, mademoiselle, you must change from those wet clothes instantly. I'll have a warm bath brought to your room.'

Ellen's teeth were chattering but she shook her head. 'I must speak to her straight away,' she said in a voice husky with nervousness, and tapped on Lady Viola's door. When she entered, she saw her stepmother reclining on the bed and, to her surprise, her father was there also, sitting in a deep chair beside her.

Quaking with consternation as much as with cold, Ellen avoided Sir Christopher's eyes, crossed the carpet to the foot of the bed, and dropped a curtsy. 'Lady Viola, I wish to apologize for my appalling rudeness to you earlier. I offer no excuses, and I beg your forgiveness.'

Viola's big, brown eyes blinked rapidly and her pursed pink lips trembled; she pushed herself up onto one elbow and looked at Ellen in astonishment. Then her face lit with delight.

There was something quite endearing about the woman's childlike ability to instantly let go all resentment, Sir Christopher decided as his wife dabbed a lace handkerchief to her nose, sat up straight and held out a hand. 'Of course you're forgiven, dear child, of course. We'll say no more about it and if you—'

'You're very kind, ma'am,' Ellen said, interrupting her stepmother, 'and now may I beg a favour? I think the time has come for me to wear my hair *up*, but I have no pins or combs and I wondered if you would be so kind as to lend—'

'No, Ellen, not yet,' Sir Christopher interjected, aware that her request was a token of complete surrender. 'I'd like you to keep your hair just as it is for a little longer.' He was touched by the relief he saw in her eyes, and had to clear his throat before he could trust his voice to continue. 'By the way, we have discussed the visit to Brighton, and Lady Viola agrees that perhaps you might prefer to remain here at Fernhill to keep me company while she is away?'

Ellen's forehead creased, as if she had misheard his words, then a faint colour washed into her cheeks. 'Stay here with you?' Her breath caught. 'Oh, thank you. Indeed, I would like that very much.'

The Rigby family and most of the other guests left for Brighton next morning But Lady Viola's departure was delayed by a last-minute change of plans when an invitation to a house party at Eversleigh Park in Somerset came from her cousin Grace, the Marchioness of Eversleigh.

'Of course you must go, Viola,' Sir Christopher said immediately. 'It will be pleasant to spend a little time with Grace and Sebastian on your way home from Brighton. Please extend my apologies, and tell them how much Ellen and I look forward to visiting Eversleigh Park on some other occasion.'

Next morning, after lengthy farewells and Sir Christopher's repeated reassurances, Lady Viola's carriage, carrying Uncle Albert and Dominique also, rolled away from Fernhill Manor.

'Goodbye, my dears,' she called to them. 'I promise to be away no more than a month or so.'

At last the house was empty, and with most of the rooms closed up until Lady Viola's return, a small bedroom for Miss Templeton was made up next to Sir Christopher's in the south wing. This arrangement had been Dominique's suggestion, and she also had Ellen's writing table and books brought into her father's room and placed near the window.

As soon as Lady Viola's vehicle rumbled away down the drive, Sir Christopher told Alfred Atkins to fetch Hannibal from the stables and bring him into the house. The manservant's disapproval was registered in the snort he gave as the hound bounded across the room to sit at Ellen's feet. 'Thank you, Alfred Now, take the afternoon off, m'good fellow, and enjoy an ale in the village. Miss Templeton will look after me, and Hannibal will make sure we're not disturbed.'

Alone at last, Ellen and Sir Christopher studied each other hesitantly. 'I'm sorry it has taken so long for us to find this time together,' he said with a sigh, 'and now I confess I'm not quite sure where to begin.'

She perched shyly on the end of his bed, and the dog sat with his head on her lap while she fondled its ear. 'Actually, I'd like you to tell me about my mother,' she said at last 'The Sharpes would never talk about her, I don't think they liked her very much. Did you love her, Papa?'

It was the first time she had called him papa, and he felt absurdly moved. He reached out a hand towards her and she came closer to put hers into it 'Yes, Ellen, I did love Margaret,' he said, choosing his words carefully. 'Our families were neighbours and I knew her from the day she was born; she always regarded me as a big brother.' He squeezed her fingers. 'And she wasn't much older than you are now when I asked her to marry me.'

Ellen took a deep breath and her chin quavered. 'Did she die because of me? The Sharpes always made me think I was the cause.'

'Oh, Lord, no, no, no!' He put his arms around her and pulled her to his chest. 'Margaret was killed in a coach accident when you were a year old. You were at home with the housekeeper and she was on her way to visit me when my regiment came back in '97.'

She stayed with her head against his shoulder. 'Tell me what she was like,' she whispered, and he realized with a jolt that – apart from the dreadful day when she'd flown into hysterics and told him that she had fallen prey to a seducer and was carrying a baby – his memories of sweet, pretty Margaret had grown very faint.

But, in order to comfort the girl now clinging to him, he spun a story of halcyon days when her mother was his childhood companion in Hampshire, when he taught her to ride a pony and to fish, and they'd played cricket with the village children.

Very slowly, he edged his tales of youth towards the sensitive issue of his health, dreading the moment he must reveal the present prognosis. 'Unfortunately, I caught rheumatic fever when I was about twelve, and it was months before I was allowed outside to run about again.'

To his surprise, Ellen sat up and looked at him searchingly. 'I once knew a boy in Littlewood who caught rheumatic fever – and eventually his heart stopped because nothing could be done.' Her voice was tight and he read the question in her blue eyes.

'Yes, my dear, sometimes the effects are felt quickly – and sometimes not for years.'

She bit down on her lip, her chin quivered, and for a moment she seemed not to breathe. 'Oh! Now I understand,' she whispered at last, and increased her pressure on his fingers. 'Lady Viola is not aware yet?'

He shook his head, and to his relief there were no flooding tears, no hysterics, no further questions. 'Oh, Papa, I'm so sorry. How I wish from the bottom of my heart that it wasn't so,' she said quietly and lay her head on his shoulder again while he continued with the story of his life in the army, of his later journeys and the people he had known.

And he chuckled when she told him tales of growing up with the Sharpes in Littlewood. 'Their lives must be so dull now that I'm not there to argue with them. I really was quite dreadful, you know, Papa, but when they tried to scold me, I'd pretend I was a hedgehog so nothing they said could ever touch me.'

As one quiet, uneventful day flowed into the next at Fernhill Manor, Ellen felt a deepening affection for her father. She asked the stableboy to take Hannibal for his long walks each morning while she stayed with Sir Christopher, and when he was too tired to talk, or even listen to her read, he liked to watch her as she sat writing at the table by the window.

Several times each week she sent a reassuring letter to Lady Viola – 'My dear Mama', they began, and after commenting on the weather and sending fond messages from Sir Christopher, she signed herself, 'Your affectionate daughter, Ellen'.

Sometimes she sat beside his bed and read to him. Sometimes she lay on the bed beside him with her head on his pillow as he talked about affairs of the world and the men who controlled those affairs – the powerful men who moved amongst the Ramsden family, the men she was likely to meet some day.

'Your face will attract men as moths are attracted to a flame, I promise,' he warned her gently, 'but keep a firm rein on a bequest that will come to you when you're twenty-one, and you'll never be forced to marry merely for security.'

'No, Papa, I don't think I'll ever marry,' she said as she helped him to a chair in a sunny corner of the walled garden one warm afternoon. 'I can think of nothing worse than being subjected to the touches of some creature like Tobias Rigby.' When he was settled, she placed a rug across his knees then stooped to touch her lips lightly on his forehead. 'Of course, should I one day be fortunate enough to find a man like you, I might be persuaded to change my mind.' She laughed and kissed him again.

'Find a man who loves you as much as I do, Ellen Templeton, and I guarantee he'll make you happy.' Emotion made his voice falter, and he lifted her fingers to his lips.

She looked at him and sighed. 'Yes, that's what I hope for, but how will I know if this man does truly love me? How will I know if I love him? Can love be assayed like gold?' She settled herself on the grass beside his chair, pulled a stalk and twirled it between her fingers.

'You'll know when it comes, I promise.' He hesitated. 'There is nothing in the world like the mystery of how love flies out of the mist to find us. The great Pascal has said that "the heart has its reason that reason does not know".'

'It sounds a very risky undertaking,' she said, half laughing. 'So tell me, Papa, were you truly, truly in love with my mother when you married her?'

'Oh, Ellen, how do I answer such a question!' he said. 'Of course I loved Margaret. She was the gentlest creature ever created and we were exceedingly happy in the short time we had together.'

She gave him a knowing smile. 'You must have been no older than thirty when she died. Was there never another love in your life?'

He clicked his tongue and gave her a wry grin. 'M'dear, this is not the kind of conversation a gentleman conducts with a youthful daughter.'

Ellen took his hand in hers. 'Who was she? Did she truly love you, too?'

'Yes, she did,' he said quietly after a long pause, and smiled as memories came rushing back. He took a deep breath. 'Her name was Antonia and I met her when I spent a year with our embassy in St Petersburg.'

'So why didn't you marry her?'

'Because, my dear, she already had a husband.'

'But if you loved each other so deeply, did you never think of running away together?'

'If only life was so simple!' he laughed and played with a strand of the dark curls lying on her shoulder. 'It wasn't a matter of morality that prevented us, I assure you, it was my lack of fortune. Nothing withers the flower of love quicker than a life of poverty.'

'But if you loved each other so deeply, I don't understand why you didn't take that risk! Surely true love can overcome anything?'

He rested his head on the back of the chair and closed his eyes. 'Just say that I loved Antonia far too deeply to gamble with her future. My inheritance had gone and I knew that I would never see old age. How could I snatch her away – and then risk leaving her alone in the world to face a life of destitution?'

Ellen shook her head slowly. 'Tell me about Antonia. Was she very, very beautiful?'

'Ah, yes! But it was much more than that.' He opened his eyes and looked into Ellen's. 'There was something about Antonia that defies description – her spirit and a courage that few could match.' He smiled at the recollection. 'She was trapped in a loveless marriage, but Antonia had the capacity to soar above the unhappiness and carry me with her.' He studied Ellen for a long moment and stroked the back of his fingers down her cheek. 'You and Antonia would have understood each other, I'm sure.'

'So, were you *very* poor before you married Lady Viola?'

'I was quite penniless, but *you* won't be, my love, now that you've become Lady Viola's ward.'

'Was that your reason for marrying her? You did it for me?' There was a catch in her voice.

'Well, m'dear daughter, let's just say that I'd spent a long, long time searching for some purpose to my life, and thanks to you, I finally found that purpose.' He stroked his hand over her head. 'Discovering the girl who was hiding behind the hedgehog quills has brought me great satisfaction. And joy.'

The weeks passed and a taste of autumn crept into the air, the leaves began to drop and a fire was kept burning in the hearth. When Lady Viola returned from her visits, full of happy gossip and family news to report, she was disappointed to find her husband still an invalid.

'Oh, poor Sir Christopher,' Viola sighed, 'I did so hope you would have recovered sufficiently for us to attend Felicity Montgomery's wedding in Bath before Christmas.'

Viola was a social creature, happiest when she was surrounded by chatter and laughter, and after several weeks spent quietly with Ellen and Sir Christopher at Fernhill Manor it was not difficult for them to persuade her to go off and attend the wedding in Bath, and even to stay and spend Christmas there with relatives.

When she arrived back at the end of January, it was Ellen herself who prepared her stepmother for the inevitable shock of facing Sir Christopher's further decline. And Viola took the news badly.

With Dominique's help, Ellen comforted her stepmother upstairs, and cared for her father downstairs. On her seventeenth birthday in March she asked to borrow pins and combs from Lady Viola and, for the first time, Dominique dressed her hair into an arrangement that swept it up to reveal a long, graceful neck. The effect was dramatic; Ellen found it daunting.

Sir Christopher smiled from his pillows when she presented herself to him. 'Well, well, so the time has come at last, has it?' He lifted a frail hand and she took it in hers. 'You're a beautiful woman, Ellen, and life is waiting for you. Don't be afraid. Embrace it,' he whispered.

'I think I'm ready.' She held his hand to her cheek. 'And I want you to know, Papa, that, in my own way, I love you every bit as deeply as your Antonia must have done.'

He looked at her tenderly. 'Then I am indeed a most fortunate man.'

She lay her head on his pillow, and he held her in his arms as she wept.

And one night, just six months after they had come to Fernhill Manor, while Ellen dozed fitfully in a chair beside his bed and his wife snored softly upstairs, Christopher Templeton murmured one name, closed his eyes, and without a sound or fuss, slipped from life as gracefully as he had lived.

CHAPTER SEVEN

Spring was late coming to Spain in 1813, and the first day of warm sunshine brought a few small rowing boats out onto the lake in Madrid's Retiro Park, though not as many as might have been expected. A wave of fear was creeping through the streets and palaces of the city as people began to realize that the unimaginable was happening: the tide of war on the Peninsula was turning against Bonaparte.

They'd heard that the emperor had lost his Grande Armée to the Russian winter, and while the British had won no great victory in Spain since Salamanca last year, Wellington was relentlessly pushing the French towards the north. And King Joseph was still openly quarrelling with Marshal Jourdan, still resisting his brother's orders to engage the British in a deciding battle.

Today, Antonia Warshensky-Rostroprovich, lounging on cushions in the stern of a boat hired for an afternoon on the lake, held her silk parasol aloft in one hand, and trailed her other in the ripples created by the oars dipping lazily in and out of the water. She gave the rower a flirtatious glance. 'I am honoured, Marqués, that you have found time for our little excursion today,' she said with an edge of sarcasm in the tone. His days were usually spent gambling, after he'd slept off the wine consumed the night before.

The man said nothing, but answered with a thin smile and a cynical lift of one eyebrow. Yet in his hard, dark eyes she read a suppressed excitement. Clearly, he had something to tell her, and out here on the lake there was no chance of their conversation being overheard.

Ever since coming to Madrid and appealing to Joseph Bonaparte – King Joseph of Spain – for protection, Antonia had been scrupulously careful to give no hint of her true purpose in the city. In the palace she mingled quietly with the swarm of Spanish aristocrats who'd thrown in their lot with the French; she said little and listened much. Several times Napoleon's brother had invited her to dine with a small party in his apartment, but Joseph was under far too much pressure these days to play his usual role of charming host.

Only Father Juan in the cathedral knew why Antonia had come to the city, yet for some unexplained reason she'd recently become aware of being watched whenever she moved – both inside and outside the palace. Today there was an orange seller sitting under a tree on the bank of the lake; and she was sure it was the same woman she'd seen selling oranges outside the palace gates an hour ago.

For some time Antonia had had the feeling that the enigmatic man now pulling on the oars was not convinced that she'd been a victim of the partisans. She twirled her parasol in one hand and, with the other, playfully splashed a few drops of water at him. He laughed.

The Marqués de Morillos el Alfonso y Melida Galindo was a tall man of fifty, a grandee of Spain, heavy featured and darkly handsome, with a carefully trimmed moustache. From a distance he looked magnificent in a dark red velvet jacket heavily embroidered with gold, its cuffs trimmed with lace, and a matching tricorne on his head. But Antonia was close enough to see the frayed edges of his collar and the skilful repairs to tears in the lace. The marqués was a refugee in Madrid also – a bored, disillusioned man whose ancestral estates had been lost; a nobleman who had allied himself with the French because, like so many others of his rank, he'd believed the British had no chance of defeating Napoleon's army.

Now he knew only too well that the moment he or any of the others stepped outside the protective circle of French bayonets around Madrid, he'd be torn apart by the Spanish people whose women and lands had for years been ravished by the French invaders.

In recent months, the marqués had discovered that seducing the beautiful Russian lady in her small room high up in the palace was a pleasant alternative to spending every day and night in the company of the other Spanish nobles living under King Joseph's protection. And seduction was a game that Madame Warshensky-Rostroprovich played as expertly as he did.

Antonia smiled invitingly at the marqués. She didn't like him, and she didn't entirely trust him, though he sometimes slipped useful information into his conversation. His wife was one of Marshal Jourdan's favourites at court, but as discretion was something totally foreign to the beautiful young marquésa, she told her husband everything she overheard Jourdan and King Joseph discussing in the marshal's private apartment. It then amused the marqués to repeat it to the delightful Russian lady, and to receive her reward.

'We live in interesting times, Doña Antonia,' he said teasingly as he began to swing the oars again. 'Would you believe that this war might soon be won by politics instead of guns?'

'And whose imagination did that little fantasy spring from?' She laughed to disguise her interest.

'Believe me, my lovely, nothing is a laughing matter when Monsieur Chevalier, the emperor's personal emissary from Paris, is involved.'

Excitement shot through her, but she shrugged one shoulder dismissively. 'I've never heard of the man.' She looked directly into the marqués's eyes as she lied.

Father Juan had whispered the name of Chevalier to her only last week. *I do not understand what lies behind his arrival in Madrid*, the priest had warned her through the grille in the confessional, *but tread even more warily now, my child, for I hear that Bonaparte is desperate and this man is powerful.*

Several times since then, Antonia had seen Napoleon's emissary coming and going from the palace, and secreting himself with King Joseph for hours at a time. Monsieur Chevalier, always dressed in unadorned black, was a small, sharp-faced man with thinning grey hair, whose alert, bird-like eyes surveyed the world from behind steel-rimmed spectacles. Physically he appeared insignificant, but she'd noted the deference shown to him by Marshal Jourdan and the courtiers.

The marqués's brow lifted now as he studied her. 'Do you know what happened to the Bourbon king five years ago when Bonaparte hauled him off the throne of Spain and placed Joseph on the warm cushion?' he asked casually.

His question surprised her, she gave a dismissive laugh and looked away. 'Everyone knows that Ferdinand the Dim was taken off to France and locked up in Talleyrand's lovely chateau at Valençay. I'm sure any other prisoner-of-war would be delighted to change places with him.'

'And that's exactly what might soon happen if Monsieur Chevalier's mission is successful.'

Her heart skipped a beat. 'Oh, Marqués, it's so tiring when you speak in riddles,' she said with a feigned yawn.

He narrowed his eyes at her. 'Tell me, señora, what is Bonaparte's most pressing need now that he's just left the greatest army in modern times lying dead in the Russian snows, and today sees Austria, Prussia and Russia gathering against him in Europe's north?' The marqués stopped rowing and leaned towards her. She held her breath.

'What the emperor desperately needs, dear lady,' he went on, 'are more men and more horses and more guns! And here on the Peninsula Wellington is keeping a quarter of a million battle-seasoned French troops engaged in a long war that is bringing no glory to France and draining the treasury.' He dipped the oars in the water again and pulled. 'The emperor wants his army out of Spain to fight the Prussians and the Russians and the Austrians.'

'Don't tell me he's going to order his men to pick up their muskets and run back over the mountains to France?'

'No, nothing so simple. He has sent Monsieur Chevalier here on a mission of the highest secrecy' – a smile flickered on his lips – 'a mission which I can reveal because my dear wife is a very light sleeper and heard last night that Napoleon proposes to restore King Ferdinand – the rightful king, the symbol of Spanish pride – to his throne.' His tone was laced with sarcasm.

'Send Joseph home to France and bring Ferdinand back to Spain?' It was impossible to hide her surprise.

'Absolutely,' the marqués said, then turned down the corners of his mouth, 'but, of course, only if he signs a treaty – the Treaty of Valençay. That's the secret. It's Napoleon's stroke of genius, because it declares that the state of war that has *unfortunately* arisen between Spain and France is now over. If Ferdinand signs, the French armies will be withdrawn, and Spain will be a free, sovereign country with its own beloved king. Spanish trophies will be restored, Spanish pride will be burnished by French flattery.'

'Unbelievable!' she gasped. If a manoeuvre of this magnitude was being proposed, British intelligence must be warned immediately. 'And what does Ferdinand have to promise in return for this remarkable French benevolence?'

'Just one thing: he has to end the alliance with Britain, cease all trade, close his ports to British ships, and order the British army to leave Spain immediately.'

'And if they don't?' Antonia felt her mouth drying.

'If they hesitate there will be no forage for the horses, food for the men, or ports for the supply ships. A starved army is no army.'

'So you're saying that, without a shot being fired, Wellington could be forced from Spain and Napoleon could take all the French troops back to march against his northern foes?' She frowned and shook her head. 'It sounds simple, but after the atrocities inflicted by the French army on the Spanish people, I can't see them eager to make peace with their bitterest enemy.' Her heart pounded as the implications of this treaty flew around her brain like bats in a cage. 'Has Ferdinand agreed to sign it?'

'I believe he's tempted, but he hasn't forgotten that the last King of France lost his head when he lost favour with his people, and it seems that our beloved Bourbon monarch is demanding reassurance that he'll not meet the same fate if he comes back here.'

'So what part does Monsieur Chevalier play in this game?' She was impatient now to get the information to Father Juan. Once Wellington heard about this treaty, British gold would flow, bribes would be offered, and the populace of Spain roused against the very thought of peace with France. Her palms were damp as the marqués spoke.

'Napoleon's emissary is here to collect *written* support from the nobility of Spain, from the Spanish generals, and most importantly of all, support from the Church. If he can show Ferdinand the evidence that enough of these people are prepared to stand behind their king, then His Majesty might feel it's safe to return.'

The news stunned her and it was some moments before she was able to speak 'And where does your loyalty lie, Marqués? Are you a king's man?'

'Loyalty?' He laughed and his proud face softened 'Ah, Doña Antonia, loyalty can be a very costly commodity, and I prefer to have none of it. I intend to stay alive, no matter whose backside sits on the Spanish throne.'

Antonia exercised great restraint as she maintained her usual evening routine in the palace, aware of watchful eyes noting her movements. Had Chevalier ordered this surveillance? Why now? At dinner there was a tension in the air – faint, but uncomfortable – and later very few people gathered at the card tables.

At midnight Antonia retired to her room. She said goodnight to the maid, pulled the curtains, locked the door and climbed into bed. She lay there quietly until all footsteps in the hall had moved away, then she slipped out of bed again and laid a shawl along the crack under the door before she lit a candle and wrote a lengthy coded report for British intelligence. Her heart raced with excitement as she folded the paper and slipped it into a pocket concealed in the lining of her cape.

It was a week since she'd made her last confession to Father Juan in the *Catedral de San Isidro*. No one would question another visit tomorrow.

A hundred miles away Major Scovell, Wellington's information officer, woke the general's adjutant and showed him a French message that had just been intercepted and deciphered.

'I agree, Major, his lordship should see this immediately,' the officer said and went to wake the general.

Wellington's opinion confirmed theirs. 'This is indeed a nasty business, gentlemen,' he said. 'If Father Juan has been arrested, he'll be taken to the court prison.' He frowned and paced the room. 'With the tools of the Inquisition still in use in those dungeons, how much torture can a fellow his age stand before he breaks? Madame Warshensky-Rostroprovich must be warned to leave Madrid immediately, but who do we have there now to help her?'

'If we can locate Don Julian Sanchez, he could well have a contact in the city,' Major Scovell suggested.

Wellington nodded. 'Ask Colonel Halifax to join us. He knows the location of Don Julian's camp and if he leaves quickly, we might be in time to organize an escape for madame.'

Within an hour, Matthew Halifax and two cavalry men were riding fast towards the mountains and at daylight they began to climb steep paths into the territory controlled by the partisans. He spurred his lathered horse over the rough terrain, driven on by the image of the woman he had once met so briefly, the woman whose face he had never been able to forget.

His shouts for Don Julian echoed from the high rocks around them, and twice they were challenged by small, armed bands of peasants. Sanchez, they all said, had taken his men to raid French supply wagons travelling north, but one man volunteered to lead the British soldiers to the hidden valley where Don Julian had made his headquarters in a cluster of dilapidated farm buildings.

Daylight was fading by the time the exhausted horses reached it. A number of women carrying muskets came from doorways and Matthew was hailed by three wounded men lying in a barn. They recognized him from the time they'd ridden together to the bridge outside the town of Tejada.

'I must get a message to the señora in Madrid,' Matthew said as he and his men dismounted, 'and again I need to ask for Don Julian's help.' He pulled a purse from a pocket and shook it to jingle the coins. 'The matter is urgent.'

'Don Julian's return here is not expected for another four or five days,' one of the bandaged partisans said as they all sat around the campfire and the women brought food and wine. 'We have little news from Madrid these days. The city is crowded with French followers, and the army keeps a heavy guard on the roads.'

'There is something happening inside those walls, my friends, and we need to know what it is,' Matthew said. 'I must find a way in, then get the señora out before it's too late.'

A tall, square-shouldered woman, whom the men addressed as Isobella, came to the fire and sat beside Matthew. The others fell silent as she spoke. 'There could be a way,' she said. 'My cousin is married to a miller who takes flour to sell in the city. I will take you to his mill, and your gold might give him the courage to help.' She stood and gestured for Matthew to follow her.

'You must come alone. Change from your uniform, señor, become a Spanish peasant and ride one of our horses.'

Two hours before dawn, Lord Matthew Halifax, wearing a broad-brimmed hat and dressed in a worn shirt and brown breeches, sent his cavalrymen back to the regiment and rode eastwards towards Madrid with Don Julian Sanchez's woman. The gold he carried was stitched into the hem of the rough woollen cloak wrapped around his shoulders, and there was a knife slipped into the leg of his ill-fitting boot. Isobella had a pistol, but he did not. And neither did he carry identification. He was no longer a British officer.

Never in his life had Lord Matthew Halifax felt so vulnerable. And never so determined.

The morning sun warmed Antonia as she strolled slowly through the palace gardens and acknowledged the salute of the soldier at the gate. There was no orange seller waiting to follow her this morning when she stepped out onto the street, but as she began to walk in the direction of the twin-towered cathedral, a shabbily dressed youth with a limp soon became her shadow.

Twenty minutes later when she climbed the steps and entered the gilded baroque splendour of San Isidro, the youth remained outside, leaning against a column.

There were even fewer people than usual in the cathedral this morning, and with an unwanted sense of deep, dark anticipation, Antonia's first act was to light a candle and drop to her knees before it. From that position she could watch the confessionals and wait her turn to enter the door at the end, the one where Father Juan sat at this time each morning. Her heart thumped with impatience; this information on the secret treaty eclipsed anything she had sent previously.

At her first meeting with Father Juan, Antonia and the priest had devised a simple ritual to confirm that it was safe for them to talk. This morning, when she at last entered the confessional, her throat was tight with excitement.

'Bless me, Father, for I have sinned.'

There was a tone in the muffled response from the other side of the screen that sent a prickle of alarm through her. This voice carried a sibilation that Father Juan's Galician accent did not have.

'For these sins I have already lit a candle to Saint Theresa of Avila,' she said warily. This was their private signal to inform the priest that she had a message to pass to him. This was the moment for him to slide aside the screen to receive it. Nothing moved, and a chill crept up Antonia's spine. She leaned closer to hear the voice more clearly.

'Confess your sins, my child, that you may receive God's forgiveness.' The words were carried on a wave of stale tobacco breath and she sat back quickly. Father Juan never smoked; he detested it. Spiders of fear crawled over her skin.

'My sins, Father, are grievous,' she said, commanding her brain to function. If she was to give this unknown man a confession, she'd give him something to be remembered 'Forgive me, Father, for the sin of lustful thoughts that assume me and for the longing I have to be ravished by the great Napoleon. My body throbs for him, and each night I see him coming to me under the stars where we are naked, and he throws me to the ground.' A little cry of joy came from her throat. 'Oh God! I see his magnificent cock so long and thick and hard, and I cry out in pleasure because it grows longer and longer when I open myself to be devoured by his passion.' She made a panting sound. 'He thrusts himself into me, he thrusts and thrusts and I feel him sliding inside me, deeper and deeper until his whole being lies within my womb.' Now she whimpered. 'Forgive me, Father, for this glorious longing that nightly haunts my dreams, and during each day—'

A deep, throaty, impatient grunt from the other side of the screen halted her words, and the sound of her own blood pounding in her ears muffled the man's response and the number of Hail Mary's he imposed.

'Thank you, Father,' she said meekly and left the confessional with trembling knees. Whoever the man was behind the screen, at least she seemed to have confused him. But how in the name of God was she to get her report out of the city?

She knelt amongst the congregation gathering for Mass and fingered her rosary while she looked surreptitiously about the cathedral for Father Juan. He had always refused to disclose the name of his courier; he said it was safer for her not to know. Perhaps if she waited here on her knees someone else would make contact with her here this morning.

But she caught no subtle signals and nobody approached, though she was one of the last to leave after the service. She pulled the cloak tightly around her as she walked down the steps. The youth with the limp was no longer there, but a burly young man wearing glasses and dressed as a student watched her as she walked past him; then he began to follow.

The band of tension around her forehead tightened. How would she find the next link in Father Juan's chain?

She was startled by a touch on the elbow, and looked up to see the marqués beside her, smiling roguishly. 'Such piety does you credit, my poor dear Doña Antonia. After spending so long on your knees on that hard cathedral floor, I now insist you permit me to escort you to a delightful coffee house I know in the Plaza Mayor. Come, I'll not take no!'

He slipped her hand into the crook of his arm as they strolled towards the square. 'Do you know, my dear, that while you have been at your devotions, I've had a most interesting morning inspecting the fresh animals brought into the corrals beside the bullring,' he said casually. 'This afternoon I will take you to the bullfight, though I'm afraid the quality of the animals they produce these days falls far short of the brave and beautiful beasts we once enjoyed watching.'

'I don't enjoy watching any kind of slaughter,' she said coldly. Her head throbbed; she needed time to think.

'Hmmmm,' he said, and led her around the plaza's grand arcade until they were greeted effusively by the owner of the coffee house and seated at a table. The marqués spent the next ten minutes in a detailed discussion with the man and his wife about the dishes to be prepared for them, and when that was settled, he turned back to the subject of bullfighting, while the student who'd been following them was nowhere to be seen.

'Yes, we Spaniards love to spend an afternoon at the bullring – Spaniards of all ranks, from aristocrats to peasants. Even priests. Did you know that Father Juan regularly attends to watch the bulls bred by a man who is his *special* friend?'

She looked at him in astonishment. 'Where did you hear that?'

'Idle men need to find some occupation, my angel, and meddling in business that doesn't concern us is one way of filling our time.' There was a new intensity in his gaze. 'But this time I've meddled deeply in *your* business because – fool that I am – I must admit that I find myself falling in love with you.' He picked up her hand, kissed it, then heaved a heavy sigh. 'Unfortunately, I'm discovering that some people in Madrid do not regard you quite as highly as I do.'

She held her breath and continued to stare at his dark, handsome face.

He rested his elbows on the table and leaned forward. 'I discovered last night that drunken tavern-talk can sometimes be most illuminating,' he went on, smiling as he watched her closely. 'You see, I drank with a man who breeds the bulls which interest Father Juan, and he boasted that he is never searched by the soldiers at the barricades when he brings in his beasts for the ring. The guards know him well now.'

Antonia's heart skipped a beat. 'And is that also the case when he leaves the city to go back to his farm?' She held her breath. Could this man be Father Juan's courier?

'Unfortunately, he was under the table and unconscious before I was able to touch on that point,' the marqués said with a shake of his head, 'but I know where he sits to watch his bulls fight. I will find him this afternoon at the ring.' He lifted his wine glass and took a sip, watching her over the rim. 'Perhaps he might regard it as an honour to meet a beautiful lady from St Petersburg.'

It was tempting to take the marqués into her confidence, but Antonia simply shrugged. 'I haven't decided whether or not I could bear to watch a bullfight,' she said in a carefully neutral tone. Nobody these days was to be trusted, even a man who had just declared his love.

He laughed softly.

And in the end, she went with him.

CHAPTER EIGHT

The marqués and Antonia sat in the shade, six rows back from a solid fence around a ring of sand the colour of burnt orange. The student who'd been following them remained outside the main gate, and while the tiers quickly filled with *aficionados*, she searched vainly for Father Juan somewhere in the crowd, which was now growing noisy and calling for the performance to begin.

The marqués flirted with her openly, whispering in her ear and lifting her fingers to his lips. 'Let them see us enjoying the afternoon, my dear,' he murmured, 'and as soon as the first bull has been killed, it will be my pleasure to go below and purchase a glass of refreshment for you.' He dropped his voice lower and smiled at her knowingly. 'The frown between your eyes leads me to believe that something today has given you a *headache*, so perhaps I might also find a remedy for that.'

'Thank you, Marqués, your consideration is most touching,' she said coolly. Then the shadow of a smile crossed her lips and she arched her brows at him. 'And, yes, I would be most grateful if you could purchase something to relieve my sudden *headache* – no matter what the price.'

His eyes burned. 'For you, Doña Antonia, no price could ever be too high.'

At that moment the *presidente* sitting in the official box beside the ring flicked a handkerchief, and a ripple of excitement ran around the audience in the tightly packed tiers. A trumpet sounded, the gate on the far side swung open, and to the sound of a band playing a *pasodoble*, the parade of the bull-fighters began.

Led by two riders in black velvet cloaks and white ruffs, whom the marqués explained were the constables of ceremony, came three slender young men in their magnificent, skin-fitting *traje de luces*, the suit of lights, and each wearing his gorgeous dress cape over one shoulder. Walking behind them were the cuadrillas, whose costumes carried just a little less glitter. These were the men who would test and try the bull and place the first *banderilla* barbs, and they were followed by the mounted picadors, dun-coloured figures in their stiff-brimmed hats and buckskin trousers, and carrying lances.

They all saluted the president in his box and then dispersed as he threw down the key of the bull-pen. A trumpet blast unwound the air's coiled spring, and to the accompaniment of the crowd's long 'Aaah!' the first black bull galloped into the sunshine, sand flying from its hoofs as it put down its head and charged at the magenta-yellow cape held by a cuadrilla man.

He played the bull past the cape, turning it sharply, and as it came at him again he slipped into a barrier bolt-hole. The bull pulled up just short of the fence and, snorting its rage, wheeled and charged for another cape farther out. That cuadrilla man played it past, and past again, and the crowd gave its first '*Olé!*'

'This is a *toro bravo*, a good bull,' the marqués said with cheerful anticipation in his tone. 'He's full of fight and charges straight. A torero can work well with a bull like this.'

The matador himself stepped out onto the sand to try the bull, standing imperiously as he pulled the animal round with his cape, drawing it close to his body and turning it in a spine-wrenching motion. When it recovered, it charged savagely again, and this time the matador performed an elegant pass that flowed the cape behind him like a dancer's skirt, while the animal brushed by within an inch of his leg. The wind of '*Olés!*' grew to a vocal gale across the arena.

Antonia found herself gripped by the performance of these fearless, slender, light-footed men in their graceful, daring dance with death. But then the first blood flowed and her stomach turned.

The bull lowered its head and she cried out when it charged a picador's horse, tossing it off its feet, slicing open its flank and exposing its entrails. But in that brief second before the impact, the man had struck with his *pic* and driven the steel point into the bull's shoulder hump of muscle. Quickly three more *pics* were piercing and weakening the animal and its blood began to run, staining the sand. Its torment continued, now with a barbed *banderilla* stuck into each wither to weaken it further, but though covered in sweat and blood, panting and frothing at the mouth, the animal lost none of its wild brute pugnacity.

'I can't sit through any more of this!' Antonia hissed. 'I must leave.'

The marqués gripped her arm. 'Not yet. Not yet. The kill will be soon. See how the matador waits for the exact moment when the bull stands with his front feet together; the sword must go straight in between the shoulder-blades for death to be swift.'

Antonia's head was in her hands and her eyes were tightly closed; she didn't open them until roars of '*Olé!*' soared around the arena. The marqués was shouting as loudly as everyone else, and when she looked at the ring, the dead bull was lying on the sand and the victor was holding aloft one hairy black ear. 'Indeed a good fight!' the marqués breathed with satisfaction.

'I will never understand how you can call this entertainment,' she sighed, gathering her cloak around her. 'I can't possibly sit through anything like that again.' She started to stand.

'Patience for just a little longer, I beg,' he whispered and sent her a tiny wink. 'Wait here while I fetch something to quench your thirst.' He pretended to be struck suddenly by an idea. 'Perhaps I can also find the breeder of that brave bull and discover if he is the one who can ease your unfortunate *headache*?'

She paused to choose her words carefully, for perhaps the bull-breeder who'd boasted he came and went freely from the city was indeed Father Juan's courier. 'Thank you, Marqués, I'm touched by your consideration, and if that gentleman is able to help my situation, I would be most happy to meet him.' He laughed, leaned towards her and kissed her lips. She didn't pull away and he kissed her again.

A number of people left the stand when the marqués did, and she watched the carcass of the bull leaving a long, red streak on the sand as it was dragged from the ring by a pair of mules. When other people began returning to their seats, she sat in a fidget of impatience waiting for the marqués. He failed to come. The trumpet sounded, the glittering parade came through the gates again, and the ritual torture of another sweating, blood-soaked beast was repeated in the ring of sand.

Antonia could watch none of it, and she even tried to close her ears to the noisy excitement of the spectators. The continuing absence of the marqués alarmed her, but she feared drawing attention to herself by leaving the stand now, so sat where she was until the next wretched bull had been despatched. As the tiers began to empty once more, she joined the congestion in the long, odorous passageway beneath the stands where vendors were selling refreshments. Her only thought was to find the marqués, and on instinct she jostled her way towards an exit that led through the stables to the bull pens outside.

Suddenly, through the crowds she caught a fleeting glance of the big, bespectacled young man who'd followed them earlier. He rushed from one of the horse stalls and was now shouldering his way roughly along the paved passage ahead, almost fighting his way past people in his rush to get out of the building.

Her progress was then blocked by a tight crowd jamming one of the doorways in the stable, and she was roughly pushed as she strained to catch a
glimpse of what was causing the interest She heard a few bursts of laughter
and some angry growls, but most people were staring dumbly at a body lying
face down on the straw, and at the rivulet of blood trickling across the cobbled
floor.

Antonia instantly recognized the marqués's red velvet coat with its once-
beautiful gold embroidery and lace cuffs, and the breath caught in her throat.
When one man walked into the stall and rolled the body onto its back, her
knees turned to water. The grandee's eyes were staring up in an expression of
wild surprise, and his fingers were curled into his palms, as if trying to grasp
onto one last moment of life as his killer struck. His throat had been cut so
deeply that the neck was almost severed, and when his body was moved, his
head lolled at a ridiculous angle on the straw, which brought a fresh burst of
laughter from some onlookers.

Antonia swayed and fought to stop her stomach from emptying itself onto
the paving stones. Her legs seemed unable to move and when her shoulders
were suddenly gripped forcefully from behind, she gave a cry of terror.

'Make no sound, madame,' a male voice whispered in her ear. 'I'm
Matthew Halifax; we've met before. Come with me quickly.'

He pushed himself in front of her and worked a path for them towards the
exit. Here, as they stepped out into the bright afternoon sunlight, they were
met by sounds of angry voices in the bull pens. Halifax pulled her behind a
group of onlookers where they huddled inconspicuously as a squad of French
soldiers marched by with a middle-aged, plainly dressed man whose head had
been badly cut. His hands were bound behind his back, and there was an angry
rumble from the crowd as the French passed with their prisoner.

'Come!' Matthew Halifax whispered urgently. 'It's not safe for you to
return to the palace; a miller's cart is waiting around the corner to take us out
of the city.'

She remembered the colonel well from their brief meeting at the bridge in
Tejada. He was a man that any woman would find hard to forget.

Beside the empty cart stood a grey-haired, thick-set man, who gave her a
baleful look, pulled aside a sheet of canvas and indicated with a jerk of his
head that she was to climb aboard.

'Apologies, madame,' Matthew whispered as he helped her onto the cart.
'Lie flat, remain silent and put your face next to the cracked board up there.
You'll see why. I'll come beside you.'

Immediately, the man covered them both with the canvas sheet and Antonia heard him urging his mules forward. They'd travelled a very short distance before the cart stopped and they heard gruff voices around it discussing the arrest. 'Damn French!' someone growled. 'Carlos always bred the best bulls for the ring. Who will supply them now?'

Antonia felt sick. Had the man been arrested because he was Father Juan's courier? Was the marqués murdered because his association with her had been discovered? In God's name, who had betrayed them? What had the British discovered to make them send Colonel Halifax into Madrid?

Now she was aware of something being thrown on the canvas above them. Something that stank. The weight grew heavier and warmer and, as she breathed in the air coming through the crack in the floor boards, she realized exactly what was being loaded into the cart.

'I'm carrying a message, Colonel,' she hissed. 'A most urgent message.'

His mouth was near her ear. 'All is arranged. Don Julian's lady is waiting for us. This cart belongs to a miller who is married to her cousin; he was persuaded this morning to bring me into the city under sacks of his flour.'

The stench hanging in the air made Antonia's head spin, but just as she thought she could stand no more, the cart jerked forward again, away from the dung pile in the bull pens, and out onto the road where a little more air, albeit dusty air, crept in though the crack in the floor boards. She sucked it into her lungs, aware that Matthew Halifax was struggling for breath, too.

She moved to ease her discomfort on the bare boards of the cart, and when her hand touched his, she pressed his fingers in a silent message of thanks. He kept a comforting hold on her hand until the cart was stopped at the military barricade on the city outskirts. The words spoken between the miller and the guards were too indistinct to be understood but, from the tone, it was clear that the soldiers were not eager to delay the reeking cart.

As they moved along the road again, Matthew listened for sounds other than the clopping hooves of the mules and the squeaking wheels. He could hear Madame Warshensky-Rostroprovich gasping for breath and felt her increasing tension in the grip on his hand. Twice the miller was forced to pull over while a company of infantry tramped past on its way towards the city, and when artillery caissons rumbled along the road, Matthew counted twenty guns. Why were they heading for Madrid? Even King Joseph must realize that Wellington was marching north.

The road was clear again after two squadrons of cavalry had clattered by, and Matthew felt a wash of relief as the mules began to trot once more. Never had a five-mile journey seemed so interminable.

The next time they stopped he felt a layer of the muck being shifted from the canvas sheet above them. Alarm gripped him and he was struggling to reach the knife lodged in the leg of his boot, when suddenly a corner of the canvas was lifted and a wedge of glorious daylight and fresh air hit his face. As he and Antonia struggled to scramble from their hiding place, he saw Isobella standing beside the cart and holding the reins of two horses. The miller was clearly frantic to rid himself of his passengers.

'Out quickly!' Isobella said, reaching up to help Antonia. 'The soldiers are at this moment searching the mill. We cannot go back there.'

Matthew called his thanks to the miller, who was whipping his mules along the road without a backward glance. Antonia dragged in several more lungfuls of fresh air as she threw Isobella a smile of relief and flapped her blue silk cloak in the vain hope of losing some of the cart's odour.

'Madame, this is Don Julian's good lady, Isobella, who led me here to find you,' Matthew said as the partisan swung her horse for Antonia to mount behind her. 'Father Juan was arrested some days ago' – he spoke rapidly – 'and I fear he has been persuaded to give names.'

The colour drained from Antonia's face at the thought of the old priest being broken under torture.

'It seems the French are now most eager to meet you, madame,' the Spanish woman said, frowning with a twinge of feminine envy at Antonia's rich apparel. 'There are patrols out everywhere.'

'We've no time to waste,' Matthew said as he swung onto his saddle, 'but first, put my cape around your shoulders and hide that blue silk, madame, or you'll be spotted a mile away.'

Wrapped in the tattered, odorous cloak and sitting behind Isobella on the horse, Antonia held on tightly as they rode fast along a track leading across the deceptively silent plain and past small damaged farms, some still smouldering The sun was dipping low and both horses were streaked with white sweat by the time the trio dismounted to water them at a shallow stream.

Nothing seemed to move in the landscape except the wind-ripple of grass and a solitary crane slowly flapping his way across the cloudless sky. Isobella announced that they would keep riding through the night, though Matthew doubted that her weary mount would be capable of carrying the two women all the way back through the hills. He was about to propose that they should both ride on ahead with the message while he followed on foot as best he could.

Suddenly Isobella looked across his shoulder and gave a hiss of alarm. Matthew turned just in time to see two French soldiers stepping from a clump of trees on the opposite side of the stream, barely ten yards away. Stragglers?

Deserters? One was already aiming a musket; a split-second later came a flash, and smoke blossomed from the muzzle.

Matthew felt his body shudder under a great blow, and it seemed then as if everything was happening at only half the speed of ordained time. He was falling backwards into a white-hot pain that tore into him, and he saw the warm, fresh blood welling from between the fingers of the hand clutching his chest. He glimpsed Isobella raising her pistol. Heard a shot. A scream.

Isobella had killed many Frenchmen. She kept her head and she was fast. The first shot from her double-barrelled pistol hit the second soldier before he could fire the musket he was aiming at Antonia, and while the first Frenchman was reloading his musket, she swiftly killed him, too. It was all over in a matter of seconds. She looked around quickly to see if the gunfire had attracted attention before she splashed across the stream to spit on the French uniforms, rifle the pockets and unstrap the packs from the soldiers' backs.

Antonia, horrified by the suddenness of what had happened, dropped to her knees beside Matthew, untied his scarf with shaking fingers and held it as an ineffective pad against the blood flowing from his wound. She looked up fearfully as Isobella ran back and dropped the French muskets and packs on the ground beside him. 'Isobella, what can we do for him?' Antonia's voice broke. 'How can we find help? Shelter?'

Isobella frowned and shook her head slowly. 'I doubt he'll live, señora,' she muttered as she swiftly opened one of the French packs to look for dressings, then gave an angry grunt 'The swine,' she growled, emptying the pack of wine bottles, ham and cheese, silver spoons, a simple gold ring, all obviously plundered from some farmhouse. But no dressings for a wound.

Matthew stirred. His eyes opened briefly then closed again. 'We're not going to let him die, Isobella,' Antonia said, with a rush of blind optimism. 'There must be a farmer nearby who'd welcome some English silver to help us, and to hear that two more of the French bastards are dead.'

Isobella shrugged, opened the second pack, and pulled out a silver dish, more wine bottles, a silk shawl, an unplucked chicken, and right at the bottom, a packet of dressings issued by the army.

Antonia snatched one and held it against the mess of open flesh and shattered rib, while Isobella edged her hand gently under Matthew's back. Her frown deepened as she withdrew it. 'Señora, the shot remains inside. There is no exit wound, and without a surgeon to remove the lead, he cannot live.'

Antonia mustered every ounce of courage she had to fight her tears. 'Isobella, I have information that must reach the British without delay, but I refuse to leave him to die alone out here!' She looked about desperately. 'We must find shelter somewhere – anywhere. I'll wait with him while you take my message to the British. They'll send someone back to help him.'

'Think again, señora,' the partisan said coolly. 'When I leave here, it would be at least six or seven days before I could return.'

Antonia drew in a shuddery breath and acknowledged that fact. 'Do your best, Isobella. I can't leave him to die alone.'

Isobella shrugged. 'If this is your decision, señora, we must find shelter for you both,' she said, shaking her head, 'and I shall send a prayer to St Jude, for he is the saint of hopeless causes.'

Together they quickly repacked the food plundered by the Frenchmen and loaded it onto one horse, and it was almost dark before they succeeded in heaving Matthew onto the back of the other. The pain caused by the initial movement dragged him briefly into an agonized consciousness, but he sank thankfully into oblivion again while they were positioning him onto the horse. Antonia sat behind his slumped form and his blood dripped onto her arms as she held him on the saddle. Isobella walked beside them, one hand helping to keep him from falling, the other holding the reins of both horses.

In this formation, the trio crossed the stream and set out across the fields, but they had gone only a mile before they met the acrid smell of smoke in the air. When they came closer to a low stone wall around a farm, they saw that fire had destroyed most of the small house, and approached it cautiously. The gate was off its hinges but the remains of a white-walled barn stood out in the darkness; Isobella led the horses through its door and under what was left of its thatched roof.

Getting Matthew down from the horse and onto the straw-covered floor was little more than breaking his fall as he tumbled into their arms. They could see little in the dim interior, but Isobella set about scratching together a bed of straw to drag him onto. He groaned, and Antonia felt fresh, warm blood running from his wound as he settled. She sat beside him, holding his hand and feeling useless, while Isobella went outside to find water, and came back quickly with a bucketful.

'The well – the well cannot be used,' she said tightly, 'but there is a rain barrel half full.' Matthew's breathing was shallow and she crouched beside him to touch his brow. 'I tell you again that there is nothing you can do for him, señora,' the Spanish woman said with a new softness in her tone. 'If he doesn't bleed to death, infection will set in. Maybe he will last two days, maybe three.' She waited a moment, giving Antonia time to change her mind.

'How can I leave him to die alone?' she repeated. 'I can't do it!'

'Very well. If that is your decision, I will go immediately with your message,' she said. 'Try not to reveal yourself. God knows where the French are now.'

Antonia fumbled inside her cape for the report and handed it to the Spaniard as they walked together from the barn. The chill of night was settling on the land and above them the stars had appeared. Antonia felt her courage shrinking.

'God's speed, Isobella,' she said shakily, and to her surprise, the partisan gripped her face between her rough hands and kissed her forehead before she swung herself into the saddle.

'May the Holy Mother watch over you, señora,' she called as she rode off. Antonia stood utterly alone in the darkness with her exhaustion and fears welling up to overwhelm her. Her shoulders shook as she wept for the young man who was dying in the barn, and she wept for Father Juan who had been broken by the tools of the Inquisition, and she wept for the marqués whose loyalty to her had cost him his life. She wept in despair for lost love. She wept in fear of the days ahead.

And when she could weep no more she clung onto the barn door to steady herself before she wiped her face, tipped it to the stars, and took a deep breath. 'Well, St Jude, are you awake up there?' she whispered. 'You might regard Antonia Warshensky-Rostroprovich as quite beyond help, but there's a young man lying in here who certainly needs you.'

Nervously, she went in and felt her way across the floor to Matthew. He was no more than a dim shape on the straw; his breathing was shallow, and he gave a low groan when she touched him. He was cold.

'Don't die, don't die, don't die!' she whispered, and fumbled in the dark to give him a fresh dressing. Then she spread her silk cloak and the rough woollen one over him, found the knife hidden in the leg of his boot and used it to prise the cork from one of the wine bottles in the French soldier's pack. She drank several strong, fruity mouthfuls and when she dripped some of the wine into Matthew's mouth, he swallowed it. Then with a sinking heart she lay down on the straw close beside him to share her warmth, and to pray.

CHAPTER NINE

Antonia had little sleep through the long night as she lay against Matthew, listening to his irregular breathing. From time to time when he stirred and moaned she gave him sips of water. And she was also kept awake by the horse that Isobella had left in the barn, as well as by the rustlings of rats scurrying through the straw and the occasional sound of a night creature in the woods at the bottom of the hill.

She was numb with exhaustion by the time a finger of daylight at last speared through the hole in the roof, and she lay for a time watching the dust motes dancing in its rays while she summoned the strength to face the new day.

Matthew mumbled faintly and stirred. There was blood frothing in the corner of his mouth and she wiped it away before she offered him a drink. The old horse nosed his way further into the barn and had just found something else to chew, when the sound of slow footsteps on a stony path outside sent a wave of terror through her. She held her breath, but to her relief, they moved past the barn and, as Antonia silently scrambled to her feet to investigate, a chilling cry rose from the farmyard.

She opened the door a crack and saw a wizened woman wrapped in a black shawl leaning over the well, then losing her grip on its edge as her legs gave way. She slumped to the ground, all the time wailing and calling down curses on Bonaparte and the whole French nation.

The woman shrieked in alarm when Antonia appeared from the barn, and tried to crawl away. 'Señora, please calm yourself, I wish you no harm,' Antonia called, and as she came closer to the well, its odour explained why Isobella had warned her last night to avoid it. There was something very dead in that water.

'My son! My son and his wife! May all Frenchmen burn in hell! They have killed my son!' The toothless old woman gave another heartbreaking wail and reached out towards the well.

'Oh, señora, I am so sorry. God will punish the men who did this, I am sure,' Antonia said. 'Is this your home?'

The woman sobbed. 'My son's wife told me to hide in the woods when they saw the soldiers coming, and I did! Oh, how I wish I had stayed and died with them.'

'This is a cruel, terrible thing that has been done here,' Antonia said and cast an apprehensive glance over the walls of the farmyard 'Please tell me, have you seen any soldiers this morning?'

The woman shook her head and her deeply lined face grimaced as Antonia helped her to her feet and took her, shuffling, into the barn. 'We have a little food in here which we can share with you,' Antonia said. 'It was taken from French soldiers we encountered – and killed – yesterday, and that is why we must stay hidden for a few days.' She held out the bottle of wine that had been opened last night 'Here, this may help.'

The woman snatched the bottle to her lips and swallowed rapidly. Then Matthew groaned and she blinked in surprise, peering into the gloom where he lay. 'The French did this to your son?' she asked when she stood beside him.

'Yes, señora, and that French shot is still in his chest.' She stopped herself from correcting the woman's perception; being called Matthew's mother was simpler than explaining the truth.

The old woman clicked her tongue sympathetically as her gnarled fingers began to ease away the dressing which was clinging to the congealed blood on his chest. He moaned again and she touched his heated forehead and frowned as his lids lifted and cloudy eyes gazed up at her, then shifted to look vacantly at Antonia.

'Is there anyone who can come to help my son, señora?' Antonia asked.

The grey head shook. 'The fever is taking hold,' she said, stating the obvious. 'He must be bathed before it consumes him. What have you—' She looked around as she spoke, then saw the two packs that Isobella had taken from the dead soldiers. They lay open on the floor, and the woman gave a cry as she reached for the silk shawl and recognized other items plundered from her house – silver pieces, the gold ring. Her howl came from the depths of misery.

'The soldiers who stole this from your family are dead now, I promise you,' Antonia said quickly, gathering the items together for the woman. 'I've searched the Frenchmen's packs for more of their dressings, but it seems I've used them all.'

The woman seemed not to hear as she gathered the family's possessions in her arms, hobbled to the barn door and set out towards what little of the farmhouse remained standing.

The horse snorted; Antonia gave it water and the last of the hay stored in the barn. Keeping the animal in here was going to pose difficulties, but if she put it outside to graze, might that create even greater problems if it was seen by someone?

Her throat was tight as she went back to Matthew; he was starting to sweat and soon his body began to shake. His teeth rattled and he mumbled in delirium, repeatedly calling a name – *William Gray?*

Antonia touched him and felt his pulse beating with a fierce, accelerated rhythm. Close to tears again, she undid his buttons, and using his knife, she slashed a panel from her blue silk cloak to bunch into a sponge. It seemed so futile to merely wipe his body with a damp cloth when what he needed to save his life was a skilled surgeon to remove the musket shot.

He continued to groan and mumble, and because she could think of nothing else to do while she brushed away the flies, she began to sing to him softly, as if he was a child she was trying to comfort. After all, the old woman had assumed that he was her son, and it was not difficult to imagine that this young man could very well have been the child she'd never had.

She dipped the cloth again in the bucket and squeezed out the water while she thought of whom amongst the men she had known she might have chosen to be his father. Certainly not the man she'd married. Her mind slipped down the years and, for a moment, closed her eyes and saw him – the Englishman whose tenderness had concealed his stubborn strength. How well she remembered the laughter in his voice, the love in his touch.

No matter what he'd said at the end, she should have followed him from St Petersburg while she'd had the chance; before her husband had made sure it was impossible for her to go anywhere. Where was Christopher Templeton now?

Thinking about that lost opportunity deflated her spirits further. She carried the stained water outside, tipped it over the wall, and after the bucket had been refilled from the barrel, she saw the old woman in a garden on the far side of the burned farmhouse, crouching to pick the leaves from whatever was growing there.

She went back to Matthew and held his head while he sipped a little of the cool water. The fever still burned in him, and she was just about to sponge him down once more when the woman shuffled into the barn with bedlinen torn into strips, and a collection of herbs soaking in a cracked bowl.

The linen smelled strongly of smoke but it appeared to be clean, and

Antonia watched as the woman made a poultice of the herbs and bandaged it against the infected wound. She frowned and clicked her tongue crossly at Antonia. 'Care for him until I return,' she said, shuffling away.

Antonia nodded wearily and poured water and wine into a soldier's tin cup for him to sip, before she began again to wipe his body with the wet silk. 'Oh, my dear, how I wish there was more I could do for you.'

Eventually exhaustion overcame her and with his hand in hers she fell asleep beside him on the straw, only to wake with a start when the old woman returned at sunset with bread and an egg wrapped in a scarf, and a small, corked jar. Without a word she lifted the dressing from Matthew's wound, took the lid off the jar, and to Antonia's horror, picked out several wriggling maggots and placed them on the raw, inflamed wound before she prepared a fresh dressing

The woman seemed surprised by Antonia's expression. 'They will eat only the putrified flesh, señora, not the healthy. They will keep the wound clean.'

Antonia swallowed hard. 'You are most kind,' she said.

'You killed French soldiers,' the old one said, 'and because of that I will help you, but be wary of those who will come here tomorrow to bury my son and his wife. Do not show yourself. It is safer that others do not know you are here.' She turned to leave, then pointed to the horse. 'It must go.'

Well before daylight next morning, Antonia led the horse away from the farm and tethered him to graze, hopefully unnoticed, on the far side of the woods. She ran back up the hill to the barn, panting as she closed the door, and went to Matthew's side. Was it her imagination or had the fever begun to recede? His breathing seemed deeper now, as if a spark of self-preservation had ignited during the night; but when he tried to move, the pain caused him to gasp. He opened his eyes and she thought she saw a glimmer of recognition in them.

Her heart leapt with relief, and she lifted his head to sip a little more wine and water from the cup. When he'd finished, he studied her face. 'I thought I was dead,' he muttered as he lay back on the straw.

'Matthew, you're not going to die. I forbid it! We're safe here, and help is on its way.' She tried to infuse her words with the confidence she didn't really have.

Again his lips moved and she leaned closer to catch his words. 'Go back. You shouldn't be here,' he mumbled. 'Go home.'

'That's not possible,' she said as she brushed aside the lank hair falling on his forehead and bathed his face. 'Anyhow, I'd find no more safety back in St Petersburg now than I knew as a girl with my father in America.' His eyelids drooped and he frowned, struggling to comprehend her words.

'Let me tell you a story about a girl who was born in Philadelphia,' she said, settling down beside him. 'This little girl had a mother who walked off and left her to be raised by other women who really didn't want her. Then one day when she was six years old, her father came back, and when he saw that she'd grown into a pretty little girl with golden curls, he decided to take her away with him on his travels.'

Matthew's eyes were wide open now.

'The little girl's father was a handsome man who preyed on lonely ladies – if they had money, of course. He was a gambler, a thief, and a swindler.' She dipped the sponge in the bucket again. 'At each new town, he'd present himself as a grieving widower, sadly left to raise a sweet little daughter all on his own. Oh, he was very convincing, and while some tender-hearted lady was being wooed by his charm, the little girl would slip through her house and collect pieces of jewellery and other pretty things and hide them in the back of her doll. She was quick-witted and she was never caught – though she had a few lucky escapes.'

She paused as memories rushed back, then shrugged and continued drily. 'All the time she was growing up, she provided quite a good living for her father, until his drinking cost him his looks and he could no longer charm the ladies. Then it was a bad time for them both when he began to lose heavily at the gaming tables—'

The sound of male voices in the farmyard made her stop abruptly, and when Matthew groaned she put her hand gently across his mouth. 'Hush, hush,' she soothed, then listened to the old woman's cries of grief when the bodies of her son and his wife were apparently pulled from the well and carried away for burial.

Matthew slipped back into unconsciousness and Antonia lay tensely beside him for a long time while her heartbeat steadied.

He stirred, calling for water, and she put the cup to his lips. 'Tell me the end of the story,' he said as she lay his head back on the straw.

'Well, when the father had gambled away everything else, he wagered his last possession – his fifteen-year-old daughter – and lost her to the captain of a Russian trading ship moored in Boston harbour.' Her tone was flat. 'It was the middle of the night when the girl was bundled out of a waterfront tavern and taken on board a ship bound for St Petersburg.'

'Good God!' Matthew's eyes were wide open again.

'Of course, the girl was terrified, but the captain was first and foremost a trader, you see, and when he'd sobered up a little, he realized that – if the girl remained *intact* – her angelic face and golden hair would fetch a good price in St Petersburg.' She heaved a long, hissing sigh through her teeth. 'So, as soon as the ship docked there, the girl was presented to a middle-aged gentleman, money changed hands and the next day a priest was paid to marry the girl to this man. He had no wife and he was well connected at court, so the captain said the girl should thank him for finding her such a husband.'

A tremor crept into Antonia's voice. 'This husband was excessively possessive of the pretty girl as he was of all the other valuable objects he owned. She spent the next fifteen years being paraded amongst the Russian aristocracy dressed in his jewels while other men ogled her. The husband took a warped pleasure in watching handsome young aristocrats flirt with his wife at court.'

Antonia paused and brushed away an insect crawling across the straw. She sighed. 'The girl flirted, too, and she developed the art of deceiving her husband, though none of her little affairs meant anything until an Englishman came into her life. Then, for the first time, she discovered how it felt to be truly loved.' She sat quietly for some time before she emerged from the daydream and shrugged. 'Sadly it all came to nothing because the Englishman went away, and before the girl could follow him, her husband learned about the affair and *persuaded* her to join a convent, far away in Suzdal.'

'Surely she refused?'

'Refuse?' She gave a bitter laugh. 'You must have heard about the quaint old Russian custom of locking away wives or sisters or daughters who become an embarrassment to their menfolk.' Tears she didn't want to shed found their way onto her cheeks and, without being aware of doing it, her tale became personal. 'It was three years before I found a way to get through that convent door and make my way to England; but I never did see my love again.'

'. . . stay in England?' he muttered.

'Remain there as a penniless thirty-year-old refugee with no connections? I think not! I had the wit to offer my unique talents to certain men in Whitehall, men who were prepared to employ me at first to carry messages to the Royalists in France. Then I came to work for them in Spain. They pay me well.'

Matthew's head rolled on the straw. 'You must leave me,' he whispered. 'Please go now. Take the horse and ride east until you meet up with an English company. You know there's nothing more you can do for me here.'

She shook her head and stroked the back of her hand across the stubble on his chin. 'I have no intention of going anywhere without you, Matthew Halifax,' she said, sniffing and trying to smile. 'I enjoy your company.'

*

His pain was unremitting and there were times during the next black days when Antonia felt he would not see another dawn. But each morning he rallied sufficiently to eat a little of the egg which the old woman found and brought to him, along with snippets of news filtering out of Madrid.

'My neighbour says that the French are preparing to leave the city!' she said breathlessly as soon as she arrived on the sixth day. 'Already they are plundering the palaces and the churches; the entire treasure of Spain is being loaded onto their wagons – hundreds of wagons! The grandees are in a state of panic,' she cackled, 'and they're preparing to run off over the mountains with King Joseph.'

'Did you hear that, Matthew? Help will be here soon.'

It was after another wretched night and late into another wretched morning when Antonia at last heard the sound of hoofs approaching. Blinking into the bright sunlight, she stumbled to the barn door in time to see Isobella arriving at the head of a group of red-coated soldiers, some on horseback and one driving a wagon.

The partisan dismounted and ran into the barn ahead of the men. 'Yes? He is alive?' she asked and strode to view the haggard, still-breathing form on the straw. 'Good! You and St Jude have done well, señora.'

A stocky, grey-haired officer came into the barn. 'Allow me to introduce myself, ma'am. I'm Doctor Ferguson. Lord Wellington was most concerned to hear of the colonel's injury.' The doctor crouched beside Matthew and lifted the dressing; his expression was grim as he examined the wound, then glanced at the surroundings. 'I hold out little hope, madame, but I'll do whatever I can,' he said, and called for his assistant to bring his box of instruments and salves.

'I need to work on a table of some sort. Out there in daylight,' he said over his shoulder, and as Antonia slumped numbly against the wall, she watched the soldiers find planks and put together a rough tressle. Matthew, barely conscious, was lifted onto it while the doctor removed his coat, set a pair of spectacles on his nose, and rolled up his sleeves. Four redcoats stood beside the table to hold the patient's limbs and one wedged a pad of well-chewed leather between his teeth while the doctor began his work with a scalpel and probe.

Matthew's muffled cries tore at Antonia's heart. Dear God! How much more could his body endure?

'Madame Warshensky-Rostroprovich,' a quiet male voice said beside her, 'I must speak with you immediately. Perhaps we should sit outside in the shade.'

He startled her; she'd been too preoccupied to notice this young man entering the barn. 'Permit me to introduce myself, ma'am. I'm Captain Thomas Field, and I have a message for you. From London.' He wore the uniform of a staff officer.

She looked at him in puzzlement and allowed herself to be escorted to a rough bench under a tree at the far end of the farmyard, away from the sounds of Doctor Ferguson's work.

'Ma'am, I regret this most inopportune moment to deliver my message, but I was told that it is of the greatest urgency.'

'I can't imagine anything more urgent at the moment than saving that young man's life,' she said shakily. 'What does London want of me?'

'My apologies for this haste, madame, but certain circumstances beyond our control' – he jerked his head towards Matthew's ordeal – 'er, have made it impossible for you to be contacted earlier.'

'Oh, please, Captain, quickly say what you must before I drop dead from exhaustion!'

'Madame, my instructions are to escort you immediately to Lisbon. A gentleman is arriving from London and is most anxious to speak with you.'

She looked at him in astonishment and rose unsteadily to her feet. 'What you're saying is impossible! Look at the state I'm in! I have nothing but the clothes on my back. No, no, I can't do it; this is too much to ask.'

The young captain stood, too, worry written on his face. 'Of course, ma'am, and I do understand your situation, but I beg you to reconsider. Here, please take this' – he swung the blue cloak from his shoulders and held it out to her – 'and at the first opportunity I will make every endeavour to secure whatever else you require.'

She looked nonplussed and continued to shake her head. 'I'm telling you, I can't do it!' She felt her emotions crumbling; tears welled in her eyes.

Now he became red faced and flustered. 'I'm stepping well beyond my authority to say this, Madame Warshensky-Rostroprovich, but I believe the gentleman coming from Whitehall wishes most urgently to have discussions with you.' He floundered and looked down, apparently studying the grey dust coating his fine leather boots. 'I understand, ma'am, that he has certain information concerning your husband in St Petersburg.'

Antonia stared at him; a shiver ran through her. 'Tell me immediately! You must tell me what you know!'

He swallowed hard and ran his tongue around his lips. 'I'm sorry, ma'am, but I overheard a report that your husband died recently, and I believe you will be asked to return to St Petersburg.'

Such a possibility had never entered Antonia's wildest dreams; her head spun. 'What – what are you saying? When did my husband die?' The news was a shock, but it could produce no grief. 'How?'

The young man looked uncomfortable. 'I have none of the details, ma'am, but I believe it was murder. He was shot.'

She stared at him, slack jawed, scarcely breathing. Vladimir Warshensky-Rostroprovich dead, and she was alive! She swayed and Captain Field put out a hand to steady her. 'Madame, please let me apologize again – but the General's orders are for Colonel Halifax to be taken to the nearest field hospital – I mean, er, if the surgeon here is successful – and he requests that you should be escorted immediately to Lisbon.'

She found it impossible to think clearly. Some murderer's bullet had freed her from her husband's power and it was a struggle to contain her whirling emotions in front of this earnest young officer. 'I – I don't know what I will do now that my husband is dead,' she whispered and began to walk unsteadily back towards the barn where Doctor Ferguson was now washing Matthew's blood from his hands and his assistant was packing away the instruments.

'Good news, madame,' the doctor called with brisk satisfaction as he reached for a towel and nodded towards the bandages swathing Matthew's chest. 'I've removed the shot and if he lasts the journey back through the Gredos hills, he might recover. Eventually.' Doctor Ferguson picked up the lead he'd dug from living flesh, tossed it in the air and caught it again. 'He can keep this as a souvenir.'

'Thank you, Doctor,' said Antonia weakly and turned to Isobella, who had observed it all. 'And thank you, too, for everything you have done. Will you see to it that the old lady here is paid well for all her help?' Her own voice seemed to belong to someone else, and she could scarcely believe the words she heard coming from her mouth. 'I won't be riding back with you because – God help me! – I'm leaving immediately with Captain Field and his escort.'

She swung the officer's cape around her shoulders and tried to smooth her hair. 'Goodbye, Matthew, my dear. God's speed,' she whispered, and kissed his forehead. His eyelids fluttered and his lips moved. She thought he smiled.

'Very well, Captain Field, I'm prepared to ride with you to Lisbon. But please make all speed to provide me with a change of clothes and a brush for my hair.'

CHAPTER TEN

Somerset

The stars were high in the heavens when the gatekeeper at Eversleigh Park was roused to open the gates for the hired chaise from Portsmouth. It rumbled up the long, tree-lined drive until the great house loomed darkly into view, then the horses were swung towards the rear of the building and halted.

'Oh, m'lord, is that *you*?' gasped the startled butler when he and two footmen ran to answer the pounding on the kitchen door and saw Lord Matthew Halifax, hunched, haggard and unshaven, standing on the step.

'Yes, Dobson, it's me,' said Matthew and nodded towards the coach. 'Will one of you show the driver to the stables? Give my apologies to the groom and have the horses taken care of.' The clock in the servants' hall whirred, then struck two as he stepped into the kitchen and dropped onto a chair. 'There's no need to disturb my brother and Lady Grace at this hour; I'm going straight up to my room.'

By now the housekeeper and the head chambermaid had arrived to investigate the visitor. 'Oh, God be praised, you're home safe at last!' The housekeeper's eyes filled with happy tears. 'But so thin, you are! Just a shadow of your old self. We heard of the terrible times you had there in Spain, m'lord – but never mind, you're here now.' She rubbed her palms together gleefully. 'Jenny,' she said to the chambermaid, 'you and Hector run upstairs and make his lordship's room ready; and light the fire there while we see to some refreshments. Quietly now!'

At that moment the cook and several other servants arrived to join in the welcome and, one by one, Matthew shook them all by the hand. 'It's good to be home,' he said, and swallowed hard. 'And now that I'm here I want nothing more than a long, quiet rest.'

'Oh, m'lord,' said the cook, who had enjoyed having Matthew play in her kitchen when he was a child, 'did you not know that the house is full of guests? They don't leave for another week or so – the whole Pettigrew family, and Lord and Lady Sutcliffe with their brood, and Lady Viola with her ward—'

Matthew groaned and rubbed a hand across his forehead. 'Damn! I was hoping to spend the time here quietly with my brother and Lady Grace. Damn, damn! I don't want to face a crowd of other people.' He looked at the servants and saw their understanding glances.

'Mum's the word, m'lord,' said the housekeeper. 'You stay upstairs and out of sight, and we'll make sure you're not disturbed.'

'And I know exactly what will put some flesh on your bones again,' the cook joined in. 'Just like the old days, Lord Matthew: beef stew and dumplings? Treacle tart?'

Matthew rallied his strength to follow the footman, who was carrying his campaign box up a back staircase to his suite, where a fire had been lit in the bedroom and the chambermaid was running a warming pan between the sheets. Warm water arrived and, while he washed, his few belongings were unpacked from the shabby box which he'd found to replace the one lost when a French cannon ball had hit the baggage train.

'This is not the grand chest ye set off with, m'lord,' the footman noted as he closed the lid. 'Perhaps Mr Gray will be able to make ye another?'

Matthew nodded. 'I'll speak to him about it, Patrick.' He turned his back to the servant while he unbuttoned his shirt. He wasn't ready yet for shocked eyes to linger on his scarred chest. 'Actually, I'd like someone to take a message tomorrow to Mr Gray and tell him I'm home again, and— Well, just tell him I'm here.'

The butler himself arrived carrying a bottle of brandy and a plate of bread and ham sent up by the cook. 'Thank you, Dobson,' Matthew said as he began to eat. 'That's all for now, but when the marquess wakes, you will inform him of my arrival?'

Once Matthew's head was on the pillow it took less than two minutes for a dream-filled sleep to overtake him. It was a dream he'd had repeatedly since he'd regained consciousness in a fetid field hospital and received Antonia's letter describing the events after he'd been shot. She'd tenderly wished him well, and said that she was leaving Spain.

The news still frustrated him; nobody had been able to tell him where she had gone or how to reach her. He held faint memories of the days she lay beside him on the straw, tending him, willing him to cling to a thread of life. During that time she'd been closer to him than anyone else ever had, and he had a hazy memory of things she had disclosed about herself. Or had all that merely been a part of his fevered ramblings?

In his dreams at night he searched endlessly for her: he could hear her calling to him and he knew she was waiting for him just around the next corner. But when he reached out to her, it was Evangeline Fenton's ghostly fingers who snatched his arm and as he fought to pull away from her, he heard himself calling for William Gray to help.

Matthew always woke at that point. Woke crying out for William Gray, the big, softly spoken village craftsman who had helped shape the character of the young Matthew. William Gray whose presence was felt everywhere in the magnificent furniture he'd crafted for Eversleigh Park. Crafted for Matthew's mother, the late marchioness.

He felt disoriented now as he opened his eyes, stretched, then gasped as sharp pain reminded him that his body still resented sudden movement. A shaft of bright sunlight speared through a gap in the curtains to touch a bowl of pink roses that had been left beside the bed. He smiled; Grace would have arranged that. The house was silent and when he glanced at his clock, he saw that he'd been asleep for more than twelve hours. God, but it was good to be home!

He sat up gingerly and rang the bell. The door flew open and the Marquess of Eversleigh's long-faced valet came into the room. 'Ah, good morning, m'lord,' he said and pulled aside the Chinese silk curtains to fill the room with light. 'My master is most anxious to welcome you, sir, whenever it is convenient, and so is her ladyship. I'll have your bath prepared and send a servant to shave you.'

Matthew looked around the room. 'God, but it's good to be home,' he said to himself again.

When he was bathed and dressed in his burgundy velvet dressing robe, he sat at the table by the window in his sitting room and ravenously ate the beef stew and dumplings sent up by the cook. The view from this window had always been his favourite and he'd often pictured it in the last four years when he'd been cold and exhausted, hungry and fearful that the next moment would be his last: the walled rose garden which his mother had planted, the great green swathe of lawn surrounding the fountain with the bronze dancing nymph, the shrubbery with its trimmed hedges and the copse of beeches on the gently rolling hill beyond.

As he sat lost in warm memories, his attention was caught by the sight of a hatless girl running down the hill, light-footed and swift, with her skirts held high and a great brown dog bounding at her side. Her pace didn't slacken until she came to the fountain, dropped to her knees and rolled onto the grass, panting. The dog wheeled around and she laughed as it tried to lick her face.

All at once the dog turned his head, stiffened, and the hairs on his back bristled. The dark-haired girl sprang to her feet; she and the dog sprinted down the steps to the walled rose garden and disappeared into a little arbour at the far end.

Looking down on it all from his window, Matthew had a clear view of a smartly dressed young man swinging his cane as he sauntered down a path between the flower-beds, then looking around expectantly when he reached the fountain. His nonchalance quickly faded and he strode to the entrance of the rose garden and stood there searching but failing to see – as Matthew could – the girl and the dog crouched behind the stone seat in the arbour.

The man spun around and marched back along the path, slashing his cane at the flowers growing on either side, while the girl and the dog came out of their hiding place. She sat on the seat, pulled a book from her pocket and began to read.

Matthew was still smiling at the episode when his brother tapped on the door and came into the room.

The Marquess of Eversleigh was a small, fine-boned man, who carried himself with authority. He was almost twenty years older than his brother, and while there was little similarity between them, either in physique or disposition, they shared a deep, undemonstrative affection.

'My dear Matthew, how good it is to have you home again! How's the wound?' The marquess held out his hand and quelled the tremor of emotion in his voice.

'Sebastian!' Matthew said, grasping the hand in both of his. 'I'm still as weak as a kitten, but it's nothing that a period of rest at Eversleigh won't remedy.' As he was speaking, the marchioness swept into the room and ran to him with her arms extended.

'Matthew, Matthew, what a wonderful surprise this is! Here, let me kiss you.' She put her face up to his. 'The house is full of guests – and I'm afraid your arrival is no longer a secret.' She gave him an apologetic smile. 'But I've asked everyone to stay away until you feel ready to receive visitors.'

'Thank you, Grace,' he said. 'The wound is healing well but, frankly, at the moment I have no inclination to share anyone's company – apart from yours and Sebastian's, of course.' He went to the window and looked down. 'But tell me, who is that girl with the dog down there?'

His brother stood beside him. 'That's Lady Viola's stepdaughter, Miss Ellen Templeton, and the dog goes everywhere with her. Did you hear that Grace's cousin married Sir Christopher Templeton last year? Surprised us all, I can tell you, but the poor fellow's heart gave out, and now his daughter is

Viola's ward. She's a pleasant young person, inclined to be reserved, but Viola seems fond of her.'

'Yes,' Lady Grace said as she joined them at the window, 'they stayed here for a few weeks after Sir Christopher died. Poor Viola was distraught and I must admit that Ellen Templeton was very attentive and kind to her. But she's an odd girl – somewhat *too* private and *too* self-contained – and I'm afraid she's not an easy person to know, though Ramsden quite dotes on her. He's told me – in confidence – that he has hopes of Miss Ellen Templeton one day taking over Viola's role as his hostess. She's very young yet, of course.'

It didn't take long for Matthew to grow impatient with his confinement indoors. He tried to strengthen his weakened muscles by walking to and fro briskly in the long gallery, but even that soon had him sagging into a chair.

'I need to get outside to exercise my limbs,' he told his brother on the second day. 'I might stroll down to the river tomorrow. Forgive me for being so infernally unsociable,' he said, 'but frankly I'm not ready yet to face the people downstairs and deal with the inevitable questions about Spain – the war, the politics, and Wellington's strategies. Just give me a few more days to myself, Sebastian, and I'll find the strength to be civil.'

The following day, while some of the guests at Eversleigh Park were preparing for a morning out with the guns and others were gathering for croquet, Matthew left the house by a side door. Dressed in clothes that hung loosely on his gaunt frame, he set out to visit William Gray. The craftsman's thatch-roofed house and workshop stood barely a mile away on the outskirts of the village – a distance that Matthew used to run easily.

But he'd walked no more than halfway there today before he was forced to admit that he'd badly overestimated his ability. He paused for a few moments to catch his breath, then urged his legs to drag themselves a dozen paces further to a big tree growing near the river-bank. He sank to the ground with a grunt, propped his back against the trunk, savouring the silence and staring down at the long reeds waving sensuously in the water's current. 'God, it's good to be home,' he muttered to a crow flying overhead.

The sun appeared from clouds banked high behind a wooded hill and lit up the stream, no wider than a stone's throw at this place. His throat tightened as he recalled the childhood days when William Gray and he had stood companionably side by side here with their fishing lines dangling in the water while his mother sat watching them. Her love for the man had never been spoken of, but Matthew had always recognized it, and understood it.

At that moment the sound of someone approaching broke through his reflections; he leaned his head back against the broad trunk and made no movement as the footsteps passed behind the tree.

It was Ellen Templeton and her dog. At that moment a duck and a line of ducklings took to the water, and the great shaggy hound instantly made to splash in after them. 'Stay, Hannibal,' he heard the girl order, and he dropped to the ground, quivering with excitement while she sat on the grass beside him, watching the birds paddle their way serenely downstream and around the bend.

Matthew made no sound or movement and, though he was sitting only a few yards away from them, the dog's attention remained riveted on the water while the girl continued to study the scene, unaware that she was being observed. She was hatless, and the sunlight glistened on the dark, wind-ruffled hair around her shoulders, and shone on her skin, creamy and unflawed, radiant with the beauty of youth. And innocence.

At last she stood, and with the dog romping along the path ahead of her, disappeared from view, leaving Matthew feeling old and battered and filled with the disillusionment of a man who had spent four years in the cesspits of hell. Four years that had stolen the last of his own innocence.

He sat ruminating for a little longer, harnessing the energy to continue his walk, though he was again short of breath when he arrived at the open doorway of William Gray's workshop, where he stood for a moment surveying the interior.

Two apprentices were working at the far end with wood shavings collecting on the floor around them; and on one side of the room, awaiting its final polish, stood a magnificent ebony table with a surface of inlaid silver and ivory. Matthew saw the cabinet maker himself about to lift a plank of Honduras mahogany from a shelf of exotic timbers.

Even at the age of sixty, William Gray was still a fine-looking, strongly built man, though Matthew noticed how his grey hair had thinned in the last four years. He was about to attract his attention when a female voice called and William crossed to the workbench to stand beside Miss Templeton.

Their backs were to the door and both heads were bent over a sheet of paper, which the girl was tapping with one finger. Matthew was intrigued to watch the pair straighten and look at each other for a moment, then look back to the paper, then look at each other again, and burst into laughter.

'No, no, Mr Gray, don't worry, it's just a matter of calculating the bottom angle first,' Matthew heard the girl say, 'then if the next angle starts just here on the right at no more than thirty degrees, it will the alter the whole perspective.'

'So, Miss Ellen, you have found a simple mathematical solution to my artistic problem.' He was still laughing.

She shook her head. 'All credit for that belongs to the old Dutch painters who discovered how to make their black and white tiled floors run off into the distance. It worked perfectly in their pictures, and it will work just as well with your marquetry.' With a ruler and pencil she drew lines on the paper. 'Now, using those angles, I guarantee this river will no longer appear to be running uphill.'

He smiled down at her and put the paper away in a drawer. 'My thanks, Miss Ellen. Now may I offer you a glass of mild cider? And some plum cake?' He turned at that moment and was startled to see Matthew standing in the doorway. His face lit up with delight. 'M'lord,' he said with a touch of breathlessness as he strode across the floor, 'I heard you had returned, but I didn't expect to see you here so soon.' They reached for each other, and shook hands before Matthew acknowledged Ellen, who was regarding him with frank curiosity.

'Forgive me, ma'am, I believe you must be Miss Templeton,' he said with a bow. 'Please allow me to introduce myself: I'm Matthew Halifax. My brother told me that you and Lady Viola were staying at Eversleigh.' Hannibal came up behind him to sniff his legs. 'Will I lose my fingers if I touch him?' Matthew asked with mock alarm.

The girl curtseyed and her blue eyes sparkled. 'He'll only attack if I tell him to, m'lord.'

'I'm greatly relieved,' he said and fondled the dog's ear while his eyes looked into hers, dark-fringed and clear as crystal. 'I hope you're enjoying your visit to Eversleigh, Miss Templeton.'

'Thank you. Yes, it's very pleasant.' She held his gaze a moment longer, then looked away. 'And I always enjoy coming here to watch Mr Gray create his beautiful marquetry.'

She indicated several works standing on the bench, and as Matthew glanced past them he saw a mahogany campaign box in the process of construction. He raised his eyebrows at the craftsman.

'Aye, m'lord,' William said, 'when you wrote that the other had been wrecked by the French, I began making this. Only the brass inlays and corners to be put on now, and a little finishing inside to be done and – and— Well, m'lord, I just hope it never has to leave England's shores.'

Matthew ran his fingers over the lid. 'I'll be rejoining my regiment when the time comes, Mr Gray,' he said flatly. 'We're going to fight the French on their own soil one day before long. I can't miss that!'

William's forehead creased. 'Ah, well, we must pray the end comes soon. But now, m'lord, would you and Miss Ellen care to come through to the kitchen and try a mug of my cider?' he said, opening the door. 'This latest hogshead is a particularly good one.'

The girl walked ahead of them into the adjoining house and, with an easy familiarity, went straight to the shelf; brought down three blue and white pottery mugs and a cake tin, and placed them on the table. William carried two jugs of cider from the pantry, poured Ellen's drink from one, and the men's from the other, while she cut slices of cake and put them out on a plate.

The conversation between the men avoided mention of the war, and drifted randomly from village news of births, deaths and marriages, to work that William had recently completed for the Duke of Moreland's estate three miles away.

Ellen listened, watching their faces closely. Though she said nothing, her eyes were alight with interest. There was an inner stillness about her that Matthew found appealing, and his gaze frequently drifted in her direction. He even felt a twinge of disappointment when she stood to leave.

'If you will excuse me, gentlemen, I should return to the house now,' she said with a warm smile. 'I've promised to read to my stepmother this afternoon.'

Matthew and William both escorted her to the gate, and stood watching as she turned to wave before rounding the bend in the lane. 'Does she come here often?' Matthew asked.

William nodded. 'Miss Templeton and I first met when Lady Viola brought her to stay at Eversleigh last year, soon after her father's death,' he said, looking at Matthew shrewdly. 'The lass felt his loss deeply, and I found her weeping alone on the river-bank one day; she told me she went there so her stepmother wouldn't see her crying. It upset her.'

'Seems a pleasant, perfectly straightforward sort of girl,' Matthew murmured, recalling Grace's comment. *Too self-contained*, she'd said. Based on today's brief encounter, that was not at all his own opinion of the youthful Miss Templeton.

When Matthew returned home he announced that he would dine downstairs this evening. And as he had anticipated, his arrival amongst the guests was met with a flurry of greetings, followed by a bombardment of questions about his campaigns and Wellington's strategies, as well as news of friends whose names had appeared in the casualty lists published in the newspapers. He answered everything as well as he could, carefully laundering his descriptions of some of the more appalling events, and making little of his own injuries.

He looked around the room quickly but caught no sight of Ellen Templeton. She arrived a few minutes later with her arm linked through Lady Viola's.

'Oh, my dear Matthew!' Viola cried. 'Allow me to present my ward, Miss Ellen Templeton. You did hear, didn't you, that I am now Lady *Templeton*? Dear Sir Christopher and I were married, and then – oh – I can't speak of it! But—'

'Lady Viola, allow me to congratulate you and commiserate, too,' Matthew said, and glanced at Ellen. 'And my condolences to you, too, Miss Templeton.'

She accepted his words with a curtsy and gave no indication that they had already met. She had lost the delightfully wind-tossed appearance he'd noted by the river, and was dressed tonight in a gown of forget-me-not-blue silk the colour of her eyes. Her hair was arranged with simple elegance and a rope of small pearls twined through the dark strands, which had been swept up to expose a long, graceful neck. A delicate necklace lay around it, sparkling in the candlelight.

Matthew thought he had never seen anyone so lovely, and saw that his admiration was shared by others, though Miss Templeton responded to all the attention with a cool reserve.

When they went in to dinner, he was seated at one end of the table and she at the other. He watched her speak occasionally with those sitting around her, but she was not at all the self-assured, laughing girl he'd met in Mr Gray's workshop this morning.

When the ladies left the table after dinner, the gentlemen moved their chairs closer to his, pressing him for further details of the war and all the horrors that he wanted to forget. By the time they made their way to join the ladies in the drawing room, Ellen was sitting at a card table, intently partnering Lady Viola in a game of whist, and giving him no opportunity to speak with her again.

He found himself quickly surrounded by a group of ladies with fluttering fans who expressed their condolences on Miss Evangeline Fenton's demise, and were then quick to colour their conversation with snippets of gossip about his late fiancée's escapades while he was in Spain.

He gave the impression of listening stoically but, in fact, none of it seemed relevant now. Her death had been tragic, but she hadn't loved him any more than he had loved her.

Before the evening drew to a close, Matthew made it clear to everyone that he was still not sufficiently fit to ride with them in the morning, and he certainly had no inclination to pick up a gun and join the shooters.

He decided that tomorrow he would simply take a little exercise again and perhaps invite Miss Templeton to join him in a walk to William Gray's workshop. Yes, he liked that idea, and glanced around the room for her.

'Ellen?' Lady Grace said when he enquired. 'Oh, I saw her taking Viola upstairs to bed a few minutes ago.' She clicked her tongue. 'My cousin *knows* she should never drink more than one glass of claret at dinner!'

CHAPTER ELEVEN

That night Matthew's sleep was again disturbed by his nightmare of a lost Antonia. But this time Evangeline Fenton made no appearance, and when he called out to William Gray, the man smiled and sent Matthew a reassuring signal. In the light of day it made no sense whatsoever, but he woke with an unaccountable sense of relief.

As soon as he was shaved and dressed he went downstairs for breakfast, expecting to speak with Ellen, but learned that she had already left the house with Viola's French maid.

'If it's company you'd like on today's walk,' Lady Grace said brightly as she lifted her porcelain teacup, 'I'm sure Juliette and Caroline would be happy to oblige.'

'Absolutely!' the Pettigrew sisters chorused. 'We'd be delighted, and so would Ralph and Humphrey, wouldn't you?'

'A stroll into the village?' the young men said. 'Splendid, and we can call in to the inn for lunch.' Even when Matthew reminded them that he was simply walking for exercise, several others decided to join the party, too.

His own slow pace wasn't noticed as the group spread out in twos and threes along the lane leading to the village, and Matthew found himself at the rear, escorting the Pettigrew sisters whose short legs were making hard work of the distance. But they were pleasant girls whom he'd known all his life, and their chatter was benign.

At the sound of fast hoofbeats coming along the lane behind them, he quickly drew them to one side before two riders galloped round the corner, then wheeled about and curbed their mounts so hard they reared and twisted.

'Good God! Can I believe my eyes? Lord Matthew Halifax is still alive and – behold! – the hero returns!' The tone was designed to provoke.

Matthew struggled for a moment to recognize the speaker – a colourless young man with a sly smile, a mass of purple pimples on his chin and a suffocating air of self-consequence. Then he remembered.

'Well, if it isn't young Lord Nettleton, the Duke of Moreland's pride and joy,' Matthew said. 'I see your manners haven't improved since we last met, Nettie. Why don't you try a year or two in a good regiment to smarten yourself up?' He acknowledged the other rider, Freddie Houghton-Blake, a young man with a rakishly good-looking face and lavishly curled blond hair hanging to his collar. It was generally agreed by those who knew him that an original thought had never entered Freddie's head; he followed wherever Lord Nettleton led.

'Come, come, Halifax, is this what you have learned in the army? Never settle for one pretty little creature on your arm when you can head off into the woods with two of 'em, eh?' Lord Nettleton edged his sweating horse closer to Juliette Pettigrew, leered suggestively at her, then turned to Matthew and lifted one brow. 'But what have you done with the other one? Where's that very tasty girl with the wolf? Now, there's one who'd be worth the effort.'

'On your way!' Matthew exploded with a sudden, livid anger. 'And for God's sake, try to learn the rudiments of gentlemanly behaviour before I meet you again – or I'll thrash it into you.'

The future Duke of Moreland sniggered and threw a look full of insolence as he jerked the rein to swing his horse around. 'Come along, Freddie, good times await!' he called over his shoulder and spurred the animal into a gallop.

The golden-haired, smirking Mr Houghton-Blake, whose father was one of the wealthiest men in the county, lifted his hat to the ladies in a pantomime of chivalry, and with a knowing look, rode off after his friend.

Matthew fervently wished he'd had the strength to whip the pair of offensive puppies on the spot. The brief incident had brought Juliette and Caroline close to tears and they now clung to his arms even more tightly. 'Oh, Matthew, that was appalling! I feel quite ill with shock.' Juliette's voice quavered.

'I want to return to the house,' Caroline whispered, and the trio had been retracing their steps for only a few minutes when a gig pulled up behind them in the lane.

'Good morning to you all,' Ellen Templeton called brightly, then saw the stricken expressions on the girls' pale faces. 'Oh, dear! Are you ill?' she said and jumped down from the vehicle, followed by the French maid.

'Good morning,' Matthew said. 'I'm afraid the ladies have had a rather upsetting encounter.' He had no intention of revealing what had taken place, but Juliette and Caroline instantly provided Ellen with a word-for-word report. Then they repeated it twice, each time adding a few embellishments and making themselves increasingly agitated.

'Goodness! That sounds frightfully unpleasant,' Ellen said with sympathy. 'Now, I insist you climb aboard the gig, and the groom can drive you straight back to the house. Dominique and I will walk.'

When the vehicle pulled off with its new passengers, Matthew felt a rush of relief to find himself walking in Ellen's company after all. 'I looked for you at breakfast, but Lady Grace told me you had set out early.'

She glanced at him in surprise as she untied the ribbons to remove her bonnet 'Yes, Dominique and I went to the village to find even more trimmings for the dress I'm to wear to the ball next week,' she said, then gave an exaggerated sigh and laughed as she slipped her arm through that of the maid walking beside her. 'Dominique knows all the rules of fashion and she is trying to teach me which buttons look best with which fabric and what lace never to put on velvet.'

'Mademoiselle has developed a very good eye for colour,' Dominique answered with mock severity, 'but her understanding of style and detail have yet to be fully grasped.'

Ellen gave a low, gurgling laugh. 'So you see how eclectic my education has become, m'lord?'

'You're part of the family now, Ellen,' he said impulsively, and felt himself smiling, 'so you must call me Matthew.'

'Not Uncle Matthew?'

He caught her gravely mischievous glance. 'In all honesty,' he said, 'I feel I could well be called Great Uncle Matthew this morning.' He gave an apologetic shrug and nodded towards a fallen log. 'I need to rest here for a few moments.'

Ellen and the maid perched themselves on the log, too, and they all sat there without speaking for some time. Then the girl turned and looked at him steadily. 'Matthew, what actually happened to you in Spain?'

She spoke artlessly, and her question made him take a deep breath. He sank into reflection before he spoke, then to his own surprise, he found himself telling this young lady, whom he barely knew, not only how he'd come to be wounded, but also how his life had been saved by a remarkable woman who had put herself at enormous risk by staying with him until help arrived. 'I'm left with only a hazy recollection of those days, but I know she was there with me the whole time, willing me to live.'

Ellen Templeton listened, and there was something in her expression that unlocked his resolve never to speak about his time in Spain. And once the words began to flow, they kept coming. He mentioned no names but she occasionally asked for clarification of some military term he'd used, and while he talked of one matter, other incidents sprang into his mind and so he told her about them, too – the noise and chaos of battle, the cold, the heat, the fear, the loneliness and the friendships.

When he stopped talking, Ellen stared off into the distance and said nothing for several minutes. Then she looked at him again and shook her head slowly. 'Tell me, Matthew, how did someone like you – a man who grew up here in these gentle surroundings – go off to war and learn to become such a soldier?'

He was struck by the innocence of her question and had to think hard before he could answer.

'It seems like a hundred years ago now, but when my friends and I rushed off to join a regiment, we expected excitement, and maybe a little glory.' He narrowed his eyes and gazed into the distance. 'There's no glory on the battle-field, Ellen, and there's not a lot to learn, actually, because for any soldier to stay alive in any war, the rules are simple: trust no one, be ever watchful, and if trouble comes, hit first and hit hard.' He saw a shiver run through her. 'So there you have it,' he said, with a sudden rush of embarrassment to realize how much of his inner self he'd just revealed. He pulled out his watch, fumbled with the catch and apologized for taking up so much of their time.

'Not at all,' Ellen said. 'I like to understand things. Thank you.'

He got up stiffly from the log and grunted. 'I need to keep on exercising,' he said and they set off once more towards the house. 'Perhaps you'd be kind enough to walk with me again tomorrow morning?'

'Of course,' she said and her face lit up. 'Hannibal and I would like that very much.'

Again that evening, when the guests assembled for dinner, Ellen Templeton came into the room on Lady Viola's arm. And again heads turned to admire her, dressed in a cloud of jonquil gauze over a slip of white satin ornamented with clasps of tiny roses to match those in her hair.

Matthew watched closely as she and her stepmother moved amongst the guests. Ellen looked strikingly beautiful, but her expression was so cool and unexpressive she seemed to be a completely different girl from the one who had charmed him with her friendly candour this morning. She was – as Grace had commented – far *too* self-contained.

But when he caught Ellen's anxious gaze he realized that she was, in fact, extremely shy.

Again at dinner they were seated at opposite ends of the table, and again she sat playing cards afterwards. But Matthew made sure he found the oppor-tunity to speak briefly to her before she and Viola retired for the night.

'Tomorrow morning?' he reminded her quietly as she was leaving the room.

'Indeed! I look forward to it,' she said, and he felt a rush of pleasure to see her eyes brighten.

'Matthew seems to be spending a great deal of time this week with young Ellen,' Lady Grace noted to the marquess as they prepared to mount their horses for a morning's ride. 'They went walking together again after breakfast.' She frowned and looked around to see if the other riders were in their saddles.

'Give him time, m'love,' Sebastian said. 'I'm delighted to see how his health is improving, and surely it's immaterial whether that has come about because of all the walking he's done, or whether it has something to do with Miss Ellen Templeton's company.'

Lady Grace leaned closer to her husband and lowered her voice. 'I think that young lady has a hidden streak of cunning, and she could well be flirting with his affections, you know.' She looked at her husband for endorsement, but he frowned at her suggestion. 'Anyhow, Viola and Ellen are leaving on Saturday morning, and matters could very well improve for Matthew at the ball tomorrow night. I've invited everyone, including that very pleasant red-headed niece of Moreland's. She's staying with them at the moment, and I can remember your brother being quite taken with her in the past. The duchess told me yesterday that the young lady still has no particular attachment.'

The marquess gave her a concerned frown. 'Have you invited everyone in the duke's family? Matthew won't be pleased to see young Nettleton here after the disgraceful way he behaved in front of Juliette and Caroline last week.'

'I did consider that, Sebastian, but thank heavens the boy has already taken himself back to London.' She turned in the saddle to signal the other riders, and the group set off with a clatter of hoofs.

On the morning of the Eversleigh Park ball the great rooms of the house were busy with servants draping floral decorations around the marble pillars, arranging gilded chairs at tables in the supper room, setting up a dais for the orchestra in an alcove at one end of the ballroom. And there was even more bustle below stairs where preparations for a lavish supper were under way in the kitchen.

Matthew and Ellen left the house earlier than usual for their walk to the river. 'Dominique has given me strict instructions to bring you back by midday,' he said as they crossed the meadow, climbed the stile and followed the path that led to the big tree beside the river. 'I must say I find it hard to believe that it will take all afternoon for her to get you bathed and rested, dressed and preened for the ball – but I haven't the courage to disobey one of Dominique's orders.' He grinned.

'That's wise,' she said lightly. 'My father told me to always listen to Dominique's advice.' They sat with their backs against the trunk of the tree and watched Hannibal splash into the water. 'But, Matthew, I'm afraid there are still things that even Dominique can't help me to understand.'

He looked at her with raised brows.

'I really dread this ball tonight,' she sighed.

'That's ridiculous,' he said, rolling a twig between his fingers. 'You know you'll outshine every other lady there.'

'My father once reprimanded me for appearing to be arrogant but I swear I have never felt that way.' She picked up a pebble and skimmed it expertly across the water. 'But neither have I ever felt entirely *comfortable* in this family.'

She saw that he was about to challenge her on that, so she gave him no opportunity to speak 'Listen, let me tell you a story about a polar bear who lived near the North Pole – a bear who lived just like all the bears do up there in the ice and snow. Then one morning she woke up to discover that a wizard had whisked her away in the night, and she was standing in the sunny desert amongst a herd of camels. Oh, the camels were very kind and welcoming, and they told her that now she could live with them in their lovely warm sandhills. They even gave her a magnificent new camel coat to wear.' She picked up another stone and skimmed it into the river. 'She tried to be like all the other camels but underneath, I'm afraid, she was still a polar bear. She didn't always understand the new language she heard around her, and sometimes she got lost amongst the sandhills.' A flush washed into her cheeks. 'I'm sorry, you must think me absolutely ridiculous.'

'No, Ellen, not at all.' Instinctively he picked up her hand and held it tightly. 'Actually, you've made perfect sense,' he said.

'Please don't imagine I'm ungrateful for all the kindness my stepmother and Lord Ramsden and Lady Grace have shown me. I'm extremely fond of them all, and I do try to be the kind of daughter Lady Viola would like me to be.' She shrugged apologetically.

'But sometimes that new camel coat doesn't fit comfortably?'

She turned her head and her eyes held his; he felt her fingers squeeze his hand, and he enjoyed the sensation. Her grip was firm, her skin soft; a smile played in the corners of her lips, and he felt a heady rush of pleasure rising like a warm tide inside him.

Oh, no! he thought, and looked away quickly while he let out a long, slow breath and began to ease his grip on her hand. She relaxed her fingers, too, and slid them slowly back onto her lap. As fond as he was becoming of Ellen Templeton, he knew he'd be an utter fool to encourage any tender feelings to develop between them.

As if she could read his mind, she stood up quickly and brushed her skirt, then turned away and whistled to Hannibal. The dog splashed up from the river, shook the water from his coat and rolled on the grass before he ran up to her.

'Come along,' she said to Matthew, 'we'll still have time to visit Mr Gray if we set off now.' Her cheeks were flushed, but her deep blue eyes looked down at him calmly. 'I must say my farewells to him because Mama and I are to leave for London early tomorrow.'

Before she went upstairs to dress, the Marchioness completed her inspection of the preparations and congratulated the staff not only on the floral decorations but also on the patriotic emblems they had erected as a tribute to Wellington's recent successes in Spain.

'Thank you, it all looks splendid,' Lady Grace said as she walked into the supper room where silver and crystal gleamed on white linen, and flowers cascaded in elaborate arrangements along the whole length of the tables.

'I'd like to start the ball with a quadrille,' she said to the leader of the orchestra when they discussed music for the evening, 'and of course we must have a cotillion and a polonaise, interspersed with waltzes.' She looked through the musician's repertoire. While Matthew's health had steadily improved, Grace knew he'd be unlikely to attempt any of the more energetic polkas and galops, and so she carefully selected music that would encourage her brother-in-law to dance with as many pretty partners as possible. It was time for Matthew to have a lady in his life again. A suitable lady. Not the young and indecipherable Miss Ellen Templeton.

Ellen's new ballgown of white satin was embellished with pink rosebuds and love knots, every one of which was studded with a tiny, glittering crystal. Under the great chandeliers in the ballroom the effect was dazzling; and Ellen's eyes caught the light, too, sparkling as brightly as the sapphire clips in her hair.

As soon as she entered with Viola, she was surrounded by gentlemen asking for their names to be placed on her dance card, and Matthew observed how she received their attention with the usual aloof civility she displayed in public. Her poise was impressive as she took the arm of a tall, fine-looking man and walked across the floor to join a set forming for the first quadrille.

Her sparkling white gown was modestly cut, with the *decollétage* giving no more than a hint of the treasure beneath the silk. Yet as she danced her way through the figures, advancing and retiring with her partner, linking arms to circle with him, weaving her way up and down the long line of dancers, the glittering fabric revealed every supple movement of the enticing female body beneath it.

She danced every dance with a different partner, but she gave little of herself to any of them beyond the requirements of etiquette. Men followed her around the room with their eyes and it was clear to Matthew that this very inaccessibility had become part of her allure.

It was well into the evening before he was able to claim her for a waltz 'Thank you, Matthew, but we don't really have to dance,' she whispered. 'I'd be very happy to sit down.'

'Your compassion for my rapidly fading stamina is much appreciated, Miss Templeton,' he whispered back, and offered her his arm as they left the ball-room and walked into the library. He sank into a chair with a sigh of relief, then stretched his legs while she went to a side table, unstoppered a brandy decanter and poured some into a glass for him.

He took it and raised the glass to her. 'Here's to your health – and to a long life of happiness.' He sipped the brandy and she gave him one of her singularly lovely smiles as she inclined her head in acknowledgement of the toast, then settled into the high-backed leather chair opposite his. Her breasts lifted in a sigh of contentment, and she leaned her head against the back of the chair, looking at him.

He studied her over the rim of the glass and recognized the heady blend of innocence and passion lying within her. Which man would win the privilege of being beside her when she realized she was no longer a child? he wondered.

She gave him a small, warm smile and an unwise tension grew in his chest. How old was she now? Seventeen? Many girls were already married at that age. He felt the impulse to sit closer to her – then quickly drained his glass and reminded himself that within a few weeks he'd be ready to rejoin his regiment. It would be grossly unfair to play with her affections at this time, tempting as it might be.

His wayward thoughts were interrupted when Lady Grace came to the door of the library. 'Oh, there you are, Matthew,' she said frigidly, seemingly vexed to find him sitting alone with Ellen. 'I'm afraid Miss Bickford is looking for you, my dear,' she said, 'and she insists you have asked her to dance the next quadrille. The sets are forming now.'

'Of course,' he said, and stood slowly while holding Grace's gaze. 'I think I've danced with every other lady in the room tonight – so why not Miss Bickford now? Thank you for allowing me a much-needed rest, Ellen.'

He offered her his arm, and they followed the stiff-backed marshioness into the ballroom.

Later, when supper was announced, Matthew escorted Lady Viola to the table, but when he glanced around the room for Ellen, she wasn't there.

'Yes, I'm afraid we must set out for London tomorrow,' Viola said to those seated around her. 'Ramsden expects us both home because Lord and Lady Castlereagh, as well as the prime minister, are coming to dine at the end of the week. My brother is quite taken with Ellen, you know, and I know he misses her when we are away. He arranged for her to take music lessons – have you heard her play, Matthew? No? And a French tutor comes to the house twice a week; Ramsden considers it essential for a young lady in her position to be fluent in that language. And you've noticed how well she dances? Yes, she has been taught by the best dancing master in London.'

Viola turned to speak to a gentleman sitting opposite, and Matthew's eyes searched the room again for Ellen. When she was still nowhere to be seen, he left the table and walked back into the ballroom, the billiard room, the library, the smoking room, the morning room. Idiotic as it seemed, he began to feel a twinge of concern. 'Has Miss Templeton come this way?' he asked the footman standing by the entrance.

'Yes, m'lord, Miss Templeton went out a few moments ago.'

Matthew hesitated. 'Was she accompanied?'

'No, m'lord. She was alone.'

His heart sank 'And which direction did she take?'

The footman averted his gaze. 'The young lady left in great haste, m'lord, and went in the direction of the lake.'

'Thank you. Say nothing of this to anyone,' Matthew said as he ran down the steps, across the lawn and into the shrouding darkness.

CHAPTER TWELVE

The moon was flying in and out of ragged clouds, giving just enough light for Ellen to see her way to the path leading towards the little Greek temple standing on the far side of the lake. Yesterday she had strolled this way with Viola and the other ladies to have afternoon tea in the temple; tonight her heart thundered as she raced towards it.

Who had let Hannibal out of the stables when he'd become ill? Panic tore at her insides and now she couldn't recall if the footman who'd given her the message had said that the dog was ill, or if he'd met with an accident. Oh, God! She hadn't listened for details when the man approached her just as she was going towards the supper room. Hearing that Hannibal was in a 'desperate state' in the temple had closed off her mind to everything but the need to find him.

She stopped running for a moment and slumped against a garden statue to catch her breath and try to clear her thoughts. Whether Hannibal had been taken ill or had been injured, why had he run all the way down here to collapse beside the lake?

She gulped air into her lungs then hurried on again towards the little Doric tea house now clearly visible in the moonlight. No sound reached her ears as she climbed the four shallow steps leading up to it, straining for some sign of the dog in the dim interior. A shiver of alarm ran through her. 'Hannibal?' she called softly. 'Hannibal, where are you?'

Something moved in the shadows and she heard a soft footstep. 'Who is there?' Her voice cracked; she took a step backwards, then another, and bumped into one of the little iron chairs, causing it to scrape loudly on the stone floor. 'What has happened to Hannibal?'

She heard the footstep again – now behind her – and terror dug talons into her throat as she swung around. 'Answer me, whoever you are. What have you done with my dog?'

The silhouette of a man's figure loomed towards her. 'Don't worry, my dear, there has been some misunderstanding,' a deep voice said in soothing tones. 'Your dog is unharmed.' Fingers brushed her arm and she instinctively swung away before they could grasp hold. She took several steps backwards and heard the man's breath coming closer, and heavier. Then she felt the wall at her back.

'Come no further,' she ordered, and began to edge her way along the cold stone towards the entrance. Her eyes were now becoming accustomed to the dim light in the temple, but before she could recognize the man's features, he threw himself against her and pinned her back against the wall with his body while his hands groped the neckline of her gown and slipped beneath its silk.

She twisted and attempted to bring her knee into contact with the hardness in his groin, but he moved swiftly to prevent that, and her scream was stifled by the pressure of his mouth forcing her lips apart, by the invasion of his tongue. Her hands and nails were her only weapons and she fought with all her strength to punish his face, his eyes—

Suddenly she became aware of a familiar scent in her nostrils, and her attacker's heavily perfumed hair triggered a memory of having danced with him tonight – a softly spoken middle-aged officer with carefully oiled and smoothed black hair tied at his neck with a velvet ribbon. Captain Connors!

She uttered a muffled sound of outrage, then succeeded at last in clamping her teeth on the man's lips as he pulled away for breath. But one of his hands grasped her throat and she felt his leg fumbling against hers, attempting to trip her onto the floor.

'Get away from me!' she cried, half choking as she struggled and fought against him. But she was unable to prevent herself from falling and he gave an animal growl as he came down on her. She cried out in terror, twisting, attempting to kick while his fingers groped her leg.

The moon reappeared as Matthew ran towards the lake, and he sent a prayer to every god in the cosmos that his instincts were wrong. But the instincts that had kept him alive during the last four years couldn't be disregarded tonight. Something was not as it should be. In God's name, what was Ellen doing out here alone?

He was almost at the temple when he heard a cry, and it was that sound which muffled his own footfall as he ran up the steps. Even in the weak light of the moon, her white gown sparkled and he saw her on the floor with a man's figure in uniform crouching over her. The officer turned his head but he was much too slow, for Matthew was already at his back with his left hand tangled in the officer's greasy hair. 'I'll kill you, Connors,' Matthew growled. He hauled the captain's head back and chopped the side of his right hand into the neck.

He hit him again, then with a snarl the captain heaved Matthew off and twisted to swing a heavy fist that caught him in the chest. Matthew gave an involuntary gasp of pain, then staggered, but came at the officer again with a punch that found its mark. Connors swore viciously as he fell, and dragged Matthew to the floor with him where they grappled, trading blows before they were on their feet again.

Matthew caught Connors on the jaw, but the captain deflected the second blow with his forearm and struck out savagely at Matthew with his right fist. Again its force landed jarringly on the old wound, and for a moment the pain of it took his breath away. As he panted hard, he saw the captain's face twist with a galling smirk of triumph. Matthew raised his own fists once more— O, God, what was Ellen about to do?

She was coming up behind Connors with one of the small iron chairs raised in her hands, and she cracked it down on the man's head, sending him sprawling face downwards on the floor with a deep, bloody gash across his crown. Though her blow had dazed him, the officer was attempting to scramble to his feet when Matthew rushed at him and, fighting his own pain, grasped the back of the captain's jacket with both hands, and hustled him down the temple steps, towards the bank of the lake a dozen yards away.

With every step, he could feel the captain rallying his strength, struggling to resist the forward thrust that was about to plunge him head first into the dark water. They were almost at the edge when a spasm tore through Matthew's wound. The pain caused him to gasp; he staggered and he swore viciously as his fingers lost their grip on Connors.

It was then he saw Ellen hurtling down the bank with arms outstretched towards the captain's back, and the force of her thrust toppled the man into the lake. While the wretch splashed and floundered, she ran to Matthew who was standing hunched with his locked arms across his chest.

'Dear God, Ellen!' he said breathlessly. 'Are you all right?'

'Yes, but I hope he drowns.' Her breath came in huge, stomach-heaving gasps. 'Oh, thank you for finding me when you did, Matthew, but – oh, dear! – now you've been hurt. Should I run for help?'

'No, no, stay here until I catch my breath,' he panted, and they sat together on the bottom step watching Connors drag himself from the muddy water and slink away towards the stables.

Matthew felt her body shaking violently as she told him of the message regarding the dog. 'How could I have been so stupid, stupid, stupid! I didn't stop to think what I was doing, and now you've been hurt because of me. I'm so terribly sorry.'

'No, you must never think that, Ellen! None of this was your doing,' he said. 'Connors, damn him, is the only one at fault here. In no way are *you* to blame for his disgraceful actions. Remember that.' She was crying now; he slipped his arm around her shoulders and pulled her against him.

She sniffed. 'I can't understand why it happened to me, Matthew, because I promise you, I gave him no encouragement when we were dancing. Or at any other time.' She sniffed again. 'I'm not a complete fool, you know, and I'm quite aware of the way things go between men and women.' Again she trembled and wiped at the flow of tears on her cheeks. He reached for his handkerchief and passed it to her wordlessly.

When her face was dry, she gave it back to him. 'I can't understand why that man would do such a thing! All I did was to dance with him – a cotillion, I think I didn't like the perfumed oil on his hair, but he did nothing ungentlemanly, apart from looking at my body the way they often do. Men, I mean. But I promise you, Matthew, that I – I did nothing, said nothing to him to suggest that I would ever be willing to – to . . . Believe me, I didn't flirt with him.'

She needed the handkerchief again, and he gave it back to her. 'My father talked to me a lot about the world, though nothing about this kind of thing,' she said as she blew her nose. 'It was the blacksmith's daughter in Littlewood who told me about men like Captain Connors – and yet I ran straight into his trap.' She shuddered again.

'Well, thank God no harm came to you.' His grip around her shoulders tightened. 'I promise that your name won't be mentioned, Ellen, but I'll make sure Captain Connors' actions tonight are known to his regiment. Will you talk to Dominique about this?'

'No, I don't think anyone else needs to know.' She thought for a long moment. 'Of course, if my father was still alive, I know I'd have told him. Will you tell Mr Gray?'

She spoke to him in her customary frank tone, but for a moment he was unable to respond. Had she just obliquely disclosed that she realized William Gray was his natural father? He felt almost glad that she was able to voice what the family never acknowledged, though his physical likeness to the craftsman had always been obvious. 'Would you object if I did tell Mr Gray?' he asked gently.

'No, not at all. He'd understand. Nobody could have been kinder to me than he was after my father's death.' Her hand was resting on his knee and he felt her fingers tighten. 'But let Mr Gray know that in future I'll practise what you once told me: *Be ever watchful, trust no one, and if trouble comes, hit first and hit hard.*'

He laughed, and it hurt his chest. 'Oh, yes, do remember those points whenever you find yourself facing a French army, Ellen Templeton, but in English society I think other strategies will be more appropriate.'

'So you're telling me to go off and behave like all the other docile young ladies in society. I've tried – I really have, Matthew – but I don't understand them any more than they understand me.' After a pause, she sniffed again. 'But I'm sure none of them would have made the stupid mistake I did tonight.' The tone of her voice lightened. 'But you and I did make a good fighting team, didn't we?'

She pressed his knee again and he instantly forgot the throbbing pain in his chest. Oh, God! It was the most innocent of touches – one that his head told him conveyed nothing but her trust and gratitude. Yet his male body responded with a rush of warmth, and he realized how simple it would be at this moment to show this enchanting young woman just what an innate power she wielded over men.

He cleared his dry throat, slid his arm away from her shoulders and made to stand unaided. 'I think another brandy is what I need to settle me now,' he said briskly. 'Are you ready to walk back to the house?'

'Yes, thank you. But first, Matthew, is there enough light here for you to see if my dress has been damaged?' She turned slowly in front of him, smoothing the front of it with her hands.

'I think the dress is fine, but stand still for a moment while I tuck these strands of hair back— Where do they belong?' The moon made a shadow on her cheek and his fingers fumbled with the sapphire clips as he pinned the wayward curls into place, aware of her eyes watching his face. Aware of a faint scent of jasmine about her. Aware that if he bent his head forward a few inches his lips would touch her forehead.

'There, it's done,' he said and took a step back.

'Thank you, Matthew, you're very kind to me,' she said softly, 'but I'm afraid you look awful. There's a cut over your eye and blood on your other cheek. What about your hands?' She took them in hers and inspected his knuckles. 'Oh! What a pickle we're in! Nobody in the house will ever believe you've simply fallen into a bramble patch.' She gave a little snort of laughter.

'You're right,' he said. 'Perhaps it would be prudent for me to retire and send my apologies to Grace. I can say that too much dancing tonight has been, um, unhelpful to the old wound.' He shrugged apologetically. 'But what about you? Will you go straight up to your room?'

She shook her head. 'Mama would be concerned if I did that,' she said, then looked across the lake towards the brightly lit house. 'No, I'll go back and dance some more, but it will create gossip if we're seen walking in together. Perhaps you should use the conservatory door?'

He smiled to himself. Clearly, Ellen Templeton was no longer thinking as a child.

Lady Viola and Ellen left Eversleigh Park next morning after breakfasting in their rooms while most of the other guests were still asleep after the ball. Their farewells to the marquess and marchioness had been said before they'd all retired, and now, apart from servants, the only person waiting to see them into the carriage was Matthew.

Ellen winced at the sight of his cuts and bruises. 'Is it painful?' she asked him quietly while Dominique was arranging cushions and rugs on the seats of the barouche.

He shrugged. 'It will fade. Ah! Good morning, Lady Viola.' She came from the house, smiling but barely awake, and seemed quite unaware of his split knuckles as he offered her his hand to climb aboard the coach. Ellen nimbly followed.

'I wish you all a safe journey,' he said as the steps were raised and the door closed. 'I hope I may have the honour of calling on you when I return to London?'

Viola stifled a yawn. 'Matthew, my dear, of course you must call to see us.'

Only then did he look directly at Ellen and they exchanged a smile that was not lost on Dominique.

Antonia Warshensky-Rostroprovich turned this way and that as she studied herself closely in the long mirror hanging in the bedroom of her secluded villa in the hills behind Lisbon. This splendid gold and cream striped gown, which had been delivered an hour ago was just as well-fitting as the others made in recent weeks by an unseen seamstress in the city.

Golden afternoon sunlight streamed through the windows and Antonia stepped closer to the mirror to examine the face gazing serenely back at her from the glass. The haggard creature who'd been smuggled into Lisbon wearing the clothes of a peasant had vanished once rest, good food and excellent wine had worked their magic. She looked closely at her skin for tell-tale lines of ageing, and smiled. Few women of forty-five could boast of a complexion to match hers. The sound of a carriage arriving in the courtyard below provided a welcome distraction and drew her to the window, and when she saw the man who stepped from the vehicle she felt a rush of excitement.

It was Mr Peter Fulton – a middle-aged man with the face of a cheerful country vicar, and the sharpest mind in Whitehall for intrigue. Antonia had met him there when she'd had her first discussions with the Secretary of State for War, and it had been Peter Fulton who had subsequently directed her intelligence-gathering activities.

She hurried downstairs and met him as he stepped into the blue and white tiled entrance hall. 'My dear Peter! How good it is to see you,' she said and gave him her hand. 'When did you arrive in Lisbon?'

He adjusted his small, steel-framed spectacles and smiled at her in a way that conveyed a feeling which had never been voiced. Mr Fulton's dealings were always scrupulously professional. 'I stepped off the packet from Falmouth a matter of hours ago,' he said as she escorted him into a small sitting room and closed the door. 'And it's a pleasure to see you looking so well after your ordeals, *Mrs Smith*.' He used her incognito name even though there were no servants within earshot.

'Yes, yes, I'm perfectly fit, thank you, but what news do you bring from London?' she asked. 'Can you tell me about Colonel Halifax? Did – has he recovered? When and how did my husband die? And what have you heard of poor Father Juan? And how much longer am I to remain here as a recluse?'

He pulled a chair for her to sit at the table, then produced several pages from his pocket and spread them in front of her. 'First, I'm happy to inform you that Colonel Halifax survived and was sent home to England to recuperate. As for Father Juan – we have no details, but we suspect he died under interrogation. I'm afraid nothing has been heard of him since that time.'

They looked at each other for a moment and Antonia shook her head sadly; her throat was too tight to speak.

Mr Fulton shuffled his papers. 'You've heard, of course, about Wellington's great victory at Vitoria. What was left of the French army has retreated into the Pyrenees and King Joseph and Jourdan were last seen scrambling from their coach in such a hurry that Jourdan forgot his marshal's baton, and Joseph went without his silver chamberpot! The Prince Regent already has them both on display at Carlton House.'

'Is Napoleon ready to surrender now?'

'Far from it. He's conscripting schoolboys and old men, and he'll fight us every inch of the way through the mountains and into France.' He sat forward with his elbows on the table and steepled his fingers. 'King Ferdinand has signed the Treaty of Valençay, y'know, and Bonaparte is sending him back to his throne in Madrid. His Majesty has sworn to rally the Spanish army and join the fight against the British.'

Antonia looked alarmed, but Fulton gave a throaty laugh. 'I'll wager every penny I possess that once Ferdinand feels the crown of Spain on his head again he'll do absolutely nothing to honour any of the promises he has made to the Emperor of the French!'

She acknowledged his prediction with a shrug, then drew in a deep breath. 'But now, you must tell me what you know about my husband's death.' She stood and turned from the table to pour sherry for them both. Her hand shook and the bottle hit the rim of the glass, spilling a little. 'Why have I been asked to return to St Petersburg?'

Peter Fulton sipped his sherry before he spoke. 'I need a correspondent there, and nobody could fulfil this task better than you, now that your husband has gone.'

'Tell me what happened to him!'

'I know only what was reported in one of the Russian newspapers we receive. It simply said that Vladimir Warshensky-Rostroprovich had been shot by an intruder in his bedroom.' He watched her closely. 'Was the assassin a thief? A jealous husband or some man seeking revenge? It seems your husband collected enemies as well as *objets d'art* and lovely ladies. The servants heard nothing, saw nothing, of course.'

For several moments Antonia sat in stunned silence before she could speak. 'I was his wife for fifteen years, but I can't pretend to be distressed by the news of Vladimir's death.' She drained her glass, then got up to pour another sherry for herself. 'I had no contact with him after he sent me away to the convent in Suzdal, and I'm sure he soon put me out of his mind.'

'Perhaps he did, but he never divorced you. You are still his widow—' Mr Fulton reached across the table quickly to take the glass from her fingers before she dropped it. 'However, before you celebrate, we hear that he was deeply in debt.'

'Vladimir in debt? Impossible! His house was full of treasures, and he was never a gambler. He'd become furious – even violent – if he discovered I'd been gambling.'

Mr Fulton removed his glasses and polished the lenses with a handkerchief while he let out a long sigh. 'Our difficulty in St Petersburg now is that the relationship between the court and our embassy is an uneasy one. Of course, Whitehall receives diplomatic communiques from the ambassador, but we get very little background information to help us read between the lines. We need to learn the mood of the country from the gossip passed in the market places, in drawing rooms and at dinner tables, and now that Warshensky-Rostroprovich is lying cold amongst his ancestors—' He gestured towards her.

She took his meaning, but it caused her to frown. 'It's well over ten years since I lived in St Petersburg; few people will remember me.' She stood and paced to and fro across the room. 'What use could I be if I returned there?'

'We need to hear whispers of how the wind is blowing in St Petersburg because the British government is about to donate two million pounds into Tsar Alexander's war chest. Simply say that providence has provided an opportunity for you to become our correspondent in St Petersburg, and I'll give you the address of an "Aunt Sophie" in London who would be most interested to hear any gossip regarding England's investment.' He picked up his glass and drained it. 'Anyhow, you might even enjoy renewing old acquaintances.'

She could feel her excitement rising. 'In that case, how can I refuse your offer? How do I travel from here? Where will I live? How will I account for my long absence from St Petersburg?'

CHAPTER THIRTEEN

Matthew Halifax came to London earlier than he had anticipated when he received news of a well-bred bay gelding which was up for sale. He wasted no time in arranging to inspect it; good horse-flesh was becoming more difficult to find these days.

His first appointment in London was to watch a groom take the horse, named Trojan, for an early-morning gallop around the ring at a time when few other riders were in Hyde Park. He noted the animal's long sloping pasterns and shoulders well laid back, its rhythmic gait and instant responses to signals; within five minutes he was in the saddle himself and cantering slowly along the path beneath the trees.

Eventually, the urge to press Trojan into a gallop became too strong and the big bay stretched himself into a pace that sent them swiftly passing other riders. Matthew felt himself smiling. This was indeed the horse for him, he decided, and reined it back into a walk. An offer of 500 guineas had already been made for the animal, he knew. He'd put in his own bid immediately at 550.

It was while he was planning how best to ship the horse with him when he returned to the regiment that he became aware of a flighty chestnut mare ahead. The young lady in the saddle was having difficulty controlling her rearing mount and, while her flustered groom was attempting to calm the animal, two smartly dressed men riding stallions were circling her, loudly calling advice and adding confusion to the situation.

Matthew pulled to the other side of the track and rode on past the group, keeping his eyes on a point far ahead – until he caught the sound of a familiar female voice: 'You will oblige me greatly, gentlemen, if you kindly take yourselves off to the ends of the earth and mind your own business!'

Matthew reined in the bay horse and swung around in the saddle, astonished to see that it was Ellen on the pretty, misbehaving mare. She was in a green velvet riding habit made in the fashionable military style now favoured by ladies, with epaulettes on the shoulders and the jacket frogged with gold braid.

The two male riders she'd rebuked were pulling away, doffing their hats while she turned to speak to her groom. Her horse began to walk, then broke into a trot, and Matthew saw the fierce concentration in her expression as she and the groom passed him without a sideways glance.

He followed them, keeping well behind and watching the groom instructing her. The gleaming chestnut mare was a beauty, with a white blaze on her head and four white socks. But it was obviously a high-spirited, poorly schooled animal who tossed her head and snatched at the bit, changed gait, shied at shadows and occasionally tried to crab-walk. In every way, the mare seemed determined to show her novice rider just how troublesome she could be.

Matthew trailed them at distance around the ring once more, until Ellen and the groom eventually rode out through the gates of the park and turned in the direction of Curzon Street. He then went immediately to settle with the owner of the bay horse, before making his first morning call – one which he knew would be difficult.

Lady Fenton and Evangeline's two younger sisters received him tearfully as he expressed his condolences. Listening to their description of Evangeline's suffering, Matthew's heart sank as he recalled the vivacious, laughing girl who, on the eve of his departure to war, he had impulsively asked to share his life. He'd been twenty-two years old, and she just eighteen – and at that moment they'd believed themselves to be truly in love.

He heard Lady Fenton's mournful words, and made the appropriate responses. Eventually he took his leave, and on his way to Curzon Street he reminded himself that Miss Ellen Templeton was still very young, and he must avoid leaving any impression at Ramsden House that his feelings for Viola's ward were growing warmer. And he was certainly not about to declare them on the eve of his departure.

'Matthew, how delightful of you to call,' Lady Viola greeted him when he was announced. 'See, Aunt Adelaide and Mrs Blessington are also here this morning.' He acknowledged each of the grey-haired women, who plunged immediately into condolences on the death of his fiancée and offered their advice not to delay in finding someone else while he was in England.

'Do sit, my dear,' urged Viola. 'Will you have tea? Ellen is having her music lesson at the moment and she will join us shortly. And do you know, she has been riding in the park this morning! Ramsden bought her a sweet horse for her birthday, and she had her first riding lesson with the head groom yesterday. I'm sure—'

'Her birthday?' Matthew interrupted. 'I had no idea. When?'

'Yes, she turned eighteen two days ago.' Viola gave a knowing glance at the two ladies. 'Actually, we have just been discussing a coming-out ball. Can you imagine what offers are likely to come her way once she's out?'

Aunt Adelaide and Mrs Blessington nodded enthusiastically and were listing the names of likely contenders for Ellen's hand, when she herself walked in with Hannibal, clipped and sweet-smelling, at her heels. Viola's lap dogs jumped from their chair, tails wagging, and ran across the room to scamper around his legs, but he ignored them and wiped Matthew's hand with his tongue.

Ellen greeted the ladies then turned her smile towards Matthew. 'What a wonderful surprise! I didn't expect to see you in London so soon.' Her eyes shone. 'I must say you are looking much better than you were at our last meeting.'

He made a polite bow and felt his pulse-rate rise a notch. 'Thank you. I hope I find you well also?'

'Frankly, I'm aching in every joint,' she said. 'Yesterday I rode a horse for the first time, and I thought my arms were about to be pulled from their sockets.' She made a long face. 'Riding is much more difficult than I ever imagined, and after we came home from the park this morning my fingers were so stiff from tugging the reins that my music teacher said poor Mozart would turn in his grave if he heard how I *mutilated* his lovely little minuet. Would you like to come to the mews and see my horse?'

He agreed. It seemed kinder not to mention that he had seen the difficulty she was having with it in Hyde Park. 'Will you excuse us, Mama?' she asked.

'Of course, take Matthew to see your horse, dear, but don't forget you have an appointment with Mr Lawrence at two o'clock.'

'The kindness Mama and Uncle Ramsden show me seems boundless,' Ellen said in a tone of wonder as they went out to the mews. 'Lord Ramsden has commissioned Thomas Lawrence to paint my portrait, and I go for three sittings each week.'

'And now Lady Viola is planning a coming-out ball?' He surprised himself by mentioning it, but Ellen slid him a sideways glance and smiled smugly.

'That won't happen, Matthew. It's the last thing in the world I want, and Dominique will convince Mama that it would be unwise to put me onto the marriage market at a time when so many of the most eligible young men are away fighting' She looked up at him with a sly smile. 'Then when they all come home again, Dominique and I will find another excuse not to have a ball. Perhaps we'll persuade Mama to take me abroad for a few years, and after that

I'll be considered too old to come out.'

Matthew was still grinning when they reached the stables and Ellen introduced him to Smithers, the wiry, grey-haired groom whom he had seen with her earlier.

'Lord Ramsden might be a clever man in runnin' the country, m'lord, but he's certainly not when it comes to buying a fittin' mount for Miss Ellen.' The man clicked his tongue and opened the door into a stall bearing the name *Honey* in fresh paint. The lovely mare turned her white-blazed nose towards them and flattened her ears warningly as the groom approached.

'I'm afraid this one has learned a basketful of bad habits, m'lord,' he said gruffly, and dodged the mare's teeth coming at him. 'His lordship went ahead and bought the animal without askin' me to see as to its suitability for Miss Ellen.'

Ellen watched tensely as Matthew walked into the stall to examine the horse while the groom held her head. 'She's a splendid animal, Mr Smithers,' he said as Honey tried to position herself to kick him, 'but I agree that her manners should be improved before Miss Templeton attempts to ride her again.'

'Indeed, m'lord,' the groom said.

'I've just bought one of the finest horses I've ever ridden,' Matthew said. 'He's named Trojan – sweet-tempered, easy-moving, and has a mouth as soft as butter. He's tall, but he'd make an excellent mount for a beginner.'

Mr Smithers caught his drift. 'And you'd take Honey in hand, m'lord?'

Matthew nodded. 'We need say nothing about this to Lord Ramsden, but I'll bring my bay here in the morning and you can put Miss Templeton's saddle on Trojan while I ride the mare and do my best to teach her how to behave like a lady.'

'Oh, Matthew to the rescue again!' Ellen said cheerfully. 'You'd blush if I told you how sharply I scolded two gentlemen who thought they could help when Honey was misbehaving in the park this morning.'

He wisely said nothing as they walked back to the house, where he immediately accepted Viola's invitation to join them for lumch – and abandoned the plans to meet friends at his club that afternoon.

Shortly before two o'clock he accompanied Ellen and Dominique to the door of Mr Lawrence's studio in Bond Street. Like the rest of London, he was well aware of the handsome, philandering painter's reputation with ladies of quality, but Dominique gave him a reassuring smile as he stood hesitantly on the doorstep.

'I always accompany mademoiselle upstairs when she poses, m'lord,' she said, straight-faced. 'Perhaps you would be so kind as to return for her in two hours?'

'I'd be delighted,' he said, and set out with a sense of urgency to find a birthday gift for Ellen. It would be a necklace, he decided – one that was delicate yet handsome.

He visited a popular Bond Street jeweller, another in Sackville Street, then set off along Piccadilly. One after another he inspected – and rejected – a variety of lovely necklaces. Some were too long, some too heavy, others too showy and sophisticated. However, it was a pleasant, time-consuming exercise, and eventually he found a light, lacy gold necklace set with amethysts and small diamonds. He was smiling as he came from the shop with its velvet, silk-lined box in his pocket.

'Only one more sitting and the portrait will be finished,' Ellen said as he escorted her back to Curzon Street, where they met Lord Ramsden returning from Westminster. He greeted Matthew warmly before drawing him into the library while he vented his anger on a proposal made by the Whigs in Parliament. 'There are some outright Bonapartists in their ranks, I tell you!' he said savagely.

While Matthew gave the appearance of listening attentively, his mind was more focused on the velvet box in his pocket. 'Indeed, sir!' he said when his lordship thumped his fist on the table after making an angry statement, the point of which had quite slipped past his listener.

'And now, m'lord,' Matthew broke in, 'may I have your permission to ask Ellen to accompany me to the theatre while I'm in London?' A perfectly innocent request, he thought.

'Ellen, eh? Splendid. Why, of course you have my permission,' said his lordship. He seemed relieved to put the business of government behind him for the moment, and sent a footman to ask Miss Templeton to join them in the library.

'I'm glad you're willing to offer her a little entertainment, Matthew; she needs to spend more time in younger society,' Ramsden said with feeling. 'My sister and I take great pleasure in having her here with us, and she goes about a great deal with Viola to tea parties and endless shopping. But I'm afraid most people her age consider Ellen to be a little too bookish.' He looked puzzled. 'She's lively enough here, though I admit she still spends a deal of time in correspondence with her old tutor.'

'Ellen has a bright mind,' Matthew added, and inwardly winced at his patronizing tone.

'Just so,' his lordship said keenly, 'and that's why I thought a little horse riding would be beneficial in bringing her out to meet younger people. Most of 'em ride.'

Ellen came into the room while Lord Ramsden was speaking and she went directly to him and kissed his cheek. 'Yes, Uncle, I've already introduced Matthew to Honey.'

His lordship's habitually dour expression brightened. 'Now, m'dear girl, Matthew has something to ask you.'

She looked to him and smiled expectantly.

'Yes,' he said, 'but first will you do me the honour of accepting this belated birthday gift?' He pulled the velvet box from his pocket.

Under the watchful eyes of Lord Ramsden, she opened the box and the small gems set in the fine gold necklace sparkled up at her. For a long moment she gazed at it, lying on the cream satin, and a flush crept up her neck. 'It's truly lovely, Matthew. Thank you so much.' She came towards him and lifted her lips to his cheek, 'I'll treasure this always.'

'And now,' he said, trying to maintain a matter-of-fact tone, despite her closeness, 'would you care to accompany me to Covent Garden tomorrow evening? *The Beggar's Opera* is playing and I think you'd enjoy the – satire and the music is lively.'

'Oh yes!' A smile lit her face and she looked quickly at Lord Ramsden. 'May I?'

'Of course,' he answered, and Matthew experienced a pleasant pulse of anticipation.

Their box at Covent Garden was close to the stage and Ellen perched on the edge of her chair, looking eagerly at everything around her – at the elaborate velvet curtains, the crowds filling the stalls, the gilded ceiling decorations, the people in their boxes on the other side of the theatre who were looking back at her through their opera glasses.

'If my father hadn't rescued me from Norfolk, I'd have come to London and become an actress,' she announced conversationally.

'You would have been a woeful actress,' Matthew said, without looking up from the programme in his hands.

'You're so wrong! I'd have soon learned how to perform in front of a theatre full of people,' she said, pretending to be offended.

'From what I've observed of your performance in a *ballroom* full of people, Miss Ellen Templeton, you appear to have great difficulty with dialogue.' At this point, he was unable to hide the laughter in his voice.

'Very well, if that's your poor opinion of me, sir,' she said, using the same tone and slanting him a sideways glance, 'take me to another ball and I'll go prepared with a long script full of civil inanities and bore everyone to death by repeating them endlessly.'

'Yes, that would be an excellent start,' he said, looking up as the curtains parted and the hubbub in the packed audience stilled, 'and you'll also be able to tell everyone about the performance we're about to see because the role of the highwayman is being played by the famous Vestris. Have you heard of her?' She shook her head. 'Well, I'm sure you won't forget her after tonight because she plays the role wearing boy's clothing – breeches.'

Indeed, the beautiful Italian singer's voice and dancing delighted the audience and when the curtain came down on the first act, Ellen joined in the wild applause. 'Oh, how I am enjoying this!' she said. 'And don't you agree that Vestris's legs look absolutely beautiful in tights?'

'They do?' he said with feigned surprise. 'I failed to notice.'

She giggled and hit his wrist with the ivory sticks of her fan.

It was so delightfully easy to make her laugh, but a knock on the door of the box interrupted their banter, and a young officer with a scarred cheek and wearing a patch over one eye came in. 'I say, Halifax, what luck finding you here tonight. I'd no idea you were back in London!'

She saw the happy surprise on Matthew's face as he stood and grasped the young man's hand. 'Ellen, allow me to present Captain Randal McAlister – we fought together in Spain. Rand, this is Miss Templeton.'

The officer bowed to her. 'Forgive me for interrupting, ma'am, but the last time the colonel and I were together was in an army hospital. I was the first to leave and I wondered—'

'Thank you, Rand, I've made a good recovery, but tell me – have you married the lovely Patricia yet?'

'Yes, indeed I thought she might have been put off by this, but—' He adjusted his patch, then grinned engagingly and pointed across the auditorium to a box where a young woman in a yellow gown was waving her fan at them. 'We're having a small dinner party next Tuesday, and we'd be delighted if you and Miss Templeton could join us.'

Ellen looked at Matthew and gave a tiny nod.

'Thank you, Rand. Tuesday evening it is, then.'

'Oh, Dominique, I'm sorry to have kept you up so late, but I've had a most wonderful evening! The performance was a little *outre*, but I did so enjoy it, and the applause for Vestris went on and on and on.' The maid smiled at Ellen's high spirits, and put the new necklace back in its box before she unbuttoned her gown.

'Matthew met several of his friends there tonight, and we were invited to have supper with a naval captain and his wife, who told me that she has often sailed on his ships *and* she has learned how to navigate by the stars! Oh, what I wouldn't give to be able to do that!'

The maid unpinned Ellen's hair and began to brush it while she barely paused to draw breath. 'Matthew has said he'll take me to visit the observatory at Greenwich soon, and we're to attend a lecture on the pyramids at the Royal Society tomorrow evening. And I might even go up in a hot-air balloon when we are at Vauxhall Gardens on Friday.'

Dominique pulled down the bedcovers and Ellen climbed into the lace-edged sheets. 'I don't know when I've ever had such a happy time,' she said with a sigh as she nestled her head into the pillows. 'I do wish my father had lived long enough to meet Matthew Halifax.'

Matthew walked slowly up the stairs to his bedroom. In his hand was the message that had come from Horse Guards while he was out. Even without opening it, he knew what it contained.

Yesterday's newspaper reports had stirred his anger when they'd shouted that Wellington's long siege of San Sebastian had been successful and now the British army had only to press on through the Pyrenees before they faced Bonaparte on French soil at last.

Idiots! Every private in the army knew that Wellington had no hope of getting through before winter set in because Bonaparte was going to throw every last man in France at them. Months of desperate fighting lay ahead in the mountains – months of hauling cannons and men and supplies and wounded over miserable, snow-covered terrain and through narrow passes.

When he reached his bedroom Matthew broke the seal and read the message. As he'd anticipated, it was an order for him to present himself at Horse Guards before returning to duty. He looked at the dates and his heart sank. Three weeks. He had barely three weeks left to teach Ellen's stubborn horse how to behave, and just three more weeks to teach Ellen how to – what?

He winced at his own arrogance and ran his fingers through his hair. Good God, she needed no tutoring from him. The only thing Ellen Templeton needed now was to make the acquaintance of people whose intellect challenged hers. Perhaps in the next three weeks he could see that it happened.

The sturdy new walnut campaign chest stood beside his bed. William Gray's skilled hands had fashioned the box, lovingly polished the timber and adorned it with gleaming brass fittings. If ever it came back to England that surface would carry the inevitable scratches and scars inflicted by travel in the regimental baggage train, but inside, hidden from the eyes of strangers . . .

Matthew opened the box to look again at the fine marquetry panel decorating the underside of the lid where hundreds of tiny, colourful fruitwood
pieces depicted his favourite view of the river bend. And to this scene the
craftsman had added the figure of a girl and a dog standing on the bank to
watch a duck and her ducklings paddling downstream.

Matthew felt his throat constrict as he looked at it. This was just as he had
seen Ellen before they'd come face to face in the craftsman's workshop later
that morning – after he'd overheard her calculating angles to ensure that this
river did not appear to run uphill.

And now William Gray had ensured that Matthew would carry the river
scene with him wherever he went. Ellen Templeton would travel with him
constantly.

CHAPTER FOURTEEN

Antonia always knew that returning to St Petersburg would stir her emotions, but standing alone at the ship's railing as it sailed up the Neva River, past the granite quays lined with palaces and classical buildings topped by gilded domes and spires, she was torn by feelings that alternated between dread and exhilaration.

There was a bustle on the deck of the Danish ship as the crew made ready to drop anchor beside the other merchant vessels berthed across the river from the long baroque façade of the Winter Palace. Antonia's breathing quickened as she gazed towards it, recalling its glittering halls lit by a thousand candles, the music and the sparkle of jewels, and the great sweeping staircase where Christopher Templeton had waited for her. Did he also carry regrets that he'd allowed his honour and his unbreakable convictions to stand in the way of a fixture they might have shared?

A round-faced, grey-haired woman joined her at the rails and broke into Antonia's daydreams. 'Madam, I can see Mikhail waiting on the landing steps.'

'Ah! Thank you, Olga.'

Peter Fulton's meticulous planning for Madame Warshensky-Rostroprovich's return to St Petersburg was unfolding precisely as he and Antonia had discussed in Lisbon. From amongst his network of information-gatherers, Mr Fulton had engaged a young Russian man and an older woman as madame's servants. 'Tell them to mention your name in the markets. Kitchen gossip rises like hot air in a house, and within two days I guarantee the news of your return to St Petersburg will have raced upstairs to the drawing rooms,' he'd said.

While Antonia and Olga had waited to board this ship at a small Baltic port, Mr Fulton had sent Mikhail on ahead to St Petersburg with instructions to find a suitably modest house and carriage in readiness for his mistress's arrival.

Now, along with their luggage, Antonia and Olga were the first to be ferried ashore in the ship's cutter and Mikhail, a deceptively bland-faced young man in livery, stood waiting at the steps to assist them from the boat.

Her arrival at the quay did not go unnoticed 'Everything is running to plan, madame,' Mikhail said quietly. 'Your name is very well remembered in this city.' There was a smile in his sharp grey eyes as he opened the carriage door and let down the steps.

She sat silently while the carriage rumbled across the bridge and past the great bronze statue of Peter the Great on his rearing horse. The sights of the city became a blur beyond the carriage windows as they drove through the wide, busy streets lined with gardens and great columned houses, one of which was the mansion that had been her home for so many years. Behind those cold stone walls, someone had killed the man who'd called himself her husband, and she had to curb an impulse to cry out with joy.

They crossed a wooden bridge over the Fontanka River and Mikhail stopped the carriage outside a modest, two-storeyed house which overlooked the Summer Gardens on the far bank. A female servant opened the front door and when Antonia inspected the reception rooms she liked what she saw for, although the house was not large, it was filled with light and furnished with a pleasantly faded elegance. 'Thank you, Mikhail, this will suit very well indeed.'

He bowed, hat in hand. 'I understand that several other parties were eager to lease this house, but when the attorney heard that it was Madame Warshensky-Rostroprovich who required it, he had no hesitation in putting your name on the contract.'

She looked at the signature on the paper and recalled the man's melancholy face more than twenty years ago when she'd told him that their brief little affair must end before her husband learned of it. Vladimir always returned in a black mood from a visit to his country estate; she shivered at the memory of it.

While Mikhail carried her boxes up to the bedroom one by one and Olga began to unpack the gowns and arrange silver-topped bottles and jars on the dressing table, Antonia stood tensely by the window, looking out over the river.

'Mikhail, what do people say here about my husband's death?' she asked.

The young man was puffing as he set down his load on the floor. 'Well, madame, the general opinion seems to be that the gentleman was killed by a thief,' he said. 'There was an investigation, but nothing came of it, I'm told. And now the house and everything in it has been sold.' He straightened and shook his head slowly. 'The biggest surprise seems to be that your husband was bankrupt.'

Everything about Vladimir's death was incomprehensible, she decided, but being murdered by an intruder was beyond belief. The house had always been as secure as a fortress, and her husband had lived amongst his ever-growing collection of treasures like a dark, long-legged spider poised to pounce with one of the loaded pistols he kept ready.

She took a deep breath and deliberately pushed all bitter memories aside while focusing her gaze across the river to the vibrant green canopy of the great oaks and elms planted a century ago when Peter the Great had laid out the Summer Gardens. What different memories lay in those tranquil acres!

'I feel like taking a walk in the gardens for an hour or so,' she announced on a sudden impulse. 'Please keep on with what you're doing; I'll not need company.'

She picked up a shawl and her parasol, and left the house bare-headed. Her throat tightened as she hurried across the wooden bridge and, with a quickening heartbeat, approached the fine filigree iron grille surrounding the gardens. At the gates she paused and looked along the avenues ahead, at the fountains and statues amongst the trees, and wiped at the foolish tears stinging her eyes.

She would not find Christopher Templeton waiting here for her today, or any other long, lilac-scented summer day such as this when they had met in years gone by to stroll beneath these trees, and embrace in the secluded arbours.

She twirled her parasol and set off slowly along paths that were filled with whispers of the times when she and Christopher had made love here in the moonless luminescence of the white nights. She walked further amongst the trees, and relived the long, dark winter days when they'd wrapped themselves in furs and watched their laughter frost on the air around them as their boots crunched through crisp snow that turned the trees, fountains and statues into a silent, white world that was theirs alone.

Strangely, the deeper she walked into the gardens, the closer she felt his presence. She looked around and a sob caught in her throat. At any moment he might touch her, he was here with her now, she could tell. He was here still because he had never stopped loving her – even on the appalling night when she'd lost her husband's diamonds. Of course, her stupidity had angered him – how could she ever forget his expression when she'd told him what she'd done! – but, in the name of love, Christopher had beggared himself to save her.

She leaned against a marble statue, the very place where they had stood when he had told her of his immediate posting to Naples. And here it was that she'd sworn to repay every rouble he'd sacrificed to retrieve that wretched necklace, and to follow him.

'I could have done it, I swear,' she said, looking up to address the uncaring marble face of the woman who had overheard her promise that night. 'I knew how to be a canny thief; I could have found a way to get the money. But I was prevented.' The pale stone face remained unmoved while Antonia's insides crawled again with the apprehension she'd lived with during the long days following Christopher's departure from St Petersburg.

He had carefully negotiated the financial arrangements to buy back the diamonds, and organized for the necklace to be returned to her discreetly. But it had failed to reach her for more than two weeks – a time filled with paralyzing dread that her husband would come back and discover what she had done. But with just hours to spare before his mud-splattered carriage pulled up at the house, the diamonds had arrived and she'd placed them safely back in his jewel safe.

Antonia had always been cautious about committing her thoughts to paper, but in her elation that night she had begun a note to Christopher in Naples. 'Everything is done, my darling, and I thank you from the bottom of my heart,' her quill had spluttered across the paper. 'Now nothing will prevent me from joining you.'

Vladimir, everlastingly suspicious, had noticed a light coming from under his wife's bedroom door in the early hours of the morning, and walked in before the ink had dried on the paper. 'So, you have plans to leave me?' he'd whispered. And the battering began.

Before dawn she'd been placed in a carriage, bleeding and barely conscious, and taken on a long journey to join the menage of aristocratic ladies already forced to live out their lives behind the locked doors of the Suzdal convent.

The news of Antonia's arrival back in St Petersburg spread quickly, and the first callers arrived barely two hours after she and Olga had returned from a visit to a silk merchant who also remembered her well.

'The Countess Volkonsky and Madame Shishkov to see you, madame,' Olga announced and, with a touching display of well-rehearsed astonishment, Antonia rose to greet the ladies. 'How very kind of you to call,' she murmured as she stood and stretched out her hands to them, well aware that she was looking her best in an afternoon gown of cream silk.

'My dear Antonia,' gushed the countess, 'what a delight to welcome you back! We heard only this morning.' Her gaze swept over Antonia's slender, flawless appearance. 'The news of your husband's death shocked us all, of course, but is it appropriate to offer our condolences?'

Antonia gave a noncommittal shrug and a watery smile.

'It has been so long since we had the pleasure of your company,' Madame Shishkov added breathlessly, barely able to contain her curiosity, 'and how well you appear.'

'It is most kind of you to say so,' Antonia said meekly to the women, both of whom she noted had gained considerable weight in the last decade. 'It's a great joy to be back in St Petersburg, though I can't pretend to have returned in triumph.'

The ladies sat forward in their chairs. 'The religious life did not suit you?' the countess asked and raised one eyebrow.

'It was a dreary existence, so I left,' Antonia said tonelessly, then turned her head aside and appeared to struggle with a sudden rush of emotion. Her breast heaved, just as Mr Fulton had suggested she might play this role.

'Oh, my dear, it must have all been so – so difficult,' the countess said, while Madame Shishkov's face crinkled with sympathy.

Antonia appeared unable to speak for a moment, then she rallied and lifted her chin. 'I'm afraid I left the convent without my husband's consent, and went to live in Prussia.' At this point she put a quaver in her voice, steepled her fingers under her chin, then sighed, seemingly lost in memory.

Mr Fulton's meticulous attention to detail had discovered the name of a Prussian officer killed in battle when General Blücher's force faced Bonaparte at Brienne a few months previously. The Prussian army had left 4,000 men lying on the field that day – and one of the names on the casualty list was that of a minor nobleman, Baron Frederik von Ehrich.

Between them, Antonia and Mr Fulton had created a fictional life for the late von Ehrich, and Antonia's eyes swam with tears now as she told the ladies how ten years previously, providence had guided her path from the convent to the baron's idyllic *schloss* located high on a hill in a Prussian forest. She carefully avoided specific details, but it was a small estate, she told them, for her hero was not a wealthy man.

'My beloved Frederik', Antonia called her paragon when she described him to the countess and Madame Shishkov. They listened, enthralled to learn that as well as his limitless manly virtues, her beloved Frederik had also composed poetry as she lay in his arms beside the fire. At this point in her story, she stole several lines from Lord Byron and recited them as examples of her lover's talent.

'When word came that my beloved Frederik had been killed by Bonaparte I thought I would go mad with grief!' Here she paused for dramatic effect. 'All I could think to do was to return to Russia and wait for the day when our tsar rids the world of the French monster.' Here she gave way to her sorrow.

Her performance touched the hearts of her visitors. 'You have taken the wisest course, my dear Antonia,' the countess said soothingly.

'Alexander is God's instrument, the saviour of Europe!' Madame Shishkov spoke rapidly and gesticulated a great deal. 'My dear young cousin, Princess Volkonskaia, is travelling with his entourage – there is a great affection between Alexander and my cousin – and she writes to me of the cheering and the adulation that is showered on the tsar wherever he goes.'

'He is as handsome as he is good – a true romantic – and so gracious to the ladies at every ball and reception—' The countess spread her hands expressively.

Antonia gave a wan smile. 'It's unlikely that invitations to such events will come to the widow of Vladimir Warshensky-Rostroprovich. Besides, I'm sure few people here will remember me after all this time.'

She laid the bait just as Mr Fulton had suggested, and it was instantly taken up by Madame Shishkov. 'You underestimate St Petersburg society, my dear,' she said.

'Indeed you do!' interjected the countess. 'My dear Antonia, you must come to my reception on Wednesday and renew acquaintances. I insist!'

'Thank you, Countess. I am overwhelmed by your kindness,' Antonia said, adding the right degree of emotion to her voice. 'Now, do please give me the news of your own family; was your Moscow house burned when the French invaded? And did the Grand Duchess Sophie eventually marry her Swedish prince?'

'Madame, what a delightful pleasure it is to see you again! You have been away far too long.'

Antonia heard these words spoken with varying degrees of sincerity throughout the evening at Countess Volkonsky's reception. Her arrival had caused a flurry of interest throughout the great, lavishly appointed rooms, but she was well prepared for the inevitable curiosity she aroused. She was dressed in a gown of sapphire-blue satin, cunningly cut to flaunt her figure and the still-flawless skin of her neck and shoulders, and while every other woman glittered with gems, Antonia wore none – and was still able to outshine them all.

There were many guests in the marble rooms whom Antonia remembered, but a number of the younger people had been children when she'd left and introductions were needed. Some of the young men who wore splendid new uniforms of blue and gold invited her to dance, and talked enthusiastically about leaving soon to join the tsar and share in the glory of Bonaparte's defeat. She smiled and offered each novice warrior a customary platitude, while her heart sank for them.

'How long do you imagine it will take for the reality of battle to overtake our brave young patriots in their pretty, clean new uniforms?' The arrestingly deep voice was familiar and she turned to face the speaker standing at her elbow.

'Good evening, Count Spiransky,' she said and extended her hand to the thick-set man who was regarding her with a cynical lift of his dark, heavy brows. In Russia he was known euphemistically as a banker, but over the years his vast wealth was known to have been involved in revolts raised to topple the ruler of a North African state, as well as in the recent downfall of a minor principality in Italy.

He raised her fingers to his lips. 'Madame, your attendance tonight lends lustre to the evening,' he said, 'but I accuse you of great cruelty to all the other bejewelled ladies when you come wrapped only in your own matchless beauty.'

She laughed. 'It's been a long time since I wore jewels, Count, but let me say that the years have been kind to you also.' There was only a little grey in the sleek dark hair swept back from his forehead, though his girth had grown somewhat wider.

He acknowledged her compliment, but she saw his pale grey eyes continue to scrutinize her while he stroked his goatee beard between his thumb and finger. He was not a good-looking man – his nose was too bulbous and mottled with red veins – and he must be over sixty now, but his wealth had always given him an aura that women found attractive. To Antonia he was still the inscrutable man who had often come to the house to view her husband's collection of *objets d'art*, paintings and antiquities, as well as the young wife on whom Vladimir Warshensky-Rostroprovich had hung a fortune in jewels. She had always been regarded as part of her husband's collection, and displayed to arouse the envy of male connoisseurs.

She watched the count draw out his gold snuff box, flick it open and take a delicate pinch. 'I hope I may have the honour of calling on you in a day or so, madame?' he asked. She gave an almost imperceptible shrug of one shoulder and made no answer. Would it be wise to be seen associating with this powerful man so soon after her arrival?

The count lifted her fingers to his lips again. 'Madame, St Petersburg rejoices in your return,' he murmured and held her hand an instant longer while his eyes searched hers. A brief smile flirted with the corners of his mouth, then he bowed and left her side as another gentleman approached and invited her to accompany him in to supper.

The next two days brought a number of callers to Antonia's small house and more invitations followed. Mikhail drove her about the city to shop, and each afternoon she walked with Olga in the Summer Gardens.

While wounded soldiers were seen occasionally on city steets, the reality of war and its trail of human tragedy in other parts of Russia seemed remote; nothing dimmed the gaiety of St Petersburg society or the adulation of Alexander. Everywhere she went, Antonia heard people affirming that God Himself was directing their tsar to expand Russian borders. But Whitehall was already well aware that Alexander had visions of Russia becoming the master of Europe, so her first communique to Mr Fulton – whom she was to address as 'Aunt Sophie' – contained little but an account of her social activities.

On the third day after the countess's reception, an imperial messenger arrived at the house with a note written in the dowager empress's own hand. It was an invitation to attend a soirée the following week at her summer palace, located sixteen miles outside St Petersburg. Antonia smiled; its arrival confirmed Mr Fulton's confidence in the speed of gossip. 'It has been far too long since we have had the pleasure of your company,' the tsar's mother had written, and Antonia immediately sent the messenger back with a note of acceptance.

When Count Spiransky called at Antonia's house that afternoon, she received him in the drawing room, which was filled with the flowers that had been arriving for her each day. The count remarked on them as he took the seat she offered, and Olga entered carrying a silver tray with porcelain cups and a silver pot of coffee. Spiransky's presence made Antonia unaccountably uneasy, but after half an hour of benign, aimless conversation, she felt herself relaxing. Until he reached into his pocket.

'I would be honoured, my dear lady, if you will accept this small token from one who has long felt a deep admiration for you.'

She tensed, but took the oblong box from his hand and opened it hesitantly. A diamond bracelet winked up at her from the satin interior and, after a brief glance, she closed the lid firmly. 'Thank you, but I'm not able to accept this; I believe the price would be too high,' she said. When he made no move to take it from her, she got up and placed it on a table beside his chair, then returned to her own.

'It is a trifling gift, madame. I assure you there is no price attached, so please do not be so swift to refuse.' His deep, fruity laugh filled the room.

'A posy of violets is a gift, Count,' she said, holding his gaze, 'but experience has taught me that diamonds inevitably carry a price. At this time in my life I have neither the means – nor the will – to pay for such things.'

He brought his palms together in applause. 'Ah! A splendid performance, my dear madame, and I could almost believe your sincerity if I did not know you better.'

Antonia felt cold inside. 'You do not know me at all!' She stood and was about to conclude their meeting, but he settled back in the chair, narrowed his eyes and pulled a cigar from his pocket.

'You're entirely mistaken, Antonia. I know you very well. And one small thing I know is that you have no objection to cigar smoke,' he said, carefully lighting the one in his hand and drawing on it slowly. Apprehensively, she resumed her seat while he lifted his chin, blew a perfect smoke ring and watched it wobble its way towards the ceiling.

Those seconds provided the time to resume her composure. 'How entertaining you are, Count,' she said drily. 'Unfortunately, I've learned no such clever little party tricks to amuse a guest.'

He drew on the cigar again, blew another smoke ring and watched it rise, before levelling his gaze to meet hers once more. 'Don't underestimate yourself, Antonia. Your ability to amuse me is infinitely superior to any feat that I could ever produce to entertain you.'

She assumed a look of bored indifference while a band of tension tightened around her temples. 'You're speaking in riddles, Count, and now I must beg you to excuse me. I have pressing matters which require my attention.' She rose regally to her feet.

He stood also, still smiling, and reached for her hand. 'My apologies, madame, I have stayed too long.' His lips brushed her fingertips and when he lifted his head, his eyes gleamed, large and intense, close to her own. 'Tomorrow morning I will call, and we will take a pleasant drive into the countryside. On our way, you can tell me how – when you were so far from St Petersburg at the time – you contrived the most entertaining feat of bringing about your husband's death.'

She gasped and pulled back from him, but he moved towards the door, still speaking as he did so. 'Of course, I know perfectly well that it was Vladimir's own finger on the trigger, but it was your ingenious little manipulation that drove him to blow out his brains. I applaud you, madame.' Then he was gone from the room, and the diamond bracelet still lay on the table.

His words left her physically winded. Her jaw dropped and she stared dumbly after him, feeling as though her head was full of moths that were fluttering away with her sanity.

CHAPTER FIFTEEN

Antonia slept little that night but when morning came her thoughts were clear. She took extra time attending to her toilette, smoothed a little cochineal ointment on her pale lips and cheeks and was ready to face Count Spiransky when he called for her in his splendid carriage drawn by four greys, with footmen perched behind.

'I'd like two things to be clearly understood, Count,' she said as soon as she was settled in the vehicle and it pulled away from the house. 'Firstly, I have no intention of continuing the kind of game you began to play with me yesterday. If you have something to say, oblige me by stating it clearly. And, secondly, I have no intention of accepting your bracelet.'

Tension made her throat dry. She took the box from her reticule and held it out to him. 'Please take this.' He laughed at her, and his hands remained in his lap. She felt her temper rising and set her teeth. 'Yesterday you claimed to know me well,' she said in an ominously low voice, 'but I'm afraid you must have me confused with a girl who was once the wife of Warshensky-Rostroprovich.' He laughed louder.

She opened the carriage window and the wind billowed the soft lace curtains as she flung the velvet-covered box out onto the road. She turned and looked at him with narrowed eyes. 'I made it clear yesterday that I was not prepared to accept your diamonds, and now perhaps you will see I'm a woman who means what she says.'

She saw the flare of anger in his eyes, but he was quick to curb a response until he had regained a measure of composure. 'My apologies, madame,' he said, bowing his head to her. 'I fear I have offended you, and that is the last thing I intended to do.'

'Is it? Well, you certainly offended me yesterday when you alleged that I was in some way responsible for my husband's death.' Her heart began to knock rapidly against her ribs. 'Surely you must know that I had no contact at all with him after—' She stopped when she found herself becoming breathless.

Spiransky regarded her thoughtfully, then signalled for the coachman to stop. 'Perhaps for you to understand the reason for his suicide you should see for yourself what part you appear to have played in it.'

'In God's name, what are you saying?' she asked nervously as the carriage was turned and they drove back towards his house.

'I'd like you to view part of your husband's collection, and give me your opinion.'

'You've already bought some of it? Was there an auction?'

He appeared to enjoy her confusion. 'No. At the moment I have the entire collection locked in my cellars, but once Bonaparte is out of the way and trade resumes across Europe, prices will rise. That's when I'll begin to sell it.'

'It's all yours now?' Antonia's puzzled frown deepened. 'What will happen to Vladimir's estate near Novgorod? He went there several times each year.'

Spiransky shook his head. 'Antonia, there was no country estate. He inherited land in his youth, but he soon sold it and came to St Petersburg with delusions of grandeur.' His voice had lost its bantering tone and his lip curled. 'The man was mad, of course. He spent all he had on buying that great house for himself, then set out – with borrowed money – to fill it with beauty.'

'And you were the one who financed his acquisitions?'

'I was indeed.' He studied his well-manicured nails. 'The man had impeccable taste and his greed was insatiable.'

Antonia sat silently for several moments, attempting to digest this revelation. 'Are you saying that you were prepared to see him falling further and further into your debt, knowing he would never be able to repay you?'

He clicked his tongue as if she was a backward child. 'Don't you see? I had no need to look for *repayment* when I was already the owner of everything under his roof.' He gave a barking laugh. 'In the end I owned most of his roof, too.'

A chill rushed through Antonia's blood. *What about me?* she wanted to cry, and shards of fear scratched inside her as she waited for him to claim possession of her, also. Did he not know that Vladimir had purchased her all those years ago from the captain of a Russian trader? Her palms began to sweat as she watched his expression, but he seemed unaware of that fact. Attack seemed the best defence. 'So, how dare you suggest that I was in some way behind his suicide, when you were the one snatching everything from him!'

Spiransky shrugged. 'Perhaps that was so, but your husband also had other disquieting matters in his life at that time' – he slanted her a sideways glance

– 'such as the death of the wife he'd kept well out of sight in Novgorod all those years. I told you the man was mad: he could never break away from his peasant woman.'

Again Antonia could only gape, swaying against the velvet cushions as the horses were turned into the circular driveway leading to the count's mansion. They came to a halt at the pillared entrance and the footmen sprang from their perch to open the door. One bowed to the count, and produced the velvet box which he had been quick to jump down and retrieve from the road.

Antonia pretended not to notice, and they entered the imposing, columned marble hall where the count gave orders to a footman before he escorted her in silence up the sinuous staircase leading to the reception rooms above. She needed to clutch the banister to steady herself as her mind whirled with the implications of everything that had just been revealed: Vladimir had been a man doomed by an obsession that drove him ever deeper into ruinous debt, yet he'd been a man who rubbed shoulders with the aristocracy. And he'd already had a wife when Antonia arrived in St Petersburg!

At the top of the stairs, she threw a challenging look at the count. 'Let me repeat that I will not be part of any of your games today. I want to hear the truth.'

'Patience, my dear Antonia,' he said, ushering her into a room of almost overwhelming opulence. He pulled aside a long velvet curtain and bright sunlight streamed through the window to strike the green malachite top of a gilded table. 'I have something of interest for you to inspect – something which I feel provided *the last straw* for poor Vladimir's sanity.'

'You're playing games with me again, Count!' she said as she took a chair beside the table and willed herself to remain calm. He sat on the other side, casually pointing out to her some of the important Italian paintings lining his walls – until there was a knock on the door and two servants entered carrying the heavy safe which Vladimir had always kept behind a panel in his dressing room. The men placed it on the floor, then bowed and left the room; the count followed them to the door and locked it behind them.

She held her breath and watched him take a key from his waistcoat pocket to open the safe's door and reveal the ten slim, velvet-covered drawers with carved ivory knobs. How well she remembered them. Vladimir had never guessed that she'd often opened this safe while he was away, and she'd needed no key because her own father had taught her to use a cleverly shaped little metal tool on this kind of lock.

The count pulled out the first drawer and placed it on the table. There, in the rays of strong sunlight, lay pearls, diamonds, jade, topaz, ruby, sapphire, emeralds of various sizes, all mounted in gold pins, clips, combs and rings, and glittering against the black velvet.

'Indulge me, Antonia, and play this little guessing game, because I think that somewhere amongst all this lies the mystery of why your late husband reached for his pistol.'

Antonia remained motionless. 'I'm no expert on the subject of gems, but I know that Vladimir dealt only with the most reputable traders. Even then, he'd have every stone inspected by a jeweller before he took it.' Spiransky pulled out the next drawer and cornflower-blue sapphires surrounded by diamonds lay sparkling in an elaborate necklace, with two matching bracelets, earrings and hair clips. 'Yes,' she breathed, 'I remember him buying this from a man who came from India, and that ruby ring once belonged to a prince in the East Indies.'

He opened the drawers one after the other for Antonia to examine the jewels she had often worn to balls and imperial receptions. 'Why, after all those years, did you decide to take the entire collection away from him?' she asked.

'War is an expensive enterprise – besides, the idea that your husband ever owned any of it was simply his illusion.' He shrugged and his face hardened. 'Naturally, I had my own experts value the contents of this safe before I took it, and that proved to be a very interesting exercise.'

Only the last drawer remained to be opened, and when he did so, Antonia's heart turned over. Lying there was the dazzling necklace once owned by the Empress Elizabeth, the one for which Christopher had paid a ransom. These were the diamonds that she had returned to this drawer before her husband could discover the drama surrounding their loss. She stared at the stones; it seemed impossible to drag her eyes away, and her nails dug painfully into her palms.

'Are these the gems once owned by the Empress Elizabeth?' Spiransky reached into the drawer to pick up the necklace. 'Here, look closely!' He held it towards her, but she found herself unable to touch it. 'You wanted to know why your husband killed himself? Well, here is the reason: he learned that this is made of paste!'

'No! That's impossible!'

'Madame, the jewellers who valued my investment had no doubt that this great beauty is a fake.' He heaved his heavy shoulders. 'That news certainly surprised Vladimir, and he showed me receipts to prove that he had bought the original, but God knows where it went. Or who put this one in its place.'

Antonia's head swam, and she forced herself to breathe deeply. 'I'm truly astonished to hear that,' she said, and arranged her facial muscles so that no hint of her inner turmoil was revealed. 'Surely you would never suggest that I played some part in this? Believe me, if I'd sold the real diamonds, I'd have run off immediately to sunny Italy. To Naples.'

He narrowed his eyes and studied her. 'I fear that Warshensky-Rostroprovich remained convinced that you had deceived him, and it wasn't simply the financial loss of the diamonds which drove him over the edge, Antonia. It was the fact that he believed himself to have been outwitted by you.'

She shook her head in disbelief. 'Then he was truly mad,' she muttered, steeling herself to take the heavy necklace and hold it up to the bright light. 'Are you sure there is no mistake? See how it sparkles – and look how the stones are mounted so perfectly.'

While she appeared to be lost in a close examination of the forgery, her mind raced back to the events surrounding the loss of the original to General Vlasova, the thin, dark-haired man with a humourless, determined face who had played so hard against her at the gaming table.

She could never prove that he'd been cheating that night, but now her suspicion was reawakened and anger rose from deep inside, so fierce that her tongue could almost taste its bitterness. That bastard! General Vlasova had cheated, taken the necklace and Christopher had immediately paid the price he'd demanded for its return. But it had taken two weeks for the diamonds to reach her, two weeks in which Vlasova had ordered a masterly paste copy to be made. And it had been this imitation which she had locked back in her husband's safe, while the general kept the real diamonds.

The scheme was diabolical in its simplicity. God! How dearly she would love to kill that man who had taken Christopher's money, and thereby ruined all hope of them finding a new life together somewhere far away from Russia. A shudder rippled through her.

'Antonia, how pale you are. Let me pour you a brandy.' The count sounded almost contrite. 'I can see now that this has been a great shock, and I must humbly apologize for my clumsy way of going about matters this morning.'

She took the brandy from him and drank it more quickly than she should have. But its soothing warmth helped to calm the waves of emotion tumbling inside her and restored her ability to sit back in the chair and assume an attitude of nonchalance.

'I'm sorry, but I can throw no light on this mystery,' she said and pushed the necklace across the table towards him.

He looked at her and tilted his head a little to one side. 'This is a forgery, my dear, and it should have no place in the collection. Will I fling it from the window? Or would you care to keep it as a souvenir?'

Antonia gave him a veiled smile. 'Everything has some value, Count. I'll give you ten roubles for it.' Some instinct demanded that she should claim the fake.

He gave a hoot of laughter. 'Twenty roubles.'

'Fifteen!'

'Done!' he said quickly and handed her the necklace. 'Madame, believe me when I say how very glad I am that you have returned to St Petersburg.'

She gave him a wavery smile and put the paste diamonds into her reticule.

When Antonia reached home that evening she called for Mikhail. 'Please discover what you can about a man named General Gregori Vlasova. I'd like to know where to find him. And enquire also if there is a lady in his life.'

That night she sat alone with the worthless necklace in her hands. By lamplight it looked convincingly authentic and she hatched a wildly improbable plot to turn the tables on Vlasova by locating the genuine diamonds and somehow substituting this in its place. But her head told her it was a hopeless idea, and she almost wept in frustration.

The next morning a basket of glorious flowers was delivered to the house with a note from Count Spiransky. 'Please accept this gift from one who admires you deeply,' he'd written. She gave a rueful smile and had them put into vases.

It took Mikhail little time to return from the markets with the news that General Vlasova had fallen in the battle at Borodino last year and his widow had gone to Denmark where she'd already remarried. The general's mistress had wasted no time in leaving St Petersburg and putting herself under the protection of a gentleman in Warsaw.

God alone knew who was now wearing the Elizabeth necklace, Antonia fumed as she strolled through the Summer Gardens. If only it was possible to turn back the clock, she said to Christopher Templeton when she felt him walking beside her in the shade of the trees. If only, if only . . .

A week later she sent a communique to Mr Fulton at the Blackheath address which she'd been directed to use.

My Dear Aunt Sophie,

How correct you were to predict that my return to St Petersburg would be an enjoyable experience. Indeed, I have been overwhelmed by invitations to renew old acquaintances, and two days ago I was entertained by the tsar's mother at Pavlovsk. What a delightful woman she is, and she speaks so proudly of the Almighty Himself communicating with Alexander by daily visions in which he is assured that Bonaparte's days are numbered and the Tsar of Russia will become the new master of Europe.

This evening Count Spiransky accompanied me to dine at the Peterhof Palace with the tsarina and Prince Adam Czartoryski, her lover. Her court is not nearly as lively as that of the dowager empress at Pavlovsk, but I flatter myself to imagine that the widow Warshensky-Rostroprovich has left a favourable impression with several members of the imperial family – both male and female.

And may I add that Count Spiransky has become a most obliging and convenient escort when he is in St Petersburg. I will miss his company when he goes away again on the 14th of next month.

Your affectionate niece,

Antonia

CHAPTER SIXTEEN

Balls given by Lord and Lady Castlereagh in their St James's Square residence were usually not noted for their gaiety, but tonight the atmosphere in the foreign minister's house sparkled with celebration: news had just reached London that Bonaparte had been defeated by the allies at Leipzig in Germany, and Wellington had crossed the Spanish border at the Bidassoa estuary, thanks to the Basque fishermen who provided British intelligence officers with vital information about the tides and the location of fords.

At last the war had reached French soil, and throughout the evening, toasts were raised in St James's Square to the British army.

Ellen's dance card quickly filled because, although she hadn't yet spoken to Matthew, she had written his name down in all the blank spaces. She'd seen him arrive but apart from being included in a brief greeting to Lady Viola and Lord Ramsden he'd made no attempt to approach her. She was peeved. Disappointed. Frustrated.

'I say, Miss Templeton, I had the pleasure of watching you handling a very showy chestnut in the park this afternoon. A new mount?'

Ellen, standing with her arm linked through Lord Ramsden's, smiled at a young man she'd met last week in a group of Matthew's friends when they'd visited the pavilion of exotic plants at Kew Gardens. Embarrassingly, now she couldn't remember the gentleman's name.

'Yes, she's a lovely horse, isn't she?' She glanced affectionately at Ramsden. 'My uncle bought her for my birthday, but it's taken me more than two weeks of early-morning lessons to gain the confidence to join the afternoon riders on the ring.' Lord Ramsden still had no idea that until two days ago she'd been riding Trojan each morning, and although Matthew had been able to modify some of Honey's more objectionable habits, she remained a somewhat capricious animal.

'Was thar Randal McAlister's wife I saw riding with you?' asked the young man.

'Yes, Patricia McAlister is a splendid horsewoman, and I was very glad to have her alongside me.' Matthew had sent a note to say he was unable to accompany her today, and that he'd asked Patricia to ride in the park with her at five o'clock – the popular time for society to be seen strolling in their fashionable attire, riding their horses, or parading in their carriages.

Actually, Ellen had had little opportunity to speak with Matthew in recent weeks, though he'd come early each morning to put Honey through her paces while Mr Smithers had ridden beside Trojan, schooling Ellen in equestrian skills. It was only yesterday that her side-saddle had been placed on Honey once again and Matthew had accompanied her around the park, instructing her on his methods of reining in the mare's occasional flights of misbehaviour. The animal, of course, knew she had an unskilled rider on her back, but Ellen pitched her own determination against Honey's and by the end of the morning she felt herself several points ahead of the horse.

She'd flushed with pleasure when Matthew congratulated her, but on their return to the mews, he'd immediately ridden off again. She missed his company and their friendly conversations; in recent weeks the only times she'd seen him after Honey's training session had been in the company of his friends. She was happy to make these acquaintances, but not at the price of losing Matthew's companionship.

Tonight, he'd arrived an hour ago at the ball, in the company of the Marquess and Lady Grace, who had come to London to say their farewells before he sailed tomorrow. He had already danced twice, but when she looked for him now it seemed he was in the smoking room with his brother and several other gentlemen.

She fingered the necklace Matthew had given her for her birthday and felt a whiff of exasperation. Apart from the business of Honey's early-morning sessions, it was nearly three weeks since he had either called on her at Ramsden House or invited her on an outing. They'd met often enough when Ellen went with a party of his friends to the theatre and exhibitions, and he'd been with a group which hired two boats yesterday afternoon and picnicked upstream on the river-bank. She'd seen him deliberately place himself in the other boat, and he'd paid little attention to her beyond the expected courtesies.

'May I have the next dance, Miss Templeton, if you are not otherwise engaged?' The gentleman beside her was someone she'd first met at a concert of Handel's music at Vauxhall, and later discovered they shared an enthusiasm for astronomy.

'Thank you, Mr Thornicroft, I'd be delighted,' she said, and Lord Ramsden smiled his approval of the tall young man with a fresh, pleasant countenance and a top of curly brown hair. They joined the lines forming for a galop, and again she looked vainly around the room for Matthew.

'Would you care to come with some of our friends on Tuesday evening to see the little observatory I've had built on my roof?' he asked shyly as they skipped their way down the line of dancers. 'I've bought a new telescope – splendid magnification – and, if the night is clear, the Great Red Spot on Jupiter should be visible.'

On Tuesday night Matthew would be on a ship somewhere bound for San Sebastian, she thought, and felt her throat tighten. She pretended that the energetic dance steps had taken her breath, and swallowed hard 'Thank you, Mr Thornicroft. Yes, I'd very much like to see your new telescope.'

When the music stopped, a flushed and happy Lionel Thornicroft brought her a glass of punch and, while she sipped it, Randal McAlister appeared at her side, requesting the next waltz.

Just as the musicians struck up the first bars, Matthew returned to the room, looked around quickly, and presented himself to the Duke of Moreland's red-headed niece, Lucinda Standish, who was looking particularly attractive in green taffeta this evening. She gave him her hand – and a heavenly smile – then, with his other hand on her waist, he swung her smoothly into the rhythm of the music.

He was a full head taller than his partner, and in his magnificent dress uniform Ellen thought he looked most distinguished as he moved about the room with a light-footed manly grace. Until now, it had never really occurred to her just how *very* good-looking he was, in a ruggedly masculine kind of way. As she watched them closely, she saw Miss Standish's left hand slowly slide higher onto his shoulder, and noticed how her fingers played with his gold epaulette while her breasts repeatedly brushed the gold frogging on the front of his splendid red jacket.

An uncomfortable and quite unfamiliar sensation jabbed under Ellen's ribs, and a strange heaviness squeezed around her heart. Miss Standish, still smiling as they whirled across the floor, was now speaking to Matthew, and he lowered his head to catch her words, which brought his face dangerously close to her cheek.

When Ellen experienced another painful thrust in her chest, she could no longer deny its source. This shocking new sensation, she realized with astonishment, this knot of rising tension, was *jealousy*, a great, green serpent of jealousy, the like of which she had never before known, and it was remorselessly slithering through her veins and blinding her to everything in the room but the tall, broad-shouldered figure who was smiling into the treacle-brown eyes of Miss Standish.

'Has Matthew mentioned his new appointment?' Randal asked. His voice seemed to come from a long way off, and it startled her. She blinked and shook her head. 'He's to become one of Wellington's staff officers.'

Her heart lurched. 'What does that mean?' *Will he be safe?* was what she desperately wanted to know.

'Ah, well, you see, the general usually commands his battles from an observation point and staff officers ride out with his orders to company commanders – to advance or withdraw, or move somewhere to reinforce another company that's getting into difficulties. With all the noise and confusion, not to mention the powder smoke across the field, it's usually difficult for the general to see exactly what's happening.'

His matter-of-fact tone couldn't disguise the inherent dangers facing any officer riding into the middle of a battle, and she regarded Randal with a look of dismay.

'Perhaps I've said too much,' he said with a grimace of apology. 'It might be better if you didn't mention this conversation to Matthew. He might prefer to tell you himself.'

'Of course,' she said and her insides churned. She knew she'd learn nothing about this from Matthew tonight because he was clearly avoiding her again. And when the dance finished, he didn't even look for her after he'd escorted the lovely Miss Standish to her chair. Ellen watched him move across the room to speak to Lady Castlereagh.

She fumed. What had caused their warm, easy friendship to evaporate so suddenly? She ran her tongue across the back of her teeth as she studied him. Perhaps his recent coolness had to do with his very understandable concern of what was waiting for him across the Channel; and perhaps not so much for himself, but for some idiotic fear of causing pain to her if he didn't return, or was to come back injured.

She bit hard on her lip as memories of her father rushed to her mind's eye. Initially, Christopher Templeton had kept her at arm's length – just as Matthew was doing now – imagining that he was protecting her from the reality facing him. But ultimately, it was their acknowledgement of the truth which had brought her close to her father and, in the process, had helped her to become strong. Very strong. And the truth they'd shared had left her with cherished memories of their time together, which she would otherwise never have had.

Oh, Matthew! she inwardly groaned. How little you know me! How can I make you understand that pushing me away now will only make matters a whole lot worse if something awful should happen to you.

Hot tears threatened to embarrass her but she swiftly blinked them away. In desperation, she was about to thread her way across the room and interrupt his conversation with their hostess when she was halted by the insufferable young Lord Nettleton with his friend Freddie Houghton-Blake in tow. She had crossed paths with this pair often enough in London to recognize the lecherous undertones lurking in almost every statement made by Nettie, and she was in no mood to tolerate his nonsense this evening.

'I'd be obliged if you would kindly step aside, Lord Nettleton,' she said and snapped open her fan. It was the prettily painted silk one with ivory sticks which Matthew had bought for her on their first evening together at Vauxhall.

Both young men now standing before her were clearly tipsy, and ogling her with heavy-lidded eyes. 'God! You're beautiful,' Nettie slurred and his sour breath hit her. 'Come upstairs with me, sweetling, and I'll make you a duchess one day.'

Freddie snorted and nudged his lordship's ribs. 'Oh, no, Nettie! You told me I could be your duchess!' They both staggered with laughter.

Ellen lifted her chin and threw them a disdainful look, but when she turned to walk away, Lord Nettleton's hand locked around her arm, knocking the fan from her hand as he prevented her escape. 'Miss Templeton, you're a fool if you try to thwart me,' he muttered as he thrust his face towards hers.

Though she was shaking inside, Ellen allowed no emotion to show, and drew in a deep breath. 'I DEMAND YOU REMOVE YOUR HAND FROM MY ARM THIS INSTANT, LORD NETTLETON,' she said loudly, enunciating each word slowly and with such clarity that they carried across the buzz of conversation in the room. 'AND I WARN YOU NEVER TO APPROACH ME AGAIN WITH SUCH VULGARITY!'

Matthew and others, including Lady Grace, swung around to gauge the scene, but he was the first to reach her side. The muscles in his neck stood out and the wrath in his eyes warmed Ellen's heart. She had to stop herself from cheering as he pushed Freddie aside to come up behind Nettleton and grasp his hair, jerking his head back violently while he delivered a kick to the back of his legs, which neatly forced the aristocratic lout onto his knees before her.

'If you ever again approach Miss Templeton, it'll be my pleasure to break your neck!' Matthew growled, and Nettie cried out as his head was jerked once more.

Ellen ran her tongue across her dry lips and suppressed a grin. Oh yes, it was very clear that Matthew Halifax still cared for her. Very much indeed. His fist was bunched, and he was just about to thump the future Duke of Moreland.

'Please don't kill him, Lord Matthew,' she said, adopting the sweetness of a saint. 'I feel it would be uncharitable to harm this poor, afflicted creature. It behoves us to show compassion for any young man who has suffered the misfortune of being born with a face that must surely frighten pigs, and a brain so small it would rattle in a walnut.'

The rush of fury that reddened Lord Nettleton's face even turned his jug ears scarlet. Matthew released his grip and stepped back. 'Your charity is overwhelming, Miss Templeton,' he said while Nettleton scrambled to his feet, muttered what was probably an obscenity under his breath, and clung to Freddie as they stumbled from the room.

Matthew stooped to retrieve Ellen's fan while others, including Lord and Lady Castlereagh as well as Lord Ramsden and Viola, rushed to express their outrage at Nettleton's misbehaviour. Lady Grace looked on tensely, and said nothing.

'I do apologize, Ellen, my dear,' Lady Castlereagh flustered, 'and I assure you that offensive young man will never again set foot in this house!'

'Please say no more about it,' Ellen said, hiding her delight that the incident had brought Matthew rushing to her side.

Lord Ramsden shook his head at her and clicked his tongue. 'But the shock of it! Perhaps you would like us to leave immediately?'

'No, thank you, Uncle. I feel perfectly well, and besides, Matthew was just about to ask me to dance.' She held out her hand to him and laughed, but it was a nervous laugh.

He bowed and, when their fingers touched, excitement surged through her and she knew exactly what she must say to him while they danced.

But the musicians struck up a lively polka – not at all the thing to encourage soft conversation between partners. And when that dance was over, Lady Castlereagh announced that supper was to be served.

As the guests began to drift from the ballroom, Ellen slipped her arm through Matthew's and kept a close hold on it. 'I'm sorry, but we don't have time to eat,' she whispered. 'Come this way with me.' She edged their way through the flow of people, pulled him along a corridor and opened the door into Lord Castlereagh's private study, which led into the morning room. Beyond this was a cold, unlit parlour opening out onto the garden.

'Ellen!' Matthew said, pulling back. 'What's this about?' He guessed exactly what she had in mind.

'It's all right – Lady Castlereagh won't be cross. She often brings Mama and me in here when we come for tea, but – brrrrrrrr – it's usually cozy.' She pulled him to the French doors and gave a huff. 'Oh, bother, now it's raining so we can't go outside.'

'We shouldn't be here like this,' he said firmly, aware that he was breathing fast. 'Ellen, I leave tomorrow—And you're still so young— This is foolishness—'

'You're wrong. This is exactly what should be happening tonight, and I'll tell you why.' She turned to him and put both hands around his waist, holding herself against his unyielding form while she looked up at his face, dimly visible in the light reflecting from the windows of other rooms. She leaned into him, but his hands remained by his side.

'Look, can't you see that I've grown up, Matthew? And I've come to love you with all my heart, just as my father said I would when the right time came – when the right man came. He told me I'd know – and I do know now – so please, please hold me close. I love you. I love you now, and I'll love you tomorrow and I'll love you for ever. I couldn't bear it if you went away without knowing how much you mean to me – and if something happened to you, I'd have to live my whole life regretting that I'd been too cowardly to tell you what is in my heart. Please don't let either of us be left with any regrets. Matthew, please, please hold me close. Kiss me.'

'No, Ellen, this can't happen now.' He quelled the emotion in his voice. 'You're very young and – I'm sorry – but this is not the time to talk of such matters.' He placed his hands on her shoulders to push her gently away from him.

Outside the wind rose and the rain began to run like tears down the windows while she frowned up at his face. 'You *do* care for me, Matthew, I know you do! And you're making a dreadful mistake when you say I'm too young. I'll be nineteen next birthday!'

The spectre of Evangeline Fenton laughed at him from the shadows of his mind. 'Then just say that I'm too old to pretend that this kind of emotional discussion on the night before my departure will serve either of us in the months to come.'

He heard her draw in a sharp breath, and her chin lifted as she took a step back. 'You're so wrong, and I'm disappointed to realize how little you really know me after all this time, and after all we've talked about!' Her voice was low and she couldn't hide the quaver in it. 'It's a mistake to underestimate me, Matthew, but if you insist that this conversation must wait for your return, then be assured that I *will* be waiting because I know that you *do* love me!' She swept to the door, walked out, and closed it behind her with a resounding bang.

The ghost of her scent lingered in his nostrils as, alone in the dark of the chilly little parlour, he stood at the window, staring out with unseeing eyes at the wind-tossed garden. The muscles in his abdomen were clenched so tightly he had difficulty in drawing breath but, of course, he told himself, his decision had been the sensible one: Ellen – in the first flush of girlish love – was far too young and inexperienced to understand how the war had aged him far beyond his own twenty-eight years. In order to hold on to his sanity, his life needed to be kept in separate compartments, and he congratulated himself on having had the strength to decline her invitation to announce his feelings. She was too young. And if his response to her hadn't been governed by his age and the experience of having made a hasty declaration of love to Evangeline, it was the dread of what he was about to face again across the Channel. God! He didn't want Ellen to know any part of that hell.

He ran a hand over the back of his neck and gave a groan. Damn, he should have handled this situation with more sensitivity, but she'd caught him by surprise tonight and he'd reacted to her declaration of love by equating it with Evangeline's shallow promises four years ago. In no way should Ellen Templeton ever be compared with Evangeline. If Ellen was like any other – he realized with a jolt – that woman was Antonia Warshensky-Rostroprovich.

He'd thought often about the exceptional courage Antonia had displayed during those dangerous days when she'd fought to keep him alive in Spain. And when he remembered how Ellen had reacted on the night she'd been attacked near the lake, he realized that she'd shown that same spirit and determination that made Antonia so remarkable. How odd it was that a girl from Norfolk and a lady from St Petersburg had been cast in a similar mould of courage and tenacity, and tenderness. His throat closed over and he cursed his own boorish behaviour towards Ellen tonight. Was it too late to attempt an explanation – if he could find the right words?

He left the room, and his heart raced as he went in search of her.

'Ellen?' said Lady Castlereagh. 'You've just missed her, I'm afraid. That's Lord Ramsden's carriage pulling away now.'

CHAPTER SEVENTEEN

The River Neva in St Petersburg froze solidly every winter, but it was a novelty for Londoners to see the Thames turn to ice in February 1814. Thousands flocked to view the white phenomenon separating Blackfriars from London Bridge, the Feathers pub at Queenhithe from Brooks Wharf in Southwark.

Within days, a Frost Fair was erected on the ice with cindered footways leading across the river to booths set up with streamers, flags and signs where gin, beer and gingerbread were sold. It had an atmosphere of carnival, with swings, skittles, toy shops, gambling booths, pedlars and stalls displaying pottery souvenir busts of Nelson, Wellington and Bonaparte. Fortunes were told, and boys charged a penny to whizz passengers around the ice on sledges quickly made by attaching runners under chair legs. An artist with sharp scissors and black paper was charging sixpence to cut clever little silhouetted profiles.

Ellen and Dominique stood bundled against the cold, watching the young man snip and clip the paper to produce a faithful image of a pretty young woman, but Ellen shook her head when he called out and invited her to be his next customer.

She slipped her arm through Dominique's and they continued to pick their way carefully across the ice. 'Why not have a silhouette cut, mademoiselle? You could send it to Lord Matthew with a cheerful note telling him all about the frozen river and – other things.' Dominique was the only one to whom Ellen had confided what had taken place in Lady Castlereagh's chilly, unlit parlour on the night before Matthew left England.

She shook her head. 'I haven't heard a word from him since he went to France.' The vapour from her words hung in the frosty air.

'And has he received one letter from you in the last four months?'

Ellen didn't reply at first, then she looked at Dominique and took a deep breath. 'You're right! If I have a silhouette cut I can send it to him and tell him about the Frost Fair and about Honey and – wish him well.' She shrugged. 'Then, if he replies, perhaps I'll write again and say how much I miss his company.'

Though she'd received no letters from Matthew, she had news of him from Mr Gray, to whom she'd written and asked to be kept informed about Matthew's well-being. And each time a letter had arrived from France, the craftsman had painstakingly sent her a reassuring message that all was well with him.

She'd also been able to follow Matthew's movements by the newspaper reports of Wellington's battles. And she'd studied every casualty list published, always dreading that she might find his name amongst the hundreds there. Last month, Lieutenant Tobias Rigby's name had appeared amongst the fallen, and yesterday she read that a distant cousin of Viola's – a fifteen-year-old ensign – had been killed in his first skirmish.

Everyone was aware of the heavy fire the British army had been under all along the high passes through the Pyrenees, and over steep, snowy slopes of rocks, trees and thorny brushwood. Now, in mid-February, Wellington had at last reached open country, but heavy rains had set in and the campaign had stagnated.

Lord Ramsden was privy to the military reports coming into Whitehall and, on the map in his library, he showed Ellen each evening exactly where the armies of Prussia, Austria and Russia were gaining victories through Europe, and pushing closer towards Paris.

'Surely Bonaparte knows he can't win now?' she asked every time. 'Why won't he surrender?'

Lord Castlereagh spent much time discussing the future of Europe with Lord Ramsden, sometimes over the dinner table at Curzon Street. Lady Castlereagh often lingered at the table when the other ladies withdrew, and with her uncle's approval, Ellen began to linger, too, listening with fascination to the propositions raised by men who were determined that England's voice must be heard on the Continent before Tsar Alexander redesigned the borders of Europe to Russia's exclusive advantage.

'I'm leaving for Basle tomorrow,' Lord Castlereagh said quietly to Ramsden one evening. 'Metternich and Alexander have begun meeting there, and I've heard they're at loggerheads already over Polish territory. As soon as Bonaparte has been dealt with, we must have a congress where these matters can be discussed openly,' he said and Ramsden nodded, frowning.

'I wish you well.'

*

Ever since the day Sir Christopher Templeton had brought Ellen into the family, Dominique had watched Lord Ramsden's deepening affection for his bright new niece. He was always delighted whenever she expressed an interest in hearing more about some matter of state that had occupied his day, and Dominique also noted how his lordship's sloping shoulders seemed to straighten with pride whenever Ellen stood at his side. And especially when he escorted her to Westminster to listen to some particularly important debate taking place.

Last night, because Lady Viola had been confined to her bed for several days with a head cold, his lordship had asked Ellen to act as his hostess at a dinner for the nephew of the late King Louis of France, the Duc de Berry, who had been living as an exile in England since the Revolution.

Dominique smiled with satisfaction when she saw the expressions on the faces of the distinguished guests as Lord Ramsden presented the enchanting Miss Ellen Templeton. She was looking strikingly lovely in a gown of dusky pink velvet heavily embroidered with silver thread, and wearing a pearl necklace which his lordship had presented to her from his late wife's collection.

Dominique had spent hours before the dinner teaching Ellen the elaborate etiquette of the French court, and last night she had performed her curtsy with a flourish that reached perfection.

'My dear, dear girl, you were a splendid hostess,' Lord Ramsden said, looking up from his newspaper next morning when she joined him for breakfast. 'Our guests were charmed, and the *duc* was delighted that you were able to converse with him in his own tongue.'

'Thank you, Uncle, but I'm afraid I was far from perfect. Actually, I was surprised that the *duc*'s command of English is still so *quaint* after having lived in this country for so long.' She accepted a cup of chocolate poured by a footman. 'He told me that he's sure the Bourbons will be back on the throne as soon as the Emperor Napoleon has lost his head!'

Ramsden pursed his lips and looked at her over the top of his glasses. 'All such matters will take much negotiation, m'dear,' he said. 'Bonaparte's ambition has cost many people dearly and, quite rightly, they'll demand to see justice done.'

In St Petersburg, the sun's rays sparkled on the frozen River Neva, twisting through the dazzling white of a vast winter landscape. Under a blue, cloudless sky, people moved along the ice on sleds, their breath frosting on the dry, razor-sharp cold air, while men with fishing lines sat hopefully around a few holes hacked through the thick ice.

Antonia stood behind the lace curtain in her drawing room, watching for Count Spiransky's new troika to arrive. Mr Fulton had encouraged her to continue the friendship with the count; 'Aunt Sophie' was interested to hear the dates of Spiransky's sporadic, sudden departures from St Petersburg because Whitehall had noted that following the count's visit to some faraway state, political volatility often followed. And political volatility was never good for British trade.

Sometimes the count was gone for many weeks. He told Antonia nothing about his travels, but Mikhail had heard that he'd been seen in Cairo a few months previously. Yesterday, after being away again for several weeks, he had sent a note to announce his return to St Petersburg, and an invitation for her to ride with him in his new *troika* this morning.

Surprisingly, the news that he was back had made her smile, and she was forced to admit to herself that she'd grown to enjoy the count's companionship and his robust sense of humour. Perhaps enjoy was not quite the correct word, but they'd developed an odd friendship which puzzled the gossips of the city. Even though Madame Warshensky-Rostroprovich, was seen frequently driving about with the count, as well as sometimes arriving on his arm at balls and concerts and court receptions, everyone seemed aware that she was not his mistress.

That title belonged to little Countess Zichy, a fluttery, bird-like woman still not yet thirty, whose husband was away fighting in Germany. The countess was always delighted to receive small pieces of jewellery from Vladimir Warshensky-Rostroprovich's safe, and Spiransky teased Antonia about these gifts.

And Antonia teased him in return, because the count was well aware that during his long absences, his 'Little Zichy', as he called her, was quite ready to bestow her favours on certain other gentlemen.

As Antonia watched through the window, a red and gold painted *troika*, pulled by three great, Russian-bred Orlovs, stopped at her door. The count himself was driving and Mikhail went out to hold the fresh horses while he came into the drawing room.

'Ah! How good it is to be back! I have missed you,' he said, lifting her hand to his lips.

'And, believe it or not, I've missed you, too, Gregori,' she laughed. She couldn't recall when they had begun to address each other by first names, but now 'Gregori' came easily to her lips. 'When you go away I have nobody at all to sharpen my claws on.'

'You have found no sparring partner amongst the glittering throng in the Winter Palace to replace me?' He watched her keenly. 'None of your escorts to the opera, the theatre, the ballet, the balls. . . ?'

'There are none who amuse me as you do, Gregori.'

'Perhaps none have come to understand you as I do, Antonia.' As he spoke, he pulled a small box from the pocket of his cloak, arched his bushy brows then, speaking in the same bantering tone, he held the gift out to her tentatively. 'I tremble, Antonia. Will my humble gift suffer rejection by the one person in the world I dearly wish to please?'

She opened the box and inside lay a small, delicately carved rock-crystal dove, mounted on a brooch. 'A token of peace?' she laughed and held it up to the light. 'Well, poor sweet, little bird – how could I turn you away when you've flown here all the way from Naples?' The name of that city was a stab in the dark, and it produced a result.

'No, from even further!' the count said as he stood in front of her to pin the brooch to her collar. 'He has flown all the way to you from the Grand Bazaar in Constantinople.'

'Oh, so far! Then, thank you, I must give him a warm, safe home,' she laughed and called for Olga to bring her fur cloak and hat. So, she mused, some matter had taken Spiransky into the Ottoman Empire. Only yesterday, Mikhail had come home from the tavern and reported gossip regarding new trouble rumbling between Russia and Turkey. Aunt Sophie might be interested to hear that the count had been shopping recently in Constantinople, and Whitehall could make whatever they wanted from that snippet of information.

A huge rug made of white fox fur waited on the seat of the *troika* and Antonia wrapped it tightly around herself while Spiransky took the reins and the three black horses plunged forward into a fast trot. The bells on the harness jingled and the runners under the sleigh hissed as they slid over the crisp snow; and once the city was behind them, the count urged the horses into a gallop.

Heavy snow had fallen all night and in the bright midday sun, every beech and birch tree they passed had become a silver-white transfiguration with twigs and boughs bent low and seemingly encased in shining crystal. Antonia laughed in sheer delight at the magic of it all, imagining that if one of these slender trunks was shaken, the glassy icicles hanging like pendants from the branches would surely tinkle.

It was an exhilarating ride, smooth and swift across a silent, empty land-scape, with the horses' black manes bouncing as they ran and snow flying from their galloping hooves. She pulled the foxskin rug higher to protect her face from the icy particles, feeling happier than she had been for months. Was it because the day was perfect? Or because Gregori Spiransky had returned to St Petersburg? That question presented her with a puzzle, but one that was entertaining to play with. She smiled at him.

He surprised her by throwing back his head to sing rousing folk songs, one after the other in a deep, rich voice, and she joined in some of the familiar choruses. They swept into a forest where the icy trees appeared to whip past the sleigh in a blur of light and shadow. There seemed to be something child-ishly magical about the ride, and her excitement mounted when they passed a lake, frozen and perfect for skating, before he slowed the horses to turn them into a long drive lined with majestic, heavily snow-laden fir trees.

Ahead, a house painted a warm ochre yellow came into view, the colour making it stand out vividly against the snow and the black and white trees in the forest behind. Spiransky said nothing, and neither did she. There was no one in sight and last night's heavy fall revealed no tracks or footprints around the building.

The horses were hot and blowing when the count brought them to a halt. He dropped the reins and, for a heavy man, sprang lightly from the sledge to offer Antonia his hand to alight. She stood on the shallow stone steps of the house and, with a play of nonchalance, looked up at the windows and at the front door, which remained closed. 'Whose house is this? Is it yours?'

'Of course it is. Come now, don't catch a chill, my dear,' he said, urging her towards the door. He turned the handle, and a comforting warmth met them as they walked into the silent, walnut-panelled hall. No servant appeared, and the count slipped off his own cape then assisted Antonia with hers.

'The horses, Gregori? You can't leave those hot horses unattended out in the snow!'

'No, indeed,' he said and, when she saw the laughter in his eyes, she went to the window. The horses had gone and their footprints and sleigh tracks led to the stables.

She laughed too. 'Gregori, are you a magician?'

'I'm not sure, Antonia. Perhaps by the end of the day you'll help me find the answer to that,' he said and, linking her arm through his, led her into a dining room where a tall, blue enamelled stove stood in one corner and a samovar steamed in another. A table in the centre of the room was laid with hot dishes of solyanka spicy soup, marinated lamb shashliks, fish dumplings, caviar to serve with blinis and a variety of savoury and sweet pastries filled with berries, fruit and cream.

Still there was no servant in sight. The count himself held a chair for her and served the food onto her plate.

'Well done, Gregori,' she said when he'd settled himself at the table. 'Your magic today has me quite intrigued.'

He bowed his head to her and the corners of his eyes creased. 'I have many ways of ensuring that certain things will happen. And today I wished to have time alone with you – away from the eyes and ears of servants.'

'I'm even more intrigued.'

He poured red wine into her glass as well as his own. 'Intrigued? You're the one who has kept me intrigued since the very first day you arrived in St Petersburg,' he said, raising his glass to her. 'I always considered you to be the most intriguing treasure in Vladimir Warshensky-Rostroprovich's collection.'

Her palms grew damp, but she said nothing as she looked into his eyes, usually so cynical, shrewd and calculating, and now shifting with a new intensity.

'Listen to me, Antonia: Bonaparte's end is approaching and, after that, Alexander and the other victors will argue about the new shape of Europe.' He spoke softly. 'What will be your future, dear lady? What will you do, where will you go, when your *Aunt Sophie* is no longer interested in receiving letters from St Petersburg?'

This was not the first time that Antonia had wondered about that reality, but it was a shock to hear the count mention it. 'It seems that I have no secrets from you, Gregori,' she said with a brittle laugh, and spooned a serving of kulebiaka on to her plate.

'Your secrets have always been my secrets, Antonia. Some time ago I realized that the British had sent you back here as an informer – just as you were in Spain. But what will they do – what will *you* do with your life – when this war is over?'

There was a new, soft tone in his words and it confused her. She drew in several deep breaths and put down her spoon. 'Frankly, Gregori, I don't know the answer to that. Perhaps I'll stay in St Petersburg, or perhaps I'll find a cottage in a warmer climate somewhere. I'm not penniless.'

He reached across the table and put his hand over hers. 'For the last thirty years every man and woman I've met has expected – demanded, pleaded for – something from me. But you've asked for nothing.' His voice dropped to a velvet murmur. 'Never before in my life have I met a woman I admire as much as I do you, Antonia, and I beg you to give me the honour of ensuring that your future is a comfortable one.'

Her eyes widened in astonishment and for a moment her lungs forgot to breathe. His spies had obviously discovered her clandestine work for Whitehall – but he seemed to harbour no suspicion that she was the one who had placed the fake Elizabeth necklace in Vladimir's safe. Apparently that secret remained exclusively hers. She swallowed hard, and bit down on her lip when it threatened to tremble.

'Antonia, I adore you, and I wish to provide for you, to care for you,' he said. 'And I promise to ask for nothing more than to continue the friendship we enjoy at this moment. No demands, I swear, no restrictions.'

She was still unable to speak and, while she stared at him, her mind grappled with his proposition – one half wondering why she didn't instantly reject it, and the other half attempting to assess all that he was offering.

At last she placed her other hand on top of his and a smile flirted with the corners of her lips. 'Gregori, it seems to me that your suggestion is – very generous and very one-sided. What could I possibly bring to any such contract between us?'

He turned his hand over, laced his fingers lightly with hers and raised them to eye level. 'All I ask from you is whatever this touch signifies, my dear. Your respect? Affection? Trust?' His chest heaved and she was astonished to see a film of moisture glistening in his eyes.

'Gregori, you've taken me utterly by surprise today and I beg for a little time to consider what you are saying.' She moistened her lips and paused, because at that moment she couldn't trust her voice to say more. It was almost as if the count had been reading her innermost thoughts – the fears that had sometimes drifted through her mind when she looked in a mirror and remembered that in ten years' time she would be standing on the cusp of old age. Alone.

Without her being aware that it was happening, her fingers were tightening their hold on his hand, and she could sense the scales of indecision tipping. 'Gregori, your offer is truly noble,' she said as her heartbeat rose. 'Yes, I do trust you, and I promise to think about what you've said – but please don't press me for an answer at this moment.'

He sat back and regarded her. 'I'll wait, Antonia. I'll wait till Doomsday, but now' – his smile grew and he pushed a dish of caviar towards her – 'come, eat well, and let us enjoy our day together.'

To her surprise, she found herself dining heartily, and at the end of the meal, he took her into the drawing room and settled her into a chair by the fireplace. Listening carefully, she heard a faint clink of china as unseen servants in the next room cleared the remains of their meal, while he picked up a balalaika propped against the wall and began to strum a plaintive Slavonic melody, a serenade. After a few moments, she recalled the words, and sang softly with him.

'This is how it could always be for us, Antonia,' Spiransky said when he plucked the final notes, laid the instrument on a table and dropped to one knee beside her chair. 'I ask for nothing more than to provide for you, and to enjoy your companionship.' He leaned on the arm of her chair and grimaced as he climbed to his feet. 'As well as to beg compassion for my stiffening joints!'

They laughed together and her heart warmed. 'Gregori, my dear friend, come and sit beside me while we talk about this, because I do enjoy being with you and I do trust you. Actually, I believe I will find it difficult to refuse your offer.' Something strange seemed to be happening to her and she felt almost lightheaded. Was she ready to let go of her exciting, precarious life and drop into a world where this secretive man appeared to be offering the first stability she'd ever known? Would there ultimately be a price to pay?

'I'll give you my answer tomorrow, I promise,' she said to him as the *troika* sped away from the house into the avenue of giant firs. Dusk had already begun to close in and a knifing wind rose to slice snow from the laden branches. Yet when he smiled down at her, bundled in the white fox-fur rug, Antonia felt a happiness she hadn't known for years. Her feelings for him were very different from the heady, reckless passion that Christopher Templeton had roused in her blood but, yes, she did trust Gregori Spiransky, and tomorrow when he called, she would probably give him the answer he sought.

He had just thrown back his head and begun to sing another lusty folk song, when they were startled by a sharp cracking sound above them, and she looked up to see a great branch, heavy with snow, tear away from a tree as they passed.

She watched in helpless horror as it plunged towards them, to crash with a bone jarring thud across the backs of the three horses. They reared and screamed in terror. One fell and the others stumbled and panicked, tangling themselves in the traces, bolting off the track, dragging the sleigh onto rough ground. She heard Gregori's roar as the vehicle tilted, then tipped.

Antonia felt herself being thrown through the air.

And her world went black.

CHAPTER EIGHTEEN

Along the road to Wellington's headquarters, a band of starving and shivering French deserters sprang from a ditch and pulled the British dispatch rider from his mount. The redcoat cried out; his horse reared and twisted from the fingers grasping at its bridle, then it bolted with saddle-bags flapping while the three frenzied youths plunged their bayonets into the soldier's neck, chest and stomach as he lay on the road.

None of the ragged conscripts killing the redcoat was above the age of sixteen. They'd kept their bayonets when their muskets were traded for bread in mountain villages after they'd fled from the British artillery barrage that had turned their redoubt into a charnel house. The fourth deserter had died of cold during the second night after they'd run away. He'd been sixty-four years old when the army had conscripted him and taken him away from his farm. He had made a very poor soldier.

'Open the redcoat's pouch, quickly! Maybe he is carrying food!' one voice cried, but the hands reaching into the leather bag found nothing but mail that was being carried to Wellington's men. One of the ragged youths burst into tears, and another swore and cuffed his ears.

'Search his pockets and open the letters, you fools,' he ordered. 'Maybe they hold something we can sell.'

They dragged the corpse off the road and sat with it in the ditch while they plundered a few pence from the soldier's uniform pockets, ripped open envelopes and threw English correspondence into the mud. 'Nothing!' one boy sobbed, then cried out as something fluttered from the page in his hand. The young men gaped at it, then sneered. 'Worthless! Nothing but black paper!'

Along with everything else looted from the man that day, the silhouette of Ellen Templeton's profile was discarded in the muddy ditch beside the soldier's corpse. As his blood soaked into the black paper, the French deserters took his boots and musket, then trudged off miserably once more in what they hoped was a homeward direction.

*

The wind howled and Matthew Halifax pulled his hat low, wrapped his cloak more tightly around him and put the brandy flask to his lips as he surveyed the Ardour River ahead. The sleet was turning to snow now and whipping around his restless horse. He stroked Trojan's neck, and wondered idly if the animal had memories of the gentle mornings when he'd carried a novice lady rider in Hyde Park. It seemed to Matthew as though a century had passed since the night he'd parted from Ellen.

She had sent no reply to the note he'd scribbled to her in the last moments before he left London. *Dearest Ellen, forgive me. You were right last night and I was terribly wrong.* He'd given it to the head footman at Eversleigh House and told him to deliver it to Curzon Street. That was over four months ago, and he'd had no reply. By now it was clear that he'd offended her so deeply at their last meeting that she'd declined to forgive his stupidity.

He called his thoughts swiftly to order, wiped the lens of his telescope, and put it to his eye again. To his right lay Bayonne where the French were firmly entrenched. Further upstream from the city, Marshal Soult had seven divisions waiting to attack the British when they attempted to cross the Ardour – and Wellington must cross the river.

But it was clear to British observers that Soult had set no guard on the river below Bayonne. Obviously the marshal didn't expect a surprise attack to be made across an estuary 300 yards wide.

'So that is exactly what we'll do!' Wellington had decided. 'We'll buy every fishing craft in the area and build a bridge of boats across the estuary.' Unfortunately, that manoeuvre was prevented by a malevolent, howling offshore wind that scattered all the local boats out to sea.

Now as Matthew looked at the wide stretch of water, another plan formed in his mind. 'M'lord,' he said when he rode back to headquarters and shook the snow from his cape, 'the weather's not improving, but I've located five pontoons and four jolly-boats which we could use to get across the estuary.' As he'd anticipated Wellington looked sceptical.

'Sir,' he argued, 'I'm aware these row-boats are inadequate, but I feel it would be better to risk a crossing with them, rather than to sacrifice our advantage of surprising the French.'

The general frowned, studied his map again and nodded. 'Very well, give the order to proceed.'

Matthew led in the first crowded jolly-boat. Working with the engineers, they took a hawser with them, and the pontoons, lashed together as rafts, were hauled to and fro across the river loaded with men and artillery. It was a slow business, especially as the tide began to flow strongly during the afternoon, but the crossing continued all night by the light of the moon. Their attack surprised the French and caught them in a skirmish that had Marshal Soult retreating further.

Winter clung to the land with cruel talons, refusing to lose its grip as 50,000 redcoats moved in a slow and cumbersome advance over ground that was water-logged and soon churned into a morass in which the artillery floundered up to its axles and wagons became bogged.

And all the way, Soult manoeuvred out of the traps Wellington set for him as the final tide of war drifted further into France over a sea of human flesh and blood and shattered bone.

Even in April the weather remained abominable, and Matthew had almost convinced himself that there would be no further fighting. Surely Marshal Soult would see by now how hopeless the French cause was and surrender, or news would reach them that Bonaparte had been defeated, and they could all go home.

Every night when Matthew opened the lid of his campaign box, the marquetry panel reminded him again of what a fool he'd been to reject Ellen's feelings so clumsily six months ago. And he felt worse when a fellow officer who'd just arrived back in France to rejoin his regiment brought London news to share over dinner. He mentioned Ellen's name amongst the social gossip, and when Matthew prised a little more detail from the young man, he learned that Miss Ellen Templeton was frequently seen about town these days with Mr Lionel Thornicroft, the amateur astronomer.

'And she rides a great deal with Randal McAlister's brother, Simon.' Some recollection made the fellow smile. 'You should see how she handles the showiest chestnut mare on the ring. What a joy that is to watch!'

Matthew was glad when he was summoned at that moment to a meeting in the general's tent, and so had no opportunity to hear more about Ellen's life in London. Damn it, why did it sting him so deeply to be confronted by the fact that she was enjoying the attentions of other men? His jaw clenched and he ground his teeth. Just one little note from her to accept his apology was all he'd expected. All he'd longed for.

'Toulouse!' Wellington announced to the staff officers who gathered in his tent. 'Marshal Soult has gone into the city and they're barricading themselves behind the walls. At last we'll have him, gentlemen!' He spread his map on the table and pointed to a two-mile ridge which overlooked the town. 'First we have to deal with this,' he said, frowning. 'They're fortifying these heights with redoubts and filling them with infantry – and their heavy artillery has been positioned along the whole length.'

Wellington immediately began to write his orders to company commanders: 'Prepare for battle at dawn.'

Matthew slept badly; he always felt apprehensive before a big battle. He recalled having told Ellen about it as they'd sat together on a log one day – a day that now seemed a century ago. This apprehension tonight, he knew, was fear – pure, naked fear – and battle by battle, the fear had grown worse for him. In the beginning he'd felt exhilarated before a fight – a young man who thought himself immortal, confident that he could kill any man who opposed him. *Hit first and hit hardest*, he grimly remembered having told Ellen. Now he was older, he'd seen too much death, and he knew he was far from immortal.

Out there, the French had dug in and considered themselves securely entrenched on their heights; tomorrow there would be work, hard work with bullet and bayonet, work for the British infantry. And for Matthew Halifax.

'The general's compliments, Colonel,' he said at dawn to the officer commanding the 57th Infantry. 'Your orders are to advance as soon as you see the Fourth and Sixth Divisions commence their attack,' he had begun to say, when a French gun boomed behind them. He turned in the saddle in time to see a dirty puff of smoke on the crest of the ridge a few hundred yards to the east and a cannon ball screamed over his head.

Trumpet calls sounded up and down the British lines, and from the city came the crump of cannon fire as artillery began to demolish French barricades. Soon there would be house-to-house fighting in the narrow streets.

Looking up at the awesome defenses on the ridge, Matthew could feel his heart thumping and sweat chill on his skin. Along the British line he saw officers' swords sweeping downwards and heard their cry: '*Charge!*' The drummers made a flurry of sound and the redcoats hurled themselves at the French columns coming over the crest of the ridge while a deadly fire rippled across the space between them.

The skull-shattering sound of heavy artillery burst over the battlefield and a cannon ball crashed into a file of infantry storming up the slope towards the largest French redoubt, leaving a number of redcoats bloody and twitching on the soaking ground in front of Matthew. He saw drummer boys running to their aid and shouted at the young lads to find shelter. The soldiers were clearly done for.

The next cannon ball thumped the earth beside him, sending mud fountaining around Trojan, who reared and skittered sideways. He steadied the horse and, amidst the crackle of musketry, galloped back to the general, who was watching the Highlanders advancing up the southern flank of the ridge, into the acrid fog of powder smoke, marching to the skirl of bagpipes.

The French cannonade continued and they saw more French infantry storming down the slope. Under a hail of fire, the Highlanders fell, while further along the ridge, one of the redoubts was captured by the British, and then bloodily recaptured by the French.

All morning, Matthew galloped in and out of the melée with the general's orders to company commanders, while bullets hissed around him and cannon balls flew over his head to tear into the infantry. The tide of battle swung from one side to another as the armies clashed, until the screams of the wounded began to rival the music of the bands and the crashing of enemy guns.

Now, as Matthew sat on his horse beside Wellington's, keeping his telescope trained on the action, he observed a wave of redcoats, broken into leaderless units, stumbling back down the muddy slopes of the southern flank of the ridge.

'The 57th have lost their officers,' Wellington said. 'The sergeants can't hold them! The whole thrust will turn into a shambles if that section is not pulled together.'

'Yes, sir,' Matthew heard himself saying, and when he received the general's nod, he spurred Trojan towards the thunderous foretaste of hell waiting for him. Trying to make sense of what was happening in the chaos ahead was difficult, as was searching for the best rallying point for the demoralized men.

'Fifty-seventh, to me! To me!' Matthew shouted, pulling his sabre from its scabbard as he reined in, standing in his stirrups and waving the blade above his head. 'Fifty-seventh, to me! Form companies!'

As he watched men running to his call, a French cannonball flew at him and took off the head of his horse in an eruption of warm blood. For a second Matthew sat disbelievingly on the headless bay, then the body tipped forward and he frantically kicked his feet out of the stirrups and threw himself sideways as Trojan's corpse threatened to roll on him. 'God damn it!' He sprawled in a puddle of warm horse blood, then clambered to his feet. 'God damn it!' The headless body was still twitching. Ellen had been truly fond of that horse, too, he thought irrationally, before he was hailed by a straggling line of the retreating infantry.

'Fifty-seventh? Close up, close up around me! Forward! We're damn well going up to take this bloody ridge.'

Matthew's fingers tightened on the grip of his sabre. Strangely, his fear had gone, and what replaced it now was a rising rage, the unreasonable rage of battle, the anger that would only be slaked by victory. He formed the remnants of the shattered units into columns of half companies and, through the gunsmoke, led them steadily up the long slope, over the bodies of dead and dying men and into the cauldron that was the redoubt's killing ground.

A musket ball slapped past his cheek, the wind of it like a small, hot puff of air. The French drummers kept up their monotonous beat, the French war cry, '*Vive l'Empereur*', led every charge. Matthew could see the faces of the French infantry now; they looked desperately young and desperately frightened. Ahead, athwart the line of attack, lay gun batteries and entrenchments, all bolstered by earthworks topped by palisades.

He split the company, leaving some to create a feint on one side of the fortification while he and the other troops attacked the rear. The air was filled with the splintering volley and the whiplash hiss of bullets as they fought their way through the palisade and clambered over the parapet, while smoke spouted thick as blood from the cannon embrasures.

'Cease fire! Fix bayonets!' Matthew roared once they were in, and 400 men drew their blades, slotted them on to hot muzzles, and the killing continued hand to hand amongst the stench of blood and powder smoke. 'Sergeant, spike those bloody cannons,' he shouted, and felt a French blade hiss past him. He lunged and plunged his own sabre into the man's belly, twisting the steel so the flesh did not grip the blade. It was all fury now, fury and hate and terror and anger, and his savage work went on relentlessly, until the hilt of his weapon was slippery with blood.

It seemed that nature herself had designed Matthew Halifax for this calling. His eye was quick, his body was strong and moved swiftly; he stood an inch or two above those around him, and those long limbs gave his sword arm a decided advantage. Now, in the heat of battle he lost all sense of time, and though he was aware of having been struck several times, he felt no pain.

Amongst the growing heaps of dead and dying men, the French fought long and hard, but eventually they broke; some surrendered, some ran, and the redcoats sounded a rousing cheer.

Matthew, panting, raised his voice to join with theirs. Around him two armies bled, but Matthew Halifax was still alive. Somewhere in the distance a bugle sounded the call of victory. They had brought defeat to the French and he wiped his sweaty face with a sleeve, then laughed as he shook hands with those around him who were still standing. The men who had taken the ridge this day had earned their pay, and the proof of it was in the horror that spread in every direction. Dead men, wounded men, dying horses, broken gun carriages, smoke, litter; it was a field after battle.

The bile began to rise in Matthew's throat as his mind cleared and he gazed numbly at it. Enough! he thought, and vowed that this had been his last taste of war. Never, *never* again would he walk into another soul-shattering obscenity such as this day had been. It was time to go home. Home was where a birdsong was to be heard across green fields; home was where a big tree stood beside a bend in a clear river; home was where the hands of a gentle craftsman created beauty; home was where a dark-haired girl said she would wait for his return.

He could see by the smoke over the rooftops and the occasional rattle of musket fire below that fighting was still continuing in the city, but he turned his back on it and trudged down from the ridge, past Trojan's mutilated carcass. Tears stung at the back of his eyes as he walked back to deliver his report to Wellington. Mud and blood caked his uniform and a red trickle running down the back of his hand reminded him that he'd received a cut somewhere on his arm. Perhaps the moisture squelching in his boot was blood from his leg. He didn't care. The killing was over, and by some miracle, he was walking away.

As soon as he'd delivered his report, and had his wounds dressed by a medical assistant in the field hospital, he took several bottles of brandy into his tent and went to bed.

He was barely sober two days later when he was woken by loud cheering in the camp: a rider had arrived from Paris – the allies had reached *Paris!* – and he brought the news of Bonaparte's abdication. When Matthew heard that the war had ended days before, he sat with his head in his hands and a great bitterness balled in his throat. If that information had come just forty-eight hours earlier, perhaps there would have been no battle here and the corpses of 8,000 English and Frenchmen butchered around Toulouse would not now be lying in their graves, God damn it! He cursed, and shouted for his servant to find him another bottle of brandy.

Antonia asked to be propped up in her bed so she could gaze through the window at the snow-shrouded Summer Gardens on the far side of the Fontanka. Cherished memories of Christopher Templeton had always lingered there amongst those trees, but now the view of them merely deepened her melancholia. Those gardens had become just one more reminder that nothing in her life had ever brought a happiness that lasted.

'Madame, please be patient! The damage done to your ankle is still far from healed,' the doctor scolded.

Two months ago the empress had sent her own physician to care for Antonia's injuries when she heard of the accident that had killed Count Spiransky. The blow to Antonia's head that afternoon had left her unconscious for a week, and her ankle had been shattered by the overturning sleigh.

'Please, Doctor, how much longer will it take for the swelling to go down? My head no longer aches, but I'm finding—' With no words to describe the emotions that made her eyes frequently sting with unwanted tears, she pressed her lips together and blinked rapidly.

'Very well, madame,' he said with a look of understanding, 'I believe you have now recovered sufficiently for your servants to carry you downstairs to receive visitors for an hour each day, and if your health continues to improve, I believe that in a few weeks – perhaps by the time the ice breaks in the river – you might be ready to drive out to watch it.'

Olga dressed Antonia in a fetching blue velvet gown that disguised her thinness, and coloured her ghost-pale lips and cheeks subtly with cochineal ointment. Mikhail carried her downstairs to recline on a chaise in the small sitting room, filled with the hothouse flowers which had been arriving regularly since the day she'd been brought home, hurt and half-frozen, by some of Gregori Spiransky's servants. They had come across the accident a little time after it had happened.

It took weeks before Antonia was able to speak of the count's death. She felt his loss more deeply than she would ever have imagined; he *had* become a friend, one she'd been prepared to trust with her own future. Her throat tightened each time she remembered the happy, companionable day they'd shared before the sleigh had tipped and smashed his skull into the trunk of a tree.

Countess Volkonsky and Madame Shishkov were regular visitors to Antonia's bedside, bringing every scrap of gossip circulating in St Petersburg, along with baskets of exotic fruit and flowers which grew all through the winter in their conservatories.

Today when the ladies called they could barely contain their excitement 'We have wonderful news, Antonia! The war is over! Bonaparte has surrendered and he's been taken away on a British warship to be an exile for ever and ever on some little island near Italy.' She clasped her hands under her chin and sighed. 'Oh, what splendid celebrations we will have! And even more splendid when the tsar arrives home again.'

'Listen! You can hear the bells of victory ringing everywhere in the city,' cried Madame Shishkov as she opened a window, and quickly closed it again

'Of course, our tsar was the one to lead the victors into Paris – and now every-thing will be back to the way it used to be!'

Antonia shivered. Nothing will ever be the way it used to be, she wanted to cry out, but instead she produced a laugh and applauded the splendid news. Her mind raced back to those who would never be able to celebrate Bonaparte's downfall – to dear Father Juan in Madrid, and the marqués who had given his life to help her, and the old woman who provided shelter for Matthew Halifax and who had found the murdered bodies of her son and his wife in the well. So many dead. And for what?

When the countess and madame returned to visit Antonia two days later, they arrived at the house just as the doctor was leaving.

'Ah! I am so pleased to meet you like this, Doctor,' the countess called, and drew him aside. 'I'm most concerned about our dear friend's low spirits, and I'm about to suggest that she leaves this dull little house and spends the rest of her convalescence with me. She needs diversions – don't you agree? – and it would be a simple matter to arrange for her comfort in our house.'

The doctor agreed and, after much persuasion, Antonia was installed regally in the great Volkonsky mansion, along with Olga and Mikhail, who continued to care for her.

The countess – who now insisted on being addressed by her first name, Marina – provided Antonia with endless distractions, and the glittering company which attended the parties, concerts and plays performed in the Volkonsky's private theatre helped to drive many of her private hobgoblins to the back of her mind.

Dazzling victory balls and brilliant receptions continued every night in palaces and mansions all over the city, and Marina had one of her own splendid carriages fitted with a support to accommodate Antonia's still-painfully-swollen ankle. This allowed her to be transported in comfort to a different entertainment each evening, where she began to cut quite a figure, reclining royally on a chaise and surrounded by attentive admirers.

The comfortable carriage also made it possible for her to drive out and watch the city welcome the arrival of spring. As the temperature rose and the days lengthened, crowds lined the river-bank to see the giant floes of Neva ice tumbling over each other as they rumbled down to the sea. The trees unfurled their leaves, white blossom of bird cherry foamed over the countryside, and wild flowers began to carpet the meadows.

And in July, Tsar Nicholas arrived home in a mood so black and irritable that he cancelled all the official parades and celebrations made for his welcome, and refused to see anyone except his mother and a tight circle of religious mystics.

Marina's husband, who had been travelling through Europe in the tsar's entourage, was in an entirely different mood when he ran into the house and embraced his wife in front of the servants. Count Andrei was a big, handsome man, endowed by nature with a large measure of common sense, and he greeted Antonia warmly. It had been a long time since the days of their youthful flirtation, and neither of them chose to be reminded of it now.

'Welcome home, Andrei,' she said as he raised her hand to his lips. 'Marina's wonderful kindness and hospitality has surely saved my sanity in recent months.'

'Now, tell us, my love,' the countess pleaded, 'what is behind the tsar's strange refusal to celebrate Bonaparte's downfall?'

He gave a guffaw. 'Ever since Alexander led the parade into Paris, he's been swamped by adulation at every turn – and how he's loved it. We've just come from London, and the population there, too, went wild with enthusiasm each time he appeared.' The count stood beside his wife and slipped an arm around her waist. 'But I'm afraid the prince regent and the tsar disliked each other from the moment they met, and it ended by them exchanging public insults at every opportunity.'

'And is that what has offended Alexander so deeply?' Marina sounded astonished.

'No, my love. It was the British foreign minister, Lord Castlereagh, who has upset the tsar, I'm afraid.' He pulled a long face. 'The British government flatly refuses to accept the revelation that the Almighty Himself has chosen the Russian tsar to become the master of Europe.'

Antonia carefully made no comment.

'I'm afraid the British – not to mention the Austrians, the Prussians and the French themselves have their own ideas about the future of Europe, and plans are afoot for the whole matter to be discussed later in the year. In Vienna, I believe. At a congress.'

Marina stamped her foot 'Oh, Andrei! I've seen so little of you in the last two years. Surely you won't be expected to leave me again?'

He laughed, lifted a dark ringlet, and kissed her ear. 'My dear, you will come to Vienna with me. In three months' time, the whole of Europe will be gathering there for the party.'

'Antonia, surely your ankle will be mended by October?' There was excitement in Marina's voice. 'You must come to Vienna with us! Oh yes, how wonderful! We will lease a house and—'

While the Count and Countess Volkonsky discussed their arrangements, Antonia hid her excitement and began to form a plan of her own. How simple it would be to leave St Petersburg with the Volkonsky party, and never return here. Now that the war was over, what reason would Mr Fulton have for keeping her in this city? And once her ankle had healed she could hardly continue to live on the charity of the Volkonsky family. If all her possessions were taken with her to Vienna, it would be simple to leave Europe after the congress and make a new life for herself – perhaps on some small, sunny Mediterranean island, far away from the world of intrigue and deception.

She attempted to rotate her ankle, and winced at the pain. Three months was all the time she had for the bones to mend, because in three months she must be ready to walk away from this life and start a new one.

She mentioned the notion in her next letter to Aunt Sophie.

CHAPTER NINETEEN

'My dear Matthew, how kind of you to call,' cried Lady Viola when he was announced by a footman at Ramsden House. She held out her arms and almost ran across the room to greet him. 'Here, let me kiss you! It has taken you far too long to return to England, and now your dear brother and Lady Grace have gone back to Eversleigh Park. Oh, but of course, you must already know that! Are you off to join them there, or will you stay in London?'

'This is a very rushed visit to London, Cousin Viola. I'm now one of Lord Wellington's aides – sorry, one of the *Duke* of Wellington's aides. You've heard, of course, that he's just become the British ambassador to Paris; I'm travelling back there with him tomorrow.'

'Oh!' Viola sounded disappointed and continued to chatter on with news of family events. But Matthew heard little because his whole attention was caught by the full-length portrait of Ellen hanging on the wall behind her. The rich colours of the blue satin gown glowed, and the afternoon light gave a lustrous sheen to the subject's skin, almost bringing her image to life. A tightness in his chest increased.

'Lawrence has produced a splendid likeness of Ellen, I see,' he said, trying to sound offhand. 'I trust she is in good health?'

'Oh, yes, indeed She's out riding this afternoon, and I know she'll be so disappointed to have missed you. When will you be in London again?'

'At this moment, it's difficult to say.' He ran a hand across the back of his neck. 'I'm about to accompany the duke on a visit to Brussels and the Low Countries.'

When he eventually took his leave, Matthew inwardly cursed this morning's long business in Whitehall which had prevented him from arriving at Curzon Street while Ellen was still at home. He strode out towards Hyde Park, determined to find her and speak with her. It would be a casual meeting of friends, he told himself, a quiet exchange of pleasantries. He quickened his pace.

Would she ask him about Trojan? Yes, she was sure to do that, and he could envisage her expression as she listened to his sanitized version of the fatal event. If she wept, he would take her arm and find some secluded corner of the park where she could be comforted.

As soon as he approached the ring, he saw her there, mounted on Honey and wearing a stunning black habit, liberally decorated with gold braid. While the chestnut pranced and danced, seemingly to show off her magnificence to the big audience in the park, Ellen sat on the saddle with a graceful ease, exuding confidence. When she urged the mare into a gallop, he watched her flash by, followed by at least half a dozen gentlemen riders.

He waited at the rail and, after completing the circuit, the group pulled up almost abreast of him. He could catch only snatches of the banter that was being tossed to and fro, but it was clear to him that Ellen was enjoying the attention. He was even more discomforted to see her then teasing the gentlemen in turn, and finally nodding to one man astride a big grey horse – laughing, and apparently granting him the honour of escorting her home.

Matthew's spirits sank lower as he watched the pair ride out of the park, and reminded himself that nine months ago he had deliberately opened doors into a broader society – and had shoved the hesitant Miss Templeton through them.

Well, that plan had certainly been damned successful! he grumbled to himself as he walked to his club and spent the rest of the afternoon with fellow officers there, endlessly dissecting the strategic blunders made by both sides in the war, and all of which induced a headache by the end of the afternoon.

He declined an invitation to yet another dinner to celebrate victory, and ate alone in the library at Eversleigh House, re-reading the documents which had been given to him that morning. And trying not to think about Ellen. He put down the report in his hand. How long had it been since she'd described herself to him as a polar bear who couldn't find her way through the sandhills? Where now was the girl who'd been too inhibited to speak with partners at balls? Or the girl he'd offended by rejecting her youthful, romantic feelings? The girl who, in turn, had apparently rejected his feeble note of apology.

Before Matthew climbed the stairs to his bedroom, he spoke to the head footman: 'Do you recall me asking you to deliver a message to Ramsden House one morning last October, just as I was leaving for France?'

The man thought for a moment. 'Curzon Street, m'lord? Yes, indeed, I remember well, because when your carriage had pulled away, her ladyship saw it lyin' on the table in the hall. She told me she intended to visit Ramsden House that very morning, and she'd take it herself, m'lord.'

'Yes, yes, of course. Thank you, and goodnight. Will you see that I'm woken at five?' As Matthew climbed the stairs he thought about the message he'd scribbled to Ellen. Was there a possibility it hadn't reached her? Grace, he recalled, had never really liked Ellen. Could she have. . . ? He felt ashamed of that unworthy thought, and tried to focus on the diplomatic work ahead of him in Paris. But perhaps he should send another note to Ellen and mention his disappointment at not finding her at home today?

He went to the writing table, took out a sheet of paper and began. After an hour, he put down the pen and tore the five closely written pages into small pieces. There were some things that were simply too complicated for words to explain.

He reached for a new sheet of paper and picked up his pen again: 'Dear Ellen, I'm sorry to have missed you when I called on Lady Viola today'. He stopped at that point and simply signed it.

Ellen recognized the handwriting on the note lying on the salver placed before her by the footman, and her knife and fork clattered onto the breakfast plate. Lady Viola and Lord Ramsden looked on with interest as she broke the seal, read the contents, and sprang to her feet.

'Matthew was here yesterday?' She looked at Lady Viola in disbelief 'Mama, tell me, is he all right? What did he say? Why didn't he wait?' Her voice grew shrill. 'Will he come again? Did he mention having received my silhouette?'

Lady Viola was flustered by Ellen's outburst, and Lord Ramsden frowned at her over the top of his glasses. 'Hush, m'dear, you know that Matthew has been given a post with Wellington and they'll be well on the way back to Paris by now.' He took a sip from his coffee cup. 'Placing Louis back on the French throne has unleashed a number of political hurdles, and the duke is just the man to handle them. I noticed how well Matthew was getting along with him during our meeting in Whitehall yesterday—'

'Oh, Uncle! You knew Matthew was coming to London and you didn't tell me?'

She sat down hard on her chair, and Lord Ramsden saw the colour drain from her face. His brow creased. 'Why, bless me, m'dear, it didn't occur to me that you'd want to know about that. Why, with so many young gentlemen taking up your time these days, I thought – I didn't think—'

Ellen became aware of her stepmother's big brown eyes widening with interest. If Viola realized her deep feelings for Matthew, the gossip would run through the family like wildfire, and that would make the whole situation even more unbearable.

'Paris must be delightful at this time of the year,' she remarked idly, reaching for a silver dish of plum jam, and Viola's interest was immediately diverted from the topic of Matthew's visit to London.

'Paris! Oh, yes, indeed,' she said with enthusiasm. 'Now the war is behind us, Ramsden, couldn't we all make a trip to France? Remember the delightful tour of Europe we had with our parents all those years ago? Why not take Ellen?'

Lord Ramsden folded *The Times*, and smiled from one to the other. 'Paris, eh? Ah! Yes, Viola, now you've just reminded me that yesterday Lord Castlereagh suggested – at the request of Lady Castlereagh, I believe – that you and Ellen might like to accompany us to Vienna in October. We're expecting the congress there to last only a few weeks, and after that, perhaps we can all visit Paris on our way home. Does that appeal?'

Ellen sprang from her chair to kiss his cheek. 'Uncle, that's a most marvellous idea! Thank you, thank you! And I must thank Lady Castlereagh, too.' She kissed him again. 'Now, Mama,' she said, trying to urge Viola up from her chair, 'quickly, come upstairs with me while we tell Dominique where we're going! She'll know exactly what we need to take.'

'Ellen, my love, October is still three months away,' Viola protested feebly, and took another mouthful of devilled kidneys. 'We have ample time to prepare.'

'Yes, of course,' Ellen said and quickly excused herself from the table. She went straight to her room and smiled as she opened her writing slope to commence her own preparations for their visit to Paris.

Dear Matthew,
    Thank you for your note this morning and I'm so sorry I was not at home when you called yesterday. However, we will be visiting Paris before Christmas, and I hope it will be possible to see you there.

She didn't trust herself to write more, so simply signed the note and addressed it to him at the British Embassy, Paris. Would he reply? And if he did, how long would it take to reach her? She opened the window, drank in the fresh air and lifted her face to the pale sunshine. Yes, the world was certainly a brighter place today.

Well before the congress opened, Vienna hummed with preparations for the greatest event in the city's living memory. Houses were refurbished, facades repainted, furniture regilded. Every square inch of lettable space in the city was needed for the thousands of visitors, and while the sons of the aristocracy were being engaged as equerries and pages, workers were turned into coachmen, footmen and valets.

A whole army of spies had been recruited by the Austrian government and were being trained before taking up their positions in the various diplomatic missions coming from all corners of Europe.

Uniforms of every kind were needed, and tailors and dressmakers faced the busiest time of their lives. The royal stables at the Hofburg Palace were reorganized to accommodate the 1400 horses required to ferry the distinguished guests, and the emperor ordered 300 carriages to be painted in a gleaming dark green with the Hapsburg coat of arms emblazoned in yellow on their doors.

The marshal of the court, Prince Trauttmansdorff, had the difficult task of not only arranging suitable accommodation for the official delegates to the congress, but of also having to handle the intricacies of protocol and precedence amongst the four kings, one queen, two hereditary princes, three grand duchesses and sundry other princelings, dukes and nobles, along with their chamberlains, ladies-in-waiting, equerries and attendant suites, none of whom were to play any part in the official proceedings, but who were streaming into Vienna, attracted by the promise of a glittering social season.

The Volkonskys and Antonia arrived ahead of the Russian imperial party. Count Andrei had been sent early to ensure that the tsar and tsarina's apartment in the vast complex of buildings that made up the imperial Hofburg Palace was of sufficient grandeur, and he thanked the Austrian empress for the elaborate preparations she had personally made for the Russian royals.

Close by, he rented a pleasant apartment on the Minoritenplatz for his wife and Antonia. It was only a few paces from the palace leased by the British delegation, and Marina and Antonia frequently sat by their windows, drinking coffee while they watched the comings and goings of their neighbours.

'Lord Castlereagh is a most handsome, distinguished man, don't you agree, Antonia?' Marina commented idly as they saw him boarding his carriage. 'What a pity his wife is so large and so *dowdy*.' She took another sip from her cup. 'But, look, the woman with her is even larger, though I think her gown is more becoming.' She fell silent for a moment. 'I saw the dark-haired girl riding out earlier with one of the young German princelings.'

Antonia made no comment. She had also watched the girl on occasions and wondered who she was.

'Shall we drive to the Prater again today?' Marina asked, smothering a yawn and stretching, 'or would you prefer to attend Princess Bagration's soirée?'

'Would you mind very much, Marina, if I remained here to rest my ankle?' Antonia lifted her foot onto a stool and revealed the swelling that even a tight bandage couldn't disguise. 'I think I've done far too much dancing in recent weeks.'

'Oooh, yes, my dear, do rest it, otherwise you might be unable to attend Prince Metternich's ball tonight. The Duchess of Sagan will be there, of course. She's been Metternich's mistress for years, but it's no secret that she has now made room in her bed for Tsar Alexander. Andrei tells me that feelings are running so high between the two men that they're talking of a duel! He said that only Lord Castlereagh's intervention will prevent it, so everyone at the ball will be watching to see what happens tonight.'

'How stupid,' Antonia sighed and closed her eyes. 'As if we hadn't seen enough bloodshed in Europe in the last twenty years.'

While the statesmen were spending their days struggling with the task of redrawing the map of Europe, the evenings and nights in Vienna were entirely given over to pleasure and frivolity. Salons, ballrooms and bedrooms were, in any case, excellent places for gathering information, or sowing disinformation.

For weeks, while the negotiators remained deadlocked behind closed doors, an endless round of social activities continued to keep everyone else amused. All over the city, balls, dinners, theatres, *tableaux vivants*, opera performances, firework displays and concerts were given. During the day, people drove through the leafy avenues of the Prater or flocked to the parklands to watch balloon ascents. Huge hunts were organized on the imperial estates outside the city, where imperial gamekeepers rounded up thousands of imperial deer, boar, hares and foxes and drove them into the guns of kings, princes, dukes, ambassadors and sundry members of European aristocracy.

As the end of the year approached and winter brought the first snow, a delegation of Polish nobles arrived with an entourage of eager ladies. Tsar Alexander was already calling himself King of Poland, and the Poles came to protest. Their demands received little attention, however, amongst the increasing tangle of matters already lying on the conference table. So, the frustrated Poles and their ladies threw themselves also into the round of Vienna's festivals, *fêtes* and *coucheries*.

Antonia's ankle sometimes ached, especially as the weather grew colder. 'Marina, forgive me, but I really can't face one more ball this week,' she said and called for her fur cloak. 'Herr Beethoven is to give another concert tonight – a brand new symphony, his seventh – and Madame de Stäel has invited me to join her party there.'

Marina pulled a sour face. 'I don't know how you can possibly bear to sit through those long, drawn-out performances, listening to music that breaks every rule of good composition.'

Antonia laughed. 'In the first place, I'd much prefer to be sitting rather than dancing tonight, and sometimes I quite enjoy hearing rules being broken.'

When Antonia arrived at the vast Redoutensaal of the Hofburg where the concert was to be given, she acknowledged a number of acquaintances amongst the audience filing in. 'Ah ha! So, madame, I see you are also one who is unafraid of Herr Beethoven's new music.'

Antonia turned to smile at the speaker, a grey-haired Frenchman who had come to Vienna with Talleyrand's mission. 'Good evening, Count de Barbier,' was all she said before their attention was caught by the arrival of a trio of English people. Antonia recognized them as some of the neighbours she frequently saw coming and going from their residence beside the Volkonsky's.

One was the middle-aged man with sloping shoulders, another was the large, talkative lady who often accompanied Lady Castlereagh, and the third was the dark-haired girl, who always made heads turn. Just as she was doing now, Antonia noted, and saw the girl return de Barbier's smile as they approached.

He made a flourishing, courtly bow. 'Ah, what a pleasure it is to see you, Lord Ramsden, Lady Viola, and my delightful ballroom partner.' Antonia saw the girl's eyes twinkle as she inclined her head to the Frenchman. She looked especially lovely this evening, Antonia thought, dressed in a velvet gown the colour of claret and embroidered with gold thread, and wearing pearls of an extraordinary lustre around her neck and threaded through her hair.

'M'lord,' said the Frenchman, 'may I present Madame Warshensky-Rostroprovich? Madame, please allow me to introduce, Lord Ramsden, Lady Viola Templeton, and Miss Ellen Templeton.'

For a moment Antonia felt the breath leave her body. She stared wordlessly at the large, benign face of the woman who was Lady Templeton. Then, as she swallowed hard, her gaze met that of Miss Ellen Templeton.

Antonia bowed in acknowledgement, and though her heart was racing, she ordered her facial muscles into an expression of polite interest. 'M'lord, Lady Templeton, Miss Templeton.' Her voice was dry but she kept the tremor out of it. 'I believe we are neighbours on the Minoritenplatz; I am delighted to make your acquaintance.' Her insides had knotted uncomfortably, but there was one question she was unable to suppress. 'The name of Templeton? Please forgive my curiosity, m'lady, but are you – perhaps – in some way related to Sir Christopher Templeton?'

Viola clutched her breast and her lips trembled. 'Oh, indeed, yes! Sir Christopher was my dear, dear husband.' Her brown eyes became moist and Antonia noted the tears, just as she noted the sudden intensity in the gaze that Miss Ellen Templeton had fixed on her.

'My father died almost two years ago, madame,' the girl said softly, then dropped her voice lower still. 'May I enquire if you were acquainted with him?'

For a heartbeat Antonia considered whether or not she should answer truthfully, then she nodded. 'Er ... yes, Miss Templeton, I believe I met Sir Christopher in St Petersburg – a long, long time ago. Yes, I'm sure we met at a reception at the Winter Palace.'

She saw the girl's eyes widen. In the press of people sweeping around them, Ellen moved to one side, so that her shoulder was turned to the Ramsdens. 'Madame, forgive me, but could it be that you. . . ?' Her words were a husky whisper. 'Antonia?'

A wave of emotion threatened to overwhelm Antonia, and she could only incline her head in confirmation. Ellen Templeton's breathing quickened. 'May I call on you tomorrow morning, madame?'

'I will be alone after eleven. Come then, Miss Templeton.'

'I warned you that Beethoven's music would bring on a headache,' Marina Volkonsky said next morning, and clicked her tongue at Antonia's reclining form on the chaise. 'I do wish you were coming with us today because it's been snowing all night and they say the ice at Schonbrunn is thick enough for skating after lunch.' She opened the window quickly and threw a coin to an organ grinder standing below. 'We're all driving out there in sleighs— Oh! I'm sorry, Antonia. That's probably the last thing you feel inclined to do after your accident.'

'Please, don't concern yourself with me today, Marina. I have correspondence to catch up with – and I confess I didn't sleep well when I came home from the concert.'

'There! Didn't I warn you that Beethoven's wild chords would be disturbing to the brain? In future you must listen to nothing but Haydn.'

Antonia stood at the window and waved farewell to the Volonskys. As soon as their sleigh had disappeared from sight, she saw Ellen Templeton run from the house next door. During the long hours of her sleepless night, Antonia had come to the decision that it would be idiotic to form any association with

Christopher's daughter. Nothing could come of it but the arousal of bitter memories of what might have been. How the girl had come to associate the name of Antonia with her father would remain a mystery, but during this morning's visit she was determined to reveal nothing of her private life. Or to hear how Christopher came to *marry* the large, silly Englishwoman. 'I'm so sorry, Miss Templeton,' she planned to say, 'I met your father long, long ago, and I'm afraid my recollections of Sir Christopher have now become very dim.'

But when the girl was announced, she swept into the room and came to Antonia with her arms outstretched. 'Oh, madame, how happy my father would be to know that here we are, meeting at last. He told me how much you loved each other, and even on the day he died, he spoke your name.'

'How did he. . . ?' Antonia's insides quaked but she held herself stiffly.

'He died, madame, because his heart had been weakened by a childhood illness. I know he didn't tell you about it, but he was always aware that his lifespan had been shortened and, you see, that's why when his money went, he couldn't—'

Tears washed into Ellen's blue eyes, and Antonia felt herself crumbling. She held Christopher's daughter against her and wept, too. 'Nobody in my life has ever meant as much to me as your father did, and it was my stupid passion for gambling that ruined everything for us. How angry I made him that night! But I was determined to follow him when he left St Petersburg – and I would have done so, I promise, if my husband had not discovered my plans, and sent me away to be locked up in a convent.'

They sat closely together on the chaise – the two women who had loved Christopher Templeton – exchanging a flow of fond recollections.

'So you see,' said Ellen, concluding her account of his marriage to Lady Viola, 'he arranged it to ensure that I would never have to marry simply for security.'

Antonia wiped her eyes. 'Did he never tell you how he came to lose everything that his father had bequeathed?'

'Never! He told me simply that it had gone, and that he had no regrets.'

Antonia's tears began again. 'Come with me, my dear; I have something for you to see,' she said, and led Ellen to her bedroom. She locked the door after them, went to her dressing table and touched a spring to open a hidden drawer under the mirror. From it, Antonia took a black velvet pouch and tipped the contents onto her bedcovers.

For a moment Ellen stared in stunned silence at the sparkling necklace, then picked it up and threw Antonia a puzzled frown. 'This?'

'It is nothing but a worthless paste copy,' Antonia said, shrugging, 'and God alone knows where the real diamonds are now' She had vowed to herself that the secret of the late General Vlasova's deception would go with her to the grave, but within minutes she was explaining to Ellen the entire story of her marriage to Vladimir Warshensky-Rostroprovich and the saga of the lost necklace.

'Oh, madame, how dreadful! The general was a wicked scoundrel to accept my father's money and have the necklace replaced by a fake. And, as you say, there was no way of knowing then whether the real diamonds had gone to Denmark with his widow, or to Poland with his mistress.'

She held the paste copy in a ray of sunlight, and the refracted light danced across the ceiling like shooting stars. 'This looks truly magnificent. If you wore it, I'm sure nobody would ever know it wasn't valuable.'

Antonia shook her head and slipped the necklace back into its velvet pouch. 'The only reason for carrying it with me is that I don't intend going back to St Petersburg when the congress is all over – but I beg you not to mention that to anyone yet.' She stood and smiled at Ellen. 'So there you have the whole story of Antonia Warshensky-Rostroprovich.' That was not strictly true, but even Christopher's daughter could not be told of the shadowy work she had done for Whitehall. 'And now, my dear, are you able to stay and have lunch with me?'

'Thank you, madame, I'd like to very much,' she said, and Antonia took her arm as they went to the dining room.

'Now, Ellen, do tell me all about yourself,' Antonia said. 'Has some handsome young man out there stolen your heart?'

'Yes, indeed, madame, but I must tell you that my heart wasn't *stolen*. I *hurled* my heart at him just before he went off to the war, and he wasn't well pleased, I'm afraid. But you see, I had to do it because – while we'd become the best of friends – it wasn't until he was leaving that I realized all the remarkable feelings I had for him were called *love*. I wanted him to know that, and to carry it with him.'

'And did he return your tender feelings?'

'Absolutely not! But I'm sure he's always been fond enough of me.'

'So, did he come back safely?'

Ellen nodded and sighed. 'I still haven't seen him because his duties are keeping him in Paris. But at least we've begun to exchange letters.'

'*Billets-doux?*'

'Oh, no, nothing like that. Just friendly letters – but they've broken the ice between us,' she said. 'And when this congress finally ends, Lord Ramsden has promised to take Lady Viola and me to visit Paris. *Then*, when I'm alone with Matthew, I'll make sure he hears what I have to say.'

'Matthew?'

'Matthew Halifax. He spent most of the war in Spain, and he's one of Wellington's aides-de-camp now.'

Antonia hid her astonishment. Ellen and Matthew Halifax? She made no comment while Ellen described how her friendship with him had grown from their first meeting in the craftsman's workshop to the time she'd slammed the door of Lady Castlereagh's chilly little parlour.

'He accused me of being too young to talk of love,' she said with a touch of smugness. 'Well, time has now dealt with that particular debate, and when we meet again, he'll see that my feelings for him haven't changed – though I've had at least a dozen proposals in the last twelve months. And on my next birthday, I'll be *twenty*. So, just let him try to argue his way out of that!'

CHAPTER TWENTY

'Gentlemen, I must leave for Vienna tomorrow,' the Duke of Wellington announced when his staff was summoned to a morning meeting in his library at the Paris Embassy. 'The prime minister is clamouring for Lord Castlereagh's return to Westminster, and I have agreed to take his place at the congress. I must be there by the beginning of February.' The duke immediately selected three aides to accompany him, and when Matthew's name was mentioned, he hid his delight under a businesslike veneer.

'I'm not happy to be leaving Paris at this time,' the duke added, 'but I must see that Castlereagh's proposals succeed because they offer the only balanced solution to the endless bickering amongst the other delegates.' He leafed impatiently through a recent report. 'All this uncertainty in Vienna is stirring a fresh uneasiness right across Europe, and I'm receiving information from all quarters regarding the remnants of armies under the command of men who are growing dangerously restless and impatient for a decision. We might have removed Bonaparte from the scene, gentlemen, but Europe has not yet been guaranteed peace.'

Few men could claim a friendship with Wellington but, as the coaches rumbled and creaked along wet, rutted roads towards Vienna, Matthew felt he understood the duke as well as anyone did. Perhaps, he decided, it was because they shared a similar stubborn, taciturn streak in their nature, and they were both as inflexible in their demands on themselves as they were on others.

But Matthew was one of the few who had witnessed Wellington weep as he wrote to the widows of men killed in battle, and had seen him swept away by emotion during a great operatic performance. And by a ravishingly beautiful Italian opera singer who'd become the toast of Paris.

Madame Guiseppina Grassini – who had once been Napoleon's mistress –

was travelling to Vienna with them now, while the duke's wife remained behind in Paris. Such domestic arrangements required consummate diplomacy, and Matthew had sent a request to Lord Castlereagh's secretary, asking him to arrange a suitable apartment to be rented for Madame Grassini in Vienna.

He had also sent a note to Ellen, advising her that he would call on her at the first opportunity. And he silently prayed that this opportunity would not be delayed by some time-consuming calamity – such as Madame Grassini disapproving of the apartment rented for her and the need to find her another.

Ellen. Every mile they travelled was bringing him closer to her. He closed his eyes and again saw her standing as he'd first seen her on the river-bank – as transparent, unsullied, cool and life-giving as the water bubbling over the pebbles at her feet. And, on one rainy night in London, she'd said that she loved him. If he offered his hand now, would she accept?

Antonia sat up in bed and opened the sealed note which had come on her breakfast tray: 'I must speak with you urgently. Alone. I will wait for you in St Stefan's.' It was from Ellen.

Antonia drank her coffee quickly and rang for a maid to help her dress. Last night she had seen Ellen leaving in high spirits for Princess Bagration's *soirée musicale*, and two days before that, they had met by arrangement at Demel's coffee house to exchange gossip and eat pastries.

Ellen had found difficulty containing her excitement that morning because she had just heard from Matthew that he was coming to Vienna with Wellington. 'Isn't it wonderful? Oh, Madame Antonia, when you meet him, I'm sure you'll approve of my choice!'

What had happened since then to alter the girl's state of happiness? Antonia screwed up the note and threw it into the fire. 'Please inform the countess when she wakes that I have decided to take a walk this morning,' she said to the footman as she left the house, then set out at a steady pace, limping only slightly, towards the cathedral.

When she stepped into the dim, hushed interior, Antonia could hear a mass echoing from a small side chapel, and saw several worshippers lighting candles while others were on their knees before the elaborate baroque altar. Ellen was standing alone beside a pillar on the far side, gazing up at the Gothic vaulting, and Antonia moved slowly towards her, giving the impression that her interest was fixed solely on the ancient statuary.

'Isn't it sublime?' Ellen said artlessly as Antonia came close to her. She pointed upwards. 'Please keep looking up there while I tell you what I discovered last night at Bagration's soirée.'

Antonia complied, twisting her neck to study the arches soaring above. 'Madame,' Ellen whispered, 'I'm sure I saw the Elizabeth diamonds being worn by one of the Polish ladies last night.'

Antonia instantly forgot about the ceiling. 'Who was she?' Her voice carried to two women sitting twenty yards away and they turned their heads.

'Now, madame,' Ellen said quietly, taking Antonia's arm and leading her into the north aisle, 'I must show you a particularly beautiful stained glass window over here.' She pointed again and Antonia looked up with unseeing eyes at the richly coloured images while Ellen spoke quickly, close to her ear.

'I was sure it was your necklace, so I asked to be introduced to the very young woman wearing it and I told her how much I admired her diamonds. I think she said her name was Zora – or something like that – but as I speak no Polish or Russian and very little German, and she had no French or English, our conversation was very limited. However—' Ellen stopped when several people moved closer to where they were standing, she led Antonia to another window.

'However, Zora is certainly much too young to have been General Vlasova's mistress, but I *think* she said that the necklace had belonged to her mother. Her dead mother.' Ellen walked Antonia along to the next window. 'Those diamonds seemed just like the ones you showed me but, to be sure, you must see the necklace for yourself, madame.'

Antonia regarded Ellen with astonishment. 'How?'

'Now, this is what I propose we should do: Prince Talleyrand is giving a ball tonight at the Kaunitz Palace, and I understood Zora to say that she would be there. You must come, too, madame, and if you confirm that the necklace is the one you lost, I'll introduce you to Zora and tell her that you can translate and help us over our language hurdle. Then we three can find some secluded corner in the garden for a chat about – about something.'

'But, Ellen, if the girl *does* have the Elizabeth diamonds, I can hardly demand their return,' Antonia whispered.

'Certainly not, but listen to my plan: you must bring the replica in your reticule tonight, and when we three are alone in the garden, I'll persuade Zora that her clasp is coming undone. Then while I'm adjusting it, I'll make sure the necklace slips off, but – heyho! – Madame Warshensky-Rostroprovich will swiftly rescue it and Zora will find the diamonds around her neck once more. While you're doing that with the paste ones, I'll have put the real necklace into my reticule, and she'll never discover the switch.'

Antonia placed a hand over her mouth; for a moment could only look at Ellen with incredulity. 'It will never work,' she said at last. 'My dear, it's too ... too complicated, there are too many chances for matters to go awry, too many—'

'It *will* work, madame, because you and I can *make* it work if we are in accord. If we rehearse—' She looked directly at Antonia and her eyes widened as a thought flashed into her mind. 'Dominique is the one to help us! Oh, madame, she's very clever, so we must go immediately and practise this with her because tonight might be the only chance we ever have.'

Antonia still shook her head.

'Madame, we have every justification for doing this because my father paid dearly for those diamonds to be returned to your husband's safe. The general was a scoundrel and a thief. The girl wearing them now – whoever she is – has no claim on the necklace because it is rightfully yours.'

Antonia thought of Count Spiransky and sighed. 'Actually, it never really belonged to my husband, but the man who *did* own it is now no longer alive.' She tilted her head and looked at Ellen shrewdly. 'I believe that, as Sir Christopher Templeton gave everything he had for the return of those diamonds, they actually belong to you.'

Ellen clicked her tongue. 'I won't hear of it, Madame Antonia. Whatever my father did, he did it for you, and only you. He went to great lengths to make sure my future is financially secure, and now getting that necklace back will do the same for you. Come with me quickly, and let's enlist Dominique's help to make sure our plan for tonight is flawless.'

When Wellington's entourage reached Vienna, the duke wasted no time in presenting himself and his aides to the congress. Matthew watched him use his reputation and his authority to dominate the proceedings at the negotiating table, and later over dinner, they discussed in detail the strategies planned for tomorrow to curb Tsar Alexander's current demands, calm Metternich's outrage, and unravel Talleyrand's latest wily proposal to promote French interests.

When at last his grace had retired to Madame Grassini's apartment, Matthew pulled out his watch. The hour was late, but there was every chance that Ellen would still be waiting for him to call. He'd thought hard about how a meeting with her should be conducted, and the conclusion he reached was that words could wait. There were other ways to apologize, and other ways to show his feelings towards her.

It was only a short walk to the British mission's residence on the Minoritenplatz, and his knock was answered by a footman. 'Will you inform Miss Templeton that Lord Matthew Halifax has called?'

'I'm sorry, sir, the family is out.'

'Ah, in that case, please—' Frustration overtook him. 'Can you tell me where they are?'

'The Kaunitz Palace, sir. Prince Talleyrand's ball.'

Matthew swung on his heel and strode away, feeling cold, desolate and extraordinarily lonely. He'd told her that he would call at the first opportunity and – damn it! this *had* been the first opportunity. Very well, if she was at the ball tonight, he'd go to the ball, too, he decided, and hailed a passing *fiaker* to take him there.

A few minutes later his head had cleared sufficiently for him to realize that he was most inappropriately dressed for a ball. He told the driver to turn the horse around and it stood waiting while he ran to change into his dress uniform. It was well past midnight when he reached the Kaunitz Palace.

He had no invitation, but his mention of Wellington's name was all that was required to open the door, and he bowed over the hand of Talleyrand's lovely young niece, Dorothee de Courlande, who filled the role of hostess for him in Vienna. Her welcome was warm, and in the ballroom she introduced him to his first pretty partner.

As he danced, his eyes scanned the room for Ellen amongst the glittering assembly. He caught sight of Viola and a group of older ladies in the card room, and when he walked into the smoking room, Lord Ramsden hailed him cheerfully. 'Ah, Matthew! Looking for Ellen?' he asked without preamble, and Matthew nodded. 'Saw her dancing not long ago. You might find her in the supper room upstairs.'

Matthew raised a hand in acknowledgement, but didn't pause to talk. He made his way across the hall towards the staircase and had begun to take the steps two at a time, when he glanced over the gilded iron banister and blinked in disbelief. He looked again. A woman with a remarkable resemblance to Antonia Warshensky-Rostroprovich was crossing the marble floor below.

He leaned over the handrail, straining for a clearer view, and had just convinced himself that the woman was truly Antonia, when he saw Ellen come through a doorway, arm in arm with a young woman – a highly painted, over-dressed young woman, who was wearing a virtual collar of diamonds around her neck.

They joined Antonia in the centre of the hall, and Matthew's jaw sagged as he watched Ellen, with every indication of familiarity, introduce her to the young woman. There was much chatter and tittering amongst the trio as they stood together for several minutes before Ellen and Antonia each linked arms with the girl and they all walked towards the doors leading into the garden. They were about to step outside when a thick-set, grey-haired man in the uniform of a Prussian general came from the ballroom to claim the girl with the glittering necklace.

The jewelled honours decorating the man's chest sparkled as he bowed to Ellen and Antonia, and they shared a brief conversation with him, punctuated by bright laughter, before the girl took the officer's arm to return to the ballroom.

Matthew moved slowly down the staircase and stood on the bottom step, watching the scene in bewilderment. Ellen was close beside Antonia in the doorway, speaking animatedly, and it was clear to him that they were both in an ill humour. Antonia shook her head vigorously and took Ellen's hands in hers, but when they became aware of two gentlemen approaching, they instantly stepped apart and presented engaging smiles.

Matthew saw Ellen apparently accepting an invitation to dance, and a pang of frustration shot through him when she walked back to the ballroom with her partner. Antonia, it seemed, had declined to dance with the second man, but agreed to have supper upstairs with him. When they turned towards the staircase, she instantly recognized Matthew standing at the foot of it, and he noted how quickly she mastered her shock.

Antonia threw him a silencing look as she and her partner approached, and Matthew lowered his gaze, stepping aside with a courtly bow when they passed close beside him to climb the stairs. He waited where he was, watching their ascent, until they reached the top and walked towards the supper room. At that moment Antonia glanced down at him and raised her hand a fraction, in what he took to be a subtle salute.

Matthew ran a hand across the back of his neck. In God's name, what game had Ellen and Antonia been playing here tonight? Surely – *surely* Antonia had not recruited Ellen into her network of information-gatherers? He felt his temper rising as fast as his confusion. What was the connection between them? Damn it! He hadn't felt this kind of apprehension since the day he'd charged a thousand Frenchmen on the ridge overlooking Toulouse. Perhaps some of the same strategy should be put into action at this moment: attack the problem.

He walked into the smoking room and, with apologies, interrupted Lord Ramsden's conversation. 'I think Ellen must be feeling weary, m'lord,' he said, leaning close and speaking quietly. 'Do I have your permission to escort her home?'

'Yes, of course, Halifax, of course,' Ramsden said, then, as an aside, he added: 'I don't expect Viola and I will leave here for another hour or so.' His lordship was not a man given to winking, but at that moment his eye twitched.

Matthew stood stiffly inside the door of the ballroom, watching Ellen and her partner lightly weaving their way up and down the lines of dancers; his heartbeat rose when he saw how she'd grown even lovelier in the last year. He had no clear plan in mind, beyond the need to be alone with her, and he waited impatiently for her to catch sight of him. When she did, her smile was like a burst of sunlight and she hurried directly to him when the dance was over.

'How splendid to see you here!' she greeted him breathlessly. 'My uncle said you'd be kept much too busy to get away from your duties tonight.'

'I've come to take you home, Ellen,' he said bluntly and took her by the arm. 'Lord Ramsden has given me permission.'

'I'm so glad,' she said, and her smile didn't slip while they collected her cloak, and he called for a *fiaker*. They sat well apart on the seat, and though neither spoke during the short drive, she kept her head turned towards him. When they reached the house, she took him into the drawing room where he dismissed the servant and lit the fire himself.

She removed her cloak and settled into a chair, watching him intently as the flames danced through the kindling to catch the log. He stood with one arm along the mantelpiece, looking down at the hearth and biting on his bottom lip.

'I don't know where to begin,' he said at last, and turned his gaze to meet hers. 'There was a time when you and I found it easy to be open and honest with each other, Ellen. So please tell me about the woman I saw you talking with in the hall tonight.' His voice was quiet; dangerously quiet.

She looked at him in astonishment, and when she answered, he sensed she was choosing her words carefully. 'Madame Warshensky-Rostroprovich? Why do you ask? I've come to know her because she lives just a stone's throw away from here, and sometimes we have coffee together, or visit an exhibition. When you meet her, I'll know you'll like her just as much as I do.' She sat forward in the chair. 'Can't we talk of other things tonight?'

He rubbed a hand across his chin. 'First, tell me honestly, Ellen, has she ever asked you to – to, er – to tell her about matters that you overhear in this house?'

'Matthew! What are you saying?' Anger sparked in her eyes. 'Do you imagine that because Madame Antonia is travelling with Count and Countess Volkonsky she'd ask me to spy for the Russians?'

'I made no such suggestion,' he said sharply. 'But I saw something happening between you tonight – something which obviously unsettled you both.'

'Aaah!' She sat back into the chair and shook her head. 'That was all about a certain matter – a very personal matter – which concerns only Madame Antonia. I'm sorry, but I'm not at liberty to reveal it.'

His lips tightened and he turned his head away from her, picked up a poker and stabbed at a log in the fire.

'Matthew, if that secret was mine, I'd tell you like a shot. But I can't, because it belongs to madame.' She rose from the chair and came towards him with a whisper of satin skirts. 'But perhaps you'd like to hear a Templeton secret? My father told me that when he was posted to our embassy in St Petersburg years ago, he met Antonia there, and they fell in love. They never stopped loving each other.' She placed her hand on his arm. 'And that's what she and I often talk about when we're alone – my father.'

The firelight made the shadows leap and dance, highlighting the contours of her face as she lifted it to him, and he felt a constriction in his throat.

'They loved each other desperately, Matthew, and when my father left St Petersburg, madame was preparing to follow him, but her husband found out and had her locked up in a convent.'

He took a deep breath and blew it out slowly. 'And life gave them no second chances?'

She shook her head 'Matthew, do you know that it's been fifteen months, one week and four days since we last spoke? Am I permitted a second chance to say again what I said that night?' The fire crackled softly in the hearth, reflecting its glow in her eyes.

'I remember exactly what we both said that night,' he said, and moistened his bottom lip, hesitating. 'Did you receive the apology I wrote before I left London?' Her puzzled look confirmed his suspicion, and his jaw tightened. Grace had played some part in this.

'And I had a silly little silhouette cut at the Frost Fair last year. Did it find its way to you? No? Oh, I'm so sorry. There was nothing at all remarkable about it, but I – I thought it might, somehow, be a reminder that I was there beside you through all those awful months.'

He reached out and cupped her face between his hands. 'You were never there with me, Ellen, because that was the last place on God's earth I ever wished you to be.' There was a sudden catch in his voice. 'I even covered over the marquetry that William Gray so cunningly placed under the lid of my box to remind me of you.' He acknowledged her look of disappointment.

'Do you think I'd want you there to be contaminated by that obscenity called war, the bloody depravity that men create and which I was forced to wade through in the name of *duty*? It was my *duty* to kill as many Frenchmen as I could, and I was always horrified to look around me afterwards and feel nothing but elation because I'd performed my *duty* so efficiently.' He was breathing fast, and there was a note of challenge in his tone. 'I needed all my thoughts of you to be kept in an entirely different compartment, to keep you uncontaminated by all that.'

She took his hands from her cheeks and laced her fingers with his. 'Well, I was there, Matthew, whether you wanted me beside you or not. My uncle always kept me informed about the campaign, and especially any mention of you which came in dispatches from Wellington. While you might say you were only doing your *duty*, I knew how gallantly you were fighting and, of course, I worried for your safety. Actually, my uncle let me read for myself how you'd rallied the 57th at Toulouse. I was so proud of you, and I wept to learn that Trojan had been killed.'

Matthew disguised his emotion. 'I was given orders and I followed them, nothing more or less.' Her brows arched in disbelief. 'I wasn't born with the blood of warriors in my veins – as I know you're aware. For me, there's no glory in battle and for years I've had to live with the fear that each new day might be my last.' He paused and looked at her with a new tenderness. 'Now, thank God, it's all over. I've done with it for ever, so dare I ask you to forgive me for the damned fool I was that night fifteen months, one week and four days ago?'

'Of course.' She lifted his hands to her lips and kissed them. 'I love you, Matthew, I loved you then and I love you now and I'll love you for ever.' Her lips parted, and after a heartbeat's hesitation, he lowered his mouth to hers, gently at first, then harder, while she held herself against him and their kisses deepened while their longing soared.

Breathless, they clung to each other while the fire crackled and their hearts thundered. He stroked her ruffled hair and kissed her forehead. 'Can you forgive the mistakes I made? Forgive the stupidity spawned by fear? Oh, Ellen, you were right that night, and I was so terribly wrong.' He kissed her again, hard and long. 'Oh, my dearest girl, will you marry me?'

'Yes, of course I will. Soon. Very soon.'

He stroked his lips down her cheek and along her jaw. 'As soon as Lord Ramsden and Lady Viola return tonight, I'll ask their permission for us to be married the moment I return to England.'

'But *when* will that be? *When* will the Duke decide he no longer requires you beside him? No, my love, it won't do at all for a man of your advancing years to wait indefinitely.' She stepped back a pace to study him, and pulled a long face. 'Goodness, you must be thirty! I absolutely insist we marry immediately, here in Vienna. I know of at least one Protestant chaplain in the city who could perform the ceremony – right in this room, if necessary.'

'Ellen, love, there are protocols and formalities to be observed, even by us. And I must inform the duke about this decision.'

She narrowed her eyes at him. 'Well, if it doesn't please his grace to see you married, I'll solve the problem by becoming your mistress and, I assure you, that would not raise an eyebrow in Vienna. I think their lordships Castlereagh and Ramsden might be the only men in the city who don't have at least one mistress.'

He laughed with her, and they sat in front of the fire, soon talking in their old, companionable way, though now his arm was around her possessively, and her head was snuggled into his shoulder. Every so often, they fell silent and exchanged a kiss.

'Heavens, Matthew, how happy I'll be when the time comes to leave Vienna. It's been like living inside a glass dome all these months, constantly meeting the same people at every ball or party. Now everybody is becoming quite worn out by the effort of keeping themselves entertained.' She gave a throaty giggle and snuggled closer to him. 'Sometimes I'm tempted to write to the cousins who raised me in Norfolk and tell them that the girl they despaired of has dined with royal princesses, ridden with archdukes, and waltzed with the Tsar of Russia. Of course, I wouldn't tell them that he invites all the ladies to dance.' She stopped. 'Oh, Matthew, do you think the Duke of Wellington will come to our wedding?'

When Lord Ramsden and Lady Viola returned home two hours later, Matthew performed the ritual of asking for Ellen's hand and outlined the wedding plans.

'Well, upon my word!' Ramsden said. 'Of course you have my blessing, of course.' He shook Matthew's hand and kissed Ellen's cheek 'Well, well – now, don't think you've surprised me with this news, m'love. I told Viola I saw it coming, didn't I, sister?'

Surprise had obliged Viola to drop onto the closest chair and, wide-eyed, she looked from Ellen to Matthew. 'Yes, yes, that's all very well, but how can you be wed here with no family to attend?'

'Mama,' Ellen said, kneeling beside her stepmother, 'we won't be able to arrange a splendid wedding like the one you and Papa had. But when Matthew and I come back to England, I'd love to have the grandest celebration ball the Ramsden family has ever known.'

Viola's eyes brightened. 'Ah, yes! Yes, that's what we'll do, my dears, and I'll ask Aunt Adelaide and Grace to help me plan it. Splendid! Now, we must have the marriage notice put in all the London papers straight away, and do something quickly about your trousseau. Oh, Ramsden, we've been here for five months! Just *when* is this congress to end?'

CHAPTER TWENTY-ONE

Since the announcement of his engagement to Ellen four weeks ago, Matthew had found great difficulty in keeping his thoughts focused on his duties. Images of the girl who would become his wife in just two days slipped into his mind's eye at the most inappropriate times – the girl who'd once likened herself to a polar bear lost in the desert. It made him smile again to recall how, at the dinner given by the duke to celebrate their engagement, this once-retiring young female had charmed his grace into granting her soon-to-be-husband a full week's leave following the wedding.

And one of the Austrian princesses had then insisted they spend that week in a royal hunting lodge located deep in the Vienna Woods.

The thought of what lay ahead for him sent a deep warmth rushing through Matthew's veins and he had to draw in a steadying breath before returning his attention to the work now before him on the table.

Two minutes later, it was Antonia who slipped into his mind, and he couldn't suppress a smile to recall the polite formality they had each adopted when Ellen first introduced them. 'There, I said you would like Madame Antonia, didn't I?' she'd said to him later. 'And she told me she approves very much of you.'

He chuckled again and took the last dispatch from the red box which had been delivered this afternoon by the diplomatic courier from Paris. He read the report carefully and placed it to one side with the others. There was nothing of an urgent nature here that warranted interrupting the duke in the middle of a congress session, and Matthew had just put all the papers back in the box and locked it, when a page entered the room.

'A woman downstairs is asking to see you, m'lord,' the youth said. 'Name of Dominique Dupres.'

With his heart racing, Matthew ran down to meet her. 'What is it, Dominique? Has mademoiselle been taken ill? Did she send you?'

She shook her head, but her distress was clear. 'May we speak in private, m'lord?'

'Of course,' he said, and hurried her upstairs to his office.

'Mademoiselle does not know I have come because – oh, I fear I am stepping far beyond my bounds – but I must break a confidence and tell you – tell you—' She wrung her hands and her throat worked violently. 'It's about a necklace that once belonged to Madame Antonia – and tonight mademoiselle and madame are planning to – to exchange it for an imitation.' Her voice broke as she described the strategy. 'It is a foolhardy, risky enterprise – mademoiselle is eager, but I doubt she can carry out the trick – and the consequences for both ladies could be most embarrassing if they are discovered tonight.'

'Dominique, in heaven's name, tell me clearly what this is about. Everything.' Matthew poured brandy into a glass and handed it to her. 'Now! From the beginning!'

He listened with growing apprehension as Dominique floundered through what she understood of the whole convoluted story regarding the Elizabeth necklace. 'So you see, mademoiselle and madame lost their opportunity to exchange it that night at the Kaunitz Palace when the Polish girl went off to dance with the Prussian general.'

Matthew clamped his jaws and recalled the scene he'd witnessed between Ellen and Antonia after the girl and the general had left them. So that was what lay behind their ill humour that night!

Dominique drained the glass and continued, somewhat more coherently now: 'After that happened, mademoiselle and madame said it was the end of the matter because they believed the young lady was to leave Vienna the following day with her Polish lover.' She shook her head slowly. 'However, today mademoiselle discovered that the young lady had not gone with him after all, but had remained in Vienna with her new lover – General Heinrich von Stellenburg!'

She declined when Matthew offered to pour more brandy into her empty glass. 'Oh, m'lord, now mademoiselle and madame have learned that the young lady and the general will be attending Princess Maria's fireworks festival at the Belvedere Palace tonight, and they are determined to carry on with their plan which now includes my participation!' While she was speaking, Dominique had opened the small bag on her lap, pulled out a black velvet pouch and tipped the necklace onto the desk. 'This one is not genuine,' she said and pushed it towards him.

He looked at it in astonishment and held it up to the light. 'But it's magnificent.' He threw her a questioning look.

'Why am I carrying it? Because mademoiselle wants me to be in attendance on her tonight, and has told me to keep this concealed until she signals for it.' She hung her head. 'I am at a loss to know what to do – that is why I have come to beg you to intervene. Oh, m'lord, I fear mademoiselle's folly might well turn into a disaster that could ruin her reputation.'

Matthew stared at her, dumbfounded; and scrubbed a hand over his chin while arguments began to fly around in his head. He didn't for one minute doubt the truth of everything Dominique had told him about the loss of the original necklace and Antonia's lawful right to possess it again. But the concept of using deceit and trickery to recover it were anathema to every principle of decency he stood for.

And yet, how could he *not* bend a few principles for the lady from St Petersburg? The debt he owed to Antonia Warshensky-Rostroprovich could never fully be repaid. His bones would now be lying in some lonely Spanish grave if it had not been for her courage. Dear God! Was there some way he could switch the necklaces for Antonia, and save Ellen from her own recklessness?

'Thank you, Dominique, I'm most grateful for this information,' he said with a sinking heart, and slipped the necklace into a drawer. 'We'll say nothing about your visit here or what we've discussed; go home now, and play along with whatever the ladies suggest. However, it's obvious that I must act quickly this evening.'

'But what are you proposing to do, sir?'

He ran a hand down the back of his neck as he always did when he was uneasy. 'I think I'll be able to recognize the Polish girl again, and perhaps all I can do is to find an opportunity to lure her away from the general and use mademoiselle's ploy of adjusting the clasp of the necklace.' He grimaced at the thought of playing such an underhanded game.

'I must warn you, m'lord,' Dominique said, pausing at the door and looking even more distraught, 'the lady speaks no English – only Russian, Polish and some German.'

While the hands of the clock in his bedroom swept towards the time to leave for the Belvedere Palace, Matthew's discomfort mounted as he flipped through the pages of a German dictionary to refresh his memory of a few words that might be useful tonight. In the faint hope that he would not be identified in the crowd as one of Wellington's staff, he'd chosen to dress soberly in black, with a grey striped waistcoat and a flowering white cravat stuck with a diamond pin.

The breast pocket in his jacket was a deep one, but even so, the necklace lying in it made a large bulge under the fabric. He studied himself in the looking glass and decided that if he bent his elbow and carried his arm in a certain position all evening, the bulge might not be noticed. Damn! It looked ridiculous, and he grumbled to himself that the sooner he married Ellen and had her completely under his control, the better!

He'd sent word to her saying that he had been delayed by pressing duties and *hoped* he would be able to join her later at the Belvedere – if he didn't find himself under arrest, he thought grimly, or challenged to a duel by an irate Prussian general.

He looked again at the name Dominique had given him – *Zora Walewska* – and walked out briskly towards the splendidly baroque palace, muttering German phrases quietly to himself. With each step, his anger mounted. If Miss Ellen Templeton had been an officer under his command right now, he'd have her courtmartialled for her part in placing him in this invidious situation.

Matthew was amongst the first guests to arrive at the Belvedere, and after a quick reconnoitre of the terraced gardens, pools and statues, he found an inconspicuous position near the entance, beside a large sculpture of an athlete taming a wild stallion. From here he could observe the long line of carriages arriving, and soon saw Antonia and her friends alight and enter the vestibule. Ellen and the Ramsdens came shortly afterwards, and he noticed Dominique looking around anxiously as she followed them into the palace.

He waited where he was for a few minutes, inwardly cringing at the prospect of what lay ahead tonight. Eventually he joined the press of guests at the entrance, all the time searching the throng for a girl wearing a valuable necklace which wasn't really hers.

He held well back when Ellen and Viola came from the ladies' retiring room after leaving their cloaks, and he caught Dominique's eye as she hovered, grim-faced, outside the doorway. He gave her a nod of encourage-ment, then sauntered out into the garden which would later be lit by a fireworks fantasy, one that was set to outdo all the other fireworks fantasies which had been produced in other gardens in recent months.

The band of tension around Matthew's head tightened as he lurked in the shadows, fostering a folorn hope that something might prevent the girl and her general from coming tonight. But a few minutes later they stepped from their carriage and mounted the steps into the palace.

He had no trouble identifying the girl – and the necklace she was wearing. He took care to avoid meeting people who might recognize him as he shad-owed the pair up the stairs into the reception room where rows of chairs had been set out for a recital. A boys' choir was presently marching in, and lining up to sing.

The general and his companion made a good deal of fuss settling themselves in chairs near the front, while Matthew stood, unobserved, against the back wall. From that position he saw Ellen send a signal to Antonia, sitting several rows away from her. Antonia returned the nod; she, too, had seen their prey arrive. Matthew wiped a film of cold sweat from his forehead.

Zora Walewska was a pretty girl, he noted, though rather too highly rouged. She had fair hair and an amply rounded figure which was expensively dressed this evening in a peach-coloured gown with a neckline that sat dangerously low across her full breasts. Antonia's necklace, fastened around her plump throat, looked like a great, sparkling collar.

Though the boys' choir sang with the voices of angels, General von Stellenburg and the man seated beside him talked loudly throughout the whole performance. And when it was announced that, next, a tenor was to sing Mozart arias, the general and his neighbour left their seats and unapologetically made for the door. The girl stood and sauntered after them; Matthew saw Ellen turn to exchange a look of concern with Antonia.

Nobody noticed when he slipped from the room and followed the sound of the general's booming voice coming from the foot of the staircase. Zora, standing at her lover's elbow, appeared to be peeved, and she hung back sulkily as von Stellenburg and his friend strolled towards the laughter coming from a group of players gathering in the card room.

'No, Heinrich! If you start playing now, we'll miss the fireworks!' the girl's angry voice called after him. But the general ignored her and, after a moment's indecision, she drifted into the room behind him.

Matthew ran down the stairs and walked into the card room too, just as the girl was taking a glass of champagne from a tray carried by a servant. He signalled to the servant and reached for a glass also, raising it to her, lifting one eyebrow, and producing what he intended to resemble an inviting smile. It was, he thought with embarrassment, probably more of a leer than a smile.

He wasn't practised in this kind of boorish behaviour, and was somewhat surprised at his instant success in attracting her attention. Her hips swayed as she walked towards him, and he saw a clear answer in her eyes. Yes, the young lady was eager for games.

'You also are not a lover of music?' she asked teasingly and inclined her head towards the applause coming from the reception room above them.

'Alas, no.' His lack of German vocabulary was a handicap to any bright repartée, but he struggled with the language to let her know that he enjoyed waltz music – when he had his hands on a lovely lady.

That wasn't at all how he'd intended to phrase it, but the girl understood him, laughed, then finished her champagne and called for another. When she tucked her arm through his, he glanced quickly towards the general, but the man's attention seemed wholly absorbed by the game. When he picked up the cards dealt to him and let out a crow of delight, the girl gave a dismissive shrug.

She jerked her head towards the men around the gaining table and feigned a yawn. 'Grandfathers!' she muttered, then slowly ran her glance over Matthew's form and fluttered her lashes suggestively. 'You are not a grandfa-ther – so perhaps you like to have a little fireworks? I very much like to have a little fireworks.' She watched for his reaction and giggled when he winked to indicate he understood her double entendre.

'Yes, I also very much like a little fireworks,' he murmured, appalled by his own licentious tone. 'Perhaps if we stroll in the garden, we can discover when the fireworks display will start.' That was what he'd attempted to say in German, but the girl's giggle told him his effort had been abysmal. But that was of little consequence because she took his drift and drained her cham-pagne glass before they left the card players.

Good grief, he thought, it was all happening much too easily, and this pantomime lacked a script. His nerve began to fail. What the hell would he do now?

But Zora needed no script. She seemed to be quite familiar with the gardens and held his arm tightly to steer him away from people walking about the parterre. A line of flares lit their way when she led him down the terraces beside the cascade, but halfway down, she tugged him onto a dim path leading off to a stone bench nestling behind a hedge. Here she flung her arms eagerly around his neck and pulled his head towards her. 'I think a little fireworks begins,' she giggled, and began to devour him with open-mouthed kisses.

Matthew curbed his initial urge to strangle the girl, and tried desperately to devise some way to cool her enthusiasm. But, when she attempted several techniques of wrapping herself around him, he discovered that her experience in this kind of sport seemed to be much wider than his. Her breathing grew heavier and faster, and by the time he'd succeeded in wrestling her hands away from the buttons on his shirt and his trousers, she was ready to reach up and grip his neck again, pulling his face down towards her rounded breasts, which by now had slipped free of their scant covering and were hanging before him, bathed in moonlight.

The bulky necklace at her throat proved to be a great annoyance as she strained to rub her cheek against his and suck his earlobe. 'Ouch!' he complained each time the setting scraped and scratched his neck and jawline. And she must have felt the discomfort, too, for to his utter astonishment, she suddenly pulled away from him, unhooked the diamonds and flung them to the ground.

The next period was one which he resolved to block from his mind for ever as he struggled to calm the panting young woman who was snatching at his clothing, ripping his buttonholes. An episode of this kind had not figured in any of his wildest plans, but when he was at last able to persuade her to rein her passion and readjust her decolletage to cover her breasts, he scooped up the diamonds and stood behind her to fasten the paste necklace around her neck.

His hands were damp and none too steady, but within seconds, the Elizabeth diamonds were lying safely in his bulging breast pocket and he was attempting to tuck in his shirt, adjust his cravat and smooth his tousled hair. It was done!

Voices in the distance warned that guests were starting to move outside in readiness for the start of the fireworks display. The girl embraced him and spoke urgently. She would like to meet with him again because the general was leaving Vienna soon and she would be lonely. She told him where she lived, and with one final kiss, left his side and hurried to mingle with the others.

He sat on the stone bench, still stunned by the ease – well, the comparative ease – with which his task tonight had been completed. How could he ever explain to either Ellen or Antonia what had happened here? he wondered, and went in search of Dominique.

'Our mission was successful,' he whispered and she sagged against the wall with relief

'Mademoiselle is furious because she believes I forgot to bring the necklace,' she said, long-faced.

'Say nothing. I'll explain to her – when I can,' he said, and set out to find Antonia amongst the audience gathering to watch the fireworks.

She was walking to join the Volkonskys when he placed a staying hand on her arm. She smiled warmly at him. 'Ah, Matthew! You've arrived just in time for the most exciting part of the evening,' she said.

'I've had more than enough excitement this evening, Antonia,' he said quietly, reaching into his breast pocket for the bulky black velvet pouch. 'I believe this belongs to you.' He slipped it into her hand discreetly.

Her fingers felt the shape of the gems under the velvet and he heard her gasp. 'But Matthew, how? Do you mean you have. . . ? This is the. . . ?

'Just say that this is one very small way to thank you for keeping me alive in Spain. But I don't know how we can ever explain any part of *that* to Ellen without disclosing your connection with Whitehall.' He gave a rueful grin 'When my head is clear, I'll provide my fiancée with an abridged version of tonight's event with the Polish girl.'

Antonia pressed his hand; her eyes were damp. 'Oh, my dear, I thank you from the bottom of my heart. This can transform my life.'

Suddenly the first rockets burst into the night sky and a fireball of brilliant blue and silver light exploded overhead. Soon every terrace was turned into a fantasy of sparkling colour, and Matthew went to find Ellen. He came up behind her, wrapped his arms around her waist and pulled her against him while he pressed his mouth against her ear.

'Sorry I'm late, my love,' he whispered, 'but I've been busy returning a certain necklace to its rightful owner.' He felt her sudden intake of breath, and kissed her lobe. 'I love you, Ellen Templeton, and in two days I'll show you just how much I do. But I give you fair warning that if you ever again even think of doing something like this without telling me, I'll lock you up in a tower and feed you bread and water for a hundred years.'

Striped sunlight was already slicing into the shuttered room when Ellen woke from her wedding night and lay for a time with her eyes closed, smiling as she listened to the soft, rhythmic breathing of her husband lying close beside her. *Her husband!* Matthew was truly her husband now. She wore his gold band on her finger, and last night when she went into the circle of his arms and stretched out against the mystery of his male body, his tender love-making had carried her to a place so far beyond her wildest imaginings that she'd thought her heart would burst with happiness. She was truly his wife.

She sighed and smiled to herself as she lay beside him, knowing that she had made him happy, too. Her body had sung to him – an unrehearsed woman-song as old as time itself – and it had made him cry out with joy. It was a song that she was ready to sing to him again and again and again. Yes, they would make love every day of their lives. She was truly a part of him and he was part of her. Now nothing, nothing could ever come between them.

She opened her eyes and raised herself slowly onto one elbow to look down at his rugged face, at the nose that wasn't truly straight, and at his mobile, well-shaped mouth which had kissed her so deliciously last night. Everywhere. Her toes curled at the memory of what he had taught her as they lay together while night noises of the Wienerwald serenaded them from the trees around the lodge.

He was sleeping now with his lips slightly parted and one arm thrown back on the pillow. The bedcovers had slipped from his bare torso and, in the golden rays of morning sunlight spearing into the room, Ellen could see his battle scars clearly for the first time – some old, some more recent. The ugly, puckered scar across his chest made her wince and she leaned forward to kiss it.

Her featherlight touch woke him with a start 'It's over, sweetheart,' he said with a sigh, stretched and smiled at her. 'That's all behind us, and there'll be no more soldiering for me, I promise.' He brushed her wildly tousled hair away from her face and she lay her head on his shoulder. She didn't question him about the nightmares which had disturbed his sleep, and hers. Several times he had tossed on the pillow and cried out; once she thought she'd heard him weep.

'Good! No more soldiering,' she repeated. 'We'll settle down and become fat and boring and make love five times every day. Oh, Matthew – I'm so happy,' she said and snuggled closer. 'You looked dashingly handsome with all the gold on your uniform yesterday, y'know, but I think I prefer you like this – *au naturel*. Am I being terribly wicked?'

'Absolutely beyond redemption, I fear,' he said in a playful growl.

She gave a giggle and snuggled dreamily in his arms. 'Oh, wasn't it a truly lovely wedding yesterday? And Mama was delighted that so many people came to wish us well. The duke seemed to be quite taken by Madame Antonia, didn't he? I must write today and thank him for his gift. By the way, did you know beforehand that my uncle was intending to give us the deeds to Fernhill Manor as a wedding present? I was astonished – but delighted too, of course. Hannibal loves it there.'

'Well, if the dog likes it, I'm sure I will too,' he said with a chuckle and rubbed his unshaven chin. 'But your uncle has given Fernhill to you, sweetheart. He's promised me a silver punch bowl.'

She seemed about to protest, but he'd have none of it. 'This is the way Lord Ramsden wants it, love, and I have no objection to living in my wife's house from time to time.' He kissed her forehead. 'It's not as though the Halifax family is short of houses around the country, y'know. Or perhaps, if you like, we can travel soon to faraway islands in the sun, or explore the antiquities of Greece, or perhaps—'

'Or perhaps we could simply lie in bed and make love, and make love, and make love,' she said with a taunting, sideways glance that made him laugh again.

'May heaven preserve me! I had no idea I was marrying a truly merciless slavemaster,' he said with a great, slow smile, and threw one leg across hers.

'But, you'll always find me willing to oblige your requests, dearest, though –
be warned – I haven't yet shaved.'

'You'll discover that I'm a true stoic,' she said, then gave a soft gasp of
pleasure as his hands slowly slid across her warm skin and his fingertips began
to explore the hidden places that roused her delight. She slid under him and
her thighs turned to fire as he kissed her neck, her throat, stroking and fondling
with an urgency that grew to match her own. She rather liked the feel of his
rough, masculine chin; her hands slipped up his back, her palms opening and
spreading wide across his shoulders while his heart thundered against her
breast. She arched into his body and rose to him, higher, until they were swept
away once more on the sublime power of their ecstasy.

They clung together, as they came back to earth, dazed and breathless, both
unwilling to break the spell and return to the world where other people trod.
'Ellen, my precious Ellen,' he murmured.

'Hmmmm.' She sighed, stretched and ran her fingers through his hair,
tousling it. 'I adore you, Matthew Halifax, but all this love-making has
suddenly given me a ravenous appetite. Is that reason enough for us to leave
this heavenly bed for a moment or two?'

He laughed, flung the covers aside and pulled on a green silk robe, but not
before she had glimpsed his tall, splendidly formed, masculine body and the
scars it carried.

He gave her a quizzical sideways glance as he tied the sash. 'Forget about
them, sweetheart They'll fade in time, I promise.' He rang for a servant to
bring hot water for bathing.

With no fixed plan, life for the newlyweds drifted pleasurably through the
unusually warm days that followed. Each morning brought new understanding, each night fresh, sweet discovery. It seemed that every moment,
every hour, was better than the moment and the hour before.Whenever the
whim took them, they set off hand in hand to walk through the woods, or to
drive out and picnic in a meadow, or visit an inn and listen to a gypsy violinist
play serenades. They made love. They told each other secrets.

Ellen was greatly amused by Matthew's light-hearted version of how he'd
retrieved Antonia's necklace. 'Well, I think you went about it in a very clever
way, my dearest,' she purred, 'even if you did have to kiss Zora – once. But,
most importantly, you've made Madame Antonia very happy – and quite rich.
Well, rich enough to live comfortably from now on. My father would have
been so happy to hear that.'

As they talked, she sat with her back against a tree trunk while he lay

stretched out on the grass with his head on her lap. The spires and domes of
Vienna were visible below in the distance, with the snaking brown and tawny
Danube glimmering silver in the glare of the midday sun. But, for Ellen and
Matthew, that scene belonged to some other world where other people lived.

'How different my life would have been if you hadn't come into it when
you did,' she said while her fingers played with his hair. 'It didn't take me
more than an hour to see that behind all the proud titles and finery, the real
Matthew Halifax was simply a very nice, strong man. A patient man. I started
to fall in love with you that day we first drank cider in Mr Gray's kitchen. He's
also a very nice, strong, patient man.'

Matthew opened his eyes and looked directly into hers. 'That's exactly
what my mother thought of William Gray, too, but, of course, the family has
never acknowledged that I'm his son.' He smiled to himself. 'I'm sure if you
can see any goodness in my character now, lovely one, it's there because
William Gray planted it in me when I was a boy.'

He lifted her hand and rubbed his thumb across the gold ring on her finger.
'In many ways I envy William Gray, y'know. He's a man who has spent his
whole life crafting beauty that will last for generations, while I've spent most
of my adult life crafting a skill for war that brings nothing but misery.' A
sudden undertone of bitterness hung in his words. 'I feel contaminated by the
things I've seen men do to each other on the field of battle.' He paused to draw
in a deep breath before he continued. 'Ellen, you are the gentlest and the most
precious thing that has ever come into my life, and I swear I'll keep you that
way for ever.

When Matthew spoke those words, he did so with heartfelt sincerity.

But when they strolled back to the lodge an hour later, a message was
waiting for him, As he quickly read it, Ellen watched his jaw tighten and saw
the shutters snap shut behind his eyes. Her heart sank, but she held herself
rigidly and waited. She was a soldier's wife now, and she would not permit
herself to crumble when she heard the unpleasant news which she instinctively
knew this message must contain.

'I'm sorry. I've been recalled.' He was forced to clear his throat 'It seems
that Bonaparte has escaped from Elba and is already on his way back to Paris.
He's gathering up his army and Wellington is leaving for Brussels in the
morning to re-form an allied force to face him.'

She went to him and he crushed her against his chest, burying his face in
her hair. 'I'm sorry, Ellen, I'm so terribly sorry,' he said, then placed his hands
on her shoulders and slowly pushed her away.

She felt as if a spear of ice had run through her when she looked into his eyes. In the name of *duty*, the gentle man who loved her was turning aside to pick up his sword and preparing to ride off again into a terrifying place where even thoughts of her were forbidden to follow.

But she was a soldier's wife now, and she also had her duty at this time.

She straightened her shoulders and lifted her chin. 'Yes, so we must leave here.' She knew what was expected of her. 'I'll pack immediately and we can be back in Vienna before nightfall.' It took great effort to keep her voice steady.

The silent sobs came as she bolted up the stairs.

CHAPTER TWENTY-TWO

'Yes, Mama, I *am* going to ride again in the Prater this morning!' Ellen said more tartly than she'd intended 'I'm sorry' – she stooped to kiss Viola's cheek – 'but I have come to the end of my patience with all the drawing-room speculation about Bonaparte's plans. I need to have a good swift canter to lift my spirits.'

'Yes, yes, dear.' Viola sighed. 'We're all as eager as you are to return home to London. Surely the congress will conclude this month. Or the next?'

While Ellen was pleased at the thought of leaving Vienna as soon as possible, it wasn't London she wanted to head towards, but Brussels. For weeks, letters had been arriving from Matthew in the Netherlands, telling her how the duke and his staff had been constantly on the move, busy building up troop numbers and supplies, and attempting to form a cohesive force from the under-trained and under-disciplined armies commanded by rival princes and rulers of various provinces. These unreliable troops were expected to make up more than half the allied force under Wellington's command when they faced Bonaparte.

'We have no idea yet where or when he is likely to cross the border,' Matthew wrote, 'but Brussels remains overflowing with visitors, all intent on enjoying themselves. It's almost like Vienna here.'

She read that part of the letter to Lord Ramsden. 'Uncle, I realize that Matthew is very busy, but I see no reason why I shouldn't go there to be with him whenever he has a little time to spare. See, he says there are lots of officers' wives and other English people staying in Brussels.'

'I'm sorry, Ellen,' his lordship said on one of the rare occasions when he refused her a request, 'but I'm sure your husband would question my judgement if I permitted you to travel all the way to the Netherlands in this time of uncertainty.'

But finding some way of getting to Brussels was still uppermost in her mind as she rode her borrowed horse along the shady paths of the Prater. It wasn't until she was nearly upon them that she saw Antonia strolling under the trees with a big man in a well-cut suit, a man who carried himself confidently, and whom Ellen was sure she had never seen before.

But even in that one brief glance, Ellen knew instinctively that the couple would not appreciate any intrusion, and she reined in quickly before they noticed her.

During the long months they'd spent in Vienna, many men had found plea-sure in Madame Antonia's company, and it was not unusual to see her driving about with one gentleman or another. But there was something different today about the apparent easy familiarity with which Antonia was holding the arm of this grey-haired man with spectacles. And from Antonia's expression, she appeared to be highly entertained by his conversation.

Unwilling to interrupt them, Ellen swung her horse and rode away.

'Oh, he is a very old friend, my dear,' Antonia explained airily when she called to see her that afternoon. She looked at Ellen's expression and laughed. 'I assure you that Mr Fulton and I are nothing more than *friends* who have not had the opportunity to meet for some time.' Her smile widened and she gave Ellen a long, sideways glance. 'Actually, he's leaving tomorrow – and I've just told Count and Countess Volkonsky that I won't be returning with them to St Petersburg, because I've accepted Mr Fulton's invitation to join him in Brussels.'

Ellen's eyes widened. 'You're going to Brussels? How wonderful! Soon? Oh, please, may I travel with you? I know Matthew will scold me for coming because he has some ridiculous male notion that his *duty* must be kept in one compartment and his heart in another.' She tapped her fingertips on the arm of her chair. 'Well, I have a *duty*, too, and my duty as a wife is to be with my husband!'

Antonia became unusually tense, and hesitated.

'Oh, come, madame! You of all the people in the world must understand how desperately I need to be with him at this time. My father told me – and so have you – about the regrets you were both forced to live with because neither he nor you had control over the circumstances that kept you apart after St Petersburg.' Her breathing quickened. 'Well, I do have control over my life, and if something awful is lying ahead for Matthew, I want us to know that at least we'd grasped every possible moment to be together.'

A little nerve pulled in one corner of Antonia's mouth. 'You're perfectly correct, my dear,' she said softly. 'That is exactly what you must do.'

*

That evening, after Antonia had persuaded Lord Ramsden and Lady Viola that her route to Brussels was to be through Prague and Frankfurt, and would not cross the French border at any point, his lordship agreed it would be safe enough for Ellen to travel with her. It was Viola's stipulation that Dominique, too, must be included in the party.

Just as dawn was breaking three days later, Lady Viola tearfully farewelled the travellers and presented Ellen with a big box of confections. 'I've always found that marzipans and sugared almonds help to make a long journey more bearable,' she said, smiling through her sniffles. Ellen kissed her warmly, then turned to Ramsden and threw her arms around him. 'I'm so fortunate to have you as my uncle,' she whispered. 'Thank you for everything.'

His lordship himself helped Ellen and Dominique into the hired coach, after he had given lengthy instructions to the driver and the footman perched beside him with a musket.

'Please give my regards to your friend in Brussels,' Ramsden murmured *sotto voce* as he took Antonia's hand.

She hid her surprise. 'I had no idea your lordship was acquainted with him.'

'Ah, yes, madame. I am acquainted with many men who have business in Whitehall,' he said, looking at her intently. 'Even Mr Fulton's business.'

'You have my assurance, m'lord,' Antonia whispered, 'that I have no *business* to conduct in Brussels. Vienna has simply lost its appeal, and I am now seeking greener pastures.'

He raised her hand to his lips. 'As you say, madame, but please take great care of my dear girl should – God forbid! – matters not go our way with Bonaparte. I promised Sir Christopher I would love and care for his daughter as my own, as indeed I do,' he said, and pulled a handkerchief from his pocket.

Antonia squeezed his fingers. 'M'lord, you have my word that I, too, will care for Sir Christopher's daughter as my own.'

At every inn where the travellers stopped to change horses and snatch a brief rest, they heard fragments of stale news regarding Bonaparte and the direction in which the French army was said to be advancing. Nobody in the countryside drained dry by years of war seemed to have any clear picture of what was actually happening in Paris, but as the iron-shod wheels of their coach eventually crossed the border into Belgium and rolled on past hamlets and fields of tall, ripening grain, the three women in the vehicle felt a mounting sense of urgency surrounding them.

Their route was now running only a few miles north of the French border and at times the roads became clogged with military activity. Frequently the coach was delayed by horse-drawn artillery, supply wagons, and columns of infantry swarming into villages along their route. Soldiers were seen everywhere haggling in broken French with shrewd Flemish farmers and flirting with giggling girls in starched white caps and voluminous skirts. Identifying the red-coated British troops and kilted Highlanders was simple, but many wore the elaborate uniforms and plumed helmets of other armies: Saxony, Prussia, Brunswick, Hanover, Nassau, as well as the Dutch-Belgians.

'Perhaps we'll discover what is happening when we reach Brussels this evening,' Antonia said as they halted for their last change of horses in a village that seemed as insignificant as any other in which they'd made a brief stop in the last two weeks. When they strolled into the inn, a serving girl first showed them upstairs and brought warm water for them to wash, before leading them to a table in the parlour.

The soup she served was thick with vegetables and herbs, the bread fresh from the oven, and Ellen had just lifted the spoon to her mouth when there was a clatter of hooves in the courtyard and soon men's voices – English voices – came from the doorway. She looked up quickly and caught the astonishment on Matthew's face when he glanced across the room and saw her there. He and another senior officer were in uniform, as were two young ensigns behind them, but the man leading the way into the parlour was plainly dressed in a blue coat and an unadorned cocked hat, which he was at that moment removing. It was Wellington himself, looking nothing like a commander-in-chief.

He was speaking as he stepped through the doorway, but he stopped mid-sentence and smiled broadly when he recognized Ellen and Antonia sitting on the benches. 'Ladies! What a surprise to meet you here.' He walked to their table and a little of Ellen's soup splashed onto the white tablecloth as she hastened to stand, all the time watching Matthew from the corner of her eye. If he was angry, he was containing it well, she thought, because though he frowned, she caught the flicker of a smile on his lips.

Antonia rose gracefully and extended her hand to the duke. 'Delighted, madame,' he said with a look that confirmed those words. 'Now, ladies, may I present my military secretary, Lord Fitzroy Somerset?'

The handsome young officer bowed, introductions followed, and Antonia, perfectly at ease, invited the gentlemen to join them at the table. 'Your husband neglected to tell me that you were visiting Brussels, Lady Matthew,' his grace said as he cast a significant look towards the culprit, and took a place on the bench beside Antonia.

Before Matthew could attempt a reply, Antonia spoke: 'I must plead guilty to stealing my dear young friend away from Vienna without her husband's knowledge, Your Grace.' She spread her hands appealingly. 'I begged her to accompany me on the long, lonely journey here.' She threw a glance at Matthew's expression and gave him a roguish smile.

'In that case, I wish both you ladies a very agreeable visit to Brussels,' the duke said. 'You'll find the city full of social activity – day and night – though my staff and I have little enough time there to enjoy it.' He looked at Ellen apologetically and began to eat the soup which had just been served. 'Even today we must be off again as quickly as possible after our meal, and I'm afraid it will be another three days before we'll be back at headquarters. I'm making a tour of the fortifications along this border area; there are several places where Bonaparte might cross, and I always find it an advantage to survey the lay of the land with my own eyes.'

All the time Wellington was talking, Ellen's fingers edged along the bench towards Matthew's leg. His hand reached out, grasped hers under the table-cloth and held it tightly.

'If I may ask a foolish question, Your Grace,' Ellen said, speaking for the first time, 'why does Bonaparte want to conquer a little country like Belgium?'

'Not a foolish question at all, Lady Matthew,' said the duke. 'It's not about Belgium; it's all about glory. Bonaparte wants to win back his old glory by winning a battle against the allies, and we happen to be in Belgium.' He broke the bread on his plate and dipped it in the soup. 'Reports from Paris show there's very little support for the emperor now amongst the general population, and they're most unwilling to hand him back his political power. His wars have bankrupted France, crippled trade and brought production to a standstill, and the only real support he can now count on is from the army. The troops are behind him still because there was no work for Bonaparte's heroes when he went into exile and the army was disbanded. They were left to beg on the streets or starve.'

The duke paused and ate several more spoonfuls of soup. 'It's not Belgium that Bonaparte wants, m'dear, but a great victory that will win him back his old glory so he can reclaim his old power in France.' He pushed his empty plate away with a murmur of satisfaction. 'But, by God, we're not going to let him have that glory!'

'Thank you, Your Grace,' Ellen said quietly. 'I know now that I've made the right decision in coming here.' She felt Matthew's grip tighten.

'Brussels is overflowing with visitors, ma'am,' said Lord Fitzroy, hastening to finish his meal. 'My own wife is staying with friends. Do you have accommodation arranged?'

'Indeed we do,' Ellen answered, not taking her eyes from Matthew's. 'Rooms for us have been arranged at the Hotel de Belle Vue.'

'A splendid establishment,' he said dryly, releasing his pressure on her hand and permitting himself to smile. 'The Hotel de Belle Vue is barely a five-minute walk from headquarters.'

With apologies, the duke and his party left the table as soon as they had eaten, and Ellen walked beside Matthew to his horse, much to the interest of the six-man escort who were already in their saddles.

'Are you very angry with me for arriving like this?' she asked him in a quiet voice. 'I promise I won't be a burden; but when your duty permits a free moment . . .'

He shook his head. 'Every spare moment I can find will be yours – ours,' he said and touched his lips to her cheek. 'Just promise that in future you'll keep me informed about anything you're planning to do.' He swung up into the saddle and rode out of the courtyard behind the duke.

The June weather in Brussels was hot and humid when Antonia and Ellen arrived, and they found the city in a state of uneasiness and rife with rumours. Companies of infantry, artillery, horses and supplies, unloaded from ships at Ostend, lumbered in a steady stream to positions around the city and there was constant movement of uniformed men in and out of Wellington's headquarters on the Rue Royale. Batteries of artillery lay in rows in the park, with the horses picketed in a long line behind them, and soldiers with their jackets unbuttoned lolled on the steps of private houses in which they'd been billeted all over the city.

At the same time, the streets were crowded with civilians – with the citizens of Brussels stolidly going about their daily business, and smartly dressed English ladies strolling in new cambrics and embroidred muslins with rows of frills around the ankles, and wearing the latest straw hats trimmed with flowers and frills of lace.

Some days a fresh rumour of an imminent French attack sent nervous visitors fleeing back across the Channel, but their beds were instantly filled by others who were eager to arrive in time to witness the forthcoming battle with Napoleon. All over the city the markets bustled and the merchants smiled.

Within an hour of settling into their rooms at the Hotel de Belle Vue, Antonia had left again. She hurried across the Grand Place, following the directions written on the paper in her hand, and soon found herself in a quiet street leading off the Rue Neuve. Her knock on the door of a tall, narrow house was answered by a servant who showed her into the drawing room.

Mr Peter Fulton glanced up from his writing table, snatched off his glasses and sprang from his chair. 'Antonia!' he cried, and moved towards her with the long-legged lope of a perpetually active man. His wide smile made him look positively boyish, she thought, as she held out her hands.

He took them, kissed them both, and let out a long sigh. 'My dear lady, I could ask politely about your health, and the journey, and a dozen other matters – but first I must know whether you have decided to raise my hopes, or dash them utterly.'

'Such impetuosity, from you of all men!' She laughed at him, but there was affection in her tone.

'Forgive me,' he said and released her hands, 'but surely you must see how unskilled I am in the ways of dealing with matters of this delicate nature.' His voice was teasing, but the message in his grey eyes was earnest.

'My dear Peter, in the past you and I have dealt with many delicate matters with complete frankness.' She smiled at him indulgently, but the recollection made him frown.

'And I've lost many a night's sleep worrying about some of the intolerable situations I found it necessary to place you in! Antonia, nobody has worked for the service as brilliantly as you have done.'

'Peter, as I told you in Vienna, my circumstances have changed for the better, and should I choose to do so, all that can now be put behind me. I have the means to lead an independent life.' There was mischief in her smile as she studied his worried expression. 'While I have the means to live an independent life, my dear, I've not said I planned to live as a hermit.'

Ellen had made it clear to Antonia that she had no intention of attending any of the balls or military revues, tea parties or moonlight picnics which kept the English visitors endlessly entertained in Brussels. 'I had my fill of all that in Vienna, but of course you must wear your diamonds and go to the theatre with Mr Fulton this evening,' she said when Antonia came to her room next afternoon for coffee. 'Dominique and I went to the library today, and I'm perfectly content to sit here and read till Matthew arrives back from his duties.'

When the duke and his staff returned to headquarters, it was late in the evening before Matthew had completed the letters which had to be sent immediately to various commanders, and he was heavy with weariness as he walked to Ellen's hotel and knocked on the door of her room.

When she opened it she was in her night attire with her hair unpinned and falling around her shoulders girlishly, just as it had been on the day he'd first seen her by the river. He leaned his shoulder against the doorframe and gazed at her. 'God, you're beautiful,' he said.

'Come,' she said, reaching out to him and kissing him hard, 'there's a bath in the dressing room and supper is waiting.' She frowned at the lines of fatigue etched into his face. 'I've had everything you need brought over from head-quarters, so now, husband, you must do exactly as I say.'

He stood beside the bath and she began to quickly undo his buttons. 'I've told your servant to come in the morning with a fresh uniform and your shaving things.' She slipped off his jacket and shirt, then urged him into a chair while she pulled off his boots and stockings. 'Breeches now, sir!' she ordered. He complied with good humour and stepped into the bath, watching the grave concentration on her face as she knelt beside the tub and began to wash him all over with the sponge. He gave a murmur of pleasure.

'Consider this just one small part of my wifely duty tonight,' she said, wrinkling her nose at him. He leaned over to kiss her, leaving soapsuds on her chin.

Later, when he was dressed in his robe, they lounged close together on floor cushions, and supper became an intimate picnic. When she saw his eyelids growing heavy, she put out the lamp and led him to her bed.

He gave a long sigh, stroked his palm across her stomach and turned to brush his lips over the curve of one breast, then the other. 'I dream of this each night,' he murmured, and when she felt him harden, she opened herself to the joy of his love-making.

Repleted, they clung to each other for a long time, as if the press of their bodies might be imprinted on their memories for ever. Then she held him tightly with his head cradled against her breast, listening to his breathing deepen as sleep swiftly overcame him. He was safe now. Nothing tonight could harm him.

As the days slipped past, Matthew's visits to Ellen became more problematic. While Wellington maintained his unshakeable sang-froid towards the impending events, his aides were constantly on the move, galloping with his orders to commanders stationed to the south. The first French attack was likely to be a feint. Where would the main thrust come? How best should the allied detachments be positioned to respond quickly? Conflicting intelligence made decisions difficult.

Antonia spent much of her time with Mr Fulton but one afternoon, to Ellen's surprise, she arranged for them to meet, and they all drove out to picnic under the beech trees in the Soignes Forest which stretched for several miles south of the city.

'Mr Fulton is a very charming, entertaining man,' Ellen told Dominique later at the hotel. 'I'm sure he's been in love with madame for a long time, but they both avoided giving any hint about where they'd become acquainted – though I did everything but ask outright how a lady from St Petersburg had met a gentleman from London.'

Dominique was clearly intrigued. 'Did madame return his affection?'

'I think so. Oh, they laughed together a lot and I noticed that her hand touched his as often as his did hers, but' – her forehead creased – 'while I'm aware that she had an unhappy marriage and that she loved my father dearly, there is still so much I don't know or understand about Antonia Warshensky-Rostroprovich. She keeps her secrets well.' She smiled and shrugged. 'But that doesn't prevent me from loving her – and I know Matthew does, too.'

'You would like to see Madame Antonia – with or without her gentleman friend – settle in England when all this is over.' It was a statement from Dominique, not a question, and Ellen laughed.

'You're either a mind reader, or you have been listening at my bedroom door,' she said, and Dominique pretended to be shocked by the allegation. 'Matthew and I discussed that very thing last night, and when the right opportunity comes along, we'll suggest to Madame Antonia that she might like to have one of the houses on the Fernhill estate.'

But when Ellen called on Antonia the next morning, she found her reading a letter that obviously contained unwelcome news.

'Well!' she said, throwing the page aside. 'Mr Fulton has been summoned to London on urgent business of some kind.' She gave a huff of annoyance. 'We had tickets to the opera this evening, so now I must go alone, unless I can persuade you to come with me? Will you? I'm sure you would be back here by the time Matthew arrives.'

Ellen shook her head. 'Thank you, but this might just be the night Matthew is five minutes early, and I won't run the risk of forfeiting even five minutes of his time.' She bit her lip. 'Tomorrow night I'll have to share him with the ladies at the Duchess of Richmond's ball, though, from what he says, he'll have little opportunity to dance with me or anyone else. The duke has already requested his staff officers to remain by his elbow.'

'So, he thinks an attack is very close?'

Ellen frowned. 'Matthew says there is French cavalry massing all along the border.' She looked at Antonia earnestly. 'But no matter when an attack comes, there are going to be casualties, and a Belgian lady, Countess de Ribaucourt, has called for volunteers to organize aid for them. Dominique and I have been going to her house each morning to prepare cherry water, scrape lint and roll bandages, and yesterday we went knocking on doors to collect pillows and blankets for the hospital tents when they're erected.' She stood frowning for a moment before she continued.

'Matthew knows nothing about this work I've been doing, and I'm not going to tell him.' She walked to the window and tapped her fingertips on the glass. 'I've gradually come to understand something about his abhorrence of the suffering and the lives wasted in this war – all in the cause of a mirage called *glory*. My husband is a truly kind and gentle man, but I'm sure that sometimes he, too, has been swept away with some kind of blood-lust in the heat of a battle, and experiences the great elation that comes with every victory. Afterwards, I think he feels appalled – and guilty – at the enormous misery his actions have played a part in creating – all in the name of duty.'

Antonia looked at her shrewdly. 'So, right from the start he has tried to keep you at arm's length from his duty with the army, to prevent you from recognizing the part of himself which he despises?'

Ellen nodded. 'So you see how it would horrify him to know that I'm now preparing to face the awful things that he has always wanted to keep me well away from.' She paced across the room and back again. 'But I'm an army wife, and though the thought terrifies me, I consider that I have a duty to offer help to any soldier who is in need of – well, whatever I might be able to do. You see that, don't you?'

Antonia stood too. 'Yes, Ellen, I think you're perfectly correct, and I'd very much like to join you and Dominique at Countess de Ribaucourt's house tomorrow.'

'Yes, please come with us! There is so much to be done.'

Antonia looked at her fondly, then reached out and cupped her face between her palms. 'My dear, dear girl,' she murmured, 'how proud your father would be of the woman you've become.'

CHAPTER TWENTY-THREE

The Countess de Ribaucourt was a wealthy woman of middle years, with a straight back and an air of unshakeable imperturbabilty. Had she been born a man, she would no doubt have been wearing a general's uniform and leading an army towards battle at this time. Instead, she commanded a company of enthusiastic ladies in her drawing room, and kept them busy rolling bandages and packing baskets with donated salves and medications, cherry water, brandy and laudanum.

After a long, industrious morning with the other volunteers, Antonia, Ellen and Dominique were on their way back to the Hotel de Belle Vue when an ominous rumble began in the distance. Clearly it wasn't thunder.

A message from Matthew was waiting when they reached the hotel, and Antonia listened intently as Ellen read it to them. 'He says that to maintain morale in the city, Wellington has sent instructions for the Duchess of Richmond's ball to continue as planned this evening.' She shrugged and looked doubtful. 'Matthew says that orders have gone out for the troops to collect at their stations and "stand to arms", but there will be no order to march until it is known just where Bonaparte's main attack is focused. And, in the meantime, the ball must go on!'

Dominique helped Ellen and Antonia dress that evening. From the streets below came the sounds of men being summoned from their billets all over town, coupled with the rumble of horse-drawn artillery on the cobbles, trumpet calls, drums beating a rhythm for marching feet as regiments formed up in the Grand Place.

The cannon fire in the distance seemed to be growing more distinct, and hundreds of panicking visitors were rushing for horses to get them to the coast, while the citizens of Brussels carried on about their usual business, and gathered to talk around tables in the taverns and cafés.

The arrival of new intelligence from the Prussians prevented Matthew

•

himself from escorting Ellen and Antonia to the ball, and he sent a shy young ensign to accompany them there, while he and the other aides were occupied at headquarters sending out the duke's orders.

The Duchess of Richmond had done everything to make her ball the most dazzling of the season, and the coach house in which it was held had been transformed for the occasion – the walls were papered with a charming trellis pattern of roses, banks of fresh flowers stood around the room, and the whole was brilliantly lit by hundreds of candles in great chandeliers.

The night was hot, and the too-bright smiles on the faces of the guests, as well as the frequent gusts of loud laughter, were a measure of the general tension in the air. Antonia's arrival caused the stir it usually did when she walked into a crowded room, especially when she was wearing her diamond necklace. She was dressed tonight in white and sparkling silver, and when she stood under a chandelier, flirting with her spangled fan, she drew every male eye in the room. All evening, officers who were about to leave the ball and ride off and join their regiments begged for one dance with her before they went, and she obliged them all.

The non-arrival of Wellington and his staff led to further speculation and anxiety amongst the guests, and heightened the noisy exuberance in the room. But at midnight he strolled calmly into the ballroom with his staff, and invited their hostess to waltz. After that dance, he took Madame Warshensky-Rostroprovich away from her group of admirers and circled the floor with her in his arms.

'Is this the lady we plan to invite to live in our quiet little corner of Dorset?' Matthew said in an amused whisper when he came to Ellen's side and slipped his hand around her waist.

She laughed and turned to him. 'Ah! At last you're here. I think I've danced with every man in the room so, quickly, take me out into the garden before my next partner comes to claim his waltz.' She urged him through the French doors, and they had barely five mintues alone to embrace in the shadows before Lord Fitzroy called to him. 'Sorry, old chap, but the duke needs you to ride out immediately and find General Blücher. We've just heard that Charleroi and Ligny have fallen and Wellington needs the Prussians to hold Bonaparte at Quatre Bras until our reinforcements arrive.'

Matthew pulled her close against him, standing for one more moment with his face against her neck and the soft underline of her jaw, breathing in the perfume of her skin. Then he straightened, ran his hands down her arms until their fingers touched, tangled, and slowly pulled apart. 'I'm so sorry, sweetheart, but I must go,' he said.

'Yes, of course you must go. I understand,' she said, trying to sound like a dutiful officer's wife, though her heart was plummeting. 'But surely you'll first change out of your dress uniform?' She could scarcely believe the inane words spilling from her mouth, a flow that effectively prevented her from voicing the panic screaming through her blood.

He took her chin between his thumb and forefinger and smiled knowingly into her eyes. 'The uniform is no consequence, my dearest, because if it does become a little tattered, I have a clever wife who will mend it for me.'

He was uttering the same kind of nonsense, and as they looked at each other a wave of understanding flashed between them. With his arm tightly around her waist, they walked back into the ballroom, where for a moment longer they stood close together, oblivious of the dancers whirling past. 'I love you, Ellen,' he whispered. 'Whatever happens, keep safe. If things turn out badly, get to the coast as quickly as you can.' He kissed her swiftly, turned on his heel and left.

The sky was already paling towards dawn when Antonia and Ellen drove away from the ball; the streets were full of confusion and the coachman was obliged to curb his horses to a walk and sometimes bring them to a complete standstill as soldiers heaving their packs and muskets came pouring from their billets, often with friends or Belgian sweethearts running beside them.

At the great Place Royale the scene looked chaotic in the ghostly grey light. Men, horses and gun carriages seemed to be inextricably mixed; wagons were being loaded and commissariat trains harnessed, regiments were forming one after the other, and the steady tramp of boots marching off towards the Namur Gate was accompanied by the shrill blare of trumpets and the ceaseless beat of the drums. Some of the marching men sang, some whistled. It was four o'clock and the sun was up when the sound of pipers leading the Highland Brigade came nearer, and the tread of feet grew to a rhythmic thunder as they passed.

By eight o'clock the last of the regiments had marched out of Brussels to bivouac near their battle positions, and a little later the duke followed with his staff. After that, a profound silence settled on the city.

Antonia was able to snatch no more than a couple of hours' sleep, and when she dressed, she discovered that Ellen and Dominique were ready, too, to return to their work at Countess de Ribaucourt's house. They had no energy for conversation as they left the hotel together and crossed the square, now lined with baggage wagons ready to move off at a moment's notice, and the tilt carts designed to transport the wounded.

The sound of guns could be heard, a dull rumble far away in the distance and the pace of work in the countess's house grew faster. Occasionally news was brought in of heavy fighting near a hamlet called Quatre Bras. The countess opened a map, and the volunteers gathered tensely around it to find the place.

The rumble of cannon fire continued all through the afternoon as Antonia, Ellen and Dominique walked back to the hotel. There was growing panic and confusion now in the streets; the duke had ordered an embargo placed on all horses in the city and none could be hired or purchased by civilians, no matter what price was offered by people frantic to escape from Brussels.

The sound of the guns ceased abruptly at ten o'clock, and Antonia, Ellen and Dominique looked at each other apprehensively. If the battle was over – who had won?

Ellen asked Antonia to stay beside her that night, and they lay together holding hands tightly until Ellen had dried her tears and slipped into a deep sleep. 'Please, please, God,' Antonia prayed, 'send him back safely. Don't let this girl's heart be broken.'

The three women awoke next morning determined to maintain a cheerful front and keep their anxious feelings hidden. It helped them all to hurry back again to the countess's house, and they were still there when a gentleman arrived with the news that the savage battle at Quatre Bras yesterday had been inconclusive, and the cost had been high 'The first wagonloads of wounded are on the way now,' he said.

'But the hospital tents haven't yet been erected!' the countess snapped, and marched off to find whoever was in charge of such matters.

'We can't simply sit here and wait for the army to get that organized,' one of the countess's volunteers suggested, and the ladies agreed to move into action immediately.

Carrying baskets of aid and blankets, the group hurried in the direction of the city gates and discovered a number of wounded already arriving. Soon the streets were full of pitiable sights of men who had dragged themselves to Brussels on foot all through the night, only to collapse and die on the cobbled streets. Before long, bundles of straw were delivered and placed on the pavements to receive the casualties – men crying out for water, shattered men with wounds that no simple bandage or kind word could save.

Not only the countess's volunteers but many other ladies of Brussels left their safe, clean houses and came onto the streets to offer what little help they could – sending their children to fetch buckets of water and bring umbrellas to shelter men who were huddled and groaning on the pavement under the burning noonday sun. Others opened their doors and took casualties into their own homes.

Amongst the stench of blood, and dirt, and human sweat, ladies who had never before bandaged more than a child's grazed knee knelt beside strangers, attempting to stem the life-blood that was draining from gaping wounds, trying to ease broken limbs, or accepting rings, diaries and scrawled letters – promising to send them home to grieving loved ones. Nuns in stiff white caps, along with Belgian doctors, joined the few army surgeons working with the seemingly endless stream of wounded pouring into the city.

Antonia watched Ellen moving from one man to another, the frills on her flowered muslin soon filthy with the dust and muck of the pavement, the front of it smeared with blood. She smiled and spoke to each grey-faced man as she lifted his head and put a cup to his lips, sponged the sweat from his face, or slit open a coat sleeve to bind a gaping flesh-wound that yesterday would probably have made her sick. 'Have you any news of Colonel Matthew Halifax?' she asked repeatedly, but learned nothing.

Antonia and Ellen passed each other occasionally as they moved about, each giving the other no more than an encouraging nod, and making no comment on the horrors surrounding them.

As the day drew on, Ellen felt her senses growing increasingly numb; the nausea she first felt had left her, and her hands no longer shook. Now, when a Belgian doctor, kneeling beside an infantryman who was lying on a truss of straw, called to her to hold the man's leg while he dug out a musket ball from his knee, she obeyed without flinching, and then bound up the wound according to his instructions when he moved away to attend to the next man.

A few minutes later he called out again for her assistance.

Late in the afternoon, word came that the hospital tents were at last ready to take the wounded, just as a thunderstorm cracked the heavens and torrential rain washed over the cobbles and overflowed along the gutters. The women's wet dresses soon clung to their bodies and the nuns' starched caps drooped over their faces.

Ellen, drenched and dishevelled, was lightheaded with hunger and exhaustion as she supported a young Highlander with a shattered ankle, helping him to slowly hop his way along the street towards shelter in the tent. When she felt a touch on her shoulder, it was the middle-aged Belgian doctor whom she had assisted earlier. 'I'll take him, madame,' he said curtly. 'Go home and rest now; come back tomorrow.'

She nodded wordlessly and went to find Dominique and Antonia. They walked back to the hotel, and after they had bathed and ordered dinner to be brought to Ellen's rooms, none of them could eat it. 'I must have asked a hundred times for news of Matthew,' Ellen said as she played with the food on her plate. 'Nobody could tell me—' She stopped when there was a knock on the door and Dominique opened it.

The shy young ensign who had escorted them to the ball two nights ago stood there with water dripping from his uniform and a bloodied bandage over one ear. 'A message from Colonel Halifax, ma'am,' he said, handing Ellen an unsealed note.

She snatched it, mumbling her thanks, and read it immediately: *Dearest, All is well. Matthew.* It was dated *Noon, Saturday.*

'Oh, thank you, thank you for bringing this,' she said and grasped the door frame when her legs threatened to give way. 'Antonia, Dominique,' she called in a shaking voice, 'Matthew wrote this just five hours ago – and he is well!' She turned to smile at the messenger. 'And you? Have you been badly hurt? Can I offer you a brandy?'

'No, thank you, m'lady – no brandy, and no – my hurt is not severe. I lost an ear at Quatre Bras, that's all, and I'm on my way back to the regiment now.'

'In this frightful storm? Oh, dear! But how far must you ride?' Ellen asked.

'The duke is making a stand not far from a village called Waterloo – a little over ten miles from here, m'lady. They say he's chosen that place to face Old Boney because he likes the lay of the land there. So if you will excuse me, I must hurry to make sure I'm there for the start tomorrow.'

'Thank you for bringing my husband's message, and when you see him again, please be so kind as to tell him that we are well also.' She held out her hand to him, and was surprised to find her fingers, which had worked so steadily all day, were now trembling.

As soon as the young man had gone, she flung out her arms to Antonia, and they both broke into a fit of gasping sobs as they clung to each other. 'Matthew is alive and well! Alive and well!' Ellen panted, and for a few moments their torn nerves found relief in this burst of weeping But presently they both made an effort towards self-control, reached for their handkerchiefs and blew their noses.

Antonia looked at Ellen's drawn, white face and the dark circles of exhaustion under her eyes. 'My dear girl, you must take some nourishment now, and get a good night's sleep. Tomorrow is going to be another busy day for us all,' she said in a motherly tone, then added softly: 'Would you like me to stay with you again tonight?'

Ellen nodded, and when they had eaten and climbed into bed, Antonia held her as if she was a child, stroking her hair, listening to her talk randomly about her father, about growing up and meeting Matthew. Antonia kissed her fore-head.

'When all this is over,' Ellen murmured sleepily, 'Matthew and I would dearly love you to come to England with us, and— Well, you'll see that between us we have no shortage of houses.'

The suggestion caught Antonia by surprise. 'What a lovely, generous offer,' she said. 'Thank you, my dear. We must talk about it more when we're rested.'

Ellen was quickly asleep, but Antonia continued to lie awake, thinking about her future. Return to England with Ellen and Matthew? Would that be the logical path to choose now that she had decided to decline the offer of marriage that had come yesterday from Peter Fulton?

The stormy rain that had lashed the countryside all night began to ease off towards morning and when daylight came, a low mist hung over the soggy fields around Waterloo. Supply wagons had become bogged all along the unpaved roads, the wheels of the artillery sank up to their axles as they were dragged into position, and few troops were not soaked to the skin by the time the sun appeared. Brussels was quiet, waiting apprehensively while the two great armies positioned themselves on either side of a wide, shallow valley filled with fields of high, ripe grain.

The activity in the hospital tent didn't slacken and Ellen found herself again working with the Belgian doctor whose name, she learned, was Marchant. He approved of the way she'd learned to change dressings and commended her ability to bandage wounds firmly. And this skill was increasingly in demand as the number of amputations mounted. Eventually Doctor Marchant requested that she come to stand beside him at the operating table and hand him his instruments as he worried away at the shrapnel lodged in a soldier's back. Then he taught her to suture torn flesh.

It was well past midday before the first cataclysmic sound of cannon shots came from the direction of Waterloo, and the bombardment continued unabated all afternoon. As the hours passed, the tide of wounded men arriving at the hospital became a flood, and the ladies moved constantly amongst the lines of stretchers, sponging mud and congealed blood from gaping wounds, offering water and words of comfort to those too badly wounded to save.

'Can you give me any news of Colonel Halifax?' Ellen asked each time she came to a man sufficiently fit to talk Yes, one rifleman said, he'd seen the colonel riding into the thick of it when the action began.

'Aye, ma'am, 'e were on 'is way to the little chateau of Hougoumont when I seen 'im,' said a cavalry sergeant struggling for breath. 'The Highlanders and the Guards is takin' a terrible poundin' there, but they're not givin' an inch.'

Ellen kept her emotions frozen and her hands steady as she tended the men who survived the surgeon's knife, while all around her the cries and groans filling the fetid hospital air failed to dim the incessant thunder of the guns. Sometimes she caught snatches of conversations between men who had been carried from the battlefield, and her mind formed a picture of the butchery that was at this moment taking place just a few miles away.

As she knelt to change the dressing on what remained of a young man's arm that had been taken off yesterday, she felt a tug on her skirt. She turned around to the soldier lying on the next stretcher and saw him attempting to raise himself on one elbow, trying to speak through the bloodied bandages across his jaw, most of which had been shot away.

'Water?' she asked gently and he frowned.

'Colonel?' The word was little more than a growl from his throat, but she braced herself. The look he gave her was filled with pity.

'Colonel Halifax?' she asked, and put her ear near his mouth. He gave a grunt of affirmation. 'You have news of my husband?' Another grunt, and his frown deepened as his tongue struggled to form words in his bleeding mouth.

'Fell . . . chateau. Cannon . . .'

She felt her world tipping off its axis and her lungs forgot to breathe as she stared at the soldier. 'Hougoumont? You saw Colonel Halifax fall there?' Another grunt of affirmation. She patted the man's arm. 'I see. Thank you for telling me. Can I get some water for you now?' While shock swept over her in great numbing waves of disbelief, she stood and calmly signalled to the stout, middle-aged lady who was carrying a water jug and cup from patient to patient.

This must be what insanity is, Ellen thought to herself, as she picked up a basin of stained water in one hand and a basket of soiled dressings in the other and carried them out to the drain. Matthew had fallen in battle, Matthew was dead and she would never again feel his touch, never again hear his voice. She should be screaming her grief and outrage, thrashing her hands wildly into something unyielding. Yet all she felt was strangely disembodied and light-headed as she went on with her work, her arms and legs continuing to function in a dreamlike slowness as she moved from one wounded man to the next, performing her duties, and bringing what comfort she could to other women's broken men.

Yes, she was mad, she told herself as she peered closely into the face of each man lying in the rows, imagining that at any instant one of them would become Matthew. He couldn't be dead. She was mad, that was all. He couldn't be dead, so she dare not tell Antonia or Dominique that he'd fallen because if she said it aloud, it might become true. So she avoided coming face to face with either of them as the afternoon wore on and the thunder of the guns refused to stop, and the wagons continued to roll up to the hospital and unload their bloody cargoes. Some men lived through their pain, some died with a hand in hers. Some with their last breath called her Mother, Polly, Meg or Betsy.

Doctor Marchant needed her again, and she walked calmly to the table where he was preparing to remove the gangrenous foot of the young Highlander whom she'd tried to help hop through the rain to the hospital tent. Had that happened last year, or the year before? The boy tried to smile at her, even though she was now a madwoman. She smiled back at him and placed the well-chewed leather pad between his teeth before taking her place beside the surgeon while two burly attendants held the Highlander down throughout his ordeal.

Afterwards, when they carried him to his stretcher, Ellen followed with a basket of dressings and bandages, and a dose of laudanum. 'God bless 'e, ma'am,' the young man whispered. 'There's a gud lassie waitin' for me a' home, and she'll thank 'e, too. Ma Mary will see t'me fine.'

'Yes. Your Mary will be overjoyed to have you home again, I'm sure, and every day of your life together will be precious.' Suddenly Ellen discovered that the pretence of madness was failing her, because there was now a dry burning in her eyes, a constriction in her throat and she could feel a surge of emotion overtaking her, threatening to erode the remnants of her self-control.

Outside, darkness had fallen and now tears threatened to undo her as she stood and picked up her basket. It was time to change the dressings on the chest of a gunner who'd been burned on the first day, and she heaved a heavy sigh when she heard yet another wagonload of wounded pulling up at the entrance.

Her stomach churned at the odour of the gunner's burned flesh, but he clamped his jaws and made no more than a murmur as she set about her awful task. He struggled to thank her when she'd finished, and she sponged the sweat that had broken out on his forehead, then lifted his head to give him water. Suddenly his eyes flew open. 'Listen, ma'am!' he croaked in a whisper. 'The bloody guns have stopped!'

A general hubbub spread throughout the hospital. If the battle was over, then who was the victor? Ellen stood, slack-jawed, looking around at the expressions on the faces of the men and women in the tent. Some wept, some stood dumbly, and she saw several run from the hospital to learn the news.

She turned away and saw a figure sitting slumped on a box against a tent pole barely ten feet from where she stood. Matthew! A bruise purpled his fore-head, one arm was in a makeshift sling, blood matted his hair. Her heart thundered and she had to steady herself as she moved slowly towards him on knees that had suddenly turned to water. Had madness overtaken her again? Was it a hallucination? No. He was no hallucination, so what could she say to a grim-faced husband who had returned from the dead and was now staring at her in angry disbelief?

'Good God, Ellen! You shouldn't be here. What the blazes are you doing in this – this—'

'What am I doing here in this hellish place? I'm doing my duty as an officer's wife, that's all. I know you wanted to keep me from seeing all this, Matthew, but now I *have* seen it and – look at me – I'm all right.'

The calm voice that spoke those words seemed to belong to another person, but she knew the roar in her head was her own blood singing. She crouched beside Matthew and ran a hand over his knee, to assure herself that he was real. 'Oh, my love, nothing matters now because you're here, and you're alive!' Her chin began to quiver. 'I thought you'd been killed. Someone told me he'd seen you fall at the chateau. I thought – I believed that you had really *fallen!*'

'I did fall, damn it! A cannon ball had blasted some poor damn grenadier's entrails all over the paving stones in the courtyard and I slipped on them – I *fell*. And when I *fell* I broke my arm and cracked my head. I've been uncon-scious for half the battle.' He sounded angry at fate for having cheated him.

Ellen clamped her hands over her mouth in an attempt to stem the joyous, hysterical laughter she could feel welling up, ready to explode inside her. 'It's a miracle! Oh, Matthew, you fell in battle – you did truly *fall* in battle, and now here you are alive – and you've come back to me!' Her shoulders shook, while the men lying on stretchers only a few feet away, pretending not to have been listening to the conversation, grinned.

Matthew's grim, grey face broke into a sheepish smile, until he tried to ease his arm into another position and grimaced. 'Yes, well, I'm here, and if you can do your duty and arrange for a bone-setter to deal with this arm as soon as possible, ma'am, I'd appreciate it greatly.'

'Of course, Colonel, but first I must attend to that gash on your scalp.' When he seemed about to protest, she stopped him. 'You won't find neater stitching anywhere in this hospital, so if—'

A commotion outside made all heads turn towards the doorway, and a man rushed in, waving his arms and shouting. 'We've won! We've whipped Old Boney and Wellington has sent him bolting back to Paris with his tail between his legs! We've won!'

Trumpet calls sounded in the distance, and a cheer went up in the tent. Matthew reached for Ellen's hand and held it tightly as they looked at each other, both breathing fast with nervous excitement. 'You know, don't you,' he said in a threatening tone, 'that when we get home, I intend to lock you up with me in a high tower and never let you out again.'

'Locked in a tower with you? Oh, my dearest, I can think of nothing more wonderful,' she said, and made no attempt to wipe away the tears that were now starting to roll down her cheeks. 'Please make sure you throw away the key!'

CHAPTER TWENTY-FOUR

Antonia and Dominique sat on a shady park bench, chatting idly as they watched the city's gardeners turning the soil and replanting the flower-beds that two weeks previously had been trampled by horses and men rushing to answer the trumpet's call to battle.

Napoleon Bonaparte's ambition had now been turned to ashes, and there were few signs left in the city that a great army had been quartered within its walls. Though most English visitors had departed, and the wounded who were fit enough to travel were being shipped home, a fresh stream of tourists was arriving to view the battlefield at Waterloo before the farmers reclaimed their land.

Antonia brushed away a bee that had become attracted to the flowers on her hat. 'I feel restless, Dominique. When I think about my life it seems as though I've been surrounded always by a tangle of loose threads that were constantly unravelling, and now those threads are at last plaiting themselves into a single, braided cord – a strong cord that's stretching into a future that still remains quite foggy.'

Dominique gave a murmur of understanding. On the other side of the park from where they were sitting, they saw Ellen and Matthew strolling arm in arm along an avenue. 'Well, there go two people who are strong enough to withstand whatever the fates choose to hurl in their direction,' she said. Tomorrow she would see to it that their luggage was packed and loaded onto a carriage for Ostend, and in two days they would all be aboard the packet sailing for Dover.

'You and I have lived through some interesting times, Dominique,' Antonia said wistfully, slanting a glance at the Frenchwoman.

She nodded. 'Indeed, madame, and now I look forward to a settled existence once again, working for those who are very dear to me. And, perhaps, before long, children will arrive in the Halifax household, and I will have them to care for, too.' She raised her brows at Antonia in an unspoken question.

Antonia Warshensky-Rostroprovich tilted her chin and stared at the big, white clouds drifting high above the city. 'You know, don't you, that when they invited me to share in their happy future, I declined? And now you would like me to reveal why I gave them that answer.' She turned and locked her gaze with Dominique's. 'But I can't tell you that, because I can't define what it is that I'm looking for, or where I might find it.'

'You're correct, madame,' Dominique said gently. 'I don't understand.'

Antonia's hands were on her lap and she laced and unlaced her fingers several times while she called her thoughts to order. 'Countess de Ribaucourt has given me an introduction to her diamond merchant in Antwerp, and I'm driving there to see him tomorrow. I'll sell the necklace if his offer is sufficiently tempting. Then, my friend, for the first time in my life, I'll have sufficient money in my pocket to be completely independent and live in style – and search for whatever it is that I'm looking for.' She shook her head slowly. 'Is happiness so elusive?'

The Frenchwoman gave a sympathetic smile. 'I was born into service, and my happiness has always been linked to that of my employers. When the guillotine took my beloved Countess Louise, my own life looked bleak until destiny put me in the path of Lady Viola; I was most fortunate to find happiness again in that family.'

Antonia seemed lost in thought. 'For the first fifteen years of my life I was controlled by my unscrupulous father; for the next fifteen years I was just one of the possessions held by my husband. It was my destiny to know – and to lose – the happiness of one great, irreplaceable love.' She heaved a sigh. 'So, I threw myself into work that was challenging and sometimes dangerous, but it also had moments of very great excitement.'

She swung around to the Frenchwoman and her eyes widened as a sudden thought struck her. 'Ah! I think I have the answer to my problem!' Her laugh was contagious. 'Perhaps excitement has become something to which I have developed an addiction?'

'That may well be so, madame, but I sincerely believe that a cure can be found for any addiction. Even the French revolutionaries who were addicted to the guillotine overcame it. In time.'

'Hmmm. In time, you say? How much time will I need? Come along, Dominique, you're a wise woman, tell me – how long will it take me to overcome this unbecoming, disrupting addiction that makes me restless? Five years? Ten years?'

'No more than five years, madame,' said the maid in an authoratitive tone, though there was a twinkle in her eyes, 'especially if you spend that time in a warm climate. I remember you recently mentioning a visit to Italy.'

Antonia tried not to smile. 'My only mention of Italy concerned the fact that Mr Peter Fulton is going to take up a diplomatic post in Florence.'

'Ah! I once travelled to Florence with Countess Louise,' Dominique said with a look of innocence, 'and I remember well the excitement my mistress discovered in that romantic city.'

Antonia threw back her head and gave a throaty laugh. 'I suppose you might well be correct, my friend. Perhaps in Florence I'll find whatever it is I'm still craving.' She sighed and stretched. 'Or perhaps somewhere else. Who knows what the future holds?'

'In that case, my dear madame, you must go quickly to find out,' Dominique said as she held Antonia's hand tightly in both of hers. 'And with all my heart I wish you well.'